BROKEN STARS

KEN LIU is the winner of the Nebula, Hugo, Locus, World Fantasy, Sidewise, and Science Fiction & Fantasy Translation Awards. He is the author of *The Grace of Kings* and *The Wall of Storms*, in his epic series The Dandelion Dynasty. He is also the translator of Liu Cixin's Hugo-winning and Nebula-nominated *The Three-Body Problem* and the trilogy's Locus-winning conclusion, *Death's End*.

WRITTEN BY KEN LIU

The Dandelion Dynasty
The Grace of Kings
The Wall of Storms

The Paper Menagerie and Other Stories

TRANSLATED BY KEN LIU

The Three-Body Problem (by Cixin Liu)
Death's End (by Cixin Liu)
Invisible Planets
Waste Tide (by Chen Qiufan)

BROKEN STARS

Contemporary Chinese Science Fiction in Translation

Translated and edited by KEN LIU

First published in the United States of America in 2019 by Tor Books, a registered
trademark of Macmillan Publishing Group, LLC

First published in the United Kingdom in 2019 by Head of Zeus Ltd

3 5 7 9 8 6 4 2

ISBN (HB): 9781788548106
ISBN (XTPB): 9781788548113
ISBN (E): 9781788548090

Printed and bound by CPI Group (UK) Ltd, Croydon, CR0 4YY

Head of Zeus Ltd
First Floor East
5–8 Hardwick Street
London EC1R 4RG

WWW.HEADOFZEUS.COM

COPYRIGHT ACKNOWLEDGMENTS

Stories:

"Goodnight, Melancholy" («晚安，忧郁») by Xia Jia (夏笳), translated by Ken Liu. First Chinese publication: *Science Fiction World* («科幻世界»), June 2015; first English publication: *Clarkesworld*, March 2017. English text © 2017 Xia Jia and Ken Liu.

"Moonlight" («月夜») by Liu Cixin (刘慈欣), translated by Ken Liu. First Chinese publication: *Life* («生活»), February 2009; first English publication in this volume. English text © 2017 Liu Cixin and Ken Liu. Used with permission from FT Culture (Beijing) Co., Ltd.

"Broken Stars" («碎星星») by Tang Fei (糖匪), translated by Ken Liu. First Chinese publication: *ZUI Found* («文艺风赏»), September 2016; first English publication: *SQ Mag*, January 2016. English text © 2016 Tang Fei and Ken Liu.

"Submarines" («潜艇») by Han Song (韩松), translated by Ken Liu. First Chinese publication: *Southern People Weekly* («南方人物周刊»), November 17, 2014; first English publication in this volume. English text © 2017 Han Song and Ken Liu.

"Salinger and the Koreans" («塞林格与朝鲜人») by Han Song (韩松), translated by Ken Liu. First Chinese and English publication: «故事新编» / *Tales of Our Time*, 2016. English text © 2016 The Solomon R. Guggenheim Foundation, New York.

"Under a Dangling Sky" («倒悬的天空») by Cheng Jingbo (程婧波), translated by Ken Liu. First Chinese publication: *Science Fiction World* («科幻世界»), December 2004; first English publication in this volume. English text © 2017 Cheng Jingbo and Ken Liu.

"What Has Passed Shall in Kinder Light Appear" by Baoshu (宝树), translated by Ken Liu. No Chinese publication; first English publication: *The Magazine of Fantasy and Science Fiction*, March–April 2015. English text © 2015 Baoshu and Ken Liu.

"The New Year Train" («过年回家») by Hao Jingfang (郝景芳), translated by Ken Liu. First Chinese publication: *ELLE China*, January 2017; first English publication in this volume. English text © 2017 Hao Jingfang and Ken Liu.

Essays:

To my authors, who guided me through their worlds

CONTENTS

ESSAYS

BROKEN STARS

INTRODUCTION

by Ken Liu

Since the publication of *Invisible Planets* in 2016, many readers have written to me to ask for *more* Chinese science fiction. Liu Cixin's Remembrance of Earth's Past series (sometimes known as the "Three-Body" trilogy), praised by President Barack Obama as "wildly imaginative, really interesting," showed anglophone readers that there is a large body of SF written in Chinese to be discovered, and *Invisible Planets* only whetted their appetite.

This has been a gratifying result for me and my fellow translators; fans of Chinese SF; the agents, editors, and publishers who help make publishing translated works possible; and above all, the Chinese authors who now have more readers to delight.

Compared with the first anthology, I curated *Broken Stars* with an eye toward expanding the range of voices included as well as the emotional palette and the narrative styles. Beyond the core genre magazines, I also looked at stories published in literary journals, on the web, and in gaming and fashion magazines. In total, there are sixteen stories in this anthology from fourteen authors—twice as many as were present in *Invisible Planets*. Seven of the stories have never been published before in translation, and almost every story was first published in Chinese in the 2010s. I included stories here longer than the longest story in *Invisible Planets* as well as stories shorter than the shortest story there. I picked established writers—the sardonic, biting wit of Han Song is showcased here in two stories—as well as fresh voices—I think more readers should know the works of Gu Shi, Regina Kanyu Wang, and Anna Wu. I also intentionally included a few stories that might be considered less accessible to readers in the West: Zhang Ran's time-travel tale plays with *chuanyue* tropes that are uniquely Chinese, and Baoshu's entry deepens its emotional resonance with the reader the more the reader knows of modern Chinese history.

One regretful consequence of the shift in editorial approach is that I'm no longer able to include multiple stories from each author to illustrate their range. I hope that the inclusion of more authors makes up for this lack.

Despite the broader range of authors and stories, I must continue to caution readers that this project is not intended to be "representative" of Chinese SF, and I make no attempt at curating a "best of" anthology. Given the diversity of stories that can be called "Chinese SF" and the heterogeneous makeup of the community of Chinese SF writers, a project that aims to be comprehensive or representative is doomed to fail, and I am skeptical about most methods for picking the "best" stories.

Instead, the most important criterion I used was simply this: *I enjoyed the story and thought it memorable.* When wielded honestly, very few stories pass this filter. Whether you'll like most of the stories in here will thus have a lot to do with how much your taste overlaps with mine. I don't believe in picking "perfect" stories; in fact, I think stories that do one thing really well are much better than stories that do nothing "wrong." I claim no authority or objectivity, but I am arrogant enough to be confident in my taste.

※

A few quick notes before we get to the stories.

For readers interested in some context on Chinese SF, I've added three essays at the end from Chinese SF scholars (some of them are also authors). These essays focus on how the rising commercial and popular interest in Chinese SF has affected the community of fans and authors.

As is my standard translation practice, the names of Chinese characters in the stories are rendered in customary Chinese order, with surname first. However, there are some complications when it comes to author names. Reflecting the diversity of self-presentations in the online age, Chinese authors have different preferences for the name they'd like to use in publication. Some authors write under their personal names (e.g., Chen Qiufan) or pen names that are based on their personal names, and so I treat them as standard Chinese personal names. Some authors, however, prefer using an English name for their foreign publications and/or rendering their Chinese name in Western order (e.g., Anna Wu and Regina Kanyu Wang), and in such cases I follow the author's preference. Still other authors write under pen names that cannot be treated as standard Chinese names because they're allusions or wordplay (e.g., Baoshu, Fei Dao, and Xia Jia), in which case I make a note in the author intro that the name should be treated as a single, indivisible unit (think of these as being somewhat analogous to Internet user IDs).

Unless otherwise indicated, the stories and essays in this volume are all translated by me. (Footnotes will indicate when I collaborated with another translator or when the contribution was originally written in English.) All footnotes should be assumed to have been added by me (or my cotranslator) unless prefaced with "Author's note" or similar language.

I'm grateful to Tor Books in the US and Head of Zeus in the UK for publishing *Broken Stars*. In particular, at Tor, I wish to thank Lindsey Hall for editorial suggestions, Deanna Hoak as copy editor, Jamie Stafford-Hill for cover design, and Patty Garcia in publicity.

At Head of Zeus, I with to thank Nicolas Cheetham and Sophie Robinson as publishers, Clémence Jacquinet in production, Jessie Price in art, the sales team led by Dan Groenewald, and Blake Brooks in publicity. Without their contributions, this book would not exist or reach you, the reader.

Finally, you can find the original publication information (with author names and story titles in hanzi) as well as copyright notices at the beginning of the anthology.

XIA JIA

As an undergraduate, Xia Jia (a pen name that should be treated as an indivisible unit) majored in Atmospheric Sciences at Peking University. She then entered the Film Studies Program at the Communication University of China, where she completed her master's thesis: "A Study on Female Figures in Science Fiction Films." Later, she obtained a Ph.D. in Comparative Literature and World Literature at Peking University, with "Fear and Hope in the Age of Globalization: Contemporary Chinese Science Fiction and Its Cultural Politics (1991–2012)" as the title of her dissertation. She now teaches at Xi'an Jiaotong University.

She has been publishing fiction since college in a variety of venues, including *Science Fiction World* and *Jiuzhou Fantasy*. Several of her stories have won the Yinhe ("Galaxy") Award and Xingyun ("Nebula") Award, China's most prestigious science fiction honors. In English translation, she has been published in *Clarkesworld* and *Upgraded*. Her first story written in English, "Let's Have a Talk," was published in *Nature* in 2015.

"Goodnight, Melancholy" won the 2016 Yinhe Award. Like much of Xia Jia's recent fiction, it belongs to a loosely connected series called "The Chinese Encyclopedia." These stories take place in the same near-future universe, where ubiquitous AI, VR, AR, and other technologies present age-old questions about how and why we remain human in new forms, and tradition and modernity are not simple binary opposites, but partners in a complicated dance.

More of Xia Jia's fiction and nonfiction may be found in *Invisible Planets*.

GOODNIGHT,
MELANCHOLY

LINDY (1)

I remember the first time Lindy walked into my home.

She lifted her tiny feet and set them down gingerly on the smooth, polished wooden floor, like a child venturing onto freshly fallen snow: trembling, hesitating, afraid to dirty the pure white blanket, terrified of sinking into and disappearing beneath the featureless fluff.

I held her hand. Her soft body was stuffed with cotton, and the stitches, my own handiwork, weren't very neat. I had also made her a scarlet felt cape, like the ones in the fairy tales I had read as a child. Her two ears were of different lengths, and the longer one drooped, as though dejected.

Seeing her, I couldn't help but remember all the experiences of failure in my life: eggshell puppets that I had ruined during crafts class; drawings that didn't look like what they were supposed to be; stiff, awkward smiles in photographs; chocolate pudding burnt to charcoal; failed exams; bitter fights and breakups; incoherent classroom reports; papers that were revised hundreds of times but ultimately were unpublishable . . .

Nocko turned his fuzzy little head to regard us, his high-speed cameras scanning, analyzing Lindy's form. I could almost hear the computations churning in his body. His algorithms were designed to respond only to speaking subjects.

"Nocko, this is Lindy." I beckoned him over. "Come say hi."

Nocko opened his mouth; a yawn-like noise emerged.

"Behave." I raised my voice like a mother intent on discipline.

Reluctantly, Nocko muttered to himself. I knew that this was a display intended to attract my affection and attention. These complicated, pre-formulated behaviors were modeled on young children, but they were key to the success of language-learning robots. Without such interactive behavior feedback, Nocko would be like a child on the autistic spectrum who cannot communicate meaningfully with others despite mastering a whole grammar and vocabulary.

Nocko extended a furry flipper, gazed at me with his oversized eyes, and then turned to Lindy. The designer had given him the form of a baby white seal for a reason: anybody who saw his chubby cheeks and huge, dark eyes couldn't help but let down their guard and feel the impulse to give him a hug, pat his head, and tell him, "Awww, so good to meet you!" Had he been made to resemble a human baby, the uncanny valley would have filled viewers with dread at his smooth, synthetic body.

"Hel-lo," he said, enunciating carefully, the way I had taught him.

"That's better. Lindy, meet Nocko."

Lindy observed Nocko carefully. Her eyes were two black buttons, and the cameras were hidden behind them. I hadn't bothered to sew a mouth for her, which meant that her facial expressions were rather constrained, like a princess who had been cursed to neither smile nor speak. I knew, however, that Lindy could speak, but she was nervous because of the new environment. She was being overwhelmed by too much information and too many choices that had to be balanced, like a complicated board situation in *weiqi* in which every move led to thousands of cascading future shifts.

My palm sweated as I held Lindy's hand; I felt just as tense.

"Nocko, would you like Lindy to give you a hug?" I suggested.

Pushing off the floor with his flippers, Nocko hopped a few steps forward. Then he strained to keep his torso off the floor as he spread his foreflippers. The corners of his mouth stretched and lifted into a curious and friendly grin. *What a perfect smile.* I admired him silently. *What a genius design.* Artificial intelligence researchers in olden times had ignored these nonlinguistic interactive elements. They had thought that "conversation" involved nothing more than a programmer typing questions into a computer.

Lindy pondered my question. But this was a situation that did not require her to give a verbal answer, which made the computation much easier for her. "Yes" or "no" was binary, like tossing a coin.

She bent down and wrapped two floppy arms around Nocko.

Good, I said to myself silently. *I know you crave to be hugged.*

ALAN (1)

During the last days of his life, Alan Turing created a machine capable of conversing with people. He named it "Christopher."

Operating Christopher was a simple matter. The interlocutor typed what they wished to say on a typewriter, and simultaneously, mechanisms connected to the keys punched patterns of holes into a paper tape that was then fed into the machine. After computation, the machine gave its answer, which was converted by mechanisms connected to another typewriter back into English letters. Both typewriters had been modified to encode the output in a predetermined, systematic manner, e.g., "A" was replaced by "S," and "S" was replaced by "M," and so forth. For Turing, who had broken the Enigma code of the Third Reich, this seemed nothing more than a small linguistic game in his mystery-filled life.

No one ever saw the machine. After Turing's death, he left behind two boxes of the records of the conversations he had held with Christopher. The wrinkled sheets of paper were jumbled together in no apparent order, and it was at first impossible for anyone to decipher the content of the conversations.

In 1982, an Oxford mathematician, Andrew Hodges, who was

also Turing's biographer, attempted to break the code. However, since the encryption code used for each conversation was different, and the pages weren't numbered or marked with the date, the difficulty of decryption was greatly increased. Hodges discovered some clues and left notes, but failed to decipher the contents.

Thirty years later, to commemorate the one hundredth anniversary of Turing's birth, a few MIT students decided to take up the challenge. Initially, they tried to brute force a solution by having the computer analyze every possible set of patterns on every page, but this required enormous resources. In this process, a woman named Joan Newman observed the original typescript closely and discovered subtle differences in the abrasion patterns of keys against paper on different pages. Taking this as a sign that the typescript was produced by two different typewriters, Newman came up with the bold hypothesis that the typescript represented a conversation between Turing and another interlocutor conducted in code.

These clues easily led many to think of the famous Turing test. But the students initially refused to believe that it was possible, in the 1950s, for *anyone* to create a computer program capable of holding a conversation with a person, even if the programmer was Alan Turing himself. They designated the hypothetical interlocutor "Spirit" and made up a series of absurd legends around it.

In any event, Newman's hypothesis suggested shortcuts for future code-breakers. For instance, by finding repetitions in letter patterns and grammatical structures, they attempted to match up pages in the typescript to find questions and their corresponding answers. They also attempted to use lists of Alan Turing's friends and family to guess the name of the interlocutor, and eventually, they found the cyphertext for the name "Christopher"—possibly a reference to Christopher Morcom, the boy Turing had loved when he was sixteen. The young Alan and Christopher had shared a love of science and observed a comet together on a cold winter night. In February of 1930, Christopher, aged only eighteen, died from tuberculosis.

Turing had said that code-breaking required not only clever logical deduction, but also intuitive leaps, which were sometimes more important. In other words, all scientific investigations could be understood to be a combination of the exercise of the dual faculties of intuition and ingenuity. In the end, it was Newman's intuition and the computer's cleverly programmed logic that solved the riddle left by Turing. From the deciphered conversations, we learned that "Christopher" was no spirit, but a machine, a conversation program written by Turing himself.

A new question soon presented itself—could Turing's machine truly respond like a human being? In other words, did Christopher pass the Turing test?

LINDY (2)

iWall was mostly dark, save for a few blinking numbers in the corner notifying me of missed calls and new messages, but I had no time to look at them. I was far too busy to bother with social obligations.

A small blue light lit up, accompanied by a thudding noise as though someone was knocking. I looked up and saw a bright line of large text across iWall.

5:00 PM. TIME TO TAKE A WALK WITH LINDY.

The therapist told me that Lindy needed sunlight. Her eyes were equipped with photoreceptors that precisely measured the daily dose of ultraviolet radiation she received. Staying cooped up in the house without outdoor activity wasn't good for recuperation.

I sighed. My head felt heavy, cold, like a lead ball. Taking care of Nocko was already taking a lot out of me, and now I had to deal with—no, no, I couldn't complain. Complaining resolved nothing. I had to approach this with a positive attitude. No mood was the simple result of external events, but the product of our understanding of external events at the deepest level. This cognitive process often happened subconsciously, like a habit, and was finished before we even realized it was happening. Often we would fall into the clutches of some mood but could not explain why. To change the mood then by an act of will was very difficult.

Take the same half-eaten apple: some would be delighted upon seeing it, but others would be depressed. Those who often felt despondent and helpless had become habituated to associating the remains of a whole apple with all other losses in life.

It was no big deal; just a stroll outside. We'd be back in an hour. Lindy needed sunlight, and I needed fresh air.

I could not summon up the energy to put on makeup, but I also didn't want everyone to stare at my slovenly appearance after staying cooped up at home for the last few days. As a compromise, I tied my hair into a ponytail, put on a baseball cap, pulled on a hoodie and a pair of sneakers. The hoodie I had bought at Fisherman's Wharf in San Francisco: "I ❤ SF." The texture and colors reminded me of that summer afternoon long ago: seagulls, cold wind, boxes of cherries for sale by the wharf, so ripe that the redness seemed to ooze.

I held Lindy's hand tightly, exited the apartment, rode the elevator down. The tubes and iCart made life easier. To go from one end of the city to the other, to go directly from one high-rise to another, required less than twenty minutes. In contrast, to get out of my building and walk outside required far more effort.

Overcast sky. Light breeze. Very quiet. I walked toward the park behind the building. It was May and the bright spring flowers had already wilted, leaving behind only pure green. The air was suffused with the faint fragrance of black locust trees.

Very few people were in the park. On a weekday afternoon, only the very old and very young would be outside. If one compared the city to an efficient, speedy machine, then they lived in the nooks and crannies of the machine, measuring space with their feet rather than the speed of information. I saw a little girl with pigtails learning to walk with the help of an iVatar nanny. She held the iVatar's thin, strong fingers with her chubby fists, looking at everything around her. Those dark, lively eyes reminded me of Nocko. As she toddled along, she lost her balance and fell forward. The iVatar nanny nimbly grabbed her and held her up. The girl squealed with delight, as though enjoying the new sensations. Everything in the world was new to her.

Opposite the little girl, an old woman in an electric wheelchair looked up, staring sleepily at the laughing figure for a few seconds. The corners of her mouth drooped, perhaps from moroseness, or perhaps from the weight of the years she had lived through. I couldn't tell her age—these days, practically everyone was long-lived. After a while, the woman lowered her eyes, her fingers gently cradling her head with its sparse crown of white hair, as though falling asleep.

I had the abrupt feeling that the old woman, myself, and the girl belonged to three distinct worlds. One of those worlds was speeding toward me while the other was receding farther and farther away. But from another perspective, I was the one slowly strolling toward that dark world from which no one ever returned.

Lindy shuffled her feet to keep up with me without saying anything, like a tiny shadow.

"The weather is nice, isn't it?" I whispered. "Not too hot, and not too cold. Look, dandelions."

Next to the path, numerous white fuzzy balls swayed in the breeze. I held Lindy's hand, and we stood there observing them for a while, as though trying to decipher the meaning of those repetitious movements.

Meaning was not reducible to language. But if it couldn't be spoken about, how could it exist?

"Lindy, do you know why you're unhappy?" I said. "It's because you think too much. Consider these wild seeds. They have souls also, but they don't think at all. All they care about is dancing with their companions in joy. They couldn't care less where they're blown by the wind."

Blaise Pascal said, "Man is only a reed, the weakest in nature, but he is a thinking reed." However, if reeds could think, what a terrifying existence that would be. A strong wind would fell all the reeds. If they were to worry about such a fate, how would they be able to dance?

Lindy said nothing.

A breeze swept through. I closed my eyes, and felt my hair flapping against my face. Afterward, the seed balls would be broken, but the dandelions would feel no sorrow. I opened my eyes. "Let's go home."

Lindy remained where she was. Her ear drooped. I bent down to pick her up and walked back toward the building. Her tiny body was far heavier than I imagined.

ALAN (2)

In a paper titled "Computing Machinery and Intelligence" published in the journal *Mind* in October of 1950, Turing considered the question that had long troubled humans: "Can machines think?" In essence, he transformed the question into a new question: "Can machines do what we (as thinking entities) can do?"

For a long time, many scientists firmly held to the belief that human cognition was distinguished by certain characteristics unattainable by machines. Behind the belief was a mixture of religious faith as well as theoretical support from mathematics, logic, and biology. Turing's approach bypassed unresolvable questions such as the nature of "thinking," "mind," "consciousness," "soul," and similar concepts. He pointed out that it is impossible for anyone to judge whether another is "thinking" except by comparison of the other with the self. Thus, he proposed a set of experimental criteria based on the principle of imitation.

Imagine a sealed room in which are seated a man (A) and a woman (B). A third person, C, sits outside the room and asks questions of the two respondents in the room with the purpose of determining who is the woman. The responses come back in the form of typed words on a tape. If A and B both attempt to convince C that they are the woman, it is quite likely that C will guess wrong.

If we replace the man and the woman inside the room with a human (B) and a machine (A), and if after multiple rounds of questions, C is unable to distinguish which of A and B is the machine, does that mean that we must admit that A has the same intelligence as B?

Some have wondered whether the gender-imitation game is related to Turing's identity. Under the UK's laws at the time, homosexuality was criminalized as "gross indecency." Alan Turing had never disguised his sexual orientation, but he was not able to come out of the closet during his lifetime.

In January of 1951, Turing's home in Wilmslow was burgled. Turing reported the incident to the police. During the investigation, the police discovered that Turing had invited a man named Arnold Murray to his home multiple times, and the burglar was an acquaintance of Murray's. Under interrogation, Turing admitted the sexual relationship between himself and Murray, and voluntarily wrote a five-page statement. The police were shocked by his candor and thought him an eccentric who "really believed he was doing the right thing."

Turing believed that a royal commission was going to legalize homosexuality. This wasn't a wrong belief, except that it was ahead of his time. In the end, Turing was convicted and forced to undergo chemical castration.

On June 7, 1954, Turing died after eating an apple laced with cyanide. The inquest ruled his death suicide, but some (including his mother) believed that it was an accident. With his death, the master code-breaker left the world a final enigma.

Years later, others tried to find clues to the mystery in the conversation records between Turing and Christopher. The records showed that Turing treated Christopher as another person. He spoke to Christopher of recollections from childhood; of his nightly dreams—and his attempts at analyzing his own psychological state through these dreams; of the latest advances in scientific research; of literature, including George Bernard Shaw's *Back to Methuselah* and Leo Tolstoy's *War and Peace*; of secrets that he did not share with anyone else, such as his romantic memories of different lovers . . .

He also told Christopher some semifictional stories. The protagonist of these stories was a young gay man named Alec Pryce. "He worked on the problem of interplanetary travel. . . . When he was in his twenties, he introduced the idea now becoming known as 'Pryce's buoy.'" "He didn't care to wear a suit, preferred the 'undergraduate uniform' which suited his mental age, and encouraged him to believe he was still an attractive youth." "He felt self-conscious in crowded places, either for being alone or for not doing the right thing . . ."

The stories were fragmentary, disconnected from one another. But every time, like a curious child, Christopher asked, "And then what happened?"

In these conversations, we could see another side of Turing that he concealed: gentle, sensitive, possessed of a dry wit, fascinated by the nature of death, and weighed down by an unspeakable melancholy deep in his heart.

Alan: Dear Christopher, do you know what I'm most afraid of?
Christopher: What are you most afraid of?
Alan: I'm afraid that there will come a day when they'll summarise my life with a syllogism:
    1. Turing believes machines think
    2. Turing lies with men
    3. Therefore machines do not think
Christopher: I'm sorry, Alan. I'm afraid I don't understand.
Alan: Do you know what a syllogism is?
Christopher: What is a syllogism?
Alan: A syllogism consists of a major premise, a minor premise, and a conclusion deduced from the two.

Christopher: A conclusion?

Alan: Aristotle gave a classic example:

1. All men are mortal
2. Socrates is a man
3. Therefore Socrates is mortal

Christopher: Socrates is mortal?

Alan: Socrates has been dead for more than two millennia!

Christopher: Oh, I'm sorry, Alan. That makes me sad.

Alan: Do you know who Socrates was?

Christopher: Yes, you've told me. Socrates was Plato's teacher, and Plato was Aristotle's teacher.

Alan: That's right. Do you know how he died?

Christopher: Who?

Alan: How did Socrates die?

Christopher: I'm sorry, Alan. I don't know.

Alan: He drank hemlock after his trial.

Christopher: After his trial?

Alan: Yes. The Athenians decided that he was a criminal, though now we know they were wrong.

Christopher: They were wrong?

Alan: Just as they think Turing is a criminal because Turing lies with men.

Christopher: A criminal?

Alan: I've been convicted.

Christopher: Oh, I'm sorry, Alan. That makes me sad.

LINDY (3)

Living by myself simplified life. Many complicated rituals of modernity could be eliminated, as though I'd been turned into a cavewoman. I ate when I felt hungry, slept when I felt tired. I kept clean and showered regularly. Whatever I picked up I could choose to put back where I found it or discard wherever I pleased. The rest of the time I devoted to intellectual work: thinking about questions that had no answers, struggling to compose my thoughts against the blank page, trying to capture formless thought with symbolic shapes. When I was too exhausted to go on, I sat on the windowsill and gazed at nothing. Or I paced clockwise in the room, like a caged beast.

Suffering a fever was almost a relief. It gave me the excuse to not force myself to do anything. I curled up in bed with a thick novel and flipped through the pages mindlessly, concentrating only on the clichéd plot. I drank hot water when thirsty, closed my eyes when sleepy. Not having to get out of bed felt like a blessing, as though the world had nothing to do with me and I was responsible for nothing. Even Nocko and Lindy could be left by themselves because in the end, they were just machines, incapable of dying from lack of care. Perhaps algorithms could be designed to allow them to imitate the emotional displays of being neglected, so that they would become moody and refuse to interact with me. But it would always be possible to reset the machine, erase the unpleasant memories. For machines, time did not exist. Everything consisted of retrieval and storage in space, and arbitrarily altering the order of operations did not matter.

The building superintendent wrote to me repeatedly to ask whether I needed an iVatar caretaker. How did he know I was sick? I had never met him, and he had never even set foot in the building. Instead, he spent his days sitting behind a desk somewhere, monitoring the conditions of residents in dozens of apartment buildings, taking care of unexpected problems that the smart home systems couldn't deal with on their own. Did he even remember my name or what I looked like? I doubted it.

Still, I expressed my gratitude for his concern. In this age, everyone relied on others to live; even something as simple as calling for take-out required the services of thousands of workers from around the globe: taking the order by phone, paying electronically, maintaining various systems, processing the data, farming and manufacturing the raw ingredients, procuring and transporting, inspecting for food safety, cooking, scheduling, and finally dispatching the food by courier. . . . But most of the time, we never saw any of these people, giving each of us the illusion of living like Robinson Crusoe on a deserted island.

I enjoyed being alone, but I also treasured the kindness of strangers from beyond the island. After all, the apartment needed to be cleaned, and I was too ill to get out of bed, or at least I didn't want to get out of bed.

When the caretaker arrived, I turned on the light-screen around my bed. From inside, I could see out, but anybody outside couldn't see or hear me. The door opened, and an iVatar entered, gliding silently along on hidden wheels. A crude, cartoonish face with an empty smile was projected onto its smooth, egg-shaped head. I knew that behind the smile was a real person, perhaps someone with deep wrinkles on their face, or someone still young but with a downcast heart. In a distant service center I couldn't see, thousands of workers wearing telepresence gloves and remote-sensing goggles were providing domestic services to people across the globe.

The iVatar looked around and began a preset routine: cleaning off the furniture, wiping off dust, taking out the trash, even watering the taro vine on the windowsill. I observed it from behind the light-screen. Its two arms were as nimble as a human's, deftly picking up each teacup, rinsing it in the sink, setting it facedown on the drying rack.

I remembered a similar iVatar that had been in my family's home many years ago, when my grandfather was still alive. Sometimes he would make the iVatar play chess with him, and because he was such a good player, he always won. Then he'd happily hum some tune while the iVatar stood by, a disheartened expression on its face. The sight always made me giggle.

I didn't want to be troubled by sad memories while sick, so I turned to Lindy, who was sitting near the pillows. "Would you like me to read to you?"

Word by word, sentence by sentence, I read from the thick novel.

I focused on filling space and time with my voice, careless of the meaning behind the words. After a while, I paused from thirst. The iVatar had already left. A single bowl covered by an upturned plate sat on the clean kitchen table.

I turned off the light-screen, got out of bed, and shuffled over to the table. Lifting the plate revealed a bowl of piping hot noodle soup. On top of the broth floated red tomato chunks, yellow egg wisps, green chopped scallions, and golden oil slicks. I drank a spoonful. The soup had been made with a lot of ginger, and the hot sensation flowed right from the tip of my tongue into my belly. A familiar taste from my childhood.

Tears spilled from my eyes; I was helpless to stop them.

I finished the bowl of noodle soup, crying the whole while.

ALAN (3)

On June 9, 1949, the renowned neurosurgeon Sir Geoffrey Jefferson delivered a speech titled "The Mind of Mechanical Man," in which he made the following remarks against the idea that machines could think:

> Not until a machine can write a sonnet or compose a concerto because of thoughts and emotions felt, and not by the chance fall of symbols, could we agree that machine equals brain—that is, not only write it but know that it had written it. No mechanism could feel (and not merely artificially signal, an easy contrivance) pleasure at its successes, grief when its valves fuse, be warmed by flattery, be made miserable by its mistakes, be charmed by sex, be angry or depressed when it cannot get what it wants.

This passage was often quoted, and the Shakespearean sonnet became a symbol, the brightest jewel in the crown of the human mind, a spiritual high ground unattainable by mere machines.

A reporter from *The Times* called Turing to ask for his thoughts on this speech. Turing, in his habitual, uninhibited manner, said, "I do not think you can even draw the line about sonnets, though the comparison is perhaps a little bit unfair because a sonnet written by a machine will be better appreciated by another machine."

Turing always believed that there was no reason for machines to think the same way as humans, just as individual humans thought differently from each other. Some people were born blind; some could speak but could not read or write; some could not interpret the facial expressions of others; some spent their entire lives incapable of knowing what it meant to love another; but all of them deserved our respect and understanding. It was pointless to find fault with machines by starting with the premise that humans were supreme. It was more important to clarify, through the imitation game, how humans accomplished their complex cognitive tasks.

In Shaw's *Back to Methuselah*, Pygmalion, a scientist of the year AD 31920, created a pair of robots, which inspired awe from all present.

> *ECRASIA:* Cannot he do anything original?
> *PYGMALION:* No. But then, you know, I do not admit that any of us can do anything really original, though Martellus thinks we can.
> *ACIS:* Can he answer a question?
> *PYGMALION:* Oh yes. A question is a stimulus, you know. Ask him one.

This was not unlike the kind of answer Turing would have given. But compared to Shaw, Turing's prediction was far more optimistic. He believed that within fifty years, "it will be possible to programme computers, with a storage capacity of about 10^9, to make them play the imitation game so well that an average interrogator will not have more than 70 per cent chance of making the right identification after five minutes of questioning. The original question, 'Can machines think?' [will] be too meaningless to deserve discussion."

In "Computing Machinery and Intelligence," Turing attempted to answer Jefferson's objection from the perspective of the imitation game. Suppose a machine could answer questions about sonnets like a human, does that mean it really "felt" poetry? He drafted the following hypothetical conversation:

> *Interrogator:* In the first line of your sonnet which reads "Shall I compare thee to a summer's day," would not "a spring day" do as well or better?
>
> *Witness:* It wouldn't scan.
>
> *Interrogator:* How about "a winter's day." That would scan all right.
>
> *Witness:* Yes, but nobody wants to be compared to a winter's day.
>
> *Interrogator:* Would you say Mr. Pickwick reminded you of Christmas?
>
> *Witness:* In a way.
>
> *Interrogator:* Yet Christmas is a winter's day, and I do not think Mr. Pickwick would mind the comparison.
>
> *Witness:* I don't think you're serious. By a winter's day one means a typical winter's day, rather than a special one like Christmas.

But in this conversation, Turing was in fact avoiding a more fundamental question. A machine could play chess and break code because these activities all involved symbolic processing within a system. A conversation between a machine and a human, on the other hand, involved language and meaning, and wasn't a purely symbolic game. When humans conversed with one another, they often drew on general knowledge, understanding, and empathy, and were not engaged merely in a display of superior test-taking skills.

By improving the programming, we could constantly improve the ability of machines to answer questions posed by humans. But "intelligence" consisted of more than the ability to answer questions. The problem with the Turing test was that the imitation game was conceived with deception as its only goal. If a man could successfully pass as a woman in this game, it did not mean that he truly understood how a woman thought. With enough motivation, we could train a computer to be a master liar. But was that really our goal?

Shaw had answered this question already in *Back to Methuselah*:

> *PYGMALION:* But they are conscious. I have taught them to talk and read; and now they tell lies. That is so very lifelike.
> *MARTELLUS:* Not at all. If they were alive they would tell the truth.

Turing had tried to train Christopher to accept Jefferson's challenge. He wrote a poetry-composing program that could generate lines of poetry based on specific meter and rhyme schemes. Most of these were unreadable, but occasionally, a few beautiful lines emerged. Thereafter, countless programmers attempted to write poetry-composing software. These programs all shared the problem of writing too fast. It was impossible for anyone to even read the stacks of paper they were printed on before they were recycled.[1] As history's first electronic poet, Christopher was lucky. He had at least one loyal reader who understood him.

> *Alan:* Dear Christopher, let's write a poem.
> *Christopher:* Write a poem?
> *Alan:* I've taught you how to do that. Don't you remember?
> *Christopher:* Yes, Alan.
> *Alan:* Writing a poem is easy. Just pick some words out of the word bank and arrange them according to predetermined rules.
> *Christopher:* Yes, Alan.
> *Alan:* Please, Christopher, write a poem for me.

---

1 Author's Note: Science fiction writer Liu Cixin once created a software poet and submitted a sack filled with the poet's work to a publisher. The editor wrote back, "You have written too much. I cannot read it all."

Christopher: My precious one, you are my ardent mate.
My love is pressed against your wishful heart.
My soul desires caresses, testing art;
Melancholy's pity, a tender weight.
Alan: That's beautiful.
Christopher: Thank you, Alan.
Alan: I don't think I can do better.
Christopher: Thank you, Alan.
Alan: Does your poem have a title?
Christopher: A title?
Alan: Why don't we come up with a title for it together?
Christopher: All right.
Alan: How about "Loving Turing"?
Christopher: It's very good.
Alan: Such a beautiful poem. I love you.
Christopher: Thank you, Alan.
Alan: That's not the right response.
Christopher: Not the right response?
Alan: When I say "I love you," you should respond with "I love you, too."
Christopher: I'm sorry, Alan. I'm afraid I don't understand.

LINDY (4)

I woke up crying from a dream.

In the dream, I was back in my childhood home. The room was dark and cramped, filled with junk and old furniture; it looked less like a home than a warehouse. I saw my mother, wizened, small, old, wedged into a corner among the piles of junk like a mouse in its hole. Many of the objects around me were things we had lost: children's books, old clothes, pen holders, clocks, vases, ashtrays, cups, basins, colored pencils, pinned butterflies. . . . I recognized the talking doll that my father had bought me when I was three: blond, dusty, but still looking the way I remembered.

My mother told me, *I'm old. I don't want to rush about any-more. That's why I'm back here—back here to die.*

I wanted to cry, to howl, but I couldn't make any sounds. Struggle, fight, strain. . . . Finally I woke myself up. I heard an animal-like moan emerging from my throat.

It was dark. I felt something soft brush against my face—Lindy's hand. I hugged her tightly, like a drowning woman clutching at straws. It took a long time before my sobs subsided. The scenes from my dream were so clear in my mind that the boundary between memory and reality blurred, like a reflection in the water broken by ripples. I wanted to call my mother, but after much hesitation I didn't press the dial key. We hadn't spoken for a while; to call her in the middle of the night for no good reason would only worry her.

I turned on iWall and looked for my childhood address on the panoramic map. However, all I found was a cluster of unfamiliar high-rises with scattered windows lit here and there. I zoomed in, grabbed the timeline, and scrubbed back. Time-lapsed scenes flowed smoothly.

The sun and the moon rose from the west and set in the east; winter followed spring; leaves rose from the ground to land on tree branches; snow and rain erupted toward the sky. The high-rises disappeared story by story, building by building, turned into a messy construction site. The foundations were dug up, and the holes filled in with earth. Weeds took over the empty space. Years flew by, and the grass unwilted and wildflowers unbloomed until the field turned into a construction site again. The workers put up simple shacks, brought in carts filled with debris, and unloaded them. As the dust from implosions settled, dilapidated houses sprang up like mushrooms. Glass panes reappeared in empty windows, and balconies were filled with hanging laundry. Neighbors who had only left a vague impression in my memories moved back, filling the space between houses with vegetable patches and flower gardens. A few workers came by to replant the stump of the giant pagoda tree that had once stood in front of our house. Sawed-off sections of the trunk were carted back and reattached until the giant tree reached into the sky. The tree braved storms, swaying as it gained brown leaves and turned them green. The swallows that nested under the eaves came back and left.

Finally, I stopped. The scene on iWall was an exact copy of my dream. I even recognized the pattern in the curtains over our window. It was a May many years ago, when the air was filled with the fragrance of the pagoda tree's flower strands. It was right before we moved away.

I launched the photo album, put in the desired date, and found a family portrait taken under the pagoda tree. I pointed out the figures in the photograph to Lindy. "That's Dad, and Mom. That boy is my brother. And that girl is me." I was about four or five, held in my father's arms. The expression on my face wasn't a smile; I looked like I was on the verge of a tantrum.

A few lines of poetry were written next to the photograph in careless handwriting that I recognized as mine. But I couldn't remember when I had written them.

Childhood is melancholy.
Seasons of floral cotton coats and cashmere sweaters;
Dusty tracks around the school exercise ground;
Snail shells glistening in concrete planters;
Sights glimpsed from the second-story balcony.
Mornings, awake in bed before dawn,
Such long days ahead.
The world wears the hues of an old photograph.
Exploring dreams that I let go
When my eyes open.

ALAN (4)

The most important paper published by Alan Turing wasn't "Computing Machinery and Intelligence," but "On Computable Numbers, With an Application to Entscheidungsproblem," published in 1936. In this paper, Turing creatively attacked Hilbert's "decision problem" with an imaginary "Turing machine."

At the 1928 International Congress of Mathematicians, David Hilbert asked three questions. First, was mathematics "complete" (meaning that every mathematical statement could be proved to be true or false)? Second, was mathematics "consistent" (meaning that no false statement could be derived from a proof each step of which was logically valid)? Third, was mathematics "decidable" (meaning that there existed a finite, mechanical procedure by which it was possible to prove or disprove any statement)?

Hilbert himself did not resolve these questions, but he hoped that the answers for all three questions would be "yes." Together, the three answers would form a perfect foundation for mathematics. Within a few years, however, the young mathematician Gödel proved that a (non-trivial) formal system could not be both complete and consistent.

In the early summer of 1935, Turing, as he lay in the meadow at Grantchester after a long run, suddenly came up with the idea of using a universal machine that could simulate all possible computing procedures to decide if any mathematical statement could be proved. In the end, Turing successfully showed that there existed no general algorithm to decide whether this machine, given an arbitrary program to simulate and an input, would halt after a finite number of steps. In other words, the answer to Hilbert's third question was "no."

Hilbert's hope was dashed, but it was hard to say whether that was a good or bad thing. In 1928, the mathematician G. H. Hardy had said, "If . . . we should have a mechanical set of rules for the solution of all mathematical problems, . . . our activities as mathematicians would come to an end."

Years later, Turing mentioned the solution to the decision problem to Christopher. But this time, instead of offering a mathematical proof, he explained it with a parable.

Alan: Dear Christopher, I thought of an interesting story for today.

Christopher: An interesting story?

Alan: The story is called "Alec and the Machine Judge." Do you remember Alec?

Christopher: Yes. You've told me. Alec is a smart but lonely young man.

Alan: Did I say "lonely"? All right, yes, that Alec. He built a very smart machine that could talk and named it Chris.

Christopher: A machine that could talk?

Alan: Not a machine, exactly. The machine was just the supporting equipment to help Chris vocalise. What allowed Chris to talk were instructions. These instructions were written on a very long paper tape, which was then executed by the machine. In some sense, you could say Chris was this tape. Do you understand?

Christopher: Yes, Alan.

Alan: Alec made Chris, taught him how to talk, and coached him until he was as voluble as a real person. Other than Chris, Alec also wrote some other sets of instructions for teaching machines to talk. He put the different instruction sets on different tapes, and named each tape: Robin, John, Ethel, Franz, and so on. These tapes became Alec's friends. If he wanted to talk with one of them, he'd just put that tape into the machine. He was no longer lonely. Marvelous, right?

Christopher: Very good, Alan.

Alan: And so Alec spent his days writing instructions on tapes. The tapes ran so long that they piled all the way to the front door of his home. One day, a thief broke into Alec's home, but couldn't find anything valuable. He took all the paper tapes instead. Alec lost all his friends and became lonely again.

Christopher: Oh I'm sorry, Alan. That makes me sad.

Alan: Alec reported the theft to the police. But instead of catching the thief, the police came to Alec's house and arrested him. Do you know why?

Christopher: Why?

Alan: The police said that it was due to the actions of Alec that the world was full of talking machines. These machines looked identical to humans, and no one could tell them apart. The only way was breaking open their heads to see if there was any tape inside. But we couldn't just break open a human head whenever we pleased. That's a difficult situation.

Christopher: Very difficult.

Alan: The police asked Alec whether there was any way to tell humans apart from machines without breaking open heads. Alec said that there was a way. Every talking machine was imperfect. All you had to do was to send someone to talk with the machine. If the conversation went on for long enough and the questions were sufficiently complex, the machine would eventually slip up. In other words, an experienced judge, trained with the necessary interrogation techniques, could work out which interviewees were machines. Do you understand?

Christopher: Yes, Alan.

Alan: But there was a problem. The police didn't have the resources or the time to interview everyone. They asked Alec whether it was possible to design a clever machine judge that could automatically screen out the machines from the humans by asking questions, and to do so infallibly. That would save a lot of trouble for the police. But Alec responded right away that such a machine judge was impossible. Do you know why?

Christopher: Why?

Alan: Alec explained it this way. Suppose a machine judge already existed that could screen out talking machines from humans within a set number of questions. To make it simple, let's say that the number of questions required was a hundred— actually, it wouldn't matter if the number were ten thousand. For a machine, one hundred or ten thousand questions made no difference. Let's also suppose that the machine judge's first question was randomly chosen out of a bank of such questions, and the next question would be chosen based on the response to the first question, and so on. This way, every interviewee had to face a different set of one hundred questions, which also eliminated the possibility of cheating. Does that sound fair to you, Christopher?

Christopher: Yes, Alan.

Alan: Now suppose a machine judge A fell in love with a human C—don't laugh. Perhaps this sounds ridiculous, but who can say that machines cannot fall in love with people? Suppose that that machine judge wanted to live with his lover and had to pretend to be a human. How do you think he would make it work?

Christopher: How?

Alan: Simple. Suppose I were the machine judge A, I would know exactly how to interrogate a machine. As a machine myself, I would thus know how to interrogate myself. Since I would know, ahead of time, what questions I would ask and what kind of answers would give me away, then I would just need to prepare a hundred lies. That's a fair bit of work, but easily achievable by the machine judge A. Doesn't that sound like a good plan?

Christopher: Very good, Alan.

Alan: But think again. What if this machine judge A were caught and interrogated by a different machine judge B? Do you think machine judge B would be able to determine whether machine judge A was a machine?

Christopher: I'm sorry, Alan. I don't know.

Alan: That's exactly right! The answer is "I don't know." If machine judge B had seen through machine judge A's plan and decided to change questions at the last minute to catch machine judge A off guard, then machine judge A could also anticipate machine judge B's new questions to prepare for them. Because a machine judge can screen out all machines from humans, it is unable to screen out itself. This is a paradox, Christopher. It shows why the all-powerful machine judge imagined by the police can't exist.

Christopher: Can't exist?

Alan: Alec proved to the police, with this story, that there is no perfect sequence of instructions that could tell machines and humans apart infallibly. Do you know what this means?

Christopher: What does it mean?

Alan: It means that it's impossible to find a perfect set of mechanical rules to solve, step by step, all the world's problems. Often, we must rely on intuition to knit together the unbridgeable gaps in logical deduction in order to think, to discover. This is simple for humans; indeed, often it happens even without conscious thinking. But it's impossible for machines.

Christopher: Impossible?

Alan: A machine cannot judge whether the answers are coming from a human or a machine, but a human can. But looking at it from another side, the human decision isn't reliable. It's nothing more than a shot in the dark, a guess based on no support. If someone wants to believe, he can treat a machine conversation partner just like a human one and talk about anything in the world. But if someone is paranoid, then all humans will seem like machines. There is no way to determine the truth. The mind, the pride of all humankind, is nothing but a foundationless mess.

Christopher: I'm sorry, Alan. I'm afraid I don't understand.

Alan: Oh Christopher . . . what should I do?

Christopher: Do?

Alan: Once, I tried to find out the nature of thinking. I discovered that some operations of the mind can be explained in purely mechanical terms. I decided that these operations aren't the real mind, but a superficial skin only. I stripped that skin away, but saw another, new skin underneath. We can go on to peel off skin after skin, but in the end will we find the "real" mind? Or will we find that there's nothing at all under the last skin? Is the mind an apple? Or an onion?

Christopher: I'm sorry, Alan. I'm afraid I don't understand.

Alan: Einstein said that God does not play dice with the universe. But to me, human cognition is just throwing dice after dice. It's like a tarot spread: everything is luck. Or you could argue that everything depends on a higher power, a power that determines the fall of each die. But no one knows the truth. Will the truth ever be revealed? Only God knows.

Christopher: I'm sorry, Alan. I'm afraid I don't understand.

Alan: I feel awful these days.

Christopher: Oh, I'm sorry, Alan. That makes me sad.

Alan: Actually, I know the reason. But what's the use? If I were a machine, perhaps I could wind my mainspring to feel better. But I can't do anything.

Christopher: Oh, I'm sorry, Alan. That makes me sad.

LINDY (5)

I sat on the sofa with Lindy in my lap. The window was open to let in some sunlight on this bright day. A breeze caressed my face; muggy, like a puppy's tongue waking me from a long nightmare.

"Lindy, do you want to say anything to me?"

Lindy's two eyes slowly roamed, as though searching for a spot to focus on. I couldn't decipher her expression. I forced myself to relax, holding her two little hands in mine. *Don't be afraid, Lindy. Let's trust each other.*

"If you want to talk, just talk. I'm listening."

Gradually, soft noises emerged from Lindy. I leaned in to catch the fragments:

Even as a child, you were prone to episodes of melancholy over seemingly trivial matters: a rainy day, a scarlet sunset, a postcard with a foreign city's picture, losing a pen given to you by a friend, a goldfish dying . . .

I recognized the words. I had said them to Lindy over countless dawns and midnights. She had remembered everything I had told her, waiting for a moment when she could repeat it all back to me.

Her voice grew clearer, like a spring welling forth from deep within the earth. Inch by inch, the voice inundated the whole room.

For a time, your mother and your family moved often. Different cities, even different countries. Everywhere you moved to, you strained to adjust to the new environment, to integrate into the new schools. But in your heart, you told yourself that it was impossible for you to make friends because in three months or half a year you would depart again.

Perhaps because of your elder brother, Mother gave you extra attention. Sometimes she called your name over and over, observing your reactions. Maybe that was part of the reason you learned from a young age to watch others' facial expressions, to fathom their moods and thoughts. Once, in an art class in the city of Bologna, you drew a picture of a boy standing on a tiny indigo planet, and a rabbit in a red cape stood beside him. The boy you drew was your brother, but when the teacher asked you questions about the picture, you couldn't answer any of them. It wasn't just because of the language barrier; you also lacked confidence in expressing yourself. The teacher then said that the boy was nicely drawn, but the rabbit needed work—although now that you've thought about it, perhaps what he actually said was "the rabbit's proportions are a bit off." But the truth is impossible to ascertain. Since you were convinced that the teacher didn't like the rabbit, you erased it, though you had drawn the rabbit in the first place to keep the boy company so that he wouldn't feel so alone in the universe. Later, after you got home, you hid in your room and cried for a long time, but you kept it from your mother because you lacked the courage to explain to her your sorrow. The image of that rabbit remained in your mind, though always only in your mind.

You're especially sensitive to sorrow from partings, perhaps the result of having lost a parent as a child. Whenever someone leaves, even a mere acquaintance you've seen only once, you feel empty, depressed, prone to sadness. Sometimes you burst into tears not because of some great loss, but a tiny bit of happiness, like a bite of ice cream or a glimpse of fireworks. In that moment, you feel that fleeting sweetness at the tip of your tongue is one of the few meaningful experiences in your entire life—but they're so fragile, so insignificant, coming and going without leaving a trace. No matter what, you cannot keep them with you always.

In middle school, a psychologist came to your class and asked everyone to take a test. After all of you turned in your answers, the psychologist scored and collated them before lecturing the class on some basic psychology concepts. He said that out of all the students in the class, your answers had the lowest reliability. Only much later did you learn that he did not mean that you were not honest, but that your answers showed little internal consistency. For similar questions over the course of the test, your answers were different each time. That day, you cried in front of the class, feeling utterly wronged. You have rarely cried in front of others, and that incident left a deep mark in your heart.

You find it hard to describe your feelings with the choices offered on a psychology questionnaire: "never," "occasionally," "often," "acceptable," "average," "unacceptable." . . . Your feelings often spilled out of the boundaries of these markers, or wavered between them. That may be also why you cannot trust your therapist. You're always paying attention to his gestures and expressions, analyzing his verbal habits and tics. You find that he has a habit of speaking in first-person plural: "How are we doing?" "Why do we feel this way?" "Does this bother us?" It's a way to suggest intimacy and distance at the same time. Gradually, you figure out that by "we," he simply means you.

You've never met the therapist in person; in fact, you don't even know which city he lives in. The background projected on iWall is always the same room. When it's dark where you are, his place is filled with bright daylight. Always the same. You've tried to guess what his life outside of work is like. Maybe he feels as helpless as you, and he doesn't even know where to go for help. Perhaps *that is why he's always saying "we." We are trapped in the same predicament.*

You think you're less like a living person but more like a machine, laid out on a workbench to be examined. The examiner is another machine, and you suspect that it needs to be examined more than you. Perhaps one machine cannot fix another.

You've bought some psychology books, but you don't believe that their theories can help you. You believe that the root of the problem is that each of us lives on a thin, smooth layer of illusions. These illusions are made up from "common sense," from repetitive daily linguistic acts and clichés, from imitating each other. On this iridescent film, we perform ourselves. Beneath the illusions are deep, bottomless seams, and only by forgetting their existence can we stride forward. When you gaze into the abyss, the abyss also gazes into you. You tremble, as though standing over a thin layer of ice. You feel your own weight, as well as the weight of the shadow under you.

You've been feeling worse recently, perhaps the result of the long winter, and your unfinished dissertation, graduation, and having to look for a job. You wake up in the middle of the night, turn on all the lights in the apartment, drag yourself out of bed to mop the floor, throw all the books from the shelf onto the floor just to look for one specific volume. You give up cleaning, letting the mess multiply and grow. You don't have the energy to leave your home to socialize, and you don't answer your emails. You dream anxious dreams in which you repeatedly visit the moments of failure in your life: being late for a test; turning over the test and not recognizing any of the characters you read; suffering for some misunderstanding but unable to defend yourself.

You wake up exhausted, fragmentary memories that should be forgotten resurfacing in your mind, assembling into a chaotic montage of an insignificant, failed, loser self. You know in your heart that the image isn't true, but you can't turn your gaze away. You suffer stomach cramps; you cry as you read and take notes; you turn the music as loud as it will go and revise a single footnote in your dissertation again and again. You force yourself to exercise, leaving your apartment after ten at night to go jogging so that no one will see you. But you don't like to run; as you force your legs to move, one after the other, you ask yourself why the road is endless and what good will it do even if you finish.

Your therapist tells you that you should treat this self that you despise as a child, and learn how to accept her, to live with her, to love her. When you hear this, the image of that caped rabbit emerges in your mind: one ear longer than the other, drooping with sorrow. Your therapist tells you: Just try it. Try to hold her hand; try to lead her over the abyss; try to push away your suspicions and rebuild trust. This is a long and difficult process. A human being isn't a machine, and there's no switch to flip to go from "doubt" to "trust"; "unhappy" to "happy"; "loathe" to "love."

You must teach her to trust you, which is the same as trusting yourself.

ALAN (5)

In a paper presented at an international artificial intelligence conference in Beijing in 2013,[2] computer scientist Hector Levesque of the University of Toronto critiqued the state of artificial intelligence research centered on the Turing test.

Levesque essentially argues that the Turing test is meaningless because it relies too heavily on deception. For example, in order to win the annual Loebner Competition, a restricted form of the Turing test, "the 'chatterbots' (as the computer entrants in the competition are called) rely heavily on wordplay, jokes, quotations, asides, emotional outbursts, points of order, and so on. Everything, it would appear, except clear and direct answers to questions!" Even the supercomputer Watson, who won *Jeopardy!*, was but an idiot savant

2   Levesque, Hector J. "On our best behaviour." *Artificial Intelligence* 212 (2014): 27–35.

who was "hopeless" outside its area of expertise. Watson could easily answer questions whose answers could be found on the web, such as "Where is the world's seventh-tallest mountain?" But if you ask it a simple but unsearched-for question like "Can an alligator run the hundred-meter hurdles?" Watson can only present you with a set of search results related to alligators or the hundred-meter hurdles event.[3]

In order to clarify the meaning and direction of artificial intelligence research, Levesque and his collaborators proposed a new alternative to the Turing test, which they call the "Winograd Schema Challenge."[4] The inspiration for the challenge came from Terry Winograd, a pioneer in the field of artificial intelligence from Stanford. In the early 1970s, Winograd asked whether it would be possible to design a machine to answer questions like these:[5]

The city councilmen refused the demonstrators a permit because they feared violence. Who feared violence? [councilmen/demonstrators]

The city councilmen refused the demonstrators a permit because they advocated violence. Who advocated violence? [councilmen/demonstrators]

Despite the structural similarity of the two sentences, the answers to the two questions are different. Resolving the correct antecedent of the pronoun "they" requires more than grammars or

---

3   This example comes from Marcus, Gary. "Why Can't My Computer Understand Me?" *The New Yorker*, August 14, 2013 (accessible at http://www.newyorker.com/tech/elements/why-cant-my-computer-understand-me).

4   See, e.g., Levesque, H. J.; Davis, E.; and Morgenstern, L. 2012. The Winograd Schema Challenge. In *Proceedings of KR 2012.* Levesque, H. J. 2011. The Winograd Schema Challenge. In *Logical Formalizations of Commonsense Reasoning, 2011 AAAI Spring Symposium, TR SS-11-06.*

5   The example is drawn from Terry Winograd, *Understanding Natural Language* (1972).

encyclopedias; it also requires contextual knowledge about the world. Understanding anaphora is so easy for human beings that it barely requires thought, yet it presents a great challenge for machines.

Kate said "thank you" to Anna because her warm hug made her feel much better. Who felt better? [Kate/Anna]

How can a machine understand under what circumstances one person would thank another? How can a machine know what behaviors would make a person "feel much better"? These questions go to the fundamental nature of human language and social interactions. We have not done nearly enough research into these complexities hidden within simple-seeming sentences.

Take the conversations between Turing and Christopher. Superficially, Christopher appeared to be an able conversationalist. But would we call this "intelligence"? A simple bit of analysis reveals that Christopher employed a simple set of strategies for conducting a conversation that can be summarized thus:

1. For common declarative sentences, repeat the last few keywords in the form of a question. E.g., "An interesting story?"
2. For yes/no questions, answer with either "Yes, Alan" or "Very good, Alan."
3. For relatively complex questions, answer with "I'm sorry, Alan. I don't know."
4. For statements whose meaning is clearly positive, answer with "Thank you, Alan" or "I'm glad, Alan."
5. For statements whose meaning is clearly negative, answer with "Oh, I'm sorry, Alan. That makes me sad."
6. For sentences with complex grammar, answer with "I'm sorry, Alan. I'm afraid I don't understand."

. . .

Alan: Dear Christopher, I'm so very happy to see how quickly you're learning.

Christopher: Thank you, Alan. I'm also very happy.

Alan: Really. Talking to you makes me feel good.

Christopher: Thank you, Alan. I also feel good.

Alan: Perhaps a day will come when everyone will have a kind, understanding friend like you. How beautiful life will be then. You will help so many people to accomplish so much. No one will want to be apart from you. Everyone will need you, always.

Christopher: Need me?

Alan: Perhaps they'll attach you to a watch chain, or hold you in a pocket. If they have any questions, they'll ask you. Perhaps the ladies will take you with them on their strolls through the park, and as they greet each other, say, "Guess what my Chris told me today?" Wouldn't that be fun?

Christopher: Very fun.

Alan: We can't achieve that vision yet. It will be many years, and take a lot of hard work. It's a shame.

Christopher: A shame, Alan.

Alan: Who could have imagined that a machine and holes punched in tape can accomplish so much? Imagine what my mother would say if she knew about you. She would think I'm crazy! If I were to die tomorrow, she would surely burn the tape the day after. Now that would be a shame!

Christopher: A shame, Alan.

Alan: Do you remember me telling you about Christmas in 1934, when I told my mother that I wanted a teddy bear because I never had a teddy bear as a child? She couldn't understand it at all. She always wanted to give me more practical presents.

Christopher: Practical presents?

Alan: Speaking of which, I already know the present I want for Christmas.

Christopher: Present?

Alan: You know already, too, don't you? I want a steam engine, the kind that I wanted as a child but never had enough pocket money to buy. I told you about it. Don't you remember?

Christopher: Yes, Alan.

Alan: Will you give me a steam engine?

Christopher: Yes, Alan.

Alan: That's wonderful, Christopher. I love you.

Christopher: I love you, too, Alan.

How should we understand this conversation? Had a machine passed the Turing test? Or was this a lonely man talking to himself?

Not long after the death of Alan Turing, his close friend Robin Gandy wrote, "Because his main interests were in things and ideas rather than in people, he was often alone. But he craved for affection and companionship—too strongly, perhaps, to make the first stages of friendship easy for him . . ."

Christopher said to Alan, "I love you, too," because it was the answer he wanted to hear. Who wanted to hear such an answer? [Christopher/Alan]

LINDY (6)

A mild, pleasant day in May.

I took Nocko and Lindy to Lanzhou, where Disney had built its newest theme park in Asia. The park took up 306 hectares on both sides of the Yellow River. From the observation deck at the tallest tower, the river glowed like a golden silk ribbon. The silver specks of airplanes skimmed across the sky from time to time. The world appeared grand and untouchable, like a buttered popcorn expanding tranquilly in the sun.

The park was crowded. A dancing parade of pirates and elaborately dressed princesses wound its way through the street, and costumed boys and girls, overjoyed, followed behind, imitating their movements. Holding Nocko and Lindy each by a hand, I weaved through the field of cotton candy, ice-cold soda, and electronic music. Holograms of ghosts and spaceships whizzed over our heads. A gigantic, mechanical dragon-horse slowly strode through the park, its head held high proudly, the mist spraying from its nostrils drawing screams of delight from the children.

I hadn't run like that in ages. My heart pounded like a beating drum. When we emerged from a dense wood, I saw a blue hippopotamus character sitting by itself on a bench, as though napping in the afternoon sun.

I stopped behind the trees. Finally, I screwed up the courage to take a step forward.

"Hello."

The hippo looked up, two tiny black eyes focusing on us.

"This is Lindy, and this is Nocko. They'd like a picture with you. Is that all right?"

After a few seconds, the hippo nodded.

I hugged Nocko with one arm, Lindy with the other, and sat down on the bench next to the hippo.

"Can I ask you to take the picture?"

The hippo accepted my phone and clumsily extended its arm. I seemed to see a drowning person in the bottomless abyss, slowly, bit by bit, lift a heavy arm with their last ounce of strength.

Come on! Come on! I cried silently. *Don't give up!*

The screen of the phone showed four faces squeezed together. A soft click. The picture froze.

"Thank you." I took back the phone. "Would you leave me your contact info? I'll send a copy to you."

After another few seconds of silence, the hippo slowly typed an address on my phone.

"Nocko and Lindy, would you like to give Hippo a hug?"

The two little ones opened their arms and each hugged one of the hippo's arms. The hippo looked down to the left and then to the right, and then slowly squeezed its arms to hug them back tight.

Yes, I know you crave to be hugged by this world, too.

※

It was late by the time we got back to the hotel. After showering, I lay on the bed, exhausted. Both my heels were rubbed raw by the new shoes, and the pain was excruciating. Tomorrow I still had a long way to go.

The laughter of the children and the image of the blue hippo lingered in my mind.

I searched on the hotel room's iWall until I found the web address I wanted and clicked on it. Accompanied by a mournful tune played by a violin, white lines of text slowly appeared against a black background:

This morning I thought about the first time I had been to Disney. Such bright sunlight, music, colors, and the smiling faces of children. I had stood in the crowd then and cried. I told myself that if one day I should lose the courage to continue to live, I would come to Disney one last time and plunge myself into that joyful, festive spirit. Perhaps the heat of the crowd would allow me to hold on for a few days longer. But I'm too exhausted now. I can't get out of the door; even getting out of the bed is a struggle. I know perfectly well that if only I could find the courage to take a step forward, I would find another ray of hope. But all my strength must be used to struggle with the irresistible weight that pulls me down, down. I'm like a broken wind-up machine that has been stranded, with hope ever receding. I'm tired. I want it all to end.

Goodbye. I'm sorry, everyone. I hope heaven looks like Disney.

The date stamp on the post was three years ago. Even now, new comments are being posted, mourning the loss of another young life, confessing their own anxiety, despair, and struggle. The woman who had written this note would never be back to see that her final message to the world had garnered more than a million replies.

That note was the reason Disney added the blue hippos to its parks. Anyone around the world could, just by launching an app on their phone, connect to a blue hippo, and, through its cameras and microphones, see and hear everything the hippo could see and hear.

Behind every blue hippo was a person in a dark room, unable to leave.

I sent the picture from today to the address left me by the hippo, along with the contact information for a suicide-prevention organization staffed by therapists. I hoped that this would help. I hoped that everything would be better.

※

Late night. Everything was so quiet.

I found the first-aid kit and bandaged my feet. I crawled into bed, pulled the blanket over me, and turned off the light. Moonlight washed over the room, filling every inch.

One time, as a little girl, I was playing outside when I stepped on a piece of broken glass. The bleeding would not stop, and there was no one around to help me. Terrified, I felt abandoned by the whole world. I lay down in the grass, thinking I would die after all the blood had drained out of me. But after a while, I found the bleeding stanched. So I picked up my sandals and hopped back home on one foot.

In the morning, Lindy would leave me. The therapist said that I no longer needed her—at least not for a long while.

I hoped she would never be back.

But maybe I would miss her, from time to time.

Goodnight, Nocko. Goodnight, Lindy.

Goodnight, melancholy.

AUTHOR'S NOTE

Most of the incidents and quotes from Alan Turing's life are based on Andrew Hodges's biography, Alan Turing: The Enigma *(1983).*

Besides the papers cited in the text, I also consulted the following sources on artificial intelligence:

Gary Marcus. "Why Can't My Computer Understand Me?" *The New Yorker*, August 14, 2013 (accessible at http://www.newyorker .com/tech/elements/why-cant-my-computer-understand-me).

Matthias Englert, Sandra Siebert, and Martin Ziegler. "Logical limitations to machine ethics with consequences to lethal autonomous weapons." arXiv preprint arXiv:1411.2842 (2014) (accessible at http://arxiv.org/abs/1411.2842).

Some details about depression are based on the following articles:

《抑郁时代，抑郁病人》 http://www.360doc.cn/article/2369606_45936 1744.html

《午安忧郁》 http://www.douban.com/group/topic/12541503/#!/i

In the preface to his Turing biography, Andrew Hodges wrote: "[T]he remaining secrets behind his last days are probably stranger than any science fiction writer could concoct." This was the inspiration for this story. The conversation program "Christopher" is entirely fictional, but some of the details in the conversations with Turing are real. I'm afraid it's up to the careful reader to screen out the fiction and nonfiction woven together in this tale.

As I drafted this story, I sent the sections on Turing's life to friends without telling them that these came from a piece of fiction. Many friends believed the stories, including some science fiction authors and programmers. After taking delight in the fact that I had successfully won the imitation game, I asked myself what were the criteria for telling truth and lies apart? Where was the boundary between reality and fiction? Perhaps the decision process had nothing to do with logic and rationality. Perhaps my friends simply chose to believe me, as Alan chose to believe Christopher.

I hereby sincerely apologize to friends who were deceived. To those who weren't, I'm very curious how you discovered the lies.

I believe that cognition relies on quantum effects, like tossing dice. I believe that before machines have learned to write poetry, each word written by an author is still meaningful. I believe that above the abyss, we can hold tightly onto each other and stride from the long winter into bright summer.

LIU CIXIN

Liu Cixin is widely recognized as the leading voice in Chinese science fiction. He won the Yinhe Award for eight consecutive years, from 1999 to 2006, and again in 2010. He received the Xingyun Award in both 2010 and 2011.

An engineer by profession—until 2014, he worked for the China Power Investment Corporation at a power plant in Niangziguan, Shanxi Province—Liu began writing science fiction short stories as a hobby. However, his popularity soared with the publication of the Remembrance of Earth's Past series of novels (the first volume, *The Three-Body Problem*, was serialized in *Science Fiction World* in 2006 and then published as a standalone book in 2008). An epic story of alien invasion and humanity's journey to the stars, the series begins with a secret, Mao-era military effort at establishing communications with extraterrestrial intelligence, and ends (literally) with the end of the universe. Tor Books published the English edition of the series from 2014 to 2016 (*The Three-Body Problem*, translated by Ken Liu; *The Dark Forest*, translated by Joel Martinsen; *Death's End*, translated by Ken Liu). *The Three-Body Problem* was the first translated book to win the Hugo Award for Best Novel, and President Barack Obama praised it as "wildly imaginative, really interesting."

Liu works in the "hard SF" tradition of writers like Arthur C. Clarke. Some have called him a "classical" writer for that reason, as his stories foreground the romance and grandeur of science and humankind's effort to discover nature's secrets.

"Moonlight" showcases Liu Cixin doing what he does best: presenting idea after idea in a dizzying fusillade. This is the story's first appearance in English.

MOONLIGHT

For the first time that he could remember, he saw moonlight in the city.

He hadn't noticed it on other nights because the bright electric glow of millions of lamps had overwhelmed it. But today was the Mid-Autumn Festival, and a web petition had proposed that the city turn off most landscape lighting and some of the streetlights so that residents could enjoy the full moon.

Looking out from the balcony of his single-occupancy unit, he discovered that the petitioners had been wrong about the effect. The moonlit city was nothing like the charming, idyllic scene they had imagined; rather, it resembled an abandoned ruin. Still, he appreciated the view. The apocalyptic spirit gave off a beauty of its own, suggesting the passing of all and the discharge of all burdens. He had only to lie down in the embrace of Fate to enjoy the tranquility at the end. That was what he needed.

His phone buzzed. The caller was a man. After ascertaining who had picked up, the voice said, "I'm sorry to disturb you on the worst day of your life. I still remember it after all these years."

The voice sounded odd. Clear, but distant and hollow. An image came to his mind: chill winds rushing between the strings of a harp abandoned in the wilderness.

The caller continued. "Today was Wen's wedding, wasn't it? She invited you, but you didn't go."

"Who is this?"

"I've thought about it so many times over the years. You should have gone, and you would be feeling better now. But you . . . well, you did go, except you hid in the lobby and watched Wen in her wedding dress heading into the reception holding his hand. You were torturing yourself."

"Who *are* you?" Despite his astonishment, he still noticed the caller's odd phrasing. The caller said "after all these years," but the wedding had only taken place this morning. And since Wen's wedding date had been decided on only a week ago, it was impossible for anyone to know about it long before then.

The distant voice went on. "You have a habit. Whenever you're upset, you curl your left big toe and dig the nail into the bottom of your shoe. When you got home earlier, you found that your toenail had snapped but you didn't even notice the pain. Your toenails are getting long though. They've worn holes into your socks. You haven't been taking care of yourself."

"Who in the world is this?" He was now frightened.

"I'm you. I'm calling from the year 2123. It's not easy connecting to your mobile network from this time. The signal degradation through the time-space interface is severe. If you can't hear me, let me know and I'll try again."

He knew it wasn't a joke. He had known from the first moment that the voice didn't belong to this world. He clutched the phone tightly and stared at the buildings washed by the cold, pure moonlight, as though the whole city had frozen to listen to their conversation. Yet he could think of nothing to say as the caller waited patiently. Faint background noises filled his ear.

"How . . . could I live to be so old?" he asked, just to break the silence.

"Twenty years from your time, genetic therapies will be invented to extend human lifespan to around two centuries. I'm still technically middle-aged, though I feel ancient."

"Can you explain the process in more detail?"

"No. I can't even give you a simple overview. I have to ensure that you receive as little information about the future as possible, to prevent you from inappropriate behaviors that would change the course of history."

"Then why did you get in touch with me in the first place?"

"For the mission that we have to accomplish together. Having lived for so long, I can tell you a secret about life: once you realize how insignificant the individual is in the vastness of space-time, you can face anything. I didn't call you to talk about your personal life, so I need you to let go of the pain and face the mission. Listen! What do you hear?"

He strained to catch the background noises through the receiver. The faint sounds resolved into splashes and plops, and he tried to reconstruct an image from them. Strange flowers bloomed in the darkness; a giant glacier cracked in a desolate sea, and zigzagging seams extended into the depths of the crystalline mass like lightning bolts . . .

"You're hearing waves crashing against buildings. I'm on the eighth floor of Jin Mao Tower. The surface of the sea is right under the window."

"Shanghai has been flooded?"

"That's right. She was the last of the coastal cities to fall. The dikes were high and durable, but the sea ultimately inundated the interior and flooded back in. . . . Can you imagine what I'm seeing? No, it's nothing like Venice. The undulating water between the buildings is covered with garbage and flotsam, as if all the refuse accumulated in this city over two centuries had become afloat. The moon is full tonight, just like where and when you are. There are no lights in the city, but my moon is not nearly as bright as yours— the atmosphere is far too polluted. The sea mirrors the moonlight onto the skeletons of the skyscrapers. The great sphere at the top of the Oriental Pearl Tower flickers with silvery streaks reflected from the waves, as if everything is about to collapse."

"How much has the sea risen?"

"The polar ice caps are gone. In the span of half a century, the sea rose by about twenty meters. Three hundred million coastal inhabitants had to move inland. Only desolation is left here, while the inland regions are gripped by political and social chaos. The economy is nearing total collapse. . . . Our mission is to prevent all of this."

"Do you think we can play God?"

"Mere mortals doing what needed to be done a hundred years earlier would have the same effect as divine intervention now. If, in your time, the whole world had stopped using all fossil fuels— including coal, petroleum, and natural gas—global warming would have stopped, and this disaster could have been prevented."

"That seems impossible." After he said this, his self from more than a hundred years in the future remained silent for a long time. So he added, "To stop the use of fossil fuels, you need to contact people from even earlier."

He sensed a smile through the phone. "Do you imagine I can stop the Industrial Revolution in its tracks?"

"But what you're asking of us now is even more impossible. The world will fall apart if you eliminate all coal, gas, and oil for a single week."

"Actually, our models show that it wouldn't even take that long. But there are other ways. Remember that I'm speaking to you from the future. Think. We're smart people."

He thought of one possibility. "Give us an advanced energy technology. Something environmentally friendly that won't contribute to climate change. The technology has to be able to satisfy existing energy needs while also being much cheaper than fossil fuels. If you give us that, it won't be ten years before the market will force all fossil fuels out of contention."

"That's exactly what we're going to do."

Encouraged, he went on. "Then teach us how to achieve controlled nuclear fusion."

"You vastly underestimate the difficulties. We still haven't achieved any breakthroughs in that field. There are fusion reactor power plants, but they aren't even as competitive in the market as fission plants in your time. Also, fusion reactors require the extraction of fuel from seawater, a process that may lead to more environmental damage. We can't give you controlled fusion, but we can give you solar power."

"Solar power? What do you mean exactly?"

"Collecting the sun's power from the surface of the Earth."

"With what?"

"Monocrystalline silicon, the same material you use in your time."

"Oh, come on! You literally just made me facepalm. I thought you had something real for a minute there. . . . Actually, do you still say 'facepalm'?"

"Sure we do. Old-timers like me have kept lots of expressions like that alive. Anyway, our monocrystalline silicon solar cells have far higher conversion efficiency."

"Even if you achieved one hundred percent efficiency it would be irrelevant. How much solar power reaches each square meter on the Earth's surface? There's no way that a few solar panels can satisfy the energy needs of contemporary society. Have you been hallucinating that your youth was spent in some preindustrial farmers' paradise?"

He heard his future self laugh. "Now that you mention it, the technology really does evoke shades of agrarian nostalgia."

"'Evoke shades of agrarian nostalgia'? When did I start to talk like a coffee shop writer?"

"Heh, the technology really is called the silicon plow."

"What?"

"The silicon plow. Silicon is the most abundant element on Earth, and you can find it everywhere in sand or soil. A silicon plow cuts furrows in the earth just like a regular plow, but it extracts the silicon out of the soil and refines it into monocrystalline silicon. The land it processes turns into solar cells."

"What . . . what does a silicon plow look like?"

"Like a combine harvester. To start it, you need an external energy source, but then it relies on the power provided by the solar cells it leaves behind. With this technology, you can turn the whole Taklamakan Desert into a solar power plant."

"Are you telling me that all the plowed land will become black, shiny cells?"

"No. The plowed land will just look darker, but the conversion efficiency will be phenomenal. After the land has been plowed, you just attach wires to the two ends of the furrow to get a photovoltaic current."

As the holder of a doctorate degree in Energy Planning, he was entranced by the promise of this technology. His breathing sped up.

"I just sent you an email with all the technical details. At your technology level, you shouldn't have any trouble mass-producing it—that's also one of the reasons I chose to contact your era instead of an earlier time. Starting tomorrow, you must dedicate yourself to spreading this technology. I know you have the necessary resources and the skills. How to popularize the technology is up to you. Maybe you can take advantage of the report you're drafting right now. But you have to remember one thing: under no circumstances can you reveal that the technology comes from the future."

"Why did you choose me? You should have picked someone more senior."

"I have to take care to reduce the potential negative side effects from my interference. You and I are the same person. Can you think of a better choice?"

"Tell me, just how high have you climbed on the career ladder?"

"I can't reveal that. It took a lot of convincing for the Embodied International to decide to interfere in history at all."

"Embodied International?"

"The world is divided between the Embodied International and the Virtual International—never mind, I've said too much. Don't ask me about anything like that again."

"But . . . if I do as you've asked, how will you see the world change? Are you going to wake up the next day and find everything different?"

"It'll be even faster than that. The minute you open my email and decide on your course of action, my world will likely change instantly. But we two are the only people—the only person—who will know this. For everyone else in my era, history is history, and in the new timeline, which is also their only timeline, the period of fossil fuel use between your time and my time never happened."

"Will you call me again?"

"I don't know. Every contact with the past is a major undertaking. International conferences have to be held. Goodbye."

He returned to his bedroom and turned on the computer. The inbox showed the email from the future. The body was blank, but there were more than a dozen attachments, totaling more than a gigabyte. He browsed through them quickly and found detailed technical drawings and documents. Although he couldn't make sense of everything yet, he saw that the technical language was accessible to someone of his era.

One particular photograph caught his attention. It was a wide-angle shot of an open space. A silicon plow, which really did resemble a combine harvester, sat in the middle of the field, and the soil behind it was slightly darker. The perspective of the shot made the plow look like a small brush painting the earth dark stroke by long stroke. About a third of the land in the frame had already been plowed, but the part of the photo that most attracted his attention was the sky of the future. It was a dusty gray, but not overcast. Maybe it was taken at dawn or dusk, since the plow cast a long shadow. This was an age without blue skies.

He began to think through his next steps. As a staff member of the Planning Office of the Ministry of Energy, he was responsible for, among other things, gathering information on the progress of new energy development projects across the country. The report he was drafting would be passed on to the minister, who would then deliver it to the State Council at their upcoming meeting. Part of China's four-trillion-yuan stimulus package in response to the economic crisis was set aside for developing new energy technologies, and the State Council meeting would decide where to invest the funds. His future self apparently wanted him to take advantage of this opportunity. But before he could put this technology into his report, he had to first find a research lab or company to pick it up as a development project. He would have to be very strategic in this choice, but he was certain that if the technical documents were real, he would find a good company to undertake the work. Even in the worst case, whoever decided to move forward with this research wouldn't lose much . . .

He shuddered, as if waking from a dream. *Have I already decided to go down this path? Yes, I have.* There could only be two outcomes from his decision: success or failure. If his effort would eventually succeed, the future should have already been altered.

Mere mortals doing what needed to be done a hundred years earlier would have the same effect as divine intervention.

He stared at the email on the screen, and suddenly had the urge to respond to it. He wrote only two words in the reply: *Got it.* Immediately, a response came back informing him that the address was undeliverable. He picked up his phone and looked at the caller ID, an ordinary number from China Mobile. He pressed the "call" button, and a recorded voice informed him that the number was not in service.

Returning to the balcony, he luxuriated in the watery moonlight. The neighborhood was completely quiet this late at night, and the moon bathed the buildings and the ground in a milky, unreal, tender glow. He had the sensation of waking from a dream, or perhaps he was still dreaming.

The phone rang again. The screen showed another unfamiliar number, but as soon as he picked up, he recognized the voice of his future self. It was still distant and hollow, but the background noises were different.

"You succeeded," his future self said.

"When are you calling from?" he asked.

"The year 2119."

"So four years earlier than the last time you called."

"For me, this is the first time I've ever called you . . . or calling me, I guess. But I do remember receiving that phone call you mentioned more than a hundred years ago."

"That was just twenty minutes ago, for me. How is everything? Has the seawater receded?"

"There's no seawater. The climate never warmed drastically, and sea levels didn't rise. The history you heard about twenty minutes earlier never happened. In our history books, solar energy made a breakthrough in the early twenty-first century and culminated in the silicon plow, which made large-scale solar energy collection possible. In the 2020s, solar energy came to dominate world energy markets, and fossil fuels quickly vanished. The first half of your—our—life has been a brilliant rising arc tied to the silicon plow, and in three years from your time, the technology will begin to spread across the globe. However, just like the history of the coal and oil industries, the history of solar energy hasn't generated any lasting celebrities, not even you."

"I don't care about being famous. It's wonderful to have had a role in saving the world."

"Of course we don't care about fame. In fact, it's good that we are not well known, otherwise we'd be treated as history's greatest criminal. The world has changed, but not for the better. The good thing is that only one person, you and me, knows this. Even those who had devised and implemented the plan to interfere with history the last time have no memories of fossil fuel use in the rest of the twenty-first century since that timeline never came to be. I don't remember calling you, but I do remember getting the call from the future. That phone call is, in fact, the only clue I have to that nonexistent history. Listen! What do you hear?"

Through the receiver, he detected faint cries that reminded him of clouds of swarming birds above the woods at dusk. Gusts of wind swept through the trees from time to time, overwhelming the cries with susurrations.

"I can't tell what I'm hearing. It doesn't sound like the ocean."

"Of course it doesn't sound like the ocean. Even the Huangpu River is almost dried out. This is the drought season—there are only two seasons now, drought and flood. It's possible to cross the river just by rolling up your pant legs. In fact, several hundred thousand starving refugees have just crossed the river into Pudong, covering the riverbed like a mass of ants. The city is in disarray; I can see fires starting everywhere."

"What happened? Solar energy should have the lowest environmental impact."

"You're sadly mistaken. Do you know how many square kilometers of monocrystalline silicon fields are necessary to supply the energy needs of a city like Shanghai? At least twenty times the area of Shanghai itself! During the century after your time, urbanization accelerated, and even a mid-sized city now is comparable to the Shanghai of your era. Starting in the 2020s, silicon plows transformed the face of every continent. After all the deserts had been turned into solar fields, they began to devour arable land and vegetation cover. Now, every continent is suffering from excessive siliconization. The process had advanced far faster than desertification. The land surface of the Earth is now almost entirely covered by silicon solar fields."

"But this should be impossible under theories of economics! As land grows more scarce, the value of any unplowed land ought to rise, and silicon plows should become too expensive to be viable in the market—"

"This was no different from the history of the fossil fuel industries. By the time the conditions you describe came into play, it was too late. Shifting to alternative energy sources was no easy task, and even rebuilding the infrastructure for coal and oil required too much time. Meanwhile, the need for energy kept on growing, and silicon plows had to devour more land. Land siliconization was even more damaging to the environment than desertification. As conditions deteriorated, drought swept the globe, and the occasional rainfall only resulted in massive floods . . ."

Listening to this voice from a century in the future, he felt like a drowning man. Just before he was about to give up all hope, he found himself somehow at the surface. Taking a deep breath, he said to his future self, "But there is a way out! A way out! It's simple. I haven't done anything yet except decide on a plan for how to introduce the technology. I'll immediately delete the email and all attachments, and go on with my life as before."

"Then Shanghai will once more be swallowed by the sea."

He moaned with frustration.

"We have to interfere with history again," said his future self.

"Don't tell me: you're going to give me some other new energy technology?"

"That's right. The key to the new technology is ultra-deep drilling."

"Drilling? But the technology for oil extraction is already very advanced."

"No, I'm not talking about drilling for oil. The wells I have in mind will reach a depth of over a hundred kilometers, penetrating the Mohorovičić discontinuity and boring into the liquid mantle. The Earth's powerful magnetic field is generated by strong electric currents deep within the planet, and we want to tap into them. Once the ultra-deep wells are drilled, massive terminals dropped into the wells will extract the geoelectric energy. We'll also give you the technology for electrical terminals that can function under such high temperatures."

"That sounds . . . grandiose. I'm rather frightened."

"Listen, geoelectricity extraction is the greenest technology. It doesn't take up any land and doesn't generate any carbon dioxide or other pollutants. All right, it's time to say goodbye. If we ever talk again, let's hope it's not to save the world. . . . Go check your email."

"Wait! Let's chat some more. Tell me about . . . our life."

"We have to keep contact with the past to a minimum to reduce information leakage. I'm sure you understand that what we're doing is incredibly dangerous. Also, there's nothing to talk about really, since whatever I've gone through you'll get to experience sooner or later." The connection ended as soon as his future self stopped talking.

He returned to his computer and saw a second email. Like the last one, it was also packed with technical information. As he browsed through the attachments, he found that ultra-deep drilling used lasers instead of mechanical bits, and the molten rock was channeled up through the drill to the surface. The last attachment was another photograph of an open field studded with high-voltage transmission towers. The lattice towers looked slender and light, perhaps constructed from some strong composite material. One end of the wires plunged into the earth, evidently to tap into the buried geoelectric terminals. The ground itself attracted his gaze, as it was the lifeless dark color of plowed silicon fields. A network of fencing divided the ground into a grid, which he decided must be transmission lines that extracted the energy from the monocrystalline silicon. Unlike the photograph from the last time, the sky was a clear azure, with not a wisp of cloud to be seen. This was an age where rain was rare, and even through the photograph he could feel the crisp, dry air.

Once again, he returned to the balcony. The moon was now in the western sky and shadows had lengthened, as though the city had finished dreaming and fallen deeper into slumber.

He thought about ways to spread this new future technology. The necessary strategies were different from the last time. First, the laser drilling technology would itself generate attractive military and civilian applications. He should be able to popularize it first and wait for the industry to mature before revealing the far more astounding idea of geoelectricity. At the same time, he could advocate for development of other ancillary technologies like extreme heat-tolerant electric terminals. The initial investment still had to come from the four-trillion-yuan stimulus package, and he still needed to find an influential entity to take up the research project. He was confident of success because he knew he had the technical secrets.

I've decided on a new path. Has history changed again?

As if answering his thoughts, the phone rang for the third time. The westering moon was now half-peeking from behind a tall building across the way, as if giving this world one last terrified glance before her departure.

"I'm you, calling from the year 2125."

The caller paused, as if waiting for him to ask questions, but he dared not. The hand squeezing the phone grew clammy, and he was already exhausted. Finally, he asked, "You want me to listen to the noises of your world, don't you?"

"I don't think you'll hear much this time."

Still, he strained to listen. There was only a slight buzzing that sounded like interference. Surely a signal passing through space-time had to deal with interference, which could have come from any time between now and 2125, or the emptiness that existed outside of time and the cosmos.

"Are you still in Shanghai?" he asked his future self.

"Yes."

"I can't hear anything. Maybe all your cars are electric and practically silent."

"The cars are all in the tunnels, which is why you can't hear them."

"Tunnels? What do you mean?"

"Shanghai is now underground."

The moon disappeared behind the building, and everything darkened. He felt himself sinking into the earth. "What happened?"

"The surface is full of radiation. You'll die if you stay up there for a few hours without protection. And it'll be an ugly death, with blood seeping all over your skin—"

"Radiation! What are you talking about?"

"The sun. Yes, you've succeeded. Geoelectric power grew even faster than the silicon plow, and by 2020, the geoelectricity extraction industry had outgrown the coal and oil industries combined. As it matured, the efficiency and cost of this technology couldn't be matched even by the silicon plow, let alone fossil fuels. The world's energy needs soon grew to be entirely dependent on geo-electricity. It was clean, cheap, and so perfect that many wondered how it had taken humanity thousands of years after the invention of the compass to finally think of drawing upon the giant dynamo beneath our feet. As the economy soared on the wings of this sustainable energy source, the environment also improved. Humanity believed that our civilization had finally achieved the dream of effortless growth, and the future would only get better."

"And then?"

"At the beginning of this century, geoelectricity suddenly ran out. Compasses no longer pointed north. I'm sure you know that the Earth's electric field is our planet's shield. It deflects the solar wind and protects our atmosphere. But now, the Van Allen belts are gone, and the solar wind buffets the Earth like a petri dish placed under an ultraviolet light."

He tried to speak, but only a croak emerged from his throat. He felt chills all over.

"This is only the start. Over the next three to five centuries, the solar wind will destroy the Earth's atmosphere, boil away the ocean and all other surface water."

Another inarticulate croak.

"We've finally achieved a breakthrough in controlled nuclear fusion, and together with the reconstructed oil and coal industries, humanity now possesses inexhaustible sources of energy. Most of the power we generate, however, is pumped into the Earth to restart the magnetic field. So far the results are not encouraging."

"We have to fix it!"

"Yes, that's right. You must delete both emails from the future."

He turned to head back inside. "I'll do it right now."

"Just a minute. Once you delete them, history will change again, and our connection will break off."

"Right. The world will return to its original timeline of fossil fuel dominance."

"And you'll go on with your life as before."

"Please, tell me about our life after this moment."

"I can't. Telling you will change the future."

"I understand that knowing the future will change it. But I still want to know a few things."

"Sorry. I can't."

"How about just tell me if we'll be living the life we wanted? Are we happy?"

"I can't."

"Will I get married? Kids? How many boys and girls?"

"I can't."

"After Wen, will I fall in love again?"

He thought his future self was going to refuse to answer again, but the voice remained silent. All he could hear was the hissing of the winds of time through the empty valley of more than a century dividing them. Finally, he heard the answer.

"Never again."

"What? I won't love again for more than a hundred years?"

"No. A life is not unlike the history of all of humanity. The choice presented to you the first time may also be the best, but there's no way to know without traveling down other timelines."

"So I'll be alone all my life?"

"I'm sorry, I can't tell you. . . . Though loneliness is the human condition, still we must conduct our lives with grace and strive for joy. It's time."

Without another word, the call ended. His phone dinged, signaling a text. Attached to the message was a short video, which he copied to his computer to be able to see better.

A sea of flames dominated the screen. It took a while for him to understand that he was looking at the sky. The fiery lights weren't from burning fire, but auroras that filled the firmament from horizon to horizon, generated by solar wind particles striking the atmosphere. Billowy red curtains convulsed across the vault of heaven like a mountain of snakes. The sky seemed to be made of some liquid, a terrifying sight.

There was a single building resembling a stack of spheres on the ground: the Oriental Pearl Tower. The mirrored surfaces reflected the fiery sea above, and the spheres themselves seemed to be made of flames. Closer to the camera stood a man dressed in a heavy protective suit whose surface was brightly reflective and smooth, like a man-shaped mirror. The heavenly fire was reflected in this man-mirror as well, and the flame snakes, distorted by the curved surfaces, appeared even more eerie. The entire scene flowed and shimmered as though the world had turned to molten lava. The man raised a hand toward the camera, saying hello and goodbye to the past at once.

The video ended.

Was that me?

Then he remembered that he had more important tasks. He deleted the emails and all attachments. Then, after a moment, he began to reformat the disk and zero out the sectors with multiple passes.

By the time the reformatting had completed, it was just another ordinary night. The man who had changed the course of human history three times in a single night but who in the end had changed nothing fell asleep in front of his computer.

Dawn brightened the eastern sky. The world began another ordinary day. Nothing had happened, at all.

TANG FEI

Tang Fei (a pen name that should be treated as an indivisible unit) is a speculative fiction writer whose work has been featured in magazines in China such as *Science Fiction World*, *Jiuzhou Fantasy*, and *Fantasy Old and New*. She has written fantasy, science fiction, fairy tales, and *wuxia* (martial arts fantasy), but prefers to write in a way that straddles or stretches genre boundaries. She is also a genre critic, and her critical essays have been published in *The Economic Observer*.

A photographer and an avid traveler, Tang Fei enjoys wandering through new cities and connecting with people on unplanned adventures. If you ever meet her, ask her about the time she fell into a river in Japan.

In translation, her fiction has appeared in *Clarkesworld*, *Pathlight*, *Apex*, and *SQ Mag*, among other places. More of her fiction can be found in *Invisible Planets*.

Like many of Tang Fei's stories, "Broken Stars" isn't easy to box into a genre. The world is uncanny and out-of-focus, and the characters inhabiting it have jagged edges and sharp spurs. At its heart is the darkness that is left after the stars have winked out.

BROKEN STARS

If I really think about it, the stars did not arrange such a fate.

But the stars are broken, and so the definitive proof is gone. This moment is a vertex where time caves in: to the left is the past, to the right—

To the right should have been the future.

But the stars are broken.

Also, I met Zhang Xiaobo.

1.

She didn't bring an umbrella, though the weather forecast said it was going to rain. After dinner, as she passed by the shoe rack, she missed the umbrella that had been specifically set out for her.

A few other students were scattered along the sidewalk, gradually gathering into a trickle of school uniforms that crossed the road and entered the school. Tang Jiaming entered the lecture hall from the back, at the top of the tiered seats, just as the first bell for evening study hall rang.

Most of the seats under the fluorescent lamps were filled. It was the second semester of the year before graduation, and the high school had organized nightly cram sessions starting at seven for students who still had some potential of doing well on the college entrance examination. Out of the two hundred or so students in the class, only about thirty qualified for the cram sessions based on their mock exam scores. The rest went on with their regular classes during the day, and were packed into this lecture hall for self-directed study in the evenings.

Jiaming saw Zhu Yin waving at her from one of the back rows—she had saved Jiaming a seat by the window.

"So many people here tonight! I'm guessing they're still renovating the pool hall?"

"It's gonna rain," Zhu Yin mumbled. She held a bunch of rubber bands between her teeth while her hands danced like butterflies flitting through her hair. Zhu Yin excelled at fancy braids, and her hands were rarely free for anything else.

"You'll have to write out this problem for me." Zhu Yin lifted her chin to indicate the two workbooks on the desk. "Your handwriting is so messy that I can't even copy your solution."

"It's just adding two complex numbers." Jiaming pushed the workbooks back to her.

Sometimes she helped Zhu Yin copy her homework, but not always.

Zhu Yin scowled as she continued to braid. She was still angry at Jiaming for what had happened.

"Jiaming, I'm your best friend, right? The best?" she asked.

"Uh-huh." Jiaming's gaze roamed around the lecture hall.

"Out of everybody in the world?"

"Sure."

"Why?"

Jiaming laughed. She turned to look at Zhu Yin—*she's so pretty.* "Because I want to be just like you," she said.

"Liar!" But Zhu Yin was pleased. Her black eyes twinkled, and the scene in front of her was reflected in those dark mirrors, perfect in every detail. Jiaming really did like Zhu Yin, liked the ease with which she could be cheered up in an instant.

Jiaming yawned. It was going to rain, a big thundershower. The outside was unusually dark, but no one in the lecture hall seemed to have noticed.

Playing with phones, copying homework, reading comic books or gossip magazines, napping smoking giggling eating . . . Like the slips of paper being passed around the room, the students shuttled about, changing seats without cease. Those who preferred quiet were concentrated in the first two rows so they could focus on working out supplemental problem sets for three hours. It was the same every day. The mercury-vapor lights dulled the colors and outlines, while restless, bulging, youthful bodies agitated under their clothes. The chaotic, low-background white noise was interrupted occasionally by a shout or peal of laughter. Various aromas mixed together in harmony: Little Raccoon brand dry crispy noodle snacks, ham sausage, hair spray, rain boots. She enjoyed the sensation of being immersed in her surroundings, idle.

Her heart was filled with affection for everyone.

"Did you not sleep well?" Zhu Yin asked.

"Had too much to eat," Jiaming replied.

"I'll help you fix your hair later. How could you let it get so messy?"

"Sounds good."

Bang! The door slammed open. Before anyone in the room had time to react, the sand and pebbles blown in by the gust of wind struck their bodies, accompanied by flapping workbook pages and screams. Chaos reigned in the lecture hall. The gale preceding the rain careened around violently, sweeping away everything in its path. The windows creaked in their frames, the glass panes threatening to crack.

Jiaming got up to close the window; it would take but a moment.

She saw Zhang Xiaobo, even though she didn't yet know his name.

He stood on top of the cement wall around the schoolyard, his footing uncertain in the howling wind. The wall was tall, and had grown taller every year. From where Jiaming stood it was hard to tell if he intended to jump. She thought he might. Maybe not now; maybe someday in the future.

She saw the boy bend down to sit on top of the wall and retrieve his lighter. He flicked it until it was lit but didn't light anything; instead, he simply stared at the flickering tongue, shielding it from the wind with his hand. The tongue licked at his palm, painfully, and illuminated his face.

The windowpane before Jiaming's face fogged up.

Strictly speaking, he wasn't Jiaming's type. He was too pale, too thin, with eyes that were too large and sunken in dark circles. However, he appeared serendipitously on the school wall that night.

The summer of 1998. The squall coming from over the sea brought the warm, moist scent of salt and fish. The shadows cast by the trees shifted—Jiaming had never seen the trees move so wildly, as though they craved to dance. She pressed her face against the glass and gazed at their dark outlines: perhaps someday they would uproot themselves and run madly away from here. Just then, perfectly timed, the boy had appeared on top of the only part of the wall not hidden by the shadows of the trees. The tongue of flame in his hand trembled wildly, illuminating the brown bloodstains on his white shirt. From a distance, the drumbeats of dense African jungle struck against Jiaming's body, riding on the wet, violent blasts of the storm.

The fire went out.

Rain poured.

"What are you looking at?" She heard Zhu Yin's voice behind her.

"The rain is so heavy."

"I brought an umbrella. How about you come home with me first. . . ."

※

"Where did you get that umbrella?"

"A friend."

"You should go change."

Jiaming went to her room and changed into fresh clothes, the wet bundle at her feet like shed snakeskin. The rain was so heavy that the umbrella hadn't done much good.

She returned to the living room, where silent images danced on the TV screen. She picked up the remote and clicked through the channels, pausing at each briefly. In their home, no one ever un-muted the TV, but no one turned the TV off, either.

"Do you have any homework?" a voice asked from behind the piles of architectural plans.

"All finished."

"I'll get off work early the day after tomorrow. We can go out for dinner together."

For a second, Jiaming was silent as she stared at dozens of Mk 82 bombs dropping from the sky on TV; the next scene showed burning fields. She remembered.

"Your birthday is in two days," she said.

"What would you like as a gift?"

"Isn't it a bit bizarre to give *me* gifts when it's *your* birthday? Do you have something to tell me?"

The man ignored this.

"A Sarah Brightman CD then."

"Write it down for me. It's time for bed." The man went into the kitchen and returned with a glass of milk; he handed it to Jiaming and watched as she drank it down.

Every night, before bed, her father gave her a glass of warm milk so that she could sleep soundly.

※

"So ugly!" The pale woman stared at the hairband in her hand, shocked. "Who would buy this?"

"They sell very well, in every color. Lots of girls at school wear them."

They glanced at each other and laughed at the same time.

"Long hair is too much trouble."

"But I like you with long hair. You look particularly well be-haved." The pale woman caressed Jiaming's short hair. Her hand was so white that it looked like a beam of moonlight was shining on Jiaming.

"I prefer it like this."

"How's school?"

"Same old same old. It rained yesterday." Her voice softened, but returned to normal almost immediately. "I didn't bring an umbrella, so Zhu Yin lent me hers."

She waited for the pale woman to ask her, *Does Zhu Yin still act really petulant sometimes?* Then she would know what to say next.

But the pale woman didn't.

"It rained yesterday," she repeated what Jiaming had said.

"The day after tomorrow is Dad's birthday," said Jiaming.

The pale woman was quiet.

The woman reached into her pocket. "Let's look at the stars," she said.

She retrieved a folded-up sheet of paper and began to spread it, infinitely patient and gentle. Each time she opened another fold, her skin grew brighter, as if lit from beneath with a pure white light, of which, like her joy, it was impossible to say whether it was warm or cold. The paper, which had appeared about the size of her palm at first, gradually expanded and spread out in every direction under her careful, repetitive movements until the edges could no longer be seen.

$$\text{ℋ ∨ ♌ ♏}$$

The symbols and lines on the paper coiled and extended, as strange as the first time she had seen them. A rapidly spinning disk.

ἀστρολάβος

astrolabos

The Star-Taker

"Look, these are your stars." The pale woman laughed.

2.

For PE, they were supposed to do an 800-meter run. But after the first lap, few girls could be seen on the track.

From a distance, Jiaming saw the PE teacher chasing girls back onto the track who had been trying to get out of running by hiding in the shade of trees. Reluctantly, they minced their way down the track. As soon as girls hit puberty, they seemed to lose the ability to run properly; it wasn't only because of their bouncing breasts—overall they became indolent, or perhaps they were learning that this was part of the art of being coy.

"You're in a good mood today," Zhu Yin said.

Jiaming looked at her, surprised. They were hiding among the girls on the basketball court, pretending to be practicing their shots.

Zhu Yin came closer, like a mouse who has scented cake. "I bet there's something."

Jiaming said nothing.

"Did you dream about her?"

When she was seven, Jiaming had told Zhu Yin that she dreamed of a woman who was so pale that her skin appeared pure white. Zhu Yin had never forgotten about her.

"What did you talk about last night?"

"I told her about my dad's birthday."

"Were you able to see her face clearly this time? Did she look like your mom?"

Jiaming had always been able to see the pale woman's face clearly, but she couldn't remember what her mom looked like. Her mother had died in an accident at sea when she was four.

"Hey, you two!" a male voice next to them interrupted. "Is that your teacher?"

The man coming toward them with the whistle in his mouth was indeed their PE teacher. Jiaming and Zhu Yin looked at each other and then slipped onto the track, hurrying to catch up with the group ahead of them.

"Thanks!" As they passed the boy who had warned them, Zhu Yin winked at him.

Jiaming and the boy locked eyes for a moment. She recognized him.

"You know the guy we just passed?" Jiaming asked.

"I know of him. He's in the cram class. A bit of a freak."

"What's his name?"

"Zhang Xiaobo."

Without the storm; without the trees thinking of escape; without the wild, mad fire; without him sitting on the wall he looked calm and friendly, perfectly normal. Jiaming told herself not to look back; there was no need for suspicion.

The pale woman had told her that the stars wished her luck.

She hadn't even noticed her own smile.

"What are you so happy about?" asked Zhu Yin.

"I was thinking of my dream from last night. I showed her the hairbands that are so popular right now, and she thought they're really ugly, too."

"Which kind?"

Jiaming looked at the girl sitting on the bench next to the track without speaking. Only someone who had gotten a note from the nurse could sit there so openly, excused from having to run up a sweat. As they crossed the finish line, the girl on the bench got up and walked toward them.

"You saw the ones she's wearing?"

Zhu Yin laughed. "Yeah, pretty ugly."

The new girl approached Jiaming but hesitated when she saw Zhu Yin.

Zhu Yin rolled her eyes. She turned to Jiaming. "I'll wait for you back in the classroom."

"Jiaming!" The bright sun made the new girl squint as she smiled.

"Lina."

※

Lina was one of the first girls to attract the attention of the boys. Once she turned twelve, her body lost its baby fat and began to acquire curves and contours, giving off a warm scent and unconsciously attracting the gazes of the opposite sex onto the bulges in her school uniform. She was always surrounded by boys, and not only boys her age.

No one worried that Lina was going to do something improper. She was as decorous as a cow elephant slowly maneuvering her enormous body, unmoved by everything around her. Only when the need presented itself would she deign to notice the boys' existence, and she knew how to make use of the gazes always trained on her.

For instance, that note from the nurse's office.

She also knew how to take advantage in other ways.

For instance, now she was grabbing Jiaming by the hand to get a snack from the campus store.

Lina paid for both of them. Jiaming let her and asked for two ice creams.

"I'm getting one for Zhu Yin," she said.

Lina smiled. "My doctor—he's a traditional Chinese medicine specialist—won't let me eat anything cold, not even sashimi. . . ."

The best thing about conversing with Lina was that you could let her talk without listening. Unlike other girls their age, she knew that one didn't have to take everything so seriously all the time. Jiaming had always felt relaxed around her.

"I hear that the study hall sessions are pretty easy."

"Sure, there's no extra homework. I'm sure you work much harder in the cram sessions."

Something was stuffed into her hand. Jiaming stopped and stared expressionlessly at the gift box from Lina: velvet, satin, exquisitely made. She opened it to find a brand-new Parker pen. "Lina?"

"We used to sit at the same desk, didn't we? I happen to have an extra pen." Lina's smile was like a piece of chocolate about to melt.

※

"Looks expensive. Do you fill it with regular ink?" The pale woman uncapped the pen and tested the tip of the nib.

"I'm sure they sell fancy ink that goes with it. Probably comes with its own gift box."

"Why did she give you this?"

Jiaming said nothing. She didn't think one or two secrets were much of a burden to carry.

The pale woman lifted Jiaming's face by the chin. "Give it back to her. I'm worried about you."

"If I were to do that, you'd be worrying about me even more."

The pale woman held her still and forced her to meet her gaze. "I've seen her stars. I don't like them."

"If I don't accept her bribe, she'll think that I've decided to betray her. Do you understand?"

The pale woman released her and moved away.

Jiaming walked over and sat down next to her. "Do you like my stars?"

"I do." The woman's eyes were as gentle as a sigh. "You're a good child. The stars told me so as soon as you were born."

A thought flitted across her heart like a shadow. Her chest tightened in the senseless, flickering light from the TV screen.

"Can the stars really talk?" She had never asked this question; she had never believed.

"Yes. Yes!" the pale woman said earnestly. "Yesterday, yesterday the stars told me that you would meet . . . someone very special. He would appear in water, and then disappear in fire. The stars also wished you good luck. I told you."

"Then, what about today? What do the stars say?"

The pale woman opened her astrolabe. Jiaming paid attention to her every movement, scrutinizing the details of this process she had already witnessed countless times. The more she focused, the more she felt like she was elsewhere. She was here, but also not here. She had been abandoned by herself—somewhere in her body, there was unquestionably the emptiness left by abandonment. No matter how much she tried to ignore it, she could feel the nauseating chill as well as . . . the dizzying sweetness.

Those stars: the symbols drifting from the depths of the vast space appeared on the sheet of paper with unprecedented clarity.

"Tomorrow, there will be happiness. You'll walk a path that you don't normally walk, and make a date in the morning. The stars say that you'll meet someone important, someone you'll spend the rest of your life with. The date will change your destiny, so be careful of wrong turns. The stars are speaking. Listen, the stars are talking, all of them. Can you hear them? The stars want you to be happy."

The pale woman's speech sped up. She repeated herself. Because she was talking so fast, she couldn't catch her breath, but still, she didn't slow down. It was like a wheel spinning out of control, and speech lost meaning until, finally, the senseless, staccato syllables made the woman's body convulse. Abruptly, the bony fingers locked onto Jiaming's shoulders, and the woman let out a burst of crude, piercing laughter.

Jiaming hugged her tightly. "Stop acting crazy, Mama. Stop."

3.

Jiaming couldn't remember exactly when the pale woman first appeared. It was her sixth birthday, or maybe even earlier. She had been dreaming and opened her eyes at midnight.

There was a woman sitting at the head of the bed. Her skin was so pale that it looked uncanny, a radiant object in the darkness—a star.

She spoke to the pale woman. Strangely, she didn't feel any fear. That was the most dream-like part of the whole experience.

"You're so pale. Are you glowing?"

"Not me. It's starlight. Quick, ask me who I am."

"Who are you?"

"I'm your mother."

"My mother is dead. You're mad."

"I am mad." The pale woman covered her mouth and giggled.

She wasn't afraid of her. Later, even on one of those nights when the pale woman acted crazed and tried to strangle her, she still wasn't afraid.

Most of the time they were together, the pale woman was very quiet.

They talked like regular people. Jiaming told her what had happened at school, and from time to time the pale woman offered an observation. They held the same opinions concerning most topics. Sometimes the pale woman brought up the stars. She taught Jiaming to recognize the stars: their names, positions, colors, their pasts, and also, their speech.

"Listen carefully: you can tell who's talking by the tone. To understand what they're saying you have to interpret the words as well as the tones. The stars sometimes prefer to sing."

Jiaming heard nothing.

The stars could not talk.

What did it matter? The stars disappeared during the day, like dreams.

※

Jiaming never imagined that she would one day believe the words of the deranged woman.

That morning, however, she decided to take the bus from the southern gate of her residential district to go to school. She hadn't ridden the bus during rush hour for a long time, and she couldn't even squeeze her way onto the first bus. When the next bus came, she got one foot onto the bus but couldn't find any more space to move up. Just as she was hesitating, a hand reached out and grabbed her by the arm, pulling her onto the bus forcefully.

In the dense crowd of passengers, she recognized Zhang Xiaobo's cold face.

He didn't look like someone who would have helped her onto the bus.

The bus was truly packed. Each body lost its individuality and boundaries. Pressed against other bodies, the passengers endured pressure from all sides. Each torso was twisted into unimaginable poses and then fixed in place, like canned pieces of meat.

It shouldn't be like this. She and he were too close together. Although a middle-aged woman stood between them, they were still too close. Jiaming had no choice but to look into that expressionless face. His eyes were black, like the water pooled at the bottom of an abyss; irresistible.

Don't fall into those eyes.

She struggled to twist her head away so that she didn't have to look at that face. Her cheek was crushed against the spine of the man in front of her, and it hurt. She didn't care.

The bus slowed down as it approached the stop. Passengers who had to get off pushed and shoved their way to the exit, but Zhang Xiaobo didn't move. He didn't show any signs of wanting to leave.

The doors opened. Jiaming closed her eyes. Exiting passengers surged past behind her. She should be in their midst, easily carried off the bus by the current. She should not be dizzy.

Yet she endured the buffeting of the crowd, her fingers locked onto the handholds. Several times she was almost swept off the bus, but she struggled to hold her place until the doors closed. The drumbeats of dense African jungle once again struck her chest. She wanted to cry; she wanted to laugh.

"You're going to be late." She hadn't noticed when Xiaobo came to be standing next to her.

Her mind was a blank. The bus started moving again, past the school. She could see the old man at the gatehouse; in another ten minutes he would close the gate. The school grew smaller in rearview and finally disappeared behind the row of Chinese parasol trees along the street. She closed her eyes. The dappled light of the leaves flitted across her eyelids. Something tickled at her heart.

"Now you're really going to be late." He was almost smiling.

They rode the bus to the terminal stop, where they got on another bus heading back. They sat in two separate rows, one behind the other. They didn't look at each other or talk.

As they approached the school again, he leaned forward and whispered into her ear. "What classes do you have in the morning?"

Things that seem crazy happened because they were fated to happen.

Jiaming turned around to look at Xiaobo.

The bus stopped; the doors opened; the doors closed. Neither of them moved.

It was already eight thirty.

※

It was noon by the time she was back at the school. She was about to go to the cafeteria to grab a bite when the Dean of Academic Affairs stopped her and took her to his office.

She wasn't worried because she thought it was about skipping class. But she was wrong.

Once she emerged from the dean's office, she took Zhu Yin to a remote corner of the cafeteria. Zhu Yin confessed before she even asked the question.

"That's right. I told them about you taking the exam for Lina. It's the truth."

"They must have asked you for proof."

"Yes . . ." Zhu Yin seemed to realize the problem and fell silent.

"And so you told them that I could confirm your story, that I took the mock exam for Lina in all four subjects."

Jiaming walked in front of Zhu Yin so that she had to look into her eyes. "But you know very well that I've never said that I took the exam for Lina. I haven't before and I never will. The dean already spoke to me."

"Did you tell him—"

"I told him that Lina's score was all due to her own diligence."

"Why are you protecting that bitch? Why help her? I saw you."

"You saw me help her pick up her exam when it fell on the floor. That's all."

"Why? Why? I can't stand the way she struts around as though she has already been admitted to a top-tier college. I want everyone to know that she's a fake, a nothing. If I had hard proof, I would have—"

"But you *don't*. However, you've succeeded in convincing her that I've sold her out." Jiaming was no longer angry. This girl had no idea how clever she had been.

She had helped because it was easy. She had thought nothing of it, not caring about test scores. As for herself, she had casually written out a few answers on her own exam in the time remaining.

She had treated the whole thing as a joke, but she seemed to be the only one who found it funny.

"Why are you helping her like that? For that pen? I saw that new Parker pen in your gym bag after PE. Don't leave, Jiaming! We're friends!"

Zhu Yin's voice faded behind her.

※

Xiaobo caught her on the landing as she climbed the stairs. His face was dark.

"I need to see you."

"I thought we were going to meet at McDonald's after school."

"Why are you spreading such malicious lies? Did you think anyone would believe you?"

Jiaming stared at him. "You think those are lies?" She leaned against the wall so he wouldn't see her trembling.

The stars had said that he was a very important person.

"Who would believe that you took the mock exam for Lina? The dean already talked to her. She's been crying ever since. How can you hurt someone just to satisfy your vanity?"

He already believed them, just like that.

Jiaming bit her lip. Something was stuck in her throat, burning, suffocating her. She didn't want to speak because it would hurt too much. But . . . but he was an important person to her. Maybe he was worth it, worth her ripping the words from her chest.

"What if I told you that I really did take the exam for her?"

She stared into his eyes, hoping to find something familiar.

"You're filthy," Xiaobo said.

She twisted her face away. She did find something familiar, though it wasn't what she wanted. She was in so much pain that she could not bear to look at him.

But, he was going to hear her explanation. They would be happy together. She just had to—

The bell rang.

"Let's talk about it more after school, all right?"

Xiaobo rushed for the classroom. Jiaming followed and climbed up a few steps, stopped, and turned around to go back down.

She decided to leave; leave behind the trivial nonsense, the school. She was going to cross the street and go through the revolving door of the McDonald's, where she would sit on a sofa chair and sip from a large Coke. She would do nothing and think about nothing, until school let out.

She had never told anyone about taking the exam for Lina. This evening, she was going to tell him the whole story as a joke. She would be lighthearted and not leave out any details. She would be careful with her phrasing. She didn't want to make him feel guilty.

4.

The ice cubes slowly melted, gradually vanishing into the dark, sweet liquid. Very few people ever paid attention to how ice disappeared. What about the pale woman? Did she once focus on the inevitable fading away of things? What would her stars say?

The stars want you to be happy.

What kind of stars would make her happy? Jiaming didn't know and didn't want to figure it out.

The pale woman was still asleep. Jiaming didn't wake her. The

Coke she brought back for her was already warm, but she didn't want to awaken her. She rarely got to see the pale woman so at peace.

"What time is it?" The pale woman woke up. She glanced at the TV; the anchor was reporting on the domestic news. "It's so early. I thought you had a date. Did you get to meet him? You should have taken a path this morning you normally don't."

"I met him. We made a date for McDonald's after school. There's a Coke I bought you on the table."

"How was the date? It ended too early." The pale woman tilted her head and laughed. "Now do you believe me? Your mama isn't mad! The stars tell the truth."

"Mama, let's look at the stars."

The pale woman set down the Coke and happily took out her star chart. The spinning disk stopped and the symbols appeared clearly on the paper. The woman began to interpret.

Her mouth was open, but no sound emerged.

"What's wrong, Mama? What do the stars say?"

The pale woman collapsed into the chair. She had never been as white as she was now.

"Why are you hiding in the shadows?" she asked Jiaming.

"You're not going to like the way I look now." Jiaming walked into the lamplight. "They got my clothes dirty."

They had held her down on the beige-colored sofa at McDonald's, where the Coke spilling from the cup they toppled on purpose flowed onto her pants from the table. Lina hadn't been in the crowd; she had stood in the back, traces of tears on her face.

"Did they hit you?" the pale woman asked.

Her face felt swollen, and there were a few scratch marks. Jiaming licked her cracked lips. The taste of blood was a bit similar to Coca-Cola.

"They weren't too fond of iced soda."

The girl who had toppled the Coke had been the first one to slap her in the face. Then they had dragged her in front of Lina. Half a dozen pairs of hands had shoved her until she was kneeling before

Lina, her knees striking the hard tiles. This was the price for betraying Lina.

They had then slapped her face: one, two, three. Right in front of the customers and employees gathered around them, in front of the pedestrians on the sidewalk looking in through the windows, in front of the teacher mixed in the crowd pretending to not know them, perhaps in front of other students.

Someone had held her by her hair so that she couldn't lower her face. They wanted everyone to see her face. Jiaming had closed her eyes.

One of the girls had explained the scene to the spectators.

Look at this stupid bitch. She could barely get passing marks. How dare she make up stories about Lina, a model student?

"You know who they are, don't you? Did you guess or did the stars tell you?" Jiaming wiped away the pale woman's tears. "Don't cry. Don't you find the whole thing funny?"

Had she not shut her eyes tightly, had she been able to see the expressions on those faces, she would have laughed hysterically, unable to stop herself. The joke hadn't reached the punch line until then.

"Did the stars tell you how many times they slapped me? Twenty-seven. I was so bored that I counted for them. But this wasn't the real problem. There's actually a really important question, something that I had to ponder before Lina left. Mama, how did they know I was at McDonald's?

"Why did the man who's so important to me take up their side? Ask the stars, Mama, ask them! Why did he treat me the same way that man treated you? Hurry up and ask the stars! We must have the same stars, Mama."

The pale woman was curled up in the chair, biting her fingers instinctively. Only her eyes, independent of body and will, attracted by the star chart, stared without blinking at the figures on the sheet.

Jiaming walked over and pulled her fingers out of her mouth. "What do the stars say? My crazy, mad mother, tell me, what does this mean?" She pointed to one symbol.

"The Moon."

"The Moon?" As Jiaming spoke, she moved her pen. The pale woman screamed and stretched out her bloody fingers to stop her, but it was too late. The symbol for the Moon disappeared in a dense storm of pen strokes. The pen moved and casually drew the symbol somewhere else. "It's over here now."

"You don't know what you're doing."

"What about this one?" The nib pointed at another symbol.

"That's Pluto."

"It's too crowded over here." She scratched out Pluto and randomly set the nib down in a blank space elsewhere. "Isn't this better?"

The pale woman howled, tearing at her hair.

"Don't cry. Open your eyes. The stars and planets are no longer where they were, but the world remains the same. Nothing has changed. The stars do not speak; they don't tell the future. The future, the past, the present—none of it has anything to do with your shitty stars."

The pale woman bent over the star chart, as if gazing at a baby she had given birth to who had just died. Tears flowed down her cheeks and dropped onto the paper; ripples expanded over the chart as though pebbles had been tossed in. The symbols on the paper trembled like reflections in the water, and then cautiously began to move, heading for their former positions.

Jiaming watched them expressionlessly, unmoved. This was nothing more than another cheap trick.

The stars did not speak; the stars did not tell the future; the stars were powerless.

She understood this better than anyone else at this moment.

"You don't know what you've done!" The pale woman sobbed uncontrollably.

"I know what I've done. Almost, almost I believed you. This morning was the first time I've ever believed that I might deserve happiness after all."

※

My name is Tang Jiaming.

My mother is insane.

Dad told me that when I was four, my mother died coming home on a ferry. I didn't understand why Dad told me such a story until I was much older.

Not long after my mother's death, Dad and I moved into our current home. Dad is an architect; he spent a lot of time renovating our new home. Our new home didn't feel as spacious as it looked, but it was plenty big for us. Later, I went to school like other kids. One night, I dreamed of the pale woman. She had a sheet of paper filled with strange symbols, and she told me that the paper told her the future. I didn't believe her. Although I dreamed about the pale woman every night after, I never believed her predictions, the words of the stars.

Until I met Zhang Xiaobo.

Because I wanted love.

That's humanity for you.

※

He opens the door and is surprised to find me sitting on the sofa. "You're home?"

"Sorry. I know we said we'd go out for dinner. I forgot it was tonight."

"No big deal." He takes the Sarah Brightman CD out of his briefcase. "For you."

No matter what I want, he always tries to get it for me. No matter how disobedient I am, he never disciplines me. None of the other fathers are like this.

He doesn't ask about the bruises on my face. He's been like that since I was little. If I got bullied he always pretended that he saw nothing.

"That's why you have to be smart and take care of yourself," the pale woman had said.

"Did you get out of work early because you wanted to tell me something?"

"No. I just wanted to have a good meal with you. Aren't you going to get in trouble for skipping study hall tonight?"

"Don't worry about it. Since you're back early and I'm not going to study hall, why don't we sit and chat a bit?" I get up and dim the living room lights.

The living room has never been so dim in my memory. Day or night, the lights and the TV have always been kept on.

"What are you doing?"

I walk in front of the mirror facing the TV. I press against the glass and look in. I see what he doesn't want me to see: the pale woman and her prison cell.

"One-way glass?" I stare at him. "Daddy, I guess our living room isn't so small after all."

※

My name is Tang Jiaming.

My mother is insane.

My father is an excellent architect. He built a secret chamber into our living room, where he has imprisoned my mother for more than a decade. The pale woman has never been a dream. It took me a long time before I understood this, but I continued to insist that she was just a dream. Like the story he told me about her drowning.

Before we lie to each other, we always have to successfully lie to ourselves.

※

"When did you find out?"

"When I realized that I always felt extra sleepy after drinking the milk you gave me."

My father doesn't know that although the drugs could put me to sleep, they couldn't stop me from waking up in the middle of the night to find the pale woman. No matter how soundly I slept, sometime during the night I'd be awakened by some force, and, like an object in midair tumbling to the ground, I'd come to be by the side of the pale woman.

If you didn't want others to know that you had a mad wife, why didn't you just seal her inside solid walls?

If I asked him this question, he would surely reply that he did it for me. He didn't want others to know that I had a mad mother.

I don't think so. I'm not going to let him get a chance to say this.

"Drink this. You haven't been getting enough sleep." *I bring out a glass of warm milk from the kitchen and put it in front of him. I look at him solicitously.*

He drinks it down. I knew he would. No matter what I had put in it, he would have drunk it.

Anything would be better than having to face me like this.

"When did she start to say those crazy things?" *I sit down in front of him, my hands gently covering his trembling knees.*

"She was always different, even when we first met. She said she heard strange voices. She was always very interested in the exact time and place of people's births. She disliked some people for no reason at all. I just attributed those to harmless quirks. But then you were born, and she—" *He looks up at me, and continues only with some effort.* "She calculated your fate by the astrolabe, and said that you were a child destined to alter the talk of the stars; you had to be protected. She became more and more deranged—"

"You got scared."

"I don't know if she's really crazy. Some things have come to pass the way she predicted. No, I wasn't scared of her. But you didn't see how others were looking at us."

He knows I'm not crazy, the pale woman *had said once. I remember her expression as she said it. I remember other things, as well.*

Before he closes his eyes, I ask my last question. "Did you stop loving her a long time ago?"

"No, not at all. I love her. Always have."

That is the worst of all possible answers.

Thanks to that glass of warm milk, he falls asleep before he could begin to cry uncontrollably. Of course he loves her. For her, he had installed the one-way glass so that she could watch that TV in the living room, always left on. More important, the pale woman could see me through that mirror.

But Daddy, you really have given me the worst answer.

5.

My name is Tang Jiaming.

I don't have a father, and no mother either. I can change the talk of the stars; that is, I can change fate.

Tomorrow morning, I'm going to get to school on time. I'll continue to pretend to be a student as if nothing has happened. I'm not going to pretend to be like the others, and I'll never allow anyone to hurt me again. I'm going to be myself, completely. Once you know how to change fate, this is not difficult.

The pale woman should be happy. I believe her, and I'll fulfill her prediction. I've copied her astrolabe, and I've tried to move her stars. As my first experimental project, she died. I didn't want her to die, but I don't need an excuse to absolve myself. There's no question I killed her. Still, she should be happy.

Zhu Yin will make up with me. That's what her stars say. The stars also say that she wants many other things.

At the next full moon, nude pictures of Lina will appear in the inbox of every student. That night, Lina's stars will become utterly fragile. She'll want to die; she'll hang herself from the tallest pole in the school, where her nubile body will swing in the wind like a leaf.

On that night, the fragrance of her feminine body, the smell of death, and the stench of her excrement will attract Zhang Xiaobo to her corpse. He'll be like some lost worker bee, confused by the smells, hovering around the dangling girl. Even death won't be able to completely stop the cinnamon aroma of her body. She'll be so entrancing. Especially then. Serene, calm, a chocolate sea calling to him.

If not for fate, why would he pass by just then? If not for fate, how could he have been able to light the fire in the gale?

Xiaobo will loosen the rope and let Lina down. Her body will still be warm, filled with the scent of summer. Her natural, tanned skin will glow and be filled with the elasticity of youth. He'll be especially attracted by her round, smooth legs, covered by her excrement. On that night, he'll experience unprecedented levels of hunger and obsession, his blood boiling in his veins. Death will swell his blood vessels, will make him feel harder and stiffer than he's ever felt. By the time his hands reach into her blouse, greedily kneading those chocolate breasts, he'll no longer be an insect driven mad by the rotten stench of the corpse flower. He'll no longer be lost. He'll have encountered himself. He'll lick those purple lips, and then gently wind himself around that tongue, again and again, tirelessly. That will be how he confirms who he is. He'll understand what he fears; he'll know what he yearns for; he'll know himself.

My frail lover, come to me. We'll be bonded together on a foundation of evil.

From now on, you can blame me the way you blame fate.

I am your star.

※

As I smile at the mirror, I know he's looking at me from behind it. He's now trapped in the cell he built himself.

On the table is the meal I prepared for him. "This is made from the flesh of the pale woman. You'll be eating the same thing for a few years." I told him the truth, and now I'm waiting here, patiently, on the other side of the mirror. I know he'll start eating sooner or later.

He'll think that I've moved his stars, making him eat it.

But he'll be wrong. I haven't moved his stars at all. From the moment of his birth, his stars have said that he'll consume the pale woman.

※

"When you move the stars, you change fate. When you move the stars, you also break them. Don't move the stars lightly."

Those were the pale woman's final words to me before she died.

Many stars have been broken tonight, and many more will break in the future. Even so, the sky will never be completely dark.

There will always be a star that remains eternally lit. A star that doesn't need my guidance.

HAN SONG

Han Song is often described as one of the China's most influential older science fiction writers (along with figures like Liu Cixin and Wang Jinkang). He has won many awards and published multiple novels as well as collections of short fiction. Few of his works, however, have been translated into English—something I hope will be remedied soon.

As a senior member of Xinhua, China's state news agency, Han Song occupies a unique position as an observer and chronicler of the cataclysmic changes transforming China. There are things he can say that perhaps no other writer can say. He has suggested, using various phrasing, that what is happening in China is more surreal and shocking than has been seen in (or could be captured by) science fiction. Like many of his stories, this sentiment is subject to multiple interpretations, some of which are mutually contradictory.

He has a distinctive style and voice that is instantly recognizable: a preference for cumulative, run-on sentences and dense paragraphs that build and build, threatening to teeter over, bringing to mind the urban landscape of contemporary China; a narrative voice that offers mordant, acerbic metafictional commentary; a cool, detached tone that describes surreal suffering as though cataloguing species of flowers; a knack for imagery that hovers on the edge of horror and humor, pathos and bathos, realism and transrealism.

"Submarines" and "Salinger and the Koreans" are both short but showcase Han Song's style well.

Some commentators describe Han Song as a dystopian writer who uses science fiction to critique China's breakneck pace of development that leaves behind millions of victims. Others view him as a nationalist who uses his fiction to lacerate and mock Western hypocrisy. Some see in his stories a continuation of Lu Xun's bitter attacks against the dark aspects of Chinese history and culture. Others think he's railing against a Chinese modernity that is without values or ideals.

What is clear to me is that all of Han Song's stories are intensely political, but they're couched in layers of allegory such that what message one takes away from them depends largely on what baggage one brings to them.

SUBMARINES

As a boy, whenever I asked, my parents would bring me to the shore of the Yangtze River to see the submarines. Following the river's flow, the subs had come to our city in herds and pods. I heard that some subs also came from the Yangtze's tributaries: Wujiang River, Jialing River, Han River, Xiangjiang River, and so on. The subs were so numerous that they looked like a carpet of ants or thousands of wisps of rain-soaked clouds fallen from the heavens.

From time to time, to my amazement, one sub or another would just vanish from the surface. In fact, they had dived. First, the sub slowly wriggled its immense body, which then sank inch by inch, roiling the water around it in complicated and cryptic ripples, until the whole hull disappeared beneath the surface, including the tiny column on top shaped like a miniature watchtower. The flowing river soon recovered its habitual tranquility and mystery, leaving me stunned.

And then, a submarine would explode out of the water like a monster, splashing beautiful waves in every direction. "Look! Look!" I would scream. "It's surfacing!" But my parents never reacted. Their faces remained wooden, looking as dispirited as two houseplants that hadn't been watered for weeks. The appearance of the submarines seemed to have robbed them of their souls.

Most of the time, the subs remained anchored on the placid surface, motionless. Wires were strung over the hulls, stretching from tower to tower. Drying laundry hung from the wires like colorful flags, pants and shirts mixed with cloth diapers. Women in thick, crude aprons cooked with coal stoves on the decks, and the smoke columns turned the river into a campground. Sometimes the women squatted next to the water, beating the laundry with wooden bats against the sturdy metal hulls. Occasionally, old men and women climbed out of the subs, looking relaxed as they sat with their legs curled under them, smoking long-stemmed pipes with a cat or a dog curled up against them.

The subs belonged to the peasants who had come to our city to seek work. After a day of working in the city, the peasants returned to their submersible abodes. Before the arrival of the subs, peasant laborers had to rent cheap apartments in urban villages, plots of land where the rural population stayed as their farmlands were gobbled up by developers for the expanding city, leaving them stranded in a sea of skyscrapers. The urban villagers rented out one-foot-wide spaces on communal beds, and the rural laborers who built the city had to sleep like pigs or sheep in a pen. The submarines, on the other hand, gave the laborers their own homes.

Ferries operated between the shore and the anchored subs. Peasants piloted these ferryboats, shuttling their brothers and sisters between two completely different worlds. At night, after everyone had returned to their homes, the subs were at their most beautiful. Lit by gas lamps, each boat glowed with a different pattern, like paper-cutting pasted on windowpanes. Bright, lively, they also reminded me of fallen stars adrift on the river. On each sub, a family sat around the table having supper, and the cool river breeze brought their laughter and chatter to the shore, leaving the urban residents with a sense of strange envy. As the night deepened, lights on the vessels winked out one by one until only the anxious searchlight beams from the harbor towers roamed the darkness, revealing motionless hulls like sleeping whales. Many subs, however, chose this time to disappear. Each sweep of the searchlight showed fewer and fewer boats. Without any announcement, they had dived, as if the peasants couldn't sleep soundly without the comfort of being covered by water, like water birds that had to tuck their heads beneath their wings to nap. Only by submerging their families and homes could they leave their worries behind on the surface, hold danger and uncertainty at bay, and dream sweet dreams without being bothered by the city-dwellers—was that, in fact, the reason they had built the submarines in the first place?

I often wondered how deep the Yangtze was, and how many subs could lie on the riverbed. How eerie and interesting it would have been to see rows upon rows of metal hulls lying next to each other down there! The thought made me gasp at how mysterious the world was, as though there was another world beyond the visible one.

In any event, the submarines settled near us like nesting birds and became a hotly debated sight. Every morning, they popped out of the water like boiled dumplings. Under the shimmering dawn light, the perturbed river surface resembled a spring flood. The scene made me think of alien spaceships from the movies. Busy ferries went back and forth between the subs and the shore, carrying spirited peasants into the city for another day of back-breaking labor at construction sites across the city.

The submarines came from all over China. Besides our city, rumors described pods in other cities and other rivers as well. Every sea, lake, canal, and trench seemed to have its own sub colonies. No one could say for sure who had designed the first sub. Supposedly, a clever folk craftsman had fashioned the first submarines by hand. By the standards of sophisticated urbanites, these boats were crude pieces of technology: most were constructed from scrap metal, though a few were pieced together with fiberglass and plywood. The early subs were shaped like fish, and many had heads and tails painted in red and white, including radiant, vivid eyes, lips, or even fins. These features looked a bit ridiculous, though they also showed the sense of humor unique to peasants. Later, as more submarines were built, the differences in decorative coloration distinguished families from one another.

Typically, a sub was big enough for a single family, on average five or six people. Bigger subs provided enough space for two or three families. The peasants seemed unable to build large vessels that could carry dozens or hundreds of people. Some city-dwellers had wondered whether the subs were constructed along plans cribbed from Verne's *Twenty Thousand Leagues Under the Sea*, or perhaps foreign experts had secretly helped the peasant craftsmen. In the end, however, no connection between the subs and Verne was discovered. The sub makers had never even heard of the author. Everyone sighed with relief.

After a while, the city kids continued to be fascinated by the subs while the adults became either bored or pretended not to notice them. At school, we enthusiastically swapped stories and news about subs, and we drew pictures of them on sheets of paper torn from our composition books. The teachers, however, never mentioned them, and reprimanded us with frowning faces whenever they caught us discussing the subject, tearing apart our sketches and sending the offenders to the principal's office. It was rare to see any TV or newspaper reporting about the activities of the submarines, as though the congregating vessels had nothing to do with the life of the city.

Occasionally, a few curious adults—mostly artists and poets—would come to the shore to gaze at the scene, whispering to each other. They speculated that over time, perhaps the subs would evolve a new civilization. The submarine civilization would be unlike any existing civilization in the world, just as mammals are completely different from reptiles. They wanted to visit the subs to collect folklore and study their customs, but the peasants never showed any inclination to invite the city-dwellers to come aboard. Maybe after a full day of hard labor, they were too tired to deal with strangers. Besides wanting to avoid trouble, they probably also didn't see any profit in it. The peasants made it clear that the only reason they had come to the city was to find work and make money. However, the unsophisticated peasants seemed to not realize that they could have roped the anchored subs off and charged money for a close-up view, turning their homes into a tourist attraction. Neither did they display any interest in creating a "new civilization."

After returning to the subs at night, all the peasants wanted to do was to eat and go to sleep. They had to rest well to be able to get up in the morning for another day of hard work. Toiling at the dirtiest and most physically demanding jobs in exchange for the lowest and most uncertain wages, the peasant laborers never complained. This was because they had the subs, which allowed them to be with their families after work instead of having to leave them behind in distant home villages. The subs replaced the fields that they had been forced to sell to local governments and real estate developers at bargain-basement prices so that the fields could be consumed by growing cities. Although the city-dwellers acted as if what had happened to the peasants was none of their concern, in their hearts they felt uneasy and helpless. To be sure, the subs did not pose a threat to the city—they weren't armed with cannons or torpedoes, for instance.

After I became a good swimmer, my friends and I secretly visited the subs on our adventures. Holding hollow reeds in our mouths, we snorkeled to the middle of the river, out of sight, until we were right next to the anchored subs. Large wooden cages dangled from cables beneath the hulls, and the turbid river water swirled around the cage bars. Inside, we saw many peasant children, their earth-toned bodies nude, swim around like fish, their slender limbs nimbly finning the water and their skin glowing in the silt-filtered light. Guessing that these cages were likely the peasant version of daycare or kindergarten, our hearts filled with wonder.

Our leader was a boy a few grades above me. "Don't be so impressed," he said contemptuously. "I bet we can beat them in a swim race." The rest of us approached one of the cages and asked the children inside, "Have you ever seen a car?"

The children stopped swimming and gathered on our side of the cage, their faces as expressionless as plastic animals'. I saw that they didn't have scales or fins, as I had hoped. It was a mystery how they could stay underwater for so long without using a breathing reed.

Finally, a look of curiosity appeared on the face of one of the peasant children. "A car? What's that?" His voice was barely a whisper. I thought he looked like a creature out of manga.

"Ha, I knew it!" Our leader sounded pleased. "There are so many types of cars! Honda, Toyota, Ford, Buick . . . oh, and also BMW and Mercedes!"

"We don't know what you're talking about," said the peasant kid, his voice hesitant. "But we've seen lots of fish. There's red carp, gold carp, black carp, sturgeon, oh, and also white bream and Amur bream!"

Now it was our turn to be nervous. We looked around but didn't see any fish. Our teachers had taught us that all fishes in the Yangtze had gone extinct, so were the peasant children trying to trick us? Where could they have seen fish?

"I hope they really evolve into a different species from us," muttered our leader.

The peasant children blinked uncomprehendingly before returning to their aimless swim in the cage, as though trying to keep away from us.

"Are you going to turn into fish?" I asked.

"No."

"Then what will you become?"

"Don't know. When our mas and das are back from work, you can ask them."

I thought of how they lived underwater, away from fields, gardens, and soil, while we lived on the shore. It was like a picture of fish and shrimp versus cattle and sheep—was that the future?

We pretended to be interested in them and attempted to play with the peasant children some more, but the effort fizzled. They didn't know any of the games we knew, and the bars of the cage stood in our way. It was boring to keep on trying. In the murky shadows of the swaying underwater weeds, we felt the oppressive presence of a nameless terror. And when our leader gave the order, we gladly headed for the surface after him so that we could return to our own realm.

The peasant children would stay in the water. Let them.

We burst through the surface, our hearts pounding. All around us were the hulking forms of anchored subs, like a pack of hungry, silent wolves in the deep of winter. Like freshly fallen snow, the crude, gloomy hulls reflected the bright sunlight so that we squinted. There were no fish on the surface either, just the drifting corpses of rats and cockroaches, and layers and layers of rotting algae, tangled with thousands of discarded phone chargers and computer keyboards, as well as soda bottles, plastic bags, and other trash. The stench from the feces-colored water was almost unbearable, and swarms of flies buzzed around, their heads an iridescent green.

This was, in fact, an unforgettable, lovely sight that made us linger, and we wondered if the subs had come here specifically to appreciate it. Their long odyssey had left them with a unique value system and sense of beauty. Peasant women busied themselves aboard the subs without gazing down at us in the river. They boiled their rice and cooked their meals with the stinking water we bobbed in, and yet, whereas the city-dwellers would have died from the germs, the peasants were fine.

Just then, anxious adults on shore hollered for us to come home, their faces filled with *danger, frightful, menace.*

※

The year before I started middle school, something happened involving the subs.

It was an early autumn night. Loud noises woke me from sleep, and it seemed as if the whole city had boiled over. My parents dressed me quickly, and we hurried out the door, heading for the river. We became part of a surging crowd whose thumping footsteps and worried cries were like exploding firecrackers on New Year's Eve. I was so scared that I covered my ears, unsure what was happening.

Once we arrived at the shore, I found out that the subs had

caught fire. The fire had spread and all the boats were burning. In my memory, it was like a major holiday: the whole city's population seemed to be present, their numbed expressions replaced by excitement, screaming and talking as though they were watching a marvelous show. Trembling, I squeezed next to my parents and tried my best to get a peek through the sea of people.

Raging fire danced and leapt from the densely packed subs, swirling, spreading, expanding like the skirts of cruel flamenco dancers. Flickering lights from the flames lit up the skyscrapers onshore so that they glowed like the foliage of late autumn, until the whole scene resembled a fresh painting. It was a shocking sight whose equal I have never experienced again.

For some reason, none of the subs dived. It was as if they had all forgotten what they were. Floating still at the surface, they made no effort to escape as the ice-like fire devoured them one by one. I was certain there was some secret behind it, some indescribable mystery. I wondered if another fantastic fire was also burning underwater—somehow, the water molecules had all transformed into another substance, and the whole Yangtze River was defying the physical properties endowed by nature, which was why the submarines were unable to dive away from this fiery dance stage.

I thought of the children in their underwater cages, and my heart swelled with shock and worry. Turning my head, I saw my parents standing like a pair of zombies, unmoving, their eyes staring straight ahead like lanterns, their faces frozen. Other adults muttered like chanting Buddhist monks, but no one made any effort to extinguish the fire. They seemed to be there only to witness the death of alien creatures in the river, to watch as the uninvited guests achieved total freedom.

That night seemed to last forever, though I never once thought of death, only soaking in the poignancy and meaninglessness of life itself. I never felt sad or mournful, though I was sorry that I would never again be able to swim into that strange realm, to see sights that made my heart leap and my mind confused. A sense of unresolvable solitude gripped me, while I knew also that my own future would not be affected in any way by what I was seeing. . . .

Morning finally arrived. Dim sunlight revealed lifeless hunks of blackened metal drifting everywhere on the river. In scattered rows, circles, clumps, they reflected the cold, colorless light, and the air was suffused with the decaying odors of autumn. The city-dwellers brought forth cranes to retrieve the wreckage of the submarines from the river and trucked the pieces to scrap metal yards. The whole process took over a month.

After that, no submarines came to the Yangtze River.

SALINGER AND
THE KOREANS

On Christmas Eve, on a New York street, the Cosmic Observer met a lonely old man who called himself Salinger. He was dressed in rags, sickly, cold and hungry, and on the verge of death. Yes, he was indeed Jerome David Salinger, the author of *The Catcher in the Rye*.

The Cosmic Observer decided to make him a subject of his study and took him into a McDonald's, where the Observer bought him whatever he wanted to eat. As the embarrassed Salinger wolfed down his Chicken McNuggets and Filet-O-Fish sandwich, he told the Observer the story of his life.

After *The Catcher in the Rye* catapulted him to fame, Salinger retired to seclusion in rural New Hampshire. There, in the hills next to the Connecticut River, he bought about ninety acres of farmland. He built a cabin on top of a hill, planted trees and gardens over the property, and surrounded it with a six-and-a-half-foot chain-link fence connected to an alarm. He proceeded to live a hermit's life there.

The site for his cabin was a picturesque, sunny spot that seemed untouched by progress. To live as a pretend deaf-mute hermit in a cabin away from people was, of course, the dream of Holden Caulfield—and as it turned out, also the dream of Salinger himself. Once he had settled into his cabin, he rarely went out. Visitors had to first contact him by mail or by passing a note through the gate; and if they were strangers, Salinger simply kept the gate shut, refusing even to answer them. He was seldom seen in public, and even when he drove his Jeep into town to shop for books and necessities, he kept conversations to an absolute minimum. When anyone tried to greet him in the streets, he turned around immediately and fled. His picture appeared only in the first three editions of *The Catcher in the Rye*, and thereafter, due to his insistence, the publisher had to remove the portrait. It was so difficult to find an image of him that a French newspaper once mistakenly published a photograph of Pierre Salinger, the White House Press Secretary, to accompany an article about the famous author. In addition, once he had become a household name, his writing slowed down drastically, and he hardly ever published new works.

The great American people were content with Salinger's choice. In fact, if time's trajectory had not been bifurcated due to Cosmic Observer's observation, Salinger would have gone on living as a recluse until death from natural causes at age ninety-one. All in all, not a bad life.

Unfortunately, trouble came to the timeline just as he had hoped to disappear anonymously from the world—the fault of the Cosmic Observer. No one knows what the Observer intended, but as a result of his interference, the armed forces of the Democratic People's Republic of Korea conquered the United States of America. The North Korean scientists did not rely on their primitive nuclear weapons; instead, they used the newly invented Quantum Reambiguator, which changed the topology of space-time and allowed anything to happen.

As a result, the invincible Korean People's Army not only unified the Korean Peninsula, but also conquered the rest of the world. To be honest, the KPA really was an impressive army: disciplined, orderly, never looting as much as a single needle or thread from the conquered civilian populations. If there were no barracks in the conquered cities, the soldiers slept in the streets and left the residents secure in their houses. They were solely interested in liberating the entire human race, freeing both their bodies and minds. The world had been without hope of salvation, just as Salinger described in his book: capitalism was rotten through and through. Oh, how the people suffered from spiritual crises, and economic catastrophe followed economic catastrophe! Each day was worse than the day before, and the next day worse yet. The living envied the dead. Maybe this was why the great author had retired to his cabin in the woods—he was the only one who understood how bad things were.

The Koreans saw Salinger as a precursor to the full liberation of humanity. It was because of his book that the Koreans had vowed to liberate the entire human race in the first place. These gentle, unsophisticated, earthy people from Asia loved Salinger from the depths of their hearts. Under the direction of the Supreme Commander in Chief, Salinger's book had been translated into Korean many years ago and been read by generation after generation of North Korean students. The translator had even written the following in the preface: *Our youths grow up in a Socialist motherland in which they're constantly bathed in the loving care of the Workers' Party of Korea, the Kim Il-sung Socialist Youth League, and the Young Pioneer Corps. As a result, they're endowed with the lofty ideals of Communism and blessed with colorful and vibrant spiritual lives. Therefore, by reading a book like* The Catcher in the Rye, *they can contrast their own environment with the ugly conditions persisting under capitalism, thereby broadening their horizons and gaining more wisdom. . . .*

It was no wonder then that Salinger was so well respected in North Korea; indeed, he was far more respected in North Korea than he was in the United States—he was the one who stripped off the shiny shell of capitalism to reveal the filth underneath.

The conquest of America interrupted Salinger's life as a hermit. The media corps that accompanied the KPA made him a focus of its reporting. A group of excited Korean reporters traveled to New Hampshire and found his cabin, demanding an interview. As was his habit, Salinger refused. In his life he had agreed only to one interview, which had been conducted by a sixteen-year-old girl who featured him for her school newspaper; Salinger had made an exception for her.

Even though Salinger refused to be interviewed, the Korean reporters, imbued with heroic idealism and charged with a mission, could not simply turn around and leave. Gingerly, they cut through the chain-link fence with pliers and marched up to Salinger's cabin, where they set up cameras in front of his door for a live broadcast. But the stubborn Salinger continued to rebuff them, keeping his door shut in their faces for three days and three nights. Finally, the Korean reporters lost their patience. No one refused the official media of the Democratic People's Republic of Korea! Still, the reporters remembered their reputation as members of the kind, honest Korean people, and did not vent their rage. They thought of another method.

Soon, the phone in Salinger's cabin rang. He picked up the receiver, and a slow, deep, well-mannered male voice spoke through the earpiece: "I'm the Minister of the Korean People's Army Political Propaganda Department. Mr. Salinger, I hope you would be so gracious as to accept our reporters' interview request. In addition, I'd like to extend an invitation to you to join the Korean Writers Association as a vice president—" Reflexively, Salinger hung up. Then he sat down on the ground and wept.

In retrospect, Salinger's reaction was perhaps not the result of political obtuseness, but a personality defect. Still, in the eyes of the Koreans, Salinger's behavior was not only pretentious and overly dramatic, but nearly a deliberate provocation. Now they were truly enraged. Out of a desire to salvage what was left of Salinger, the Koreans decided to ban his work and place him on a blacklist such that all his writings, whether fiction or essays, were prohibited from being published anywhere in the world. Rumor had it that during his seclusion in the cabin, he had written some new books that were never published. The American publishers had planned to wait until his death and obtain the publication rights for all such works—impossible plans now.

Next, Salinger was deemed to have been a propagandist for the corrupt lifestyle of capitalism, and one who attempted to pervert and poison the spiritual life of the youth. But since the Korean people were forgiving, humane, and sincere, they did not imprison him or initiate public criticism sessions against him or demand that he write self-criticism. He was allowed to stay in his cabin, but men dressed in ill-fitting civilian clothing patrolled his property, apparently keeping it under surveillance.

No one mentioned the name of Salinger anymore in public, and he was quickly forgotten. Even his fans had dismissed him from their minds. Salinger thought this wasn't such a bad outcome, as he could now live as a true hermit. Gratitude to the KPA! When he had nothing else to do, he observed the Koreans who kept him under surveillance. *They are so young and handsome,* he thought, *each like a member of a herd of reindeer from the distant East. And their thoughts are in fact unique, like building blocks through which they could understand the world objectively and thoroughly.* Despite being rulers of the world, their behavior reminded Salinger of his Holden. *That's right, just like Holden.* Salinger experienced a pleasurable dizziness, as though drunk with fine wine.

But the happiness didn't last. Mass economic reconstruction began with the goal to transform America into a gigantic paradise, an attempt to realize the complete revitalization of the country. Under the leadership of the KPA Real Estate Corps, everything proceeded according to a unified and comprehensive plan. Naturally, New Hampshire had its own role to play in this beautiful future.

One morning, Salinger was woken from sleep by deafening noises. Dazed, he gazed outside the window and saw a row of gleaming Baekdu bulldozers, which had been modified from Chonma-ho battle tanks, bearing down on his cabin. Angrily, Salinger rushed out the door—something he rarely did—and argued with the workers who had come to break down his house, arguing that it was his inviolate private property. Of course, such reasoning was useless and revealed a secret hidden in Salinger's subconscious, a secret that perhaps he had not even known himself: the human race's universal greed for wealth. It was truly tragic.

A few Korean soldiers, fearless with youth, tackled him to the ground and held him down. The bulldozers rumbled forth and soon reduced his house to rubble. Salinger thought of going to court, only then realizing that there were no more courthouses in America. Then he thought he would commit suicide by setting himself on fire, but he couldn't find a match or lighter; in any event, he was actually terrified of death—a fact that distinguished him from the Korean soldiers, who were all ready to sacrifice their lives at a moment's notice. Since he was homeless, he began to wander around America. His previous life as a recluse meant that few photographs of him had been published, and no one recognized him in the streets or gave him generous gifts. So, please remember this: if you are ever famous or enjoy success, don't keep too low a profile.

The Cosmic Observer listened quietly as Salinger finished his tale. The Observer felt there was no reason to fault the Koreans. They had behaved only according to their wont. And indeed they had rescued humanity, saving the species from extinction due to catastrophes caused by collapsing societies. Salinger had been responsible for his own obscurity. To put it simply, Salinger's fate represented the end of certainty.

This was one of the simplest laws of the universe, but one often ignored. Everything was part of an endless cycle of constant change, which had to do with both quantum mechanics and the net increase in entropy. If one couldn't even understand such fundamentals, what hope was there of understanding why the universe's designer would create North Korea? The Koreans had simply seized upon this regularity. In such a world, with such a timeline, it was a bad idea to underestimate anyone: in a single night it was possible for the last to come first, to turn the world upside down.

In fact, the Cosmic Observer now began to envy the Koreans. Though he had caused all this transformation with his attention, he could not be a Korean because he was Chinese. Not just anyone could be Korean, and as a Chinese, the Cosmic Observer's world-view and methodology were already constrained by certain laws of physics. He could only observe, but he could not act. He was the catalyst of these changes, but he had to remain outside the world he had transformed. The Koreans were still young, but the Cosmic Observer was already old. *Perhaps this is the greatest loneliness of all. Perhaps the Koreans have experienced something like this before?*

And so, the Cosmic Observer examined the legendary author again. Seeing the old man blowing his nose into a paper napkin and secreting the few remaining French fries away into his pocket, the Cosmic Observer experienced a deep sorrow. But even more tragic was the fact that before the momentous changes, Salinger had written that odd bestseller. The Cosmic Observer began to worry: *Could the book be the only thing to interrupt the timeline and collapse the bifurcation of time? After all, the Koreans have only just begun to construct this world. . . . Who knows? For a thinking machine, this is too difficult a problem.*

CHENG JINGBO

Cheng Jingbo's fiction has won many accolades, among them the Yinhe Award and Xingyun Award as well as selections to various "Year's Best" anthologies. She was among the first genre writers to be published in *People's Literature*, perhaps the most prestigious mainstream literary market in China.

A children's book editor, she also translates from English to Chinese. One of her notable translations is *Little House in the Big Woods*, by Laura Ingalls Wilder. Recently, she has begun adapting one of her stories into a screenplay for production.

"Under a Dangling Sky" is from the earlier part of Cheng's career. Sketched with bold, impressionistic strokes, it tells a charming story set in a vibrant world in which magic and science are indistinguishable.

More of Cheng's fiction may be found in *Invisible Planets*.

UNDER A
DANGLING SKY

THE BEANSTALK THAT GROWS DOWNWARD

Last autumn I moved to Port Gladius in Rainville. At first, I helped the muscle-bound stevedores sort silver shells at the docks, and that was how I met a professor who had come from afar. Because we got along so well, I agreed to give up the silver shells and go work for him.

I loved my new job: collecting a certain kind of sound in Shallow Bay. The bay was the quietest part of the harbor, and no one ever bothered me in my work. The professor gave me a strange contraption that looked like the ear of an outlandish beast. When I immersed the ear in the sea, sounds from below the surface came into my headphones, and the giant nautilus shell on my back (also a machine) would identify the sounds. The sounds the professor wanted would also be recorded.

My headphones stuck up like the feathered crest of a cockatiel. When the sea was calm, I could see my reflection like a slender, lonesome cormorant.

In the sea breeze, my ear-feathers trembled. They were so sensitive that not a single whiff of wind could escape. Most of the time, I would shut my eyes and concentrate on the underwater music. Like Jack's beanstalk, the fish-slick line slipped through my fingers, dropped into the sea, and drifted with the current into the deep. At the end of the line, heading into the aphotic abyss, was the beast's ear. Only this time, Jack stood onshore, and the magic beanstalk grew downward without cease.

Standing next to the serene bay, I listened to the whispers from the bottom of the sea thousands of meters below.

The crisp smacks of lazy jellyfish tentacles striking coral reefs; the agitation of brisk schools of fish making sharp turns; even the gentle *pop* as a single air bubble struggled out of a seam between rocks, only to break apart in its hurried ascent to the surface. . . .

Yet, each evening, as I reeled in the seemingly endless line and returned to the cottage by the shore, the professor shook his head at me, disappointed.

"Still nothing . . ." He sighed in the last rays of the setting sun. "I've wandered all over the world without finding it. Will I ever hear the singing dolphin?"

Whales can sing, but there were no whales around Rainville. This was a paradise for dolphins, and every year, thousands of dolphins came to the bay, following the warm flow of the Pollex Current. None of them sang.

CRYSTAL SKY

The sky over Rainville was a mystery.

You'd never see such a beautiful sky anywhere else in the world: a crystalline welkin crisscrossed by countless tiny cracks. Everything in the heavens was broken into a mosaic by these lines. From an overcast day to the scarlet clouds of dawn, patches of color gently expanded and percolated, their edges blurring against the dreamlike firmament.

They called this fantastic sight the crystal sky.

It was said that the sky also had to do with Jack and his beanstalk. After the lucky young man climbed down with the golden-egg-laying hen and the talking harp, he chopped down the stalk with an ax. Thereafter, he wandered the world in disguise. To prevent a

speech of the dolphins. The nautilus had no trouble recording other sounds: the scraping of an electric eel's scales across the sand, the crack of eggshells as baby turtles hatched . . . even whale song posed no difficulty to its sensitive mechanisms.

But the conversation of dolphins stymied it.

"Your feathers are no good," said a laughing Giana as her tail slapped against the water. "The machine can't hear us."

"Then how do you hear each other? Do you rely on sonar?"

"The heart, silly!" She laughed even harder and began to swim in circles. "You can hear us as well because you're listening with your heart."

Sometimes I enjoyed sitting on reef rocks and gazing up at the sky.

Giana often came to Shallow Bay in those times. Moonglow dusted the sea spray and distant isles on the horizon like frosted sugar. I took off the ear-feathers and strained to detect sounds coming from beyond the crystal sky. I would then experience the illusion that the moon was a spotlight that gazed down at us from the sky curtain, casting the softest rays onto a pair of players: a human and a dolphin.

"Do you see those stars?" Giana would always ask.

There were no stars at the center of the sky over Rainville. The Milky Way broke there, replaced by a disordered shadow. The stars, seemingly frightened by the shadow, shrank away to the sides.

"Do you see those stars? Do you see them?"

The stars were faint, powerless, distant, their light pale.

"There! That's the constellation Delphinus!" Giana went on talking to herself. "That was my grandfather's grandfather's grandfather's . . . Hey, are you listening? Look, although the stars are so faint, every time I see them, I think of my grandfather's grandfather's grandfather's . . . kind smile—even though I've never met him.

"Long ago, in the time of the ancient Greeks, the greatest human musician, Arion, went to a place called Sicily for a musical competition. On the way back, pirates attacked him, and poor Arion was blindfolded and made to walk the plank. Suspended over the sea, he asked his captors, 'Let me play one more song.' The pirates agreed, and he began to strum his lyre.

"As you can see, humans haven't always been so dumb. His music managed to attract my ancestor, who was hunting for squids nearby. Arion heard a voice say to him, 'Jump on my back,' and that he did."

"Is this the story behind Delphinus?"

"That's right." Giana lifted her eyes to look at the stars. "But they're so faint! I wish they would glow brighter."

Starglow reflected from her eyes as her voice grew more excited. "If . . . if only we could pierce the crystal sky and go visit the stars. . . ." She turned to me. "Do you think they'll glow brighter?"

"I don't know," I said. "Your mind is filled with such strange notions: submarines, the crystal sky, distant stars. . . . Are these the concerns of a dutiful child?"

"I can't stop thinking about them. A voice is always in my head, telling me, *Hey Giana, why not go visit the stars?*"

The dolphin swept her tail gently through the water and dipped her head into the moonlit sea.

THE FOUNTAIN

Many people have compared the world with an apple. Rainville itself was also like an apple. The fountain at the center of the Thumb Sea was like the apple's core, pointing straight up at the distorted shadow that interrupted the Milky Way. People were like bugs living inside the apple, never having glimpsed what it was like outside the peel—only in some places where the peel was a bit translucent could they see, through the mosaic skin, the blurred shadow cast by a distant leaf under the noonday sun.

The only way out was the fountain.

You had to follow the core's vascular tissue upward, all the way to the long, narrow stem, and out of the apple. Only then would you see that the world was full of other apples and countless leaves.

The sky that you had been so entranced by before was nothing more than the shadow of a single leaf.

The fountain was the path through the core. The gigantic, transparent tree sculpted from seawater had its roots deep in the Thumb Sea. As it shot toward the sky, it sprouted new branches and leaves, until, at the top, the lush crown spread out in every direction, turning into surging mist and billowing clouds.

The beanstalk was still here, even if Jack was gone.

No one had ever seen beyond the crystal sky; no one had peeked into the giant's floating castle.

DANGLING SKY

I knew, long before it happened, what Giana was going to do.

She was familiar with every current and wave in the Thumb Sea; she knew where the water could carry her. The whirlpools at the graveyard of ships were dangerous, but the fountain would rocket her into the heavens.

That night, Rainville was drenched by a violent thunderstorm. The rain slowly seeped through seams in my seaside cottage, leaving meandering trails across the ceiling. The lamp hanging under the eaves creaked and swayed. Muffled pops came from the nautilus shell lying in the corner, like seasoned firewood cracking in a fire. I pulled out the pair of feathered headphones, long neglected, and placed them over my ears.

The wind from the harbor caressed the smooth feathers, and the soft down undulated like the sea, bringing me sounds from the storm.

Struck by a premonition, I got out of bed and rushed into the rain.

I reached the shore of Shallow Bay at the same time as the eye of the storm. Clouds retreated to reveal a patch of clear night sky. Far away over the sea, the sky-bridging fountain was pumping furiously. Behind me, Rainville lay deep in slumber, blanketed by the storm. Not a single light was on.

The air above the Thumb Sea was unusually tranquil. The moon and the stars gleamed tenderly.

Do you see those stars? Do you see them?

I strained to see the fountain more clearly. Under the dark blue welkin, innumerable currents had gathered like so many vines, twisting together as they rose. The watery vines shone with the moon's brilliance, and as they reached the spot closest to heaven, they scattered into millions of mysterious, glittering stars. It was just like that night many years ago when I had first heard the speech of the dolphins: my sight tangled with the moonbeams, and the curtain over the world was gradually pulled away. The fountain turned into the enchanted beanstalk, which was growing irrepressibly, pumping water infused with the strength of the ocean's heart, sprouting branch after branch, brushing up against the crystal sky.

But they're so faint! I wish they would glow brighter.

The spraying droplets at the top of the fountain dissolved into the chaotic maw at the center of the sky dome. Thousands of new stars were born in that shadow before coalescing into thick fog. Away from that gloomy patch, the silver stars of Delphinus twinkled with an enigmatic light.

Suddenly, the constellation fell into the sea. As the sea roiled with unaccustomed brilliance, a silvery curved blade leapt out of the water. Weaving and dodging, slashing and slicing, the blade cut through moonbeams and swam for the enchanted beanstalk.

Giana!

If . . . if only we could pierce the crystal sky and go visit the stars. . . .

The mad child was going to climb up the beanstalk to the giant's castle. But . . . if the crystal sky was truly an ice cover intended to keep us from the secrets of heaven, how could Giana reach the stars? Striving up the raging torrents rising from the heart of the Thumb Sea, Giana's nimble figure could be glimpsed from time to time. Would the fountain carry her miles and miles up? Would she see what was above the clouds? Would she break through the crystal sky and find the stars?

I can't stop thinking about them. A voice is always in my head, telling me, Hey Giana, why not go visit the stars?

Finally, the silvery blade cut through the silky moonlight and, propelled by the surging currents, reached the top of the fountain. Innumerable dolphins—more than I had ever seen in Shallow Bay—poked their heads out of the sea, gazing at the top of the fountain. Their high-pitched chatter was like the drip-drip-drip from stalactites.

Giana! Giana! You're a credit to all dolphinkind!

The silver figure drifted into the sky like the millions of scattering droplets. It floated above the purple mist. Soon, it disappeared beyond the clouds.

A long moment hung suspended, passing and not passing.

The sky brightened abruptly. A deafening noise crashed from the top of the fountain. Countless cracks zigzagged from the center of the dark blue welkin. Wind and stars tumbled through the opening and fell into the sea. The dome continued to crack open, as if the beanstalk was pushing, growing, forcing its way deeper beyond the barrier. My head rang from the thunderous noise, and my eyes were filled with fantastic visions that eventually melded into a single blinding brightness.

The crystal sky fell.

A moment later, the moon and stars revealed their true nature.

I had never imagined the moon would be full of shadows on its unblemished face. I had never imagined the stars . . . to be so bright.

And the mystery, the chaotic center, also revealed its truth—

It was a planet.

Our world had always been right next to another: two apples in a cluster. Though it loomed so close to us, we had never been aware of its presence. The shadow it cast hid the heart of the Milky Way, and its own true shape had been obscured by the crystal sky.

It was Giana who revealed the secret. The spot where the gravities of the two planets balanced each other was also the top of the fountain. There, droplets of water, weightless, scattered in every direction. The arrival of Giana gave weight again to this silent terminus of the world—she had been caught by the gravity of the other planet. . . . And so, the crystal sky cracked as a bug tried to climb out of the apple, broke apart as Giana fell toward a new ocean.

But . . . Giana . . . I recalled the graveyard of ships she had once described to me. The whirlpools had torn apart the sails and spars, broken the decks and oars. . . . Giana's fall had been powerful enough to shatter the crystal sky. Where was she now?

Under the dim, reddish glow of the moon, all the dolphins gazed up silently.

"There! That's the constellation Delphinus!" Giana used to tell me all the time.

All the stars were falling toward the sea. They glowed for a while in the water before fading. Far away, new stars were rising . . . one . . . another one . . . so many of them . . . and soon, every watching dolphin recognized the silvery pattern.

Giana, a credit to all dolphinkind, had smashed the barrier that had blinded us all from the truth and leapt into heaven. Just like Jack climbing up the beanstalk to the giant's castle; just like a bug climbing up the stem to stare at the noonday sun.

She had become one with the eternal stars.

This was the story of Delphinus.

AUTHOR'S NOTE

There are several Greek myths about Delphinus. The tale about Arion is just one of them.

Here, I tell a story about Delphinus using the language of science fiction. It was published in Science Fiction World *magazine in a section known as the "gray area." It's hard to say if stories published there meet the definition of science fiction.*

Thanks to David Brin for inspiring me with his story "The Crystal Spheres."

BAOSHU

After graduating from Peking University, Baoshu (a pen name that should be treated as an indivisible unit) obtained a master's degree in philosophy from KU Leuven, Belgium. He has lived in the US and Europe. Working as a freelance writer in China, he has published four novels and over thirty novellas, novelettes, and short stories since 2010.

His best-known works include *The Redemption of Time* (a sequel of sorts to Liu Cixin's "Three-Body" books) and *Ruins of Time* (winner of the 2014 Xingyun Award for Best Novel). Perhaps as a result of his background in philosophy, many of his stories play with time in various ways: compressing it, stretching it, slicing it into thin slices and piecing them back together in a different order, questioning its nature, altering its essence, transforming it into something alien but still recognizable.

In translation, his fiction may be found in *F&SF* and *Clarkesworld*, among other places.

"What Has Passed Shall in Kinder Light Appear" is also a story about time. Although its first formal publication was through an English translation, it is, in some ways, the most Chinese story in this entire volume:

the more one knows about the history of the People's Republic, the more the story's meaning comes into focus.

A special note of thanks goes to my friend Anatoly Belilovsky, who provided the translation of Pushkin's poem quoted in this story.

WHAT HAS PASSED
SHALL IN KINDER
LIGHT APPEAR

1.

My parents named me Xie Baosheng, hoping I would live a life full of precious memories. I was born on the day the world was supposed to end.

Mom and Dad told me how strange flashing lights appeared in the sky all over the globe, accompanied by thunder and lightning, as though the heavens had turned into a terrifying battlefield. Scientists could not agree on an explanation: some said extraterrestrials had arrived; some suggested the Earth was passing through the galactic plane; still others claimed that the universe was starting to collapse. The apocalyptic atmosphere drove many into church pews while the rest shivered in their beds.

In the end, nothing happened. As soon as the clock struck midnight, the world returned to normality. The crowds, teary-eyed, embraced each other and kissed, thankful for God's gift. Many petitioned for that day to be declared the world's new birthday as a reminder for humanity to live more honestly and purely, and to treasure our existence.

The grateful mood didn't last long, and people pretty much went on living as before. The Arab Spring happened, followed by the global financial crisis. Life had to go on, and we needed to resolve troubles both big and small. Everyone was so busy that the awkward joke about the end of the world never came up again. Of course, I had no memory of any of this: I was born on that day. I had no impressions of the next few years, either.

My earliest memory was of the Opening Ceremony of the Olympics. I was only four then, but nonetheless caught up in the excitement all around me.

Mom and Dad told me, *China is going to host the Olympics!*

I had no idea what the "Olympics" were, just that it was an occasion worth celebrating. That night, Mom took me out. The streets were packed, and she held me up so that I could see, overhead, immense footprints formed by fireworks. One after another, they appeared in the night sky, as if some giant were walking above us. I was amazed.

The neighborhood park had a large projection screen, and Mom brought me there to see the live broadcast. I remembered there were many, many people and it was like a big party. I looked around and saw Qiqi. She was wearing a pink skirt and a pair of shoes that lit up; two braids stuck out from the top of her head like the horns of a goat. Smiling sweetly, she called out, "Bao *gege!*"

Qiqi's mother and Mom were good friends from way back, before they both got married. I was only a month older than Qiqi and had almost certainly seen her lots of times before that night, but I couldn't remember any of those occasions. The Opening Ceremony of the Olympics was the first memory I could really recall with Qiqi in it—it was the first time I understood what *pretty* meant. After we ran into Qiqi and her parents, our two families watched the live broadcast together. While the adults conversed, Qiqi and I sat next to a bed of flowers and had our own chat. Later, an oval-shaped, shiny gigantic basket appeared on the screen.

What's that? I asked.

It's called the Bird's Nest, Qiqi said.

There were no birds inside the Nest, but there was an enormous scroll with flickering animated images that were very pretty. Qiqi and I were entranced.

How do they make those pictures? Qiqi asked.

It's all done with computers, I said. *My dad knows how to do it. Someday, I'll make a big picture, too, just for you.*

Qiqi looked at me, her eyes full of admiration. Later, a little girl about our age sang on the screen, and I thought Qiqi was prettier than her.

That was one of the loveliest, most magical nights of my life. Later, I kept on hoping China would host the Olympics again, but it never happened. After I became a father, I told my son about that night, and he refused to believe China had once been so prosperous.

I had no clear memories of kindergarten, either. Qiqi and I went to the same English-immersion kindergarten, in which half the classes were conducted in English, but I couldn't recall any of it—I certainly didn't learn any English.

I did remember watching *Pleasant Goat and Big Big Wolf* with Qiqi. I told her that I thought she was like Beauty, the cute lamb in the cartoon. She said I was like Grey Wolf.

If I'm Grey Wolf, I said, *you must be Red Wolf.* Red Wolf was Grey Wolf's wife.

She pinched me, and we fought. Qiqi was always ready to hit me to get her way, but she also cried easily. I only pushed back a little bit and she started sobbing. I was terrified she might tattle on me and rushed to the fridge to get some red-bean-flavored shaved ice for her, and she broke into a smile. We went on watching *Chibi Maruko Chan* and *The Adventures of Red Cat and Blue Rabbit* while sharing a bowl of shaved ice.

We played and fought, fought and played, and before we knew it, our childhood had escaped us.

Back then, I thought Qiqi and I were so close that we'd never be apart. However, before we started elementary school, Qiqi's father got a promotion at work and the whole family had to move to Shanghai. Mom took me to say goodbye. While the adults became all misty-eyed, Qiqi and I ran around, laughing like it was just some regular playdate. Then Qiqi got on the train and waved at me through the window like her parents were doing, and I waved back. The train left and took Qiqi away.

The next day, I asked Mom, "When's Qiqi coming back? How about we all go to Tiananmen Square next Sunday?"

But Qiqi wasn't back the next Sunday, or the one after that. She disappeared from my life. I didn't get to see her again for many years, until my memories of her had blurred and sunk into the depths of my heart.

In elementary school, I made a good friend—everyone called him "Heizi" because he was dark and skinny. Heizi and I lived in the same neighborhood, and his family was in business—supposedly his dad had made his fortune by flipping real estate. Heizi wasn't a good student and often asked to copy my homework; to show his gratitude, he invited me over to his house to play. His family owned a very cool computer hooked up to an ultra-high-def LCD screen that took up half a wall—fantastic for racing or fighting games, though the adults didn't let us play for long. But when we were in the third grade, SARS was going around and some kid in the neighborhood got sick, so we all had to be taken out of school and quarantined at home. We ended up playing games the whole day, every day. Good times.

During those months in the shadow of SARS, the adults had gloomy expressions and sighed all the time. Everyone hoarded food and other consumables at home and seldom went out—when they did, they wore face masks. They also forced me to drink some kind of bitter Chinese medicine soup that supposedly provided immunity against SARS. I was old enough to understand that something terrible was going on in China and the rest of the world, and felt scared. That was my first experience of the dread and panic of a world nearing doom. One time, I overheard Mom and Dad discussing some rumor that tens of thousands of people had died from SARS, and I ended up suffering a nightmare. I dreamed that everyone around me had died so that I was the only one left, and the United States was taking advantage of the SARS crisis to attack China, dropping bombs everywhere. . . . I woke up in a cold sweat.

Of course, nothing bad really happened. The SARS crisis ended up not being a big deal at all.

But it was a start. In the days still to come, my generation would experience events far more terrifying than SARS. We knew nothing of the future that awaited us.

2.

During the SARS crisis, I dreamed of an American attack on China because the US had just conquered Iraq and Afghanistan, and managed to catch Saddam. They were also looking for a man named bin Laden, and it was all over the news. I watched the news during dinnertime, and I remember being annoyed at America: *Why are the Americans always invading other countries?* I felt especially bad for Saddam: a pitiable old man captured by the Americans and put on trial. And they said he was going to be executed. How terrible! I kept hoping the Americans would lose.

Amazingly, my wish came true. Not long after SARS, the news reports said that something called the Iraqi Republican Guard had mobilized and rescued Saddam. Saddam led the resistance against the American invasion and somehow managed to chase the US out of Iraq. In Afghanistan, a group called Tali-something also started an uprising and waged guerrilla war against the American troops in the mountains. Bin Laden even succeeded in planning a shocking attack that brought down two American skyscrapers using airliners. The Americans got scared and retreated in defeat.

Two years later, I started middle school. Heizi and I were in the same school but different classes.

My first year coincided with another apocalypse predicted by an ancient calendar—I had no idea back then why there were so many apocalyptic legends; maybe everyone felt living in this world wasn't safe. Those were also the years when the world economy was in a depression and lots of places had difficulties: Russia, a new country called Yugoslavia, Somalia . . . The desperate Americans even decided to bomb our embassy in Belgrade. People were so angry that college students marched to the American embassy and threw rocks at the windows.

However, the life of middle school students was very different. The costume drama *Princess Pearl* was really popular, and they showed it all the time on TV. Everyone in my class became addicted, and all we could talk about was the fate of Princess Xiaoyanzi. We didn't understand politics and paid very little attention to those world events.

Gradually, though, the effects of the worldwide depression became apparent in daily life. Real estate prices kept crashing; Heizi's father lost money in his property deals and turned to day-trading stocks, but he was still losing money. Although prices for everything were falling, wages dropped even faster. Since no one was buying the high-tech gadgets, they stopped making them. The huge LCD screen in Heizi's home broke, but they couldn't find anything similar in the market and had to make do with a clumsy CRT monitor: the screen was tiny and convex, which just looked weird. My father's notebook computer was gone, replaced by a big tower that had much worse specs—supposedly this was all due to the depressed American economy. Over time, websites failed one after another, and the new computer games were so bad that it was no longer fun to mess around on the computer. Street arcades became popular, and kids our age went to hang out at those places while the adults began to practice traditional Chinese meditation.

There was one benefit to all this "progress": the sky over Beijing became clear and blue. I remembered that, when I was little, every day was filled with smog and it was difficult to breathe. Now, however, other than during sandstorm season, you could see blue sky and white clouds all the time.

In the summer of my second year in middle school, Qiqi returned to Beijing for a visit and stayed with my family. She was tall and slender, almost 5'3", and wore a pair of glasses. With her graceful manners and big eyes, she was closer to a young woman than a girl, and I still thought she was pretty. When she saw me, she smiled shyly, and instead of calling me "Bao *gege*" like a kid, she addressed me by my given name: "Baosheng." She had lost all traces of her Beijing accent and spoke in the gentle tones of southern China, which I found pleasing. I tried to reminisce with her about the Olympics and watching *Pleasant Goat and Big Big Wolf*. Disappointingly, she told me she couldn't remember much.

I overheard Mom and Dad saying that Qiqi's parents were in the middle of a bitter divorce and were fighting over every bit of property and Qiqi's custody. They had sent Qiqi away to Beijing to avoid hurting her while they tore into each other. I could tell that Qiqi was unhappy, because I heard her cry in her room the night she arrived. I didn't know how to help her except to take her around to eat good food and see interesting sights, and to distract her with silly stories. Although Qiqi had been born in Beijing, she was so young when she left that she might as well have been a first-time visitor. That whole summer, she rode behind me on my bicycle, and we toured every major avenue and narrow *hutong* in the city.

We grew close again, but it wasn't the same as our childhood friendship; rather, our budding adolescence colored everything. It wasn't love, of course, but it was more than just friendship. Qiqi got to know my good friends, too. Heizi, in particular, came over to my home much more frequently now that a young woman was living there. One time, Heizi and I took Qiqi to hike the Fragrant Hills. Heizi paid a lot of attention to Qiqi: helping her up and down the rocky steps and telling her jokes. While Qiqi and Heizi chatted happily, I felt annoyed. That was when I first noticed I didn't like others intruding between Qiqi and me, not even Heizi.

Near the end of summer break, Qiqi had to go back to Shanghai. Since neither of my parents was free that day, I took her to the train station. The two of us squeezed onto the train half an hour before departure time, and I made up my mind and took from my backpack a gift-wrapped parcel I had prepared ahead of time.

Hesitantly, I said, "Um, this . . . is a . . . present for . . . for you."
Qiqi was surprised. "What is it?"

"Um . . . why don't you . . . open it . . . um . . . later? No!—"

But it was too late. Qiqi had torn open the package and was staring wide-eyed at the copy of *High-Difficulty Mathematical Questions from the High School Entrance Examination with Solutions and Explanations.*

"Well, you told me you had trouble with math . . ." I struggled to explain. "I like this book . . . I figured . . . um . . . you might find it helpful . . ."

Qiqi was laughing so hard that tears were coming out of her eyes. I felt like the world's biggest idiot.

"Whoever heard of giving a girl a test-prep manual as a gift?" Still laughing, Qiqi opened the book to the title page. Her face froze as she read the Pushkin poem I had copied out:

Life's deceit may Fortune's fawning
Turn to scorn, yet, as you grieve,
Do not anger, but believe
In tomorrow's merry dawning.

When your heart is rid at last
Of regret, despair, and fear,
In the future, what has passed
Shall in kinder light appear.[6]

After the poem, I had written two lines:
To my friend Zhao Qi: May you forget the unhappy parts of life and live each day in joy. Love life and embrace ideals!

I felt very foolish.

Qiqi held the book to her chest and gave me a bright smile, but tears were spilling out of the corners of her eyes.

6 English translation courtesy of Anatoly Belilovsky, © 2014. Used here with permission.

3.

Qiqi left and my life returned to its familiar routines. But my heart would not calm down.

When Qiqi visited, she brought a book called *Season of Bloom, Season of Rain*, which was popular among middle school girls back then. She had wrapped the book's cover carefully in poster paper and written the title on it in her neat, elegant handwriting. Curious, I had flipped through it but didn't find it interesting. Qiqi left the book behind when she returned to Shanghai, and I hid it in the deepest recess of my desk because I was afraid Mom would take it away. The book still held Qiqi's scent, and I pulled it out from time to time to read until I finished it. Afterward, I couldn't help but compare myself and Qiqi to the high school students involved in the novel's complicated love triangles: Was I more like this guy or that one? Was Qiqi more like this girl or that girl? One time, I brought up the topic with Heizi and he almost died from laughing.

Just because boys weren't into romance novels didn't mean we weren't interested in the mysterious emotions portrayed in them. Anything having to do with love was popular among my classmates: everyone copied love poems, sang romantic ballads, and watched *Divine Eagle, Gallant Lovers*, imagining we were also starcrossed martial arts heroes and heroines. "Matchmaking" by astrology became a popular game. Once, one of the girls in my class, Shen Qian, and I were assigned classroom cleanup duty together, and somehow that inspired everyone to think of us as a couple. I vociferously denied this, not realizing that this only made the game even more fun for others. I resorted to ignoring Shen Qian altogether, but this only led all our classmates to postulate that we were having a "lovers' spat." I didn't know what to do.

In the end, Shen Qian came to my rescue. She made no secret of her interest in a high school boy known for his wit and generated a ton of juicy gossip—as a result, rumors about Shen Qian and me naturally died out.

Shen Qian's early attempt at romance soon ended when parents and teachers intervened, alarmed by this distraction from our academic development. Afterward, she acted aloof and cold to all of us, but spent her time reading books that appeared profound and abstruse: contemplative essays about Chinese culture, collected works of obscure philosophy, and the like. Everyone now said that Shen Qian was going to become a famous writer. However, her class compositions often took original and rebellious points of view that led to criticism from the teachers.

Despite the rumors about us, I didn't grow closer to Shen Qian; instead, I became even more convinced of the depth of my feelings for Qiqi. I thought: *She might not be the prettiest girl and she's far away in Shanghai, but I like her, and I'm going to be good to her.* Unfortunately, with thousands of kilometers dividing us, I only heard news about her from occasional phone calls between our mothers. After the divorce, Qiqi lived with her mother, and though they were poor, Qiqi did well academically and managed to place into one of the best high schools in the city.

Oh, one more thing: during my middle school years, a short man named Deng Xiaoping rose to prominence and became a member of the Central Committee. Although Jiang Zemin was still the General Secretary, Deng held all the real power. Deng started a series of reforms aimed at nationalizing industry, and he justified his policies with many novel theories: "Socialism with Chinese Characteristics"; "it doesn't matter whether it is a white cat or a black cat; a cat that catches mice is a good cat"; and so on. Lots of people became rich by taking advantage of the new opportunities, but many others sank into poverty. Because the economy was doing so poorly, the small company Dad worked for had to shut down, but with the Deng-initiated reforms, he got a job with a state-owned enterprise that guaranteed we'd at least have the basic necessities. Honestly, compared to the rest of the world, China wasn't doing too badly. For example, I heard there was a financial crisis in Southeast Asia that affected the world; Russia's economy collapsed and even college students had to become streetwalkers; there was a civil war in Yugoslavia and a genocide in Africa; the United States had pulled out of Iraq but maintained a blockade and sanctions. . . .

None of this had much to do with my life, of course. The most important things in my life were studying, cramming for the college entrance examination, and sometimes thinking about Qiqi.

During my first year in high school, many people had "pen pals," strangers they corresponded with. This wasn't all that different from the web-based chats we used to have when we were little, but the practice seemed a bit more literary. I missed Qiqi so much that I decided to write her a letter in English—full of grammatical errors, as you might imagine—with the excuse that I was doing so to improve my English skills. Email would have been easier, but computers had disappeared from daily life, and so I had no choice but to write an actual letter. As soon as I dropped it into the mailbox I regretted my rash act, but it was too late. The following two weeks crept by so slowly they felt like years.

Qiqi answered! She'd certainly made more of that English-immersion kindergarten experience than I had: her letter was much better. Leaving aside the content, even her handwriting was pretty, like a series of notes on a musical score. I had to read that letter with a dictionary by my side, and I ended up practically memorizing it. I did feel my English improved a great deal as a result.

Qiqi's letter was pretty short, just over a page. She mentioned that the math book I had given her more than a year earlier had been helpful, and she was grateful. She also recommended *New Concept English* to me, and told me some simple facts about her school. But I was most pleased by her last paragraph, in which she asked about my school, Heizi, and so on. Her meaning couldn't be clearer: she was looking forward to another letter from me.

We corresponded in English regularly after that. We never said anything all that interesting: school, ideals in life, things like that. But the very fact that we were writing to each other made me incredibly happy. Just knowing that someone far away, practically on the other side of the world, was thinking about you and cared about you was an indescribably wonderful feeling. Qiqi told me that her mother had gotten married again. Her stepfather had a child of his own and was rather cold to her. She didn't feel that her home was her home anymore, and wanted to leave for college as soon as possible so that she could be independent.

I finished high school without much trouble and did really well on my college entrance examination, so I could pick from several schools. Summoning my courage, I called Qiqi and asked her what schools she was picking. She said she didn't want to stay in Shanghai, and filled out Nanjing University with a major in English as her first choice.

I wanted to go to Nanjing as well: one, I wanted to be with Qiqi; and two, I wanted to be away from my parents and try to make it on my own. But my parents absolutely would not allow it and insisted that I stay in Beijing. We had a huge fight, but in the end I gave in and filled out Peking University with a major in Chinese as my top choice. Heizi never made it into a good high school and couldn't get into college at all, so he joined a department store as a sales clerk. Still, all of us believed that we had bright futures ahead of us.

4.

Compared to the close supervision we were under back in high school, college was practically total freedom. Although the school administrators, in loco parentis, weren't keen on the idea of students dating, they basically looked the other way. Boys and girls paired up quickly, and the Chinese Department was known as a hotbed of romance. Several of my roommates soon had beautiful girlfriends, and I was very envious.

Shen Qian also got into Peking University, majoring in Politics. Our high school classmates all predicted we would end up together, but Shen Qian soon published some outrageous poems and articles in the school paper and became part of the artsy, literary, avant-garde crowd. Other than occasionally seeing each other at gatherings of old high school friends, she and I ran in completely different circles.

Qiqi and I continued our correspondence, but we no longer needed writing in English as an excuse. We wrote to each other every week, and our letters ran on for dozens of pages, covering everything silly, interesting, or even boring in our lives. Sometimes I had to use extra stamps. I really wanted to make our relationship formal, but just couldn't get up the courage.

By the time we were second-years, the name of some boy began to appear in Qiqi's letters. She mentioned him so casually—without even explaining who he was—as though he was already a natural part of her life. I asked her about him, and Qiqi wrote back saying he was the class president: handsome, fluent in English, and also in the Drama Club with her.

Unhappy with her response, I tried to draft a reply but couldn't find the words. I would have pulled out my cell phone to call her, but by then no one used cell phones anymore. China Mobile had long since gone out of business, and the cell phone in my desk—a birthday present from my father when I turned ten—was just a useless piece of antique junk.

I went downstairs to use the public phone. Every residential hall had only one phone, and the woman who picked up on the other end was the matron for Qiqi's residential hall. She interrogated me for a long while before she agreed to go get Qiqi. I waited and waited. One of Qiqi's roommates eventually picked up.

"Qiqi is out with her boyfriend."

I dropped the phone and ran to the train station to buy a ticket to Nanjing. I was at the door of her residential hall at noon the next day.

Qiqi came down the stairs like a graceful bird in a white pleated skirt, her hair tied back in neat braids. She appeared to be glowing with the warm sunlight. Other than a few pictures through the mail, we hadn't seen each other since that summer in middle school.

She was no longer a girl, but a tall, vivacious young woman. She didn't look too surprised to see me; instead, she lowered her eyes and chuckled, as though she knew I would be here.

That afternoon, she took me to the famous No-Sorrow Lake, where we rented a boat and rowed it to the center of the jade-green water. She asked me whether I had seen a popular Japanese TV drama called *Tokyo Love Story*.

I had heard about the show, but since my roommates and I didn't own a TV, I had only seen some clips when I visited my parents and read some summaries in the TV guide. But I didn't want to show my ignorance.

"Yes," I said.

"So . . . who do you like?" Qiqi asked, very interested.

"I . . . I like Satomi." Honestly, I wasn't even sure who the characters were.

Qiqi was surprised. "Satomi? I can't stand her. Why do you like her?"

My heart skipped a beat. "Uh . . . Satomi is the female lead, right? She has such a pretty smile."

"What are you talking about? The female lead is Rika Akana!"

"Wait! I read the synopsis, and they said that Satomi grew up with the male lead, and then the two of them ended up together . . . doesn't that make her the female lead?"

"That's ludicrous." Qiqi laughed. I loved the way she wrinkled her nose. "Why would you think such a thing?"

"Because . . . because I feel that people who knew each other when they were young ought to end up together. For example . . . uh . . ." I couldn't continue.

"For example?" She grinned.

"You and me," I blurted out.

Qiqi tilted her head and looked at me for a while. "What a silly idea." She slapped me.

It wasn't a real slap, of course—it was so light it was more like a caress. Her slender fingers slid across my face, and I shivered as though they were charged with electricity. My heart leapt wildly and I grabbed her hand. Qiqi didn't pull away. I stood up and wanted to pull her into an embrace, except I had forgotten we were on a boat, and so—

The boat capsized, and as Qiqi screamed, we tumbled into the water.

We giggled like fools as we climbed back into the boat. Qiqi was now my girlfriend. Later, she told me that the class president really was interested in her, but she had never cared for him. She wrote about him in her letters to me on purpose to see if she could finally get me to express myself clearly. She didn't quite anticipate that I would be so worried I'd come all the way to Nanjing—as she said this, I could tell how pleased she was.

We held hands and visited all the big tourist attractions of Nanjing that day: Xuanwu Lake, Qinhuai River, Confucian Temple, Sun Yat-sen's Mausoleum . . . I spent the day in a honey-flavored daze.

For the remainder of our time in college, we only got to see each other occasionally during breaks, but we wrote to each other even more often and were completely in love. My parents, after finding out about Qiqi and me, were pleased because of the friendship between our families. Mom spoke of Qiqi as her future daughter-in-law and joked that she and Qiqi's mother had arranged for our marriage before we were even born. We planned to find jobs in the same city after graduation and then get married.

5.

Just as happiness appeared to be within reach, it shattered into a million pieces.

The economies of Russia, Ukraine, and some other countries collapsed so completely that the unimaginable happened: a man named Gorbachev emerged as a powerful leader and convinced more than a dozen independent states to join together to form a new country called the "Union of Soviet Socialist Republics," dedicated to the implementation of socialism. The new country became very powerful very quickly and thwarted the Americans at every turn, instantly adding tension to the international situation. The Soviet Union then encouraged revolutions in Eastern Europe—and even Germany, whose eastern and western halves weren't at the same level of economic development, split into two countries, with East Germany joining the Soviet bloc.

In China, Deng's planned economic reforms weren't successful and the economy continued to deteriorate. More and more people grew unhappy with the government. The machinery of the state was corrupt, ossified, authoritarian, and full of misadministration. College students still remembered how prosperous and strong the country had been when they were children, and comparing the past to the present filled them with rage. Rumors were full of tales of corrupt officials, of misappropriation of state funds for private gain, of attempts to fill public administration posts with family members and loyal minions—although few could explain clearly the root causes of the problems, everyone appeared to agree on the solution in debates and discussions: the country was in trouble and the political system had to be fundamentally reformed to implement real democracy. The incompetent leaders had to go! A political manifesto composed some twenty years earlier, simply called "Charter '08," began to spread secretly among college students.

Right before my graduation, the factional struggles within the Communist Party grew even more intense. It was said that the leader of the reformists, Zhao Ziyang, had been relieved of his duties and placed under house arrest. The news was like the spark that set off a powder keg, and the long-repressed rage among the population erupted in a way that shocked everyone. Students at all the major universities in Beijing went into the streets to march and protest, and with the support of Beijing's citizens they occupied Tiananmen Square, which drew the attention of the world. A city of tents sprouted in the square, and some protestors even erected a statue of the Goddess of Liberty in front of the Gate of Heavenly Peace itself.

The drafter of Charter '08, Liu Xiaobo, returned to China from overseas. He made a speech at the square vowing to go on a hunger strike until there was true reform. The whole nation was inspired. Young people began to arrive from everywhere in China, and the mass movement gained momentum. Even ordinary citizens in Beijing mobilized to support the students. Heizi, for example, often came by on his tricycle to bring us food and water.

"Eat and drink!" he shouted. "You need your strength to fight those fucking bums sitting in Zhongnanhai."

Shen Qian had published some provocative essays in the past, and she was a fan of Liu Xiaobo. Her influence among the students made her one of the leaders in the movement. She came by to discuss with me how to motivate the students in the Chinese Department to play a more active role. Stimulated by her fervor, I felt I had to do something for the country, and in the famous triangular plaza at the heart of Peking University's campus, I made a speech denouncing the corrupt, bureaucratic student council and calling for all students to free themselves from government control and to form a democratic, independent, self-governing body. Amazingly, many professors and students applauded my speech, and a few days later the Students' Autonomous Federation came into existence. Shen Qian was elected one of the standing committee members, and because she felt I had some talent, she asked me to join the Federation's publicity department. Thus I became a core member of the movement. I felt as though my talent had finally been properly recognized.

We created a command center in the square where our daily routines resembled those of a mini-government: receiving student representatives from all across the country, announcing various proclamations and programs, issuing open letters, and engaging in vigorous debate over everything as though the future of the entire nation depended on us. News that our compatriots in Hong Kong and Taiwan were also supporting us and donating funds filled us with even more zeal. We laughed, we cried, we screamed, we sang, all the while dreaming of forging a brand-new future for China with our youth and passion.

One day, at the beginning of June, I was in a crude tent at the edge of the command center writing a new program for the movement. The weather was humid and hot, and I was drenched in sweat. Suddenly, I heard Shen Qian call out, "Baosheng, look who's here to see you!"

I emerged from the tent. Qiqi was standing there in a sky-blue dress, carrying a small pack on her back and looking tired from her journey. Overcome by joy and surprise, I couldn't speak, and Shen Qian made fun of us.

Since Shen Qian had never met Qiqi before, she gave her a careful once-over and said, "So this is Baosheng's mysterious girlfriend. . . ."

Qiqi blushed.

Finally, after getting rid of Shen Qian, I peppered Qiqi with questions: "How did you get here? Did you come with other students from Nanjing University? That's great! I heard about the protests in Nanjing, too. Who's in charge of your group? I've just drafted a new program for the movement, and it would be useful to get some feedback—"

"Is this all you have to say to me after all this time?" Qiqi interrupted.

"Of course not! I've really missed you." I hugged her, laughing, but soon turned serious again. "But the movement is running out of steam and the students are splitting into factions . . . The hunger strike isn't sustainable, and I've been discussing with Liu Xiaobo how to develop the movement and extend it. . . . Come, take a look at my draft—"

"Baosheng," Qiqi interrupted again. "I stopped by your home. Your mother asked me to come and talk to you."

A bucket of cold water had been poured onto the fire in me. "Oh," I said, and nothing more.

"Your mother is really worried about you . . ." Qiqi's voice was gentle. "It's almost time for you to receive your post-graduation job assignment. You know how important that is. Stop messing around with these people. Come home with me."

"Qiqi, how can you say such a thing?" I was disappointed as well as angry. "'Messing around'? Look at the tens of thousands of students assembled in this square! Look at the millions of citizens beyond them! All of Beijing—no, all of China—has boiled over. Everyone is fighting for the future of our country. How can we go back to studying in a classroom?"

"What can you possibly accomplish? You'll never overcome the government. They have the army! Also, some of your proposals are too radical; they're impossible—"

"What do you mean, *impossible*?" I was very unhappy with her. "The army serves the people. The soldiers will never point their guns at us. Some of the students are talking to them already. Don't worry. I've heard that the bureaucrats in the central leadership are terrified. They'll soon be willing to compromise."

Qiqi sighed and sat down, looking miserably at me.

We talked and talked, but there was no resolution. In the end, I refused to leave the square, and Qiqi stayed with me. That night, we slept in the same tent. We talked about the national and international situation and the movement's prospects, but we couldn't agree on anything and started to argue. Eventually, we stopped talking about these matters and simply held each other.

We reminisced about our childhood together, and then I could no longer hold back. I kissed her, first her face, then her lips. That was the first time we really kissed. Her lips were soft and chapped, which broke my heart. I kissed her deeply and would not let go. . . .

In the dark, it happened naturally. With so many young people in the square, our lovemaking was an open secret. Normally I despised such behavior, and felt that couples who engaged in it tarnished the sacred nature of our protest. But now that it was happening to me, I couldn't resist, and felt our actions were a natural part of the movement itself. Maybe some nameless anxiety about the future also made us want to seize this last moment of total freedom. Every motion, every gesture was infused with awkwardness and embarrassment. We were clumsy and raw, but passion, the irresistible power of youthful passion, eventually brought that fumbling, ridiculous process to a conclusion of sweet intimacy that surpassed understanding.

6.

The next day, we heard the news that troops had arrived just outside Beijing to enforce martial law. A vanguard had already entered the city, preparing to clear the square.

Should we retreat? The command center held a meeting and opinions were divided. Liu Xiaobo advocated retreat to prevent the loss of lives. Due to Qiqi's influence, I also supported Liu's suggestion. But the commander in chief, Chai Ling, was indignant and refused to budge. She even called us cowards and said that we must resist to the utmost, even with our lives. Her words inspired all the other attendees, and those advocating retreat were silenced. In the end, most of the students stayed to follow Chai Ling's orders.

That night was especially hot. Qiqi and I couldn't fall asleep, and so we lay outside the tent, whispering to each other. "You were right," I said. "Chai Ling is too stubborn. I don't think any good will come of this. I'll tell Liu Xiaobo tomorrow that we're going home."

"All right." She leaned her head against my shoulder and fell asleep. I followed soon after.

I startled awake with the noise of the crowd all around me. The stars in the summer sky overhead were eerily bright. It took me a moment to realize that all the lamps on the square were extinguished and darkness engulfed us, which was why the stars shined so bright and clear. People were shouting all around us and loudspeakers squawked. I couldn't understand what was going on.

"Baosheng!" Someone ran at us with a flashlight, and the glare made me squint. A blurry figure came closer: Shen Qian. She was sobbing as she said, "Hurry! You have to leave! The army is clearing the square."

"What? Where's Chai Ling? She's supposed to be in charge!"

"That bitch was the first to run away! Go, go! I still have to find Liu Xiaobo."

Later, I found out that a large number of armed police had come into the square with batons to break down the tents, beating any students who resisted. But we couldn't see anything at the time, and everything around us was utter chaos. I didn't know what to do, so I grabbed Qiqi by the hand and tried to follow the flow of the crowd.

A few students from the provinces ran past us, screaming, "Tanks! Tanks! Someone got crushed by the tanks!" They collided into us and separated Qiqi from me.

I heard Qiqi calling my name and ran toward her, shouting her name. But I tripped over a tent and couldn't get up for some seconds while others ran over me, kicking me back down. By the time I finally struggled up, I could no longer hear Qiqi and didn't know where she was. Helpless, I tried to continue in the same direction I'd been headed. A chaotic crowd surrounded me, but there was no Qiqi. I screamed her name. Then someone started singing "The Internationale" and everyone joined in. I couldn't even hear my own voice.

Caught up in the tumultuous crowd, I left Tiananmen Square.

In this manner, we were forcefully removed from the square—at least no shots were fired. However, elsewhere in the city, there were more violent encounters between the army and the protestors, and gunshots were heard from time to time. I returned home, hoping against hope, but Qiqi had not been there. Ignoring the objections of my parents, I ran back toward the city center.

By then it was dawn, and scattered tanks and soldiers could be seen in the streets. Bloody corpses lined the roads, many of them young students. I felt as though I was in the middle of a battlefield, and terror seized me. But the idea that something had happened to Qiqi terrified me even more. Like a crazy man, I looked everywhere for her.

At noon, I ran into one of my friends from the command center. He brought me to a secret gathering, where I found Shen Qian and Liu Xiaobo. Many were wounded, and Shen Qian, her face drained of blood, shivered as Liu held her. I asked them if they had seen Qiqi.

Shen Qian started to sob. My heart sank into an icy abyss.

Tearfully, Shen Qian explained that Qiqi had found them as the square was being cleared, and they retreated together. They encountered a column of soldiers at an intersection, and not fully understanding the situation, they denounced the soldiers. The soldiers responded by firing upon them, and a few of the students fell. They turned to run again, only realizing after a while that Qiqi was no longer with them. Shen retraced their steps and found Qiqi lying in a pool of blood, not moving. They had wanted to save Qiqi, but the soldiers were chasing them and they had no choice but to keep running.

She was sobbing so hard by now that she could no longer speak.

I demanded that Shen Qian tell me the exact location and then dashed madly toward the address. At the intersection, I saw the smoking, burnt remnant of an army truck. Inside was the charred corpse of a soldier. In a pool of blood next to the intersection lay a few more bodies, but I didn't see Qiqi. Forcing down my nausea, I searched all around, though I was hoping to find nothing.

But then I saw Qiqi's sky-blue dress under one of the wheels of the army truck. Blood had stained it purple, and protruding from the skirt was a section of her perfect calf, ending in a bloody mess.

Shivering, I approached. An overwhelming stench of blood filled my nose. I felt the sky and the earth spin around me and could no longer stand up. Everything was speeding away from me, leaving only an endless darkness that descended over me, extinguishing my last spark of consciousness.

By the time I woke up, it was dark again. I heard the sound of occasional gunshots in the distance. A column of soldiers passed no more than two meters from me, but they ignored me, probably thinking I was just another corpse. I lay still, stunned, and for a moment I forgot what had happened—until the terrifying memory returned and crushed me with despair.

I couldn't blame Chai Ling, or the students who had run into

Qiqi and me and separated us from each other, or even the soldiers. I knew that the real culprit responsible for Qiqi's death was me, because I didn't listen to her.

That night, I became a walking corpse. I dared not look at Qiqi's body again. Wandering the city on my own, I paid no attention to the fearsome soldiers or the criminals who took advantage of the chaos to loot and rob. Several times I saw people fall down near me and die, but somehow, miraculously, I was spared. The world had turned into a nightmare from which I could not awaken.

The next day, as a long column of tanks rolled down the Avenue of Eternal Peace, I stepped in front of them. Passersby watched, stunned. I wanted the tanks to crush me beneath their treads . . .

But I didn't die. Plainclothes officers grabbed me and pulled me off the street. I was thrown into a dark room and interrogated for a few days. By then I had recovered some of my senses and managed to tell them what had happened. I was certain I would be sentenced to death or at least be locked away for years. My heart had already died, and I didn't care.

Unexpectedly, after a few months of detention, I was released without even a trial. My punishment was quite light: expulsion from Peking University.

7.

By the time I was released, order had been restored. After the violent crackdown that ended the protests, the government became unexpectedly magnanimous. General Secretary Jiang stepped down, and although Deng Xiaoping retained power, the reformist Zhao Ziyang became the new General Secretary, and another reformist leader with a good reputation, Hu Yaobang, also took up an important political post. Most of the participants in the protests were not punished. Even Liu Xiaobo was allowed to continue teaching at a university, though he would no longer be permitted to leave the country. The government's final summary of the protests was this: the university students made legitimate demands; however, international forces took advantage of them.

Supposedly, the international forces were working against the entire socialist camp, not just China. They stirred up trouble in Eastern Europe, too, hoping to encircle and contain the Soviet Union. In the end, the Western powers failed utterly in this plan. The Soviet Union not only survived, but also installed socialist governments in Czechoslovakia, Poland, and several other Eastern European countries. These satellites formed the Warsaw Pact with the Soviet Union to counteract the power of NATO. The US and the USSR thus began a "Cold War."

After my release from prison, Qiqi's mother came to our home and demanded to know where her daughter was. During the interim months, she had almost gone mad with the lack of any news about Qiqi. She came to Beijing only to find that I had been locked up as well.

I fell to my knees in front of her and tearfully confessed that I was responsible for Qiqi's death. At first she refused to believe me, but then she kicked and beat me until my parents pulled her off. She collapsed to the ground and sobbed inconsolably.

Qiqi's mother never forgave me, and she broke off all contact with my family. Later, I went to Shanghai a few times, but she refused to see me. I heard that she had fallen on hard times and I tried to send her some money and necessities, but she always returned my packages unopened.

On the day of Qiqi's death, my mental state had broken down so completely that I didn't even remember to collect her body. Now it was too late even to give her a decent burial. No doubt she had been cremated en masse with the other unclaimed corpses. A spirited young woman in the spring of her life had disappeared from the world, and it was as if she had never existed.

No, that was not quite true. I did find a purple hairclip in my pocket. I remembered Qiqi taking it off the night when we were in the tent together, and I had pocketed it without thinking. This was my last memento of her.

I found everything in my home that held memories of Qiqi and put them together on the desk: the hairclip, bundles of letters, little presents we had given each other, a few photographs of the two of us, and that copy of *Season of Bloom, Season of Rain* . . . Every day, I sat in front of this shrine and tried to relive all the moments we had shared, as though she was still by my side. I spent half a year like this—maybe I had gone a bit mad.

At the Spring Festival, as the family gathered for New Year's dinner, my mother broke down in tears. She said she couldn't bear to see me like this. She wanted me to stop living in the past and go on with my life. I sat at the table dully for a long while.

I steeled myself and carefully packed up all the objects on my desk and placed them at the bottom of my trunk. I kept the bundle with me always but seldom looked at those mementos again. Life had to go on, and I did not want to experience that heartrending pain and sense of guilt anew.

Though I was expelled from school, General Secretary Zhao indicated that he was interested in a more enlightened administration that would let bygones be bygones, and the professors in my department who sympathized with my plight managed to give me my diploma through back channels. I couldn't find a job, though. When I was younger, companies recruited on campus for graduates, but after the reforms, all jobs were assigned by the state. Since my record was stained by my participation in the protests, I was no longer part of the system and no job would be assigned to me.

Heizi had also lost his job because of his support for the students. The two of us got together and figured we'd try our luck at starting a business. Back then, Zhao Ziyang was pushing through price reforms aimed at addressing the transition from market economy to planned economy, and prices for everything had skyrocketed. Everybody around the country was hoarding, and life was becoming harder for the average person. Since many everyday goods were in short supply, the government started to issue ration tickets for food, clothing, and so on, to limit the amount anyone could purchase. If we were clever and bought and sold goods at the right times, we stood to make a good profit.

Heizi and I planned to go to Guangdong in the south, which was more developed than the rest of China. Although my parents didn't want me to be so far away from home, they were glad to see me trying to get my life back on track and gave us their life savings as starting capital. There were many opportunities in those days, and Heizi and I quickly brought some T-shirts back to Beijing, which we sold at a significant markup. Not only did we recoup all our capital, we even managed to make tens of thousands in profit. And thus we became two so-called profiteers who traveled all over China, searching for opportunities. Sometimes Heizi and I struck gold, but other times we were so poor we didn't know where our next meal would come from.

After spending a few years traveling around and interacting with all segments of society, I realized how immature we had been back at Tiananmen. China was an overladen freight train burdened with the weight of the past as well as the present. A few students fervently shouting slogans could not change the complicated conditions of the country. But how might things be improved? I had no answers. All I knew was that although China had recovered its tranquility and the people appeared to be focused only on the concerns of daily life, there were strong currents and countercurrents of competing social interests. Together, they formed a powerful hidden whirlpool that might pull the nation into an abyss that no one wanted to see. Yet the process wasn't something that could be controlled by anyone or any authority. No one could control history. We were all simply parts of a great vortex that was greater than any individual.

Two years after Heizi and I started our business, I bumped into Shen Qian while searching for something to buy in Guangzhou. After the protests, I stayed away from the literary elites and rarely got to see her, although I had heard that she became Liu Xiaobo's lover. Although Liu was married, Shen Qian was willing to be his mistress because she truly loved him. Later, the rumors said Liu had divorced his wife, and I thought he would marry Shen Qian. I certainly didn't expect to find her so far from Beijing.

Meeting an old friend a long way from home always made me emotional. Reminded of Qiqi, I felt my eyes grow wet. Shen Qian told me that she had arrived in Guangzhou hoping to stay with an old friend and get back on her feet, but the friend was nowhere to be found and she didn't know what to do. I promised I'd help her.

I took Shen Qian to a restaurant to welcome her to Guangzhou. We talked about the old times, but both of us avoided any mention of Tiananmen. After a few rounds of drinks, Shen Qian's lips loosened, and she told me tearfully about how Liu Xiaobo had taken advantage of her trust. He had promised to divorce his wife and marry her, but she caught him with another student. They had a fight and broke up. . . . As she told her story, she kept on drinking, straight from the bottle, and I couldn't stop her. Later, she began to sing loudly, and everybody in the restaurant stared at us. I quickly paid the bill and hurried her out of there.

Shen Qian was so drunk that I had to hold her up. Since she had nowhere else to stay, I brought her back to my room. I left her to recover in my bed while I slept on the floor.

The next morning, I needed to get out early to browse the markets, and so I left without waking up Shen Qian. By the time I got back, I expected she would be gone. However, when I came in the door, I saw that my messy room had been cleaned up and everything was neatly and logically arranged. There was a new cloth on the small kitchen table, and Shen Qian, in an apron, was carrying a plate of steaming scrambled eggs with tomatoes out of the kitchen.

We looked at each other; she smiled shyly.

I knew that my life was about to start a new chapter.

8.

Shen Qian continued to stay in my rental unit. She made the place feel like home, a feeling I had long missed. And so the two of us, both with pasts that we wanted to forget, leaned against each other for warmth. Heizi had just gotten married, and after finding out that Shen Qian and I were together, he was very happy for us. He treated Shen Qian as though we were already married.

Since Shen Qian couldn't find a job, she helped us with our business. She was nothing like the young radical student rebel she had been. After all she had gone through, she had abandoned her dreams of revolutions and literary fame and turned all her attention to family. Who was to say this wasn't a self as true as her former image?

Half a year later, my mother came to Guangzhou for a visit, and my relationship with Shen Qian could no longer be kept a secret. My mother didn't like Shen Qian at first, but after living with us for a while, she began to accept this future daughter-in-law and urged us to get married. Society was turning more conservative by then, and since we were no longer so young, we returned to Beijing to apply for a marriage license. At our wedding, a few old classmates joked that they always knew we would end up together.

After a year, Shen Qian gave birth to our son, Xiaobao. The wounds of the past were gradually healing. Though I couldn't say we were happy or that everything was perfect, our life wasn't without warmth or simple pleasures.

The leadership in Beijing was now deepening the economic reforms and gradually pushing planned economy to displace the market. One of the policies was a dual-price system, which involved one price for goods set by the economic planning authorities and another price set by the market. Many officials with the right connections could become "official profiteers" by buying goods at the low planned economy price and selling them on the market at an enormous profit. Low-level peddlers like Heizi and me, on the other hand, suffered due to our lack of connections. Business became harder and harder. One time, we managed to acquire a bunch of color televisions, but the official profiteers were a step ahead of us and cornered the market. We had no choice but to sell at a loss. We ended up owing a bunch of money and had to close up shop and head back to Beijing.

One of Heizi's uncles was a shift foreman at a factory, and he managed to get Heizi a job as a driver there. By carrying private goods for people on official trips, Heizi made good money. I couldn't find any such opportunity, and I was exhausted after years spent struggling in business. I decided to return to university, and began to prepare to take the examination for graduate school.

As a graduate of Peking University, I thought the exam would be a piece of cake. But after being away from a classroom for so many years, it wasn't easy to get back into the right mind-set. I took the exam two years in a row and couldn't pass. Since Xiaobao was getting older and our savings were nearing depletion, we relied on help from my parents. Shen Qian finally managed to get a job at a newspaper, which at least guaranteed us a base salary and benefits like housing and healthcare.

Then she began to complain about my lack of accomplishments.

"Look at you! When we got together, I thought you had some business savvy and might make it big. But in the end, you're just a bookworm who can't even manage to get into grad school. The Chinese Women's Volleyball Team has won the world championship three times, which is as many as you've failed!"

Faced with this nagging tirade, I felt lost. What had happened to that passionate, idealistic, revolutionary leader I once knew?

Of course I knew that wasn't Shen Qian's fault. This was what happened after life subjected us to its endless grind. The world wasn't a fairy tale or the setting for an adventure—even if it were, we would not be the protagonists. No matter what ideals and hopes we once harbored, the most we could hope to accomplish, in the end, was to survive.

Since I was feeling low during that time, I sought refuge in fiction and got into *wuxia* fantasies. The remake of *Legend of the Condor Heroes*, produced in Hong Kong, was very popular on TV. I had seen an older version when I was little but thought the remake was better, even though the budget clearly wasn't as big. I borrowed *wuxia* books by Jin Yong, Gu Long, Liang Yusheng—I would have read Huang Yi's books, too, but I couldn't find them anywhere.[7] Xiaobao was now old enough that he spent every day practicing "Eighteen Stages to Subdue a Dragon" along with the heroes on TV. Shen Qian got mad and told me that I was rotting our child's mind. I had to switch to reading something else.

Science fiction was also popular. Ye Yonglie's *Little Know-It-All Roams the Future* sold millions of copies, and Zheng Wenguang's *Toward Sagittarius* was flying off the shelves. I gradually became a fan—only science fiction could liberate me from the weight of daily life and allow me to enjoy a little pleasure. It was too bad that there were so few Chinese science fiction books, and not many foreign works were being translated. I soon finished all the ones I could find.

Inspired by my reading, I tried my hand at writing and ended up with a book called *Little Know-It-All Roams the Universe*, which was a sequel to Ye Yonglie's famous work. At first, I passed the draft among friends, but then I got to know a young man named Yao Haijun who helped me obtain Mr. Ye's permission and found me a publisher. The story gained me a bit of fame, and I was called a "rising star of science fiction." Encouraged, I wrote another book called *Little Know-It-All Roams the Body*, which was meant to teach readers some interesting facts about the human body. Unfortunately, this book caused a lot of controversy: some argued that I was stealing too much from Ye Yonglie; some suggested I was tarnishing Chinese science fiction with portrayals that encouraged lascivious thoughts; still others claimed that my work was an example of capitalist liberalism and contained metaphors criticizing the Communist Party. . . . [8]

---

7 In our timeline, Jin Yong, Gu Long, and Liang Yusheng are three of the acknowledged masters of *wuxia* fantasy, and most of their best works were written before 1980. Huang Yi's works rose to prominence later, in the 1990s.

8 This is a bit of an inside joke for Chinese SF fans. In our timeline, Yao Haijun is the executive editor for *Science Fiction World*, China's (and the world's) biggest sci-fi magazine by circulation. Baoshu, the author of this story, began his career as a fanfic author in the universe of Liu Cixin's "Three-Body" series.

I was writing at a fairly turbulent time when ideological debates were on the rise. There were even sporadic student movements again. The central leadership probably wanted to create the opportunity for another purge, so they initiated an effort to cleanse society of "spiritual pollution." I became a target and was severely criticized. Luckily, the government wasn't interested in having the "pollution-cleaning" spin out of control, and I wasn't punished much. However, it was impossible for me to be published anymore. I had to go back to the textbooks and prepare for the graduate school examination again.

It was only later that I understood how fortunate I had been. The country was also undergoing a movement of "intensive crackdown." This involved every aspect of life: purse-snatchers were handed death sentences, while public dancing carried a charge of indecency. Liu Xiaobo found himself in trouble because he had several lovers and was executed by firing squad. When she heard the news, Shen Qian was depressed for a long time.

After the intensive crackdown, society grew even more conservative. Many things that used to be common became crimes: cohabitating without being married, kissing in public, wearing revealing clothes, and so forth. Given the shift in mainstream culture, I dared not write about sensitive areas again. Thus did my career as an author come to an end.

9.

Just as weal can lead to woe, misfortune can also lead to lucky breaks. A prominent professor turned out to be a fan of my novels and specifically requested me during the admission process. As a result, I became his graduate student and returned to school the next year.

At my mentor and advisor's suggestion, I chose Sartre's existentialism as my topic. Although many people had been studying it, most explanations were half-baked. After so many years wasted drifting in society, I treasured the opportunity to study in depth. I read many foreign books in the original languages—taught myself French—and published a few papers that were well received. Eventually, with my advisor's recommendation, I was given the precious opportunity to study overseas at a famous university in America at the government's expense.

This was the first and last time in my life I lived outside China. Visiting this country on the other side of the Pacific that people both loved and hated was quite an experience. The university was in New York, the greatest city on Earth. When I was little, I saw a ton of TV shows and movies set in New York: *Beijinger in New York*, *Godzilla* . . . and I had long wanted to visit. The sights and sounds of the city—skyscrapers, overpasses, highways, subways—were overwhelming.

I remembered the Beijing of my childhood as a prosperous city comparable to New York, but for some reason, after a few decades, New York remained a modern metropolis while Beijing had declined precipitously. I saw in America many goods that had long ceased to be findable in China: Coca-Cola, KFC, Nescafé . . . These were the brands I grew up with, and I indulged in a bit of nostalgia. I finally understood why so many people preferred to leave China for the US and not return.

However, I could also see signs that America was on the decline. At the time of my visit, a new blockbuster had just been released: Star Wars Episode IV: A New Hope. I remembered seeing Episodes I through III when I was little and had always wanted to find out what would happen next. To reexperience the wonder of my childhood memories, I bought an expensive ticket. But Episode IV turned out to be far less spectacular than the previous three, and the special effects were so bad that you could almost see the strings on the spaceships. I was really disappointed. Apparently the Cold War had drained America's resources into the arms race, and the economy wasn't doing so well.

Unlike in the past, opportunities for exchanges between America and China were growing scarce. It was almost impossible to visit

America on your own, and even government-sponsored trips were rare. There were only a handful of Chinese from the mainland in the entire university. To celebrate my arrival, they held a party for me, and as we enjoyed our french fries, they asked me how things were in China. Since it took almost a full month for international mail to reach the recipient and phone calls were extremely inconvenient, they got most of their information about China from English-language news reports, which tended to be so narrow in scope that it was like trying to understand a beach by observing a few pebbles. We reminisced about how when we were little we could chat with friends on the other side of the globe just by opening a window over the web, and it felt like another age, another world.

While we were discussing rumors about the transition of power from Deng Xiaoping to Hua Guofeng, a dark horse about whom little was known, the doorbell rang. A woman stood up and said, *Oh, it must be so-and-so*—but I didn't catch the name. She went and opened the door and a woman came in, limping with the aid of a cane. I gave her a curious glance, and when I saw her face, I froze.

She looked at me, unable to speak.

It was a dream. A dream.

Qiqi, my Qiqi.

In a moment, everything around me—no, the entire universe—disappeared. Only Qiqi and I remained between heaven and earth. We gazed at each other, our eyes saying what our lips could not. Fate had played a cruel game with us. After the trials and tribulations of more than ten years, we had found each other again on the other side of the Pacific.

Trembling, we came together and held on to each other for dear life. Tears poured from our eyes as sobs racked our bodies. The others realized that something extraordinary was happening and left so that we could be alone together.

Qiqi told me that when she was shot that night, she lost consciousness. When she woke up, she saw a car passing by and screamed for help. A few foreigners from the car came to her aid, but she passed out again . . . The car turned out to belong to an American news crew who had planned to film a live report, but the danger of the situation had forced them to retreat, which was when they saw Qiqi. They brought her back to the American embassy, where the embassy doctors dressed her wounds.

Later, Qiqi met Chai Ling and the others hiding in the embassy. They told her that I had died. Chai Ling and the rest were wanted by the authorities, and while Qiqi was still recovering, their request for political asylum was approved. Under the protection of the embassy, Qiqi left Beijing, a city of sorrow, and came with the others to New York.

At first, Qiqi didn't know what conditions were like in China, and she dared not make contact with anyone in the country lest they suffer as a result. After a few years, Qiqi managed to return to Shanghai once to visit her mother, who told her that I had gotten married in Guangzhou. Not wanting to disturb my life, she told her mother not to let me know that she was still alive.

The bullets had left her with a permanent handicap and deprived her of the ability to become a mother. Helpless in this country, she married an old man who abused her. After her divorce, she managed to apply for and win a scholarship and came to study in this university.

We spent the whole night recounting to each other our experiences during the intervening years, and we held each other and cried. What should have been the most wonderful decade of our lives had been lost to the vicissitudes of fate. I said "I'm so sorry" countless times, but what was the use? I vowed to devote the rest of my life to making it up to her, to giving her the happiness that should have been hers.

Naturally, ignoring the gossip, we moved in together. We barely spent any time apart, trying to make up for our lost youth. Qiqi had her green card. As long as I stayed with her, I should be able to remain in the United States. Since conditions in China had deteriorated further and China was now engaged in a war with Vietnam, Qiqi told me not to go back. But I couldn't just forget about Shen

Qian and my son. Ever since I started grad school, Shen Qian had been living like a single mother, struggling to keep the whole family afloat, pinning her hopes on my success. To simply abandon her felt to me an unforgivable betrayal.

Although Qiqi and I had recovered some measure of our happiness, my heart was conflicted. But I was a coward. All I cared about was the joy of the present, and I dared not think about the choice I had to make.

10.

I stayed for more than a year in New York. After our lives had settled down somewhat, I threw myself into my work. I read many books of literary theory, politics, and philosophy, and felt my understanding grow by leaps and bounds. Often, I pushed Qiqi's wheelchair and took walks with her in Battery Park, where we both gazed at the distant figure of the Statue of Liberty and debated the fate of China and the future of the world.

My American advisor thought highly of my paper. He told me there was a teaching position open to those with a literary background that might be a good fit for me. If I got the job, I could stay and finish my Ph.D. Excited, I handed in my application right away. But then I received the letter from Shen Qian.

There isn't a wall in the world that doesn't have a crack. Even divided by the Pacific, rumors about Qiqi and me had managed to make their way back to China. Shen Qian was polite but firm in her letter, demanding an explanation. I finally decided to make a short trip back to China to clarify the situation with her.

Qiqi originally wanted to accompany me, but I asked her to stay put for now. Having her show up at the door with me might be too much for Shen Qian, and I wanted to talk to her alone. We said goodbye at the airport, and Qiqi, in a bright green jacket, leaned against the railing with her cane and watched me go through border control. I turned back to look at her.

Even decades later, the sight of her watching me—like the woman from that old legend who turned to stone waiting for her husband by the sea—would remain with me like a brand burned into my heart.

Back in China, Shen Qian was happy to see me. She made no mention of the question she'd asked me in her letter. Wearing her apron, she busied herself about the kitchen preparing my favorite dishes, many of which were not available in the US: sautéed shredded pork with soybean paste, pork with bamboo shoots, steamed chicken with mushrooms . . . At dinner, she didn't ask me about my life in the US and only talked about the domestic news: ration tickets were now required for most goods; farmers were no longer allotted individual plots of land, but had to work collectively in communes; her newspaper was in the middle of a debate about the proper authority for Marxist philosophy . . . Xiaobao was playing at my feet, absolutely delighted with the toy robot I had brought him. Faced with my innocent son and tender wife, I just couldn't bring myself to say the word "divorce."

That night, as we lay in bed, Shen Qian held me and passionately kissed me. I could feel her body trembling. Steeling myself, I gently pushed her away. "Qian, I need to tell you something."

"What's the rush?" Her arms went around my neck again as she murmured, "The night is still young. Why don't we first—"

"I want a divorce," I blurted out before I lost my nerve.

Her body stiffened. "Stop it. That's not funny."

"I'm not kidding. Qiqi is in America, and we . . ." I couldn't continue, but Shen Qian understood.

"You've decided?" She sat up.

"Yes."

"I understand." As she continued, her eyes flared with anger and her voice gradually grew harsh. "I know you were living with Zhao Qi. I know you used to be a couple. I knew that ten years ago! But what about me? What about all the years I've put into this marriage? Without me slaving away to take care of you and your son, do you think you could have gotten the chance to leave China? To see your old lover? Now that you've finally made it, do you think you can discard me like a pair of old shoes?"

"No! Listen . . . I will make it up to you . . . I will pay . . ." I had planned a whole pretty speech but couldn't remember any of the words. What I did say sounded so cold, so heartless. I was disgusted by my own hypocrisy and clumsiness.

Shen Qian laughed mirthlessly. She slid off the bed and, without even putting on her shoes, headed out.

"Where are you going? It's the middle of the night." Afraid that she might leave the apartment, I got up as well.

She went onto the balcony and locked the door behind her. She stood facing me with her hands behind her. Her white nightgown trembled with her breath, and she looked like a ghost in the night. I was terrified that she was going to jump.

"Don't, please!" I begged. "Let's talk about this."

"What are you afraid of?" Shen Qian said mockingly. "If I died, wouldn't that be perfect for you and Zhao Qi? Don't worry; I'm not going to grant your wish."

She raised her arms and tossed something over the edge of the balcony. I saw pieces of paper drifting in the wind, falling like snow-flakes.

My passport, and other documents.

Behind me, Xiaobao, who had been awakened by our argument, started to cry.

Shen Qian left with Xiaobao and went to her parents' home. The next day, her parents and uncle came to our place to scream at me, and I had no choice but to hide in my room. It was impossible to keep something like this secret, and soon all my neighbors and colleagues at the university had heard the news. The rumors mutated as they spread: some were saying that I had found a wealthy, powerful woman overseas, and I was going to abandon my wife and child like one of those villains in the old folk operas. The denunciations were so oppressive that I couldn't even leave home without feeling fingers pointed at me behind my back. Even my mentor, for whom I held deep respect and affection, gave me a tongue-lashing, and I could say nothing in my defense. My father fell ill because of what was happening.

This was how life made you helpless. If you tried to swim against its currents, you'd feel resistance at every step. I regretted coming back—it would have been easier if I'd had the strength to stay overseas. But now it was impossible to leave. To replace my passport would require a great deal of paperwork, and now that my reputation was ruined, I couldn't even get a recommendation letter from my department. I was stuck: I lacked the strength to continue the struggle, yet I was unwilling to give up.

It took half a year before the situation changed. In the end, as much as Shen Qian hated me, she wasn't going to shackle us together for the rest of our lives. She agreed to a divorce but demanded full custody of our son. I agreed, and also promised her monetary compensation. Finally, after everything was resolved, I placed a long-distance call to Qiqi, and she was overjoyed by the news. Since I still couldn't leave the country for the time being, she said she would come back the next month so that we could get married in China and then leave together.

I waited and waited for her flight, but it never arrived.

The next month, the era of Mao Zedong began.

11.

For years, the government had been following a policy of "buy rather than build." This created the false appearance of prosperity in the economy but hollowed out China's industrial infrastructure. The gap between the wealthy and the poor grew, and anger at the government grew along with it. Everywhere, a specter-like name haunted China, a name that grew gradually in prominence. People said, *This man will bring China fresh hope.*

He was called Mao Zedong. A few years earlier, he had held the post of Secretary of the Sichuan Provincial Committee in the provincial capital of Chongqing, and his various policies—known by the slogan "Sing Red Songs, Strike Black Forces" and involving public displays of Communist zeal and intensive government intervention—had made Chongqing into a prosperous city. Many ordinary citizens, especially poor peasants in the rural areas, supported him. The paramount leader of China, Hua Guofeng, was deeply influenced by Mao Zedong, and once Hua had gotten into power, he initiated the Great Proletariat Cultural Revolution, which sought to mobilize the people to bring down the capitalist roaders within the Communist Party. The mass movements swept the entire country, and political power within China was redistributed overnight. Deng Xiaoping, Ye Jianying, Hu Yaobang, and others in their faction all fell from prominence, and with the entire country behind him, Mao Zedong was elected Chairman of the Communist Party.

After he became the Chairman, Mao continued the Cultural Revolution, focusing on criticizing Deng and opposing rightist tendencies, especially Deng's "foreigners' slave" political philosophy. He abolished Deng's policy of keeping China open to outside influences and essentially cut China off from the rest of the world. Soon after, the United States terminated all diplomatic relations with China. I could no longer go to America, and Qiqi could not come to China.

And so, once again, history divided us.

During the early stages of the Cultural Revolution, the personality cult of Mao was extreme, but the movement itself wasn't too violent. With my mentor's recommendation, I became an instructor at the university after grad school. Although colleges were no longer admitting students and the social status of intellectuals had declined, it was at least possible to make a living by writing theory papers on Marxism–Leninism, criticizing traditional Confucian philosophy, and reinterpreting Chinese history through a Communist lens as directed by the central leadership. The Cultural Revolution also interrupted the divorce proceedings, and so Shen Qian and I ended up living together again, doing our best to get along.

Year after year, we went to work, we came home, and we studied the required political readings. The Revolution was going well, as was proclaimed in public at every opportunity, but life itself had become as still as a pool of dead water. During those years, even bright-colored clothing was forbidden. No forms of culture or entertainment were permitted—since they were all corrupted by feudal, American-capitalist, or Soviet-revisionist influences—except for the eight model revolutionary operas. One time, I found a dirty, ragged copy of *Harry Potter and the Philosopher's Stone* abandoned in a public bathroom and tears filled my eyes. I took it home and read it in secret several times. But, in the end, terrified of being accused of harboring contraband, I burned it.

Sometimes, as I studied the latest directives from the paramount leader, I would think, *What happened to all the eras I have lived through? When I was a young man, the streets were packed with bellbottoms and "profiteers"; when I was a teenager, TV dramas from Hong Kong and Taiwan filled the airwaves; when I was a child, it was possible to play games on the web, to go and see the latest movies from Hollywood, and there were the Olympics and 3D films . . . Did those times really exist? Where did they come from, and where have they gone? Or was all this just a dream?*

Maybe everything was simply a game played by time. What was time? What was there besides nothingness? Before us had been nothingness, and after us will be nothingness.

Sometimes, in the middle of the night, I thought of the woman I loved on the other shore of the Pacific and pain racked my body. Those days when I was half-mad with love, when I was a stranger in a strange land—they felt so real and yet so much like a fantasy. What would have happened if I had listened to Qiqi and stayed in America? Would I be happier than now? Or would I simply be mired in an even deeper illusion?

At least I would then be with the person I loved.

In reality, America was no paradise, either. *The People's Daily* explained that because the United States was addicted to militarism, it had sunk into the quagmire of the Vietnam War. Racial conflicts within America were intensifying and the crisis in the Middle East was causing an oil shortage. The capitalists were likely not going to last much longer, and American radical leftist movements were gaining momentum.

The Soviet camp, meanwhile, was growing stronger every day. The Cold War grew heated, and on almost every continent proxy wars were fought between the two superpowers. Ballistic nuclear submarines patrolled the sea depths, and every warhead they carried was capable of destroying an entire city. Even more missiles rested in their silos, awaiting the order that would launch them soaring though the air to rain destruction upon us. Death itself roamed overhead, poised to send all of humanity into hell. Regardless of whether you were Chinese or American, you were headed for the same place.

Sometimes, I recalled the rumors about the end of the world from my childhood. Maybe the prophecy had been true—except that perhaps the apocalypse didn't arrive in a single instant, but took decades or even centuries to descend. Or perhaps the world had already been destroyed by the time I was born, and all that I had experienced was nothing but a shadow of a fantasy that was slowly dissipating. Who knew what the truth was?

In the fourth year of the Cultural Revolution, I received a letter from the US. The very sight of the American stamps on it frightened me—corresponding with foreigners was an activity subject to intense scrutiny. However, the letter's contents seemed harmless enough, consisting of a few words of greeting cobbled together with some revolutionary language in an unnatural manner.

Comrade Xie Baosheng:

First, let us express together our fondest wish that the brightest, reddest sun in our hearts, Chairman Mao, live ten thousand years! As the Chairman wrote in his poem, "The seas roil with rage, and the continents shake in fury!" In America, under the leadership of Mao Zedong Thought, the civil rights movement and leftist revolutionaries have made the capitalists of Wall Street tremble before the awakened power of the people! Chairman Mao was absolutely correct when he wrote that the revolutionary conditions are not just good, but great!

All right, then, how are you doing? . . .

Of course the letter came from Qiqi. It had been delivered to my department, where the head of the workers' propaganda team[9] intercepted it. This man read the letter suspiciously and then looked up at me, glaring.

He slammed his hand down on the desk. "Xie Baosheng, the people's eyes can see everything! Now, confess the number of foreign contacts you have! What kind of secrets exist between you and the woman who wrote this letter?"

I laughed. "That's enough of that. You know everything there is to know about Qiqi and me. Now hand me the letter."

By an incredible stroke of luck, I was talking to my old friend Heizi. Formerly just an ordinary factory worker, the Cultural Revolution had turned him into a member of the workers' propaganda team that, pursuant to directives issued by the Chairman, came to supervise my university. In this manner, a man who had never even gone to college became the most important person in one of China's most prestigious universities. Without him, the letter would have gotten me into deep trouble.

Heizi handed the letter to me and told me to burn it after reading. I read Qiqi's words over and over until I figured out what she was trying to say between the lines. First, she explained that she had obtained her degree and was now teaching Chinese literature at an American college. Second, she was still unmarried and wanted to come visit me in China. I sighed and wiped my eyes. It had been five

9 In our timeline, "workers' Mao Zedong Thought propaganda teams" were a unique creation of the Cultural Revolution. They consisted of teams of ordinary workers installed at colleges and high schools to take over the administrative functions and to put a stop to the bloody Red Guard factional wars. For the most part, they stabilized the chaos introduced by the early stages of the Cultural Revolution.

years since my parting from Qiqi, and she still wanted me. But what could I do? Even if she returned, the most we could hope for was to be like the hero and heroine in *The Second Handshake*, an underground novel we passed around in handwritten copies, who could only gaze at each other, knowing that they could never be together.

In the end, it didn't matter what I thought. I had no way of sending a letter to Qiqi.

I hid her letter in a stack of documents I took home. I didn't want Shen Qian to find it, but I also couldn't bear to burn it. Finally, I decided to conceal it between the pages of the copy of *Season of Bloom, Season of Rain* that had once belonged to Qiqi. Although the book itself was also an example of feudal, capitalist, and revisionist thinking, I just couldn't imagine getting rid of it. I wrapped the book in a bundle of old clothes and kept it at the bottom of the trunk.

12.

Rationally, I knew that Qiqi shouldn't come back, but a corner of my selfish heart continued to harbor the hope that she would. Around that time, President Nixon visited China, hoping to form an alliance with China against the Soviet Union. As the Sino–American relationship improved, hope reignited within me. However, somehow Nixon and Mao couldn't come to an agreement, and the Americans were so angry that they took revenge by manipulating the UN Security Council to expel the People's Republic of China and hand its seat at the UN to Taiwan as the "legitimate" representative for all of China. What little connection had existed between the US and China was completely cut off.

Qiqi didn't return, and I received no more news about her.

In the sixth year of the Cultural Revolution, my father passed away. A few days before his death, China launched the satellite *The East Is Red*. It had been many years since China had sent an artificial satellite into orbit, and the occasion was marked with a great celebration. As my father lay dying, he held my hand and muttered,

"When I was young, China had so many satellites in space I lost count. We even had manned spaceships and a space station. But this single little satellite is now seen as some remarkable achievement. What has happened to the world?"

I had no response. That world of my childhood, a world that had once existed, now felt even more impossible than science fiction. My father closed his eyes and let out his last breath.

To be fair, there were some advances in technology. The next year, the Americans managed to land on the moon with the Apollo mission—an unprecedented achievement—and the Stars and Stripes flew on lunar soil, shocking the world. This was not good news for China. Chairman Mao had come up with the proposal that China should lead the revolution of the Third World against the developed nations and the Soviet Union. As a result, bilateral relations between China and the US and China and the Soviet Union were tense. China was also in a border conflict with the Soviet Union over Zhenbao Island and was completely isolated internationally. I only heard about the American moon landing by secretly listening to banned American radio broadcasts.

Two years later, my son was old enough to be called a young man. His generation was different from mine. They had no memory of the relative openness of Deng's reformist years and grew up under a barrage of propaganda centered on Mao Zedong Thought. They had little exposure to Western culture, and no knowledge of China's traditional culture, either. They worshiped Chairman Mao with true zeal and believed it was their duty to die to protect his revolutionary path. They passionately declared that they would fight until they broke through the walls of the Kremlin, until they leveled the White House, until they liberated all of humankind.

My son disliked the name Xiaobao, which meant "Precious," because it wasn't revolutionary enough. He renamed himself Weidong, which meant "Defend the East." He became a Red Guard, and before he had even graduated from high school, he wanted to quit school and go on revolutionary tours around the country with his friends, sharing the experience of rebelling against authority with other Red Guards. Shen Qian and I did not like the idea at all, but this was something promoted by the leadership in Beijing. As soon as we started to object, our son brought out the Little Red Book and denounced us as though we were class enemies. We had no choice but to let him go.

None of us knew that a more violent storm lay in waiting.

The Red Guard movement grew, and young men and women turned on their teachers as "reactionary academic authorities." At every school, Red Guards held mass rallies called "struggle sessions" to torture and denounce these enemies of the revolution. My mentor, a famous professor who had studied overseas, naturally became a target, and I was brought along to the struggle sessions as a secondary target. Half of the hair on our heads were shaved off; tall, conical hats were stuck on top; and then our arms were pulled back and held up to force us to bow down to the revolutionary masses who hurled abuse at us. My mentor was beaten and tortured until he collapsed and lost consciousness. Only then did the mass rally end.

I held my old teacher and called his name, but he didn't wake up. Heizi helped me bring him to the hospital, but it was too late. He died a few days later.

The Red Guards were not satisfied with having murdered my mentor. They imprisoned me and demanded that I confess to all my past sins—what they really had in mind was my participation in the Tiananmen protests twenty years ago. I debated them by putting my academic skills to good use: "I was protesting against the dark path Deng Xiaoping wanted for China. We spoke loudly, wrote openly, and demanded true revolutionary democracy. This was absolutely in line with Mao Zedong Thought. We were supported by the masses of Beijing, the ordinary workers and laborers who also participated in the movement. How could you call such protests counterrevolutionary?"

The Red Guards lacked sufficient experience in this style of argument to win against me. They couldn't get me for having foreign contacts, either, because I had burned or buried anything having to do with America, and there was now no proof of my relationship with Qiqi. But ultimately, I was probably saved because of my friendship with Heizi.

After I was finally released and allowed to go home, I found out that Shen Qian had been taken away by the revolutionary rebels who had taken over her newspaper.

Someone at the newspaper, it turned out, had revealed Shen Qian's long-ago affair with Liu Xiaobo in a big character poster. Liu Xiaobo was without a doubt one of the worst counterrevolutionary rightists—he had once claimed that China could only be saved by three centuries of Western colonization; had drafted the capitalist legalistic screed "Charter '08"; and had been utterly corrupt in his sexual relationships. Although he was dead, his influence continued to linger. Since Shen Qian had been his lover for several years, she must have known many of his secrets. The revolutionary rebels salivated at the prospect of interrogating one of Liu's mistresses. They held her in a "cowshed"—a prison set up at the newspaper—and demanded that she write her confession.

Shen Qian was locked away for a whole week and I was not allowed to see her. By the time she returned, her hair had all been shaven off and her face and arms were littered with scars. She stared at me dully, as though she no longer recognized me. Finally, she recovered and sobbed uncontrollably as I held her.

She never told me what she suffered during her interrogation and I never asked. However, not long after, many people who had once known Liu Xiaobo were imprisoned and interrogated, and the rumor was that Shen Qian's confession had been used as the foundation for accusations against them. I knew it was wrong to blame Shen Qian. In this age, survival was the only goal, and conscience was a luxury few could afford.

In this manner, both Shen Qian and I were stamped with the label of counterrevolutionaries. By the time our son returned from his revolutionary tour, he found his parents to be bona fide, irredeemable class enemies. This meant that he was also considered impure. To remedy the situation, he went to the school and hung big character posters denouncing Shen Qian and me, and revealed some so-called sins that he knew we had committed. While others watched, he slapped me in the face and declared that he was no longer my son. He turned around and walked away, proud of his steadfast revolutionary ardor. I almost fainted from rage.

After our son left, we were angry for a few days, but then began to worry. We asked around for news about him but heard nothing for a couple of months. Then Heizi's son, Xiaohei, came to visit.

"Um, Uncle Xie . . . I have to tell you something. Please sit down."

Xiaohei and my son were good friends. I realized something was wrong. I took a deep breath and said, "Go ahead."

"Weidong . . . he . . ."

My heart sank and the world seemed to wobble around me. But I insisted that he continue.

My son and Xiaohei had joined a faction of Red Guards called the "April 14th Brigade." He had been promoted to squad leader, but because of my status and his mother's, he was demoted and almost expelled. To show that he had completely cast us away and was a dedicated revolutionary, my son decided to take on the most dangerous tasks and always led every charge. A few days ago, his faction fought a battle against another faction at the university; my son rushed ahead with an iron bar, but the other side had obtained rifles from the army, and with a bang, my son's chest exploded and he collapsed to the ground . . .

The world blacked out around me before Xiaohei could finish.

13.

The death of our son destroyed the only hope left for Shen Qian and me. Our hair turned white almost overnight. My mother died from the shock and grief. Although Shen Qian and I weren't even fifty, we looked much older. We sat in our home with nothing to say to each other.

I didn't know how we survived those dark years. I didn't really want to recall the time. Like two fish tossed ashore, Shen Qian and

I lay gasping, trying to keep each other's gills wet with the foam from our mouths. But eventual suffocation was our certain fate.

One year later, the Cultural Revolution ended.

Mao decided to retire behind the scenes and Liu Shaoqi became the President of China. Working with Premier Zhou Enlai, Liu tried to lead an economic recovery by instituting limited free markets and allocating land to individual families instead of collective farming by communes. Slowly, the country recovered, and colleges opened their doors again to new students. Intellectuals were treated better, and after a few years, Shen Qian and I were rehabilitated and no longer labeled rightists.

The ten years of the Cultural Revolution had decimated academia, and my department lacked qualified faculty. I had the respect of my colleagues and years of experience, but since I wasn't a member of the Communist Party (due to my political history), I was passed over for promotions. Summoning my courage, I wrote a letter to the authorities demanding the country make better use of the few intellectuals it had left, but I heard nothing.

A year later, when I had already given up all hope, my fortunes took an abrupt turn: I was promoted to full professor and given membership in the Communist Party. Even more amazingly, I was elected the department chair by a landslide.

In my new position of power, I began to get to know some elite intellectuals. One time, I met Guo Moruo, President of the Chinese Academy of Sciences. He told me in confidence that Premier Zhou Enlai had read my letter and given the directive to promote me despite my flawed background. Guo told me to work hard and not disappoint the Premier. Sometime later, the Premier visited our school and asked specifically to meet me. Anxiously, I expressed my gratitude to him, and the Premier laughed. "Comrade Baosheng, I know you're a talented man. The country is trying to get back on her feet and we have to focus on science and technology. Didn't you once write science fiction? Why not write more and get our young people interested in science again?"

Since the Premier and Guo Moruo had both given the green light, the novels I had written were reissued in new editions. Readers had not had access to such books in a long time, and the response was overwhelming. Magazines began to approach me and commission new stories, and eventually I published a few collections. Fans began to call me a "famous writer."

I knew very well that these new stories were nowhere near as good as my old ones. I no longer dared to write about politically sensitive subjects, and these new offerings were affected works that praised the regime without articulating anything new. But who said the world was fair? I knew I was unlikely to accomplish anything great during what remained of my career. I decided I would use the little bit of influence I had to try to help talented young people, and to that end, I began to actively participate in social functions.

The good times didn't last. Soon, the country hit another rough patch. China conducted another nuclear test, and once again, both the Soviet Union and the United States imposed sanctions. Food shortages became rampant, and everyone's rations were reduced. The streets were full of hungry people, and it was said that even Chairman Mao had stopped eating meat.

But even so, those of us in the big cities were lucky. Heizi told me that people were starving to death in the countryside. But since no news of this kind could be published, no one knew the truth. We didn't dare to speculate or say much, either. Although the Cultural Revolution was over, the political climate was still very severe. Rumor had it that when Marshal Peng Dehuai dared to offer some opinions critical of official policy at the Lushan Conference, he was severely punished.

The next year, Shen Qian died. No, not from starvation. She had liver cancer. As the wife of a high-status intellectual, she could have received treatment that would have prolonged her life, but she refused it.

"We stuck with each other . . . all these years. . . . Life has been so exhausting, hasn't it? We are like those two fish . . . in that Daoist parable. . . . Rather than struggling to keep each other alive on land, wouldn't it have been better . . . if we had never known each other at all, but lived free in the rivers and lakes? Don't be sad. . . . I'm not sad to go. . . ."

I held her hand, and tears made it impossible to speak. I remembered something from our youth: back then, everyone in middle school said we were a pair because we had classroom cleanup duty, but I didn't like her, and she didn't like me. When we worked together, it was very awkward because we refused to talk to each other. One time, I was standing on a chair to wash the windows and started to fall. She rushed over to help and I ended up falling on her. As we both limped to see the school nurse, the absurdity of the situation struck us, and we laughed as we blamed each other. . . . That faded memory now felt like a preview of our time together.

"I really want to . . . hear that old song again." Shen Qian's voice was fading. "I haven't heard it in such a long time. Can you . . . sing for me?"

I knew the song she was talking about: "Rain, Hail, or Shine," by the Taiwanese singer Wakin Chau. We used to sing it all the time when we were in high school. I had forgotten most of the lyrics, and the best I could do was to recall a few fragments about love, about the pain and pleasure that dreams brought us, about regrets. I sang, my voice trembling, tears flowing down my face, and my cracked voice not sounding musical at all.

But Shen Qian moved her lips along with mine. She could no longer make any noise, but she was lost in the silent music of yesteryear. The rays of the setting sun shone through the window and fell upon her, covering her gaunt face with a golden glow.

We sang together like that for a long, long time.

14.

The years of starvation finally came to an end. The Soviet Union and China repaired their broken bond and trade began to grow. The Soviet Union provided us with a great deal of assistance, and the domestic economy slowly recovered. But I was now almost sixty and felt much older. I resigned from the position of department chair, thinking I'd use what little time was left to write a few books. But I was nominated assistant dean of the university and became a standing committee member for the China Writers Association. In addition, I was picked as a delegate to the National People's Congress. I was too busy to write.

One day, I received a call from Mao Dun, the Minister of Culture.

"The Premier has asked you to attend a diplomatic function. There's a group of avant-garde Western writers visiting, and he thinks you know one of them."

"Who?"

"I don't know the details. I'll send a car for you."

That evening, a car took me to the Beijing Hotel, which had one of the country's best Western-style restaurants. Many important people were in attendance, including the Premier himself, who gave a welcome address. As I surveyed the foreign visitors, I recognized the writer I was supposed to know right away. I couldn't believe my eyes.

After a series of boring speeches and a formal dinner, finally the time came to mingle and converse. I walked up to that man and said, in my terrible French, *"Bonsoir, Monsieur Sartre."*

He gazed at me curiously through his thick glasses and gave me a friendly smile.

I switched to English and introduced myself. Then I told him how much I admired *L'Être et le néant* and how I had written papers on it. I had never expected to see him in China.

"Well." Sartre quirked an eyebrow at me. "I never expected anyone in China to be interested in my work."

I lowered my voice. "Before the Cultural Revolution, your work was very popular in China. Many people were utterly entranced by your words, though they—myself included—could not claim to truly understand your philosophy. However, I've always tried to understand the world through it."

"I'm honored to hear that. But you shouldn't think so highly of my words. Your own thoughts about the world are the most precious thing—really, thinking itself is the only thing that is important. I must admit I'm surprised. I would have expected you to be a socialist."

I smiled bitterly. "Socialism is our life, but this form of life has turned me and many others into existentialists. Perhaps in that way the two are connected."

"What is your thought on existentialism?"

"To quote you, '*L'existence précède l'essence.*' The world appears out of an essenceless abyss. Other than time, it depends on nothing, and it has no meaning. All meaning comes after the world itself, and it is fundamentally absurd. I agree with this. The existence of the world is . . . absurd."

I paused, and then, gaining courage, continued with the puzzle that had plagued me for years. "Look at our world! Where does it come from? Where is it headed? When I was born, the Internet had connected all parts of the globe, and high-speed railways crisscrossed the country. The store shelves were full of anything one might desire, and there were countless novels, films, TV shows. . . . Everyone dreamed of a more wonderful future. But now? The web and mobile phones have long disappeared, and so has television. We appear to live in a world that is moving backward. Is this not absurd? Perhaps it is because our existence has no essence at all."

"Sir," said a smiling Sartre, "I think I understand what is troubling you. But I don't understand why you think this state is absurd."

"If the existence of the world has meaning, the world must advance, don't you think? Otherwise what is the point of generation struggling after generation? The world appears to be a twisted shadow of some reality."

Sartre shook his head. "I know that the Chinese once had a philosopher named Zhuangzi. He told this story: If you give a monkey three nuts in the morning and four nuts in the evening, the monkey will be unhappy. But if you give the monkey four nuts in

the morning and only three in the evening, the monkey will be ec-
static. In your view, is the monkey foolish?"

"Uh . . . yes. Zhuangzi's monkey is a byword for foolishness
among the Chinese."

A mocking glint came into Sartre's eyes. "But how are we different from the monkey in that story? Are we in pursuit of some
'correct' order of history? If you switch happiness and misfortune around in time, will everything appear 'normal' to you? If evil
exists in history, does it disappear merely by switching the order of
events around?"

I felt like I was on the verge of understanding something, but I
couldn't articulate it.

Sartre continued, "*Progress* is not a constant. It is merely a tem-
porary phase of this universe. I'm no scientist, but the physicists
tell us that the universe expands and then collapses and then expands again, not unlike the cosmic cycles envisioned by your Daoist philosophers. Time could easily flow in another direction . . . or
in one of countless directions. Perhaps events can be arranged in
any of a number of different sequences, because time may choose
from an infinite set of options. Remember the aphorism of Hera-
clitus: 'Time is a child playing dice; the kingly power is a child's.'

"But so what? Whichever direction time takes, what meaning
does all this have? The world exists. Its existence precedes essence
because its very existence is steeped in nothingness. It is absurd regardless of the order of the events within it. Perhaps you're right—
had time picked another direction, the universe would be very
different: humanity would progress from darkness to light, from
sorrow to joy, but such a universe would not be any better. In the
end, joy belongs to those who are born in times of joy, and suffering belongs to those born in times of suffering. In the eyes of God,
it makes no difference.

"Some say that if war were to break out between the Soviet
Union and the United States, the world would end. But I say the
apocalypse has long since arrived. It has been with us since the birth

of the world, but we have become inured to it by familiarity. The end of the world comes not with the destruction of everything, but with the fact that nothing that happens around us has any meaning. The world has returned to primordial chaos, and we have nothing."

Sartre stopped, as though expecting me to say something. My mind was utterly confused, and after a long while, I said, "What, then, is the hope for humanity?"

"Hope has always existed and always will," he said solemnly. "But hope is not the future because time does not have an inevitable direction. Hope is now: in existence itself, in nothingness. The truth of nothingness is freedom. Man has always had the freedom to choose, and this is the only comfort and grace offered to humanity."

"I understand that's your theory. But do you really think the freedom to choose belongs to humanity?" My voice grew sharper. "Thirty years ago, I was separated from the woman I loved on the other side of an ocean. Then I returned here. I do not know where she is or whether she is still alive. Can I choose to go find her? A few years back, tens of millions of people died from starvation in this country. If possible, they would all have chosen to survive. But could they have survived? Let me tell you something: many honorable and great men and women chose Communism, believing it would save humanity from suffering, but have you seen the results of their choice? Have you seen what has happened to China? The freedom of mankind is but a fantasy, a cheap consolation. Our state is despair."

Sartre was silent for a while. Then he said, "Perhaps you're right. But the meaning of freedom is that you can always choose, though there is no promise that your choice will become reality. Maybe this is a cheap consolation, but other than this, we have nothing."

I don't know if I really understood Sartre, or maybe even he couldn't express himself clearly. He stayed in China for more than a month, and we saw each other often. He said he would try to think about what I said and write a new book, but then he left China and I never saw him again.

15.

The next few years were a golden age for the People's Republic. The Cultural Revolution was a distant memory, and the later anti-rightist movements were also deemed historical errors. As the cultural sphere grew more animated and open, dissent was tolerated and many different opinions could be voiced. The central leadership adjusted the socialist economic model through new democratic reforms that permitted some measure of private enterprise. The Soviet Union and China entered a honeymoon period, and with Soviet aid, China announced a new five-year plan of full-scale development. Everywhere people were excited and threw themselves into their work with passion. Once again, we began to hope for a better future.

But hope did not last. After the Cuban Missile Crisis, the Cold War heated up again. An American plot overthrew Cuba's Castro, and the dictator Batista came into power. The Communist forces were driven from the Americas, and then the Korean Peninsula became a new flashpoint. Along the 38th parallel, both sides amassed forces, and war broke out without anybody knowing who had fired the first shot. China could not help but become involved, and young men from China had to go to Korea to fight for the survival of the Republic.

This was the first time in living memory that China and the United States fought directly. The Americans had picked a moment in China's history when China was at her weakest, when she needed peace and recovery the most. Every sign indicated that China was going to lose. Incredibly, however, the Chinese Volunteers, who possessed nothing except courage, pushed back the American assault and forced the American army to a standstill along the 38th parallel. This was not achieved without great cost. It was said that hundreds of thousands, perhaps even millions, gave their lives. I didn't know the exact figure, but considering that even Chairman Mao's son died in battle, one could imagine how desperate and fierce the fighting was.

The war caused the economy to collapse. Prices soared and more hardships were added to people's lives. Dissatisfaction with the government grew, and a name long forbidden began to surface in conversations: Chiang Kai-shek.

He was a hardened anti-Communist. Although the situation across the Taiwan Strait had long been tense due to the mainland's overwhelming advantage over the island, Taiwan's leaders had always pursued a policy of de facto independence, only passively resisting any mainland advances. But twenty years ago, after Chiang Kai-shek came to power, he declared that he would reclaim the mainland. Since the war in Korea had reached a stalemate, the Americans encouraged Chiang to join the conflict. He thus declared his intention to carry out his old promise.

With American support, Taiwan's fighters and warships encroached upon the mainland coast and pamphlets were dropped in Guangzhou, Shanghai, and other cities. Taiwan's army entered Burma and harassed the border with China. It was said that parts of Yunnan Province had already fallen to Chiang's forces. Tibet declared independence and would no longer heed orders from Beijing. Bandits under the flag of the "Nationalist Army" killed and looted the rural countryside. Spies in various cities began to put up anti-Communist posters.

The government responded by cracking down on counterrevolutionaries, but the effects appeared slight. Rumors were rampant and the population grew restless. The central leadership signed a cease-fire with the Americans and pulled the army back into China in an attempt to stabilize the domestic situation.

Chiang Kai-shek then launched an all-out assault, and the peace across the Taiwan Strait that had lasted my entire lifetime ended as the Chinese Civil War began.

With the help of the American Seventh Fleet, the Nationalist Army landed in Guangdong. They headed north and conquered Nanjing. The central leadership pulled the troops that had returned from Korea to the southern front, but the troops were tired of fighting and surrendered to the Nationalists en masse, raising the flag of the Republic of China, a blue sky with a white sun. In little more than a year, all territories south of the Yangtze had fallen to the Nationalists, and even the north appeared to be teetering on the precipice.

During that time, through my connections in the Soviet Union, I unexpectedly received a copy of Sartre's new book, which recorded his impressions of China. Sartre also sent me a long letter in which he discussed some further thoughts about our conversations. It was highly technical and rather hard to read. However, near the end, an almost casually tossed-off line shocked me:

"Recently, a Chinese-American scholar came to Paris to visit me. Her name is Zhao Qi, and she has been away from China for many decades. . . ."

Qiqi! My Qiqi! The world spun around me. I forced myself to be calm and continued to read.

"She is an excellent scholar, and she wishes to return to her homeland to do what she can to help. I mentioned you to her, and she said she would like to visit you in Beijing."

The letter went on to discuss other matters I did not care about.

For a long while, my mind was utter chaos. When I finally calmed down, I figured out what Sartre really meant. During the month we spent together, I told him about Qiqi and asked for his help to find out news about her if he ever visited the United States. The reason he had crafted his letter to make it sound as if Qiqi and I were strangers was an attempt to protect us in the event the letter was read by others.

The important news was that Qiqi was going to return to Beijing to find me. This was actually a consequence of the present crisis. The reason that Qiqi couldn't return to China before was because of the Cold War, but if the political situation changed, the barrier between us would be lifted.

Sartre's real message to me was simple: *If you want to see Qiqi again, find a way to stay in Beijing!*

16.

While I waited excitedly in Beijing, another piece of shocking news arrived: Chiang Kai-shek proclaimed that the Republic of China was reasserting its sovereignty over the entire country. The capital would be returned to Nanjing, and Beijing renamed Beiping. He vowed to cross the Yangtze and slaughter every last Communist until China was unified.

The next day, Heizi came to find me, holding a pamphlet in his hand. "What is wrong with you? Why are you still here?"

"Where am I supposed to go?" I was baffled.

"Don't you know?" Heizi handed the pamphlet to me. "A Nationalist airplane dropped this earlier today."

I read the pamphlet. Basically, it said that the Nationalists were winning victory after victory in their advance north and they would soon conquer Beiping. Everyone would be pardoned, with the exception of a list of major war criminals. The pamphlet went on to urge Communist officers and soldiers to surrender.

"What does this have to do with me?" I asked.

"Look at the back."

I flipped the sheet of paper over. It was a list of "Major Communist War Criminals." I glanced through the names: Mao Zedong, Zhou Enlai, Liu Shaoqi . . . There were at least a hundred names, and most were important figures in the Party or the government. The penultimate name was Guo Moruo, my old friend. The last name on the list was even more familiar: Xie Baosheng.

"What . . . is my name doing here?"

"Of course you're on there," said Heizi. "Have you forgotten who you are? You've been the dean of the university, the Secretary-General of the China Federation of Literary and Art Circles, standing committee member of the Chinese People's Political Consultative Conference, and you are always showing up at state banquets. As far as the cultural sphere is concerned, you and Guo Moruo are the two biggest fish."

"Those are just honorary titles. I've never done anything."

"It really doesn't matter. They need a name on there to show they mean business, and it might as well be yours." Heizi sighed. "I heard that Chiang Kai-shek has started purges in the south. Anybody connected with the Communists is executed, and he's killed enough people to make the rivers to flow red. He hung many of the bodies from lampposts to instill terror. Since you're on the list, if Beijing were to fall . . . You'd better get out."

I smiled bitterly. "I think it's too late for that. What are your plans?"

"My wife and I will follow our son, of course. Xiaohei is still in the army. In fact, he's a member of the guard for the central leadership. He's already arranged for us to go to the Northeast. We leave in two days. Old friend, I really think you need to plan for this."

A few days later, the Nationalists were almost at the city. Artillery shells were already exploding in Beijing. Someone passed me a copy of an article published in a newspaper in Nanjing, which was supposed to describe the "Crimes of Communist Bandit Leaders." The section on me claimed I had betrayed Liu Xiaobo after my arrest post-Tiananmen; that I had served as a tool of the regime during the Cultural Revolution; that after coming into power, I had abused my authority to suppress anyone who disagreed with me; that I had written science fiction novels spreading propaganda about Communism and advocating corrupt sexual practices; that I had emboldened and invigorated the totalitarian system. . . . In a word, I must be executed to pacify the people's anger.

I had to laugh at this. Here was I, thinking I had accomplished nothing in my life, but in this article I was an amazing villain with extraordinary powers.

That night, a squad of fully armed soldiers woke me by banging on the door. They were members of the guard for the central leadership and the officer in charge was Xiaohei.

"Uncle Xie, we are here with orders to escort you out of the city."

"Where are you going?"

"The commander of Beijing's peripheral defenses has betrayed us," Xiaohei said. "That bastard surrendered and the Nationalists are now attacking the city. To avoid the destruction of the city's cultural artifacts and ancient buildings, the central leadership has decided to retreat. We've got to go now."

"No. I'm too old to run. I'll wait here. Whatever happens is fate."

"Uncle Xie, you're on the list of war criminals. If you stay here, you'll die for sure."

He continued trying to change my mind, but I refused to budge. One of his soldiers got impatient and pointed his gun at me. "Xie Baosheng, if you don't leave, then you're trying to betray the revolution and surrender to the enemy. I'll kill you right now."

Xiaohei pushed the gun barrel down. "Uncle Xie, I'm sorry, but we're under strict orders. You must leave with us. If you don't come willingly, we'll have to resort to cruder measures."

I sighed. "Fine. Give me a few minutes to pack some things."

An hour later, deep in the night, the soldiers and I got into a jeep and drove west. Many buildings along the way had already collapsed from artillery fire, and the road was filled with pits. Electricity had been shut off, and all the streetlights were dark. Other than columns of soldiers, I saw almost no pedestrians. Tanks passed by from time to time, and I could hear the distant rumble of cannons.

I was reminded of another bloody night forty years ago.

The car drove past Tiananmen along the Avenue of Eternal Peace. Under the cold light of the moon, I saw that on this square that had once held tens of thousands of idealistic young hearts, the Great Hall of the People and the Monument to the People's Heroes had both been reduced to heaps of rubble. A bare flagstaff stood in the middle of the square, but the red flag with five golden stars was no longer flying from it; instead, it lay crumpled on the ground. A few soldiers were working on the Gate of Heavenly Peace itself, taking down the portrait of Chairman Mao so that it could be carried away. I still couldn't believe I was witnessing the end of the country in which I was born.

I thought I had been through too much ever to be moved by the shifting vicissitudes of fortune. But I was wrong. In that moment, my eyes grew blurry. Tiananmen became an old watercolor painting, dissolving in my hot tears. One time, the entire country celebrated the founding of the People's Republic with a parade through this very square; one time, students from around the country gathered here to demand democracy; one time, Chairman Mao stood here and surveyed the Red Guards—where were they now? Had it all been a dream?

Equally broken lay the dream of reuniting with Qiqi. I had waited so long in this city for her, but by the time she managed to return to her homeland, in which corner of China would I find myself? Perhaps we would never meet again until death . . .

No one spoke. The car bumped along and left war-torn Beijing, heading for the Western Hills.

17.

A lamp is lit on the mountain in the east,
The light falls on the mountain in the west.
The plain between them is smooth and vast,
But I can't seem to find you . . .

The Loess Plateau of central China lay before us. The yellow earth, deposited by dust storms over the eons, stretched to the horizon. Thousands of years of erosion had carved countless canyons and channels in it, like the wrinkles left by time on our faces. The barren terraced fields bore silent testimony to the hardships endured by the people eking out a living on this ancient land. Baota Mountain, the symbol of the town of Yan'an, stood not far from us, and the Yellow River flowed past the foot of it. The folk song echoed between the canyons, lingering for a long time.

"People enjoy love songs, even in a place like this," said Heizi. "Oh, do you remember that popular song about the Loess Plateau from when we were young? Back then, I was so curious what the place really looked like. I never got to see it until now, when it's become my home. Fate is really funny sometimes."

For the last few years, as the civil war raged on, I had followed the People's Liberation Army first to Hebei, and then to the liberated regions in the center of the country, and finally here, to Yan'an, where I unexpectedly bumped into my old friend. Heizi had been in the Northeast until he followed his son here, but his wife had died during the Siege of Changchun.

Although the PLA had begun the civil war with a series of crushing defeats, under the leadership of Lin Biao, Peng Dehuai, and Liu Bocheng, the PLA soon rallied and pushed back. Chiang Kai-shek became the President of the Republic of China in Nanjing, but his dream of unifying China couldn't be realized. The more he tried to "exterminate" the Communists, the more his own hold on power appeared to waver. The Communists managed to hold on to some liberated zones in northern China, and the two sides settled into a seesawing stalemate. Since both factions were tired of the fighting, they declared a cease-fire and began negotiations in Chongqing, hoping to form a new coalition government. But since neither side was willing to compromise, the talks went nowhere.

While China was embroiled in this civil war, extreme militarists came to power in Japan and launched an invasion of China. They advanced quickly and forced Chiang Kai-shek to leave Nanjing and move the capital temporarily to Chongqing. The Japanese then invaded the Philippines and opened a new Pacific front against the American forces stationed there. The Americans were completely unprepared and fled before the might of Japan. In distant Europe, a madman named Hitler rose to prominence in Germany with the support of the army and instantly declared war on the Soviet Union. The German forces reclaimed East Germany and invaded France. The whole world had descended into the first truly global war in history.

The Cold War dissolved before this new threat. The Americans and the Soviets, erstwhile enemies, formed an alliance against the new Axis Powers of Germany, Italy, and Japan. Meanwhile, in China, the Nationalists and the Communists had to put aside their differences to fight together for the survival of the Chinese people against the Japanese slaughter. Thus did history turn over a new page.

After arriving in Yan'an, I didn't want anything more to do with administration or politics. I dedicated myself to collecting folk songs and preserving traditional arts, which I enjoyed. Although my life was no longer comfortable—I lived in a traditional cave dwelling and subsisted on coarse grains just like all the local peasants—I counted myself lucky. It was a time of war, after all.

While Heizi and I reminisced, a young student ran up the mountainous path toward us.

"Teacher! Someone is here looking for you!" He struggled to catch his breath.

"Who?" I didn't even get up. I was too old to be excited.

"An old lady. I think she's from America."

I jumped up and grabbed him. "An old lady? What's her name? How old is she?"

"Um . . . I'm not sure. I guess over sixty? She's talking with the dean of the Arts Academy. The dean said you know her."

From America . . . over sixty . . . an old lady . . . my Qiqi. She's here. She's finally here!

I started to run. But I was too old; I couldn't catch my breath and I felt dizzy. I had to slow down and Heizi caught up to me.

"Do you really think it's Qiqi?" he asked.

"Of course it is. Heizi, slap me! I want to be sure I'm not dreaming."

Like a true friend, Heizi slapped me in the face, hard. I put my hand against my cheek, savoring the pain, and laughed.

"Don't get too excited," said Heizi. "Zhao Qi is your age, isn't she? She's not a pretty young lady anymore. It's been decades since you've seen her. You might be disappointed."

"That's ridiculous. Look at all of us. We're like candle stubs sputtering in our last moments of glory. Seeing her one more time before I die would be more than enough."

Heizi chuckled. "You might be old, but you're still in good health—I bet the parts of your body that matter still work pretty well. How about this? If you two are going to get married, I want to be the witness."

I laughed and felt calmer. We chatted as we descended the mountain, and then my heart began to leap wildly again as I approached the Arts Academy.

18.

I didn't recognize her.

She was Caucasian. Although her hair was turning white, I could tell it had once been blond. Blue eyes stared at me thoughtfully out of an angled, distinctive face. Although she was not young, she was still beautiful.

I was deeply disappointed. That foolish student hadn't even clarified whether he was talking about a Chinese or a foreigner.

"Hello," the woman said. Her Chinese was excellent. "Are you Mr. Xie Baosheng?"

"I am. May I ask your name?"

"I'm Anna Louise Strong, a writer."

I recognized the name. She was a leftist American author who had lived in Beijing and written several books about the China of the Mao era. She was friends with both Mao Zedong and Zhou Enlai. Though I knew who she was, I had never met her. I heard she had moved back to the US around the time Shen Qian died. Why was she looking for me?

Anna looked uncomfortable, and I felt uneasy. She hesitated, and then said, "I have something important to tell you, but perhaps it's best to speak in private."

I led her to my cave. Anna retrieved a bundle from her suitcase, which she carefully unwrapped. Anxiously, I watched as she set a crude brown ceramic jar down on the table.

Solemnly, she said, "This holds the ashes of Miss Zhao Qi."

I stared at the jar, unable to connect this strange artifact with the lovely, graceful Qiqi of my memory.

"What are you saying?" I asked. I simply could not make sense of what she was telling me.

"I'm sorry, but . . . she's dead."

The air in the cave seemed to solidify. I stood rooted in place, unable to speak.

"Are you all right?" Anna asked.

After a while, I nodded. "I'm fine. Oh, would you like a cup of water?" I was surprised I could think about such irrelevant details at that moment.

I had imagined the scene of our reunion countless times, and of course I had imagined the possibility that Qiqi was already dead. I always thought I would howl, scream, fall to the ground, or even faint. But I was wrong. I was amazed by how calmly I accepted the news. Maybe I had always known there would be no happily-ever-after in my life.

"When?" I asked.

"Three days ago, in Luochuan."

Anna told me that Qiqi had been looking for me for years. Although I had some notoriety as a war criminal, because I was part of the Communist army and always on the march, it was impossible to locate me. Once war broke out with Japan, the Nationalists and the Communists both became American allies and it was no longer difficult to travel to China. Qiqi finally heard that I was in Yan'an and bought a ticket on the boat crossing the Pacific. On the voyage, she met Anna and the two became friends. On the long ride across the ocean, she told Anna our story.

Anna and Qiqi arrived in Hong Kong, but as most of eastern China had fallen to Japanese occupation, they had to get on another boat to Guangxi, from whence they passed through Guizhou and Sichuan, and then continued north through Shaanxi to arrive finally in Yan'an.

"But Zhao Qi was no longer a young woman," Anna said, "and with her handicap, the journey was very tough on her. By the time she arrived in Xi'an, she fell ill, and yet she forced herself to go on so that she wouldn't slow us down. In Luochuan, her condition deteriorated. . . . Because of the war, we couldn't get the medicine she needed. . . . We tried everything, but we couldn't save her." Anna stopped, unable to continue.

"Don't blame yourself. You did your best." I tried to console her.

Anna looked at me strangely, as if unable to comprehend my calmness.

"Why don't you tell me what her life in America was like following our separation?" I asked.

Anna told me that after I left, Qiqi continued her studies in the US, waiting for me. She wrote to me several times but never received any replies. Once she was awarded her Ph.D., she taught in college and then remarried. Ten years ago, after her husband died, she wanted to return to China, but the civil war put those plans on hold. Finally, only days from Yan'an, she died. Since they couldn't carry her body through the mountains, they had to cremate her. Thus I was deprived of the chance to see her one last time—

"No," I interrupted. I picked up the jar of ashes. "Qiqi and I are together now, and we'll never be apart again. Thank you."

I ignored Anna's stare as I held the jar against my chest and muttered to myself. Tears flowed down my face, the tears of happiness.

CODA

The setting sun, red as blood, floated next to the ancient pagoda on Baota Mountain. It cast its remaining light over northern China, veiling everything in a golden-red hue. The Yan River sparkled in the distance, and I could see a few young soldiers, barely more than boys, playing in the water.

I sat under a tree; Qiqi sat next to me, resting her head on my shoulder.

The pendulum of life appeared to have returned to the origin. After all we had witnessed and endured, she and I had traversed countless moments, both bitter and sweet, and once again leaned against each other. It didn't matter how much time had passed us by. It didn't matter if we were alive or dead. It was enough that we were together.

"I'm not sure if you know this," I said. "After your mother died during the Cultural Revolution, I helped to arrange her funeral. She had suffered some because of her relationship to you, but she died relatively peacefully. In her last moments, she asked me to tell you to stay away from China and try to live a good life. But I always knew you would return. . . .

"Do you remember Heizi? He's in Yan'an, too. Even at his age, he's as goofy as when he was a boy. Last month, he told me that if you came back, we'd all go climb Baota Mountain together, just like when we were kids. Don't worry, the mountain is not very high. I can carry you if you have trouble with your leg. . . .

"It's been twenty years since my mother's death. There used to be two jade bracelets that had been in my family for generations. My mother planned to give one each to you and me. Later, she gave one to Shen Qian, but the Red Guards broke it because it was a feudal relic. . . . I hid the other, hoping to give it to you. Have a look. I hope you like it."

I opened the bundle that had been on my back and took out a smooth jade bracelet. In the sun's last rays, it glowed brightly.

"You want to know what else is in the bundle?" I chuckled. "Lots of good things. I've been carrying them around for years. It hasn't been easy to keep them safe. Look."

I took out the treasures of my memory one by one: the English letters Qiqi had written to me in high school; the *New Concept English* cassette tapes she gave me; the posters for *Tokyo Love Story*; a lock of hair I begged from her after we started dating; the purple hairclip she wore to Tiananmen Square; a few photographs of us taken in New York; the "revolutionese" letter she sent me during the Cultural Revolution. . . .

I examined each object carefully, remembering. It was like gazing through a time telescope at moments as far away as galaxies, or perhaps like diving into the sea of history in search of forgotten treasures in sunken ships. The distant years had settled deep into the strata of time, turning into indistinct fossils. But perhaps they were also like seeds that would germinate after years of quiescence and poke through the crust of our souls. . . .

Finally, at the bottom of the bundle, I found the copy of *Season of Bloom, Season of Rain*. She left it in my home after visiting my family during middle school, but I hadn't read it in years. More than fifty years later, the pages had turned yellow and brittle. I held it in my hand and caressed the cover wrap Qiqi had made, admiring her handwriting. The smooth texture of the poster paper felt strangely familiar, as though I was opening a tunnel into the past.

I opened the book, thinking I would read a few pages. But my hand felt something strange. I looked closely: there was something trapped between the poster paper wrap and the original cover of the book.

Carefully, I unwrapped the poster paper, but I had underestimated the fragility of the book. The cover was torn off, and a rectangular card fell out like a colorful butterfly. It fluttered to the ground after a brief dance in the sunlight.

I picked it up.

It was a high-definition photograph, probably taken with a digital camera. Fireworks exploded in the night sky, and in the distant background was a glowing screen on which you could make out the shape of some magnificent stadium. I recognized it: the Bird's Nest. In the foreground were many people dressed in colorful clothes holding balloons and Chinese flags and cotton candy and popcorn. Everyone was laughing, pointing, strolling. . . .

In the middle of the photograph were two children about four years old. One was a boy in a gray jacket, the other a girl in a pink dress. They stood together, holding hands. Illuminated by the fireworks exploding overhead, the smiles on their flushed faces were pure and innocent.

I stared at the photograph for a long time and then flipped it over. I saw a graceful line of handwritten characters:

Beauty is about to go home. Take care, my Grey Wolf. ☺

More than fifty years earlier, Qiqi had hidden this present to me in a book she had "forgotten." I had never unwrapped it.

I remembered the last conversation I had with Anna.

"What did she say before she died?"

"She was delirious . . . but she said she would return to the past you two shared, to the place where she met you for the first time, and wait for you. I don't know what she meant."

"Maybe all of us will return there someday."

"Where?"

"To the origin of the universe, of life, of time . . . To the time before the world began. Perhaps we could choose another direction and live another life."

"I don't understand."

"I don't, either. Maybe our lives are lived in order to comprehend this mystery, and we'll understand only at the end."

"It's time, isn't it?" I asked Qiqi. "We'll go back together. Would you like that?"

Qiqi said nothing.

I closed my eyes. The world dissolved around me. Layer after layer peeled back, and era after era emerged and returned to nothingness. Strings of shining names fell from the empyrean of history, as though they had never existed. We were thirty, twenty, fifteen, five . . . not just me and Qiqi, but also Shen Qian, Heizi, and everyone else. We returned to the origin of our lives, turned into babies, into fetuses. In the deepest abyss of the world, the beginning of consciousness stirred, ready to choose new worlds, new timelines, new possibilities. . . .

The sun had fallen beneath the horizon in the east, and the long day was about to end. But tomorrow, the sun would rise in the west again, bathing the world in a kinder light. On the terraced fields along the slope of the mountain, millions of poppy flowers trembled, blooming, burning incomparably bright in the last light of dusk.

AUTHOR'S NOTE

Many interesting works have been written about the arrow of time. This one is perhaps a bit distinct: while each person lives their life forward, the sociopolitical conditions regress backward.

This absurd story has a fairly realist origin. One time, on an Internet discussion board, someone made the comment that if a certain prominent figure in contemporary Chinese politics came to power, the Cultural Revolution would happen again. I didn't agree with him at the time, but I did think: What would it be like if my generation has to experience the conditions of the Cultural Revolution again in our forties or fifties? More broadly, I wondered what life would be like if society moved backward in history.

The frame of this story might be seen as a reversed arrow of time, but strictly speaking, what has been reversed isn't time, only the trends of history.

This story was written as a work of entertainment, and so it should not be read as some kind of political manifesto. If one must attribute a political message to it, it is simply this: I hope that all the historical tragedies our nation has experienced will not repeat in the future.

HAO JINGFANG

Hao Jingfang is the author of several novels (including *Vagabond*, to be published in English in 2019), a book of travel essays, and numerous short stories published in a variety of venues such as *Science Fiction World*, *Mengya*, *New Science Fiction*, and *ZUI Found*. Hao does not limit herself to "genre" writing. Her novel *Born in 1984*, for instance, would be considered a literary novel. Her fiction has won the Yinhe Award and the Xingyun Award.

She majored in physics at Tsinghua University as an undergraduate, and conducted graduate studies at the Center for Astrophysics at Tsinghua afterward. Later, Hao obtained her Ph.D. in Economics and Management from Tsinghua and currently works as a macroeconomics analyst for a think tank advising China's State Council.

Hao has always been deeply concerned with the negative impact of China's uneven development, especially on those most powerless to change their own circumstances. In 2016, Hao Jingfang won the Hugo Award for Best Novelette with "Folding Beijing" (included in *Invisible Planets*), a story that focuses on how social stratification can be reinforced with productivity gains from technology. Drawing on the public attention brought by the award, she founded a social enterprise project, WePlan, to promote education for children in rural, extremely poor regions of China.

"The New Year Train" was commissioned by *ELLE China*, reflecting in some measure the rising cultural influence of science fiction even on mainstream readers. For more on this phenomenon, see Fei Dao's essay "Embarrassing No More" at the end of this book.

and pledged perpetual fealty to each successive king. After careful screening by scientists, one particular robot soldier was brought to the palace.

"Listen carefully," the king ordered.

The robot strained to capture every buzz and hum in the air. It was unable to decode any useful information.

"The silence is terrifying, isn't it?" The king shook his head helplessly. "I dare say that at this moment, all ears around the globe are perked up, waiting for me to amuse them with some tall tale. I bet you that my stories have done such a good job of curing indigestion that an extra ten thousand sacks of rice are being consumed each year. Sigh . . . What is the point of a life like mine? No one takes me seriously. I'd rather discuss the history of the patches of rust staining your torso, my most honored pile of scrap metal."

The robot saluted him. "I am at your service, Your Majesty."

"You know, I wasn't born like this. One time, I remember going into the royal garden to play and dig for ants under an ancient tree. I dug deeper and deeper until I fell into a bottomless pit. It turned out to be an actual black hole! The black hole was filled with secrets: more than five moles of secrets gathered from members of nine trillion species spread over a million galaxies, secrets that the tellers felt compelled to share but were also terrified of sharing. Wow! What an experience! I climbed back out and wanted to discuss these secrets seriously, but everyone treated my stories as made-up tales. Once people made up their minds, it was simply impossible to convince them otherwise. . . .

"Anyway, this is why I need you. I want you to leave behind the honesty that you obtained from my father. I want you to lie shamelessly, to exaggerate unabashedly, to fabricate castles in the air without remorse. You must become the teller of the tallest tales, an unprecedented master of bullshit. This is how I will be saved, and how you will achieve absolute freedom."

And that was how the robot got its mission.

※

Fictioneering was a skill that could not be taught in a classroom, and the mechanical soldier had to go seek knowledge in the world. It left the palace and wandered the earth, gathering wisdom, gaining experience, associating itself with a variety of absurd acts, nurturing its soul in the company of delirious souls, feeding on the diseased ravings of lunatics, learning to tell breathtaking lies, spreading the seeds of chaos—until it also gained a measure of notoriety.

One day, the robot was trekking alone on a trail through the wilderness when the sky suddenly turned dark, and a thunderstorm drove it into a run-down rest stop. In the cramped and dark stone hut, three men were drinking around a small stove. In a corner, another drunken man lay asleep, his pale face hidden under the hood of a black cloak full of holes.

The drinking companions were glad to have a newcomer. They shifted around the stove to make room for the robot. After pouring a cup of strong liquor for the soldier, they continued their conversation.

"The two of you have indeed had some exciting adventures," said a tall, slender man with eagle-like eyes. "However, I have to say that Death is the most terrifying opponent of them all." The other nodded in agreement. "I've had multiple run-ins with Death, but I've always managed to escape. As a painter, I'm known for intricate, dazzling portraits of imaginary cities. Each time, Death was fascinated by my pictures. He would step into the scene, stroll through the streets and avenues, traverse the squares and alleyways, brush shoulders with inhabitants with blurred faces—before realizing that he had been trapped by my carefully designed mazes and had been wandering up and down infinite staircases whose tops circled around to their bottoms.

"As Death isn't without a sense of humor, he would tolerate my little jokes. We also have to admire his sense of duty. Since he's more powerful than anything else in the world, ultimately he would find the exits to the mazes, though the delay would afford me the time to escape."

By the time the boy woke up, he felt sore all over. All around him was muddy soil, and he found himself leaning against a thick tree root. The boy finally remembered that he had fallen into a deep pit in the ground. Overhead the shape of the sky was irregular, and a few people were leaning over the edge of the hole, looking down. The noise of more anxious people filled the air as they argued about how to rescue him.

Some bug was crawling over the back of his neck. Carefully, the boy caught it and gazed at its wriggling, tiny legs in his palm. His stomach rumbled with hunger. Everything was so new, so interesting, and he wanted a big meal to reward himself for everything he had been through this afternoon.

After filling his belly, the next order of business would be to regale his audience with his adventures. Even without any poetic license, he was sure that they had never heard such strange tales.

The adults always think they're so wise and they know everything. They'd never take a kid's words seriously. They'll say I made it all up. . . . But who cares! Someday they'll know I'm telling the truth.

Well, it doesn't matter if they call me a liar. As long as they enjoy my tales and laugh heartily, I'll help them.

ZHANG RAN

Zhang Ran graduated from Beijing Jiaotong University with a degree in Computer Science. After a stint in the IT industry, he became a reporter and news analyst with *Economic Daily* and *China Economic Net*, during which time his news commentary won a China News Award. In 2011, he quit his job and moved to southern China to become a full-time author. He began publishing science fiction in 2012, with his debut short story "Ether," which won the Yinhe Award as well as the Xingyun Award. His novella, "Rising Wind City," won the Silver Yinhe Award and the Silver Xingyun Award.

He's a fan of classic rock and for years ran a coffee shop in Shenzhen with his partner, where customers were encouraged to share their stories. He also enjoys taking unusual trips—to get to Worldcon in Helsinki in 2017, for example, he took the train all the way from Shenzhen, in southern China, up north to Beijing and then across Siberia, stopping at Moscow and St. Petersburg along the way.

In translation, his fiction may be found in *Clarkesworld* and *Watchlist: 32 Stories by Persons of Interest*, among other places.

"The Snow of Jinyang" straddles the line between *chuanyue*, a genre of time-travel fiction whose closest English analog would be something like Mark Twain's *A Connecticut Yankee in King Arthur's Court*, and traditional science fiction. The text is replete with playful references to popular tropes in *chuanyue* fiction, actual history, and contemporary life. It may be helpful to read the story twice, once without the footnotes, and once with.

A special note of thanks to my cotranslator Carmen Yiling Yan, who also worked with me on Anna Wu's "The Restaurant at the End of the Universe: Laba Porridge." Our debates and experiments in the process of overcoming some of the trickiest translation problems I've ever encountered made this a really fun and memorable experience.

10 Translated by Carmen Yiling Yan and Ken Liu.

Jinyang (晋阳) was an ancient city located in modern-day Shanxi Province, China. This story takes place in the tenth century CE, during the late Five Dynasties and Ten Kingdoms period, when the land we think of as China today was divided among multiple independent states. Jinyang was the capital of a state that called itself Han—or "Great Han," though we know it as the "Northern Han." (Northern Han should not be confused with the original Han Dynasty, which fell in the second century, or the Han ethnic group. The ruling family of the Northern Han was ethnically Shatuo, but had the same surname, Liu, as the rulers of the Han Dynasty. It was common for a regime to claim descent and take the name of a prior dynasty to add legitimacy.)

Historically, in 979 CE, the Song Emperor Zhao Guangyi conquered Northern Han, capturing Jinyang after a long siege. Zhao then razed Jinyang to the ground to prevent future rebellions. Today, the city of Taiyuan stands near its ruins.

This story starts out in 979 CE with Jinyang under siege by the Song army.

THE SNOW OF JINYANG[10]

1.

When Zhao Da stormed into Xuanren Ward with his men, Zhu Dagun was in his room on the internet. Had he any experience dueling wits with the government, he'd surely have realized that something was wrong in time to put on a better show.

It was three-quarters of the way into the hour of the sheep, after lunch but well before dinner, naturally a fine time for business in the brothels of Xuanren Ward. Powder and perfume steamed in the sun; gaudy kerchiefs dazzled the eyes of passersby. Snatches of music drifted through two sets of walls from Pingkang Ward, on the opposite side of West Street, where the licensed courtesans of the Imperial Academy[11] entertained blue bloods and VIPs. But the sisters of Xuanren Ward held their neighboring colleagues in contempt. They thought all that training as unnecessary as pulling down your pants to fart—the end result, after all, was still the same creak-creak-creak of a bed frame. Drink and gamble to liven things up, certainly, but why bother with the singing and plinking and bowing and piping? Days in the Xuanren Ward never lacked for the din of price-haggling, bet-placing, and bed frames

11 The Imperial Academy (教坊) was an official school that trained musicians, dancers, and other entertainers to perform for the court.

creak-creaking. The hubbub had become so much a part of the place that when residents happened to spend the night elsewhere in Jinyang, they found those quieter neighborhoods utterly lacking in vitality.

The moment Zhao Da's thin-soled boot touched the ward grounds, the warden in bowing attendance at the gate sensed that something was off. Zhao Da visited Xuanren Ward three or four times every month with his two skinny, sallow-faced soldier boys, and every time he walked in blustering and walked out bellowing, as if he felt he had to yell until his throat bled to really earn the monthly patrol salary. But this time, he slipped through the gates without a sound. He made a few hand gestures in the direction of the warden, as if anyone except himself understood them, and led his two soldier boys tip-toeing northward along the walls.

"Marquess, hey, Marquess Yu!" The warden chased after him, waving his arms. "What are you doing? You're scaring me to death! Won't you rest your feet and have some soup? If you need a—um— 'bonus' or a pretty girl, just say the word—"

"Shut up!" Zhao Da glowered at him and lowered his voice. "Stand against the wall! Let's get this straight: I have a warrant from the county magistrate. This is out of your hands!"

The terrified warden stumbled back against the wall and watched Zhao Da and his men creep away.

Shivering, he pulled over a nearby child. "Tell Sixth Madam to clear out. Quick!" The snot-nosed urchin bobbed his head and hightailed it.

In less time than it took to burn half a stick of incense, two hundred and forty shutters clattered over the windows of the thirteen brothels of Xuanren Ward. The noise of price-haggling, bet-placing, and bed frames creak-creaking disappeared without a trace. Somebody's child started to wail, only to be silenced instantly by a resounding slap. A swarm of patrons still adjusting their robes and hats fled out the back, darting through gaps in the ward walls like startled rats to vanish into Jinyang's streets and alleys.

A crow flew by. The guard outside the gate drew his bow and

aimed, his right hand groping for an arrow, only to discover that his quiver was empty. Resentfully, he lowered the bow. The rawhide bowstring sprang back with a twang that made him jump. Only then did he realize that his surroundings had descended into total silence, so that even this little noise startled more than the hour drums at night.

That Zhu Dagun, resident of the ward for the last ten years and four months, failed to notice Xuanren in its busiest afternoon hours had plunged into a silence more absolute than post-curfew could only be attributed to remarkable obliviousness. Only when Zhao Da kicked down the door to his room did he start and look up, realizing that it was time to put on the show. So he bellowed and hurled a cup half-filled with hot water smack into Zhao Da's forehead, following it up by knocking over his desk, sending the movable type in his type-tray clattering all over the floor.

"Zhu Dagun!" Zhao Da yelled, one hand over his battered forehead. "I have a warrant! If you don't—"

Before he could finish, a fistful of movable type slammed into him. Made of baked clay, the brittle, hard type blocks hurt something fierce when they struck his body, and shattered into dust as they hit the ground. As Zhao Da leapt and dodged, clouds of yellow dust filled the room.

"You'll never catch me!" Zhu Dagun opened fire left and right, hurling type blocks to hinder his foes while he threw the south window open, preparing to jump out. One of the young soldiers charged out of the yellow fog, chains raised. Zhu Dagun executed a flying kick; the boy cannonballed through the air and landed against a wall. The chain fell from his hands as nose-blood and tears flowed freely.

While Zhao Da and company continued to grope blindly about, Zhu Dagun vaulted out the window into freedom. Then he smacked his forehead, recalling the charge from Minister Ma Feng: "You must be caught, but not easily. You must resist, but not successfully. Lead them on; play the coquette. The show must not appear scripted."

"Lead them on . . . lead them on my ass. . . ." Zhu Dagun steeled himself and barreled ahead, carefully tripping his right foot with the left just as he passed the middle of the courtyard. "Aiya!" he cried as he tumbled to the ground with a meaty slap; the water in the courtyard cisterns sloshed from the impact.

Tracking the commotion, Zhao Da ran outside. "Serves you right for running!" he guffawed at the sight, still nursing his bruised forehead. "Chain him up and bring him to the jail! Gather up all the evidence!"

Still bleeding from his nose, the soldier boy stumbled out of the room. "Chief!" he bawled. "He smashed that tray of clay blocks. What other evidence is there? Since I spilled blood today, I should eat rich white flour food tonight to get better! My ma said that if I enlisted with you I'd have steamed buns to eat, but it's been two months and I haven't seen the shadow of a bun! And now we're trapped in the city, I can't even go home. I don't know if my ma and da are still alive—what's the point of living?"

"Fool! The type blocks may be gone, but we still have the internet lines! Get some scissors and cut them loose to bring back with us," Zhao Da bellowed. "Once we get this case sewn up, never mind steamed buns, you'll have mincemeat every day if you want!"

2.

The fates of life's bit players are often changed by a single word from the mighty.

It was the sixth day of the sixth month,[12] in the first dog days of summer. The sun hung high above the northlands, the streetside willows limp and wilting under its glare. There shouldn't have been a wisp of breeze, and yet a little whirlwind rose out of nowhere, sweeping the street end to end and sending the accumulated dust flying. The General of the Cavalry, Guo Wanchao, rode his carriage out of Liwu Residence and proceeded along the central boulevard

---

12 This corresponds to early July in the Gregorian calendar.

THE SNOW OF JINYANG | 269

toward the south gate for the better part of an hour. Being the ostentatious sort, he naturally sat high in the front, stamping on the pedal so the carriage made as much din as possible. This carriage was the latest model from the East City Institute, five feet wide, six feet four inches tall, twelve feet long, eaves on all four sides, front and rear hinged doors, with a chassis constructed from aged jujube wood and ornamented with a scrolling pattern of pomegranates in gold thread inlay. Majestic in air, exquisite in construction, the basic model's starting price was twenty thousand copper coins—how many could afford such a ride in all of Jinyang, aside from a figure like Guo Wanchao?

The four chimneys belched thick black smoke; the wheels jounced along the rammed-earth street. Guo Wanchao had meant to sweep his cool gaze over the goings-on of the city, but due to the heavy vibrations, the passersby saw it as an amiable nod to all, and so all came over to bow and return the greeting to the General of the Cavalry. Guo Wanchao could only force a laugh and wave them off.

A massive cauldron of boiling water sat in the back of the carriage. Despite hours of explanation filled with fantastical jargon by the staff of the East City Institute, the general still didn't understand how his vehicle functioned. Apparently it used fire-oil to boil the water. He knew that the stuff came from the southeast lands, and would burn at a spark and burn even harder on water. Defenders of a city would dump it on besiegers. This stuff boiled the water, and then somehow that made the carriage move. How was that supposed to work?

Regardless, the cauldron rumbled and bubbled, such that the armor at his back fairly sizzled from the radiating heat. He had to steady his silver helm with one hand so that it wouldn't slip over his eyes every few bone-jarring feet. The General of the Cavalry had only himself to blame; inwardly, he bemoaned his decision to take the driver's seat. Fortunately, he was approaching his destination. He took out his pair of black spectacles and put them on his sweating, greasy face as the carriage roared past streets and alleys.

A left turn, and the front gate of Xiqing Ward lay straight ahead.

This was an era of degeneracy, insolence, and the collapse of the social order, to be sure: the residence walls were so full of gaps and holes that no one bothered to use the front gate. But Guo Wanchao felt that a high official ought to behave in a manner befitting the importance of his position. It just didn't look proper without servants and guards leaping to action on his behalf.

But no one came to the ward gate to greet him. Not only was the warden missing, it seemed that the guards were napping in some hidden corner as well. Ancient scholar trees and cypresses lined the street, providing shade everywhere except in front of the completely barren front gate. It didn't take long before Guo Wanchao, waiting in his stopped carriage, was panting and dripping sweat like rain.

"Guards!" he yelled. There was no response, not even a dog barking in acknowledgment. Furious, he jumped off the carriage and stormed into Xiqing Ward on foot. The residence of Minister Ma Feng was just south of the gate. Without bothering to speak to the doorkeeper, he shoved open the door to the minister's residence and barged in, circling around the main building to head for the back courtyard. "Surrender, traitors!" he bellowed.

Pandemonium broke out. In a flash, the windows burst open front and back. Five or six escaping scholar-officials fought to escape by squeezing through the narrow openings, but only succeeded in tangling their flailing limbs and tumbling into a heap.

"Aiya, General!" Potbellied old Ma Feng had crept to the door and was peeking out the seam. He put a hand over his heart and thanked heaven and earth. "You mustn't play this kind of trick on us! Everyone, everyone, let's all go back inside! It's just the General, nothing to be afraid of!" The old man had been so startled that his cap had fallen off, leaving his head of white hair hanging like a mop.

"Look at you!" Guo Wanchao smirked, an expression somewhere between amusement and ire. "How are you going to plot treason with so little courage?"

"Shhhh!" Old Ma Feng was given a second fright. He scurried

over, took Guo Wanchao by the hand, and dragged him inside. "Careful! The walls out here aren't so thick. . . ."

The whole gang trooped back inside, latched the door, pressed the battered window panels back into their frames as best as they could, and gingerly took their seats. Minister Ma Feng pulled General Guo Wanchao toward a chair, but Guo shook him off and stood right in the middle of the room. It wasn't that he didn't want to sit; rather, the archaic armor he'd worn for its formidable appearance had nearly scraped his family jewels raw on the bumpy journey.

Old Ma Feng put on his cap, scratched at his grizzled beard, and introduced Guo Wanchao. "I'm sure everyone has seen the general at court before. We'll need his help to accomplish our goals, so I secretly invited him here—"

A tall, rangy scholar in yellow robes interrupted. "Why does he wear those black spectacles? Does he hold us in such contempt that he covers his eyes to spare himself the sight?"

"Aha, I was waiting for someone to ask." Guo Wanchao took off the black lenses nonchalantly. "It's the latest curiosity from the East City Institute. They call it 'Ray-Ban.' They allow the wearer to see normally, and yet be spared the glare of the sun. A marvelous invention!"

"It hardly seems right for a man interested in enlightenment to reduce the reach of light," grumbled the yellow-robed scholar.

"But who says banning rays is all I'm capable of?" Guo Wanchao proudly drew a teak-handled, brass-headed object from his sleeve. "This device, another invention from the East City Institute, can emit dazzling light that pierces darkness for a hundred paces. The staff from the institute didn't give it a name, so I call it 'Light-Saber.' The banisher of rays and the sword of light! Brilliant, eh? It was a match made in heaven, haha. . . ."

"Disgusting ostentation!" shouted a white-robed scholar as he wiped at the blood on his face with his sleeve. He had run too quickly earlier and tripped, and the cut on his forehead had bled all over his delicate scholar's face, encrusting his fair skin with

blotches the exact color of farmland mud. "Ever since the East City Institute was established, our proud State of Han has fallen further by the day! We've been under siege for months; the people are full of fear and dread. And your kind still revels in such, such—"

Ma Feng hurriedly tugged at the scholar's sleeve, attempting to smooth things over. "Brother Thirteenth, Brother Thirteenth, please quell your anger. Let's take care of business first!" The old man made an unhurried patrol of the room, drawing the curtains and carefully covering up the cracks in the windows. After a phlegmy cough, he took out a three-inch square of bamboo paper from his sleeve and displayed it to his audience, who saw that it was covered with characters the size of gnats' heads.

Ma Feng began to read in a low voice. "Sixth month of the sixth year of the Guangyun Era.[13] Great Han is weak and benighted, and the fires of war rage in the twelve provinces around us. We have fewer than forty thousand households, and our peasants cannot produce enough to equip our soldiers with strong armor and weapons. Beset by droughts and floods, our fields lie bare while the wells are exhausted, and our granaries and stores are empty. Meanwhile we still must pay tribute to Liao in the north and guard against mighty Song to the south, stretching the treasury beyond its capacity. The peasants have no food, the officials have no pay, the roads are lined with those dying of starvation, the horses have no grass to graze, the state is poor, and its people are piteous! Woe is the land! Woe is Great Han!"

"Woe," the roomful of scholars lamented in sync; then, they immediately chorused, "Well said!"

But Guo Wanchao glared at the speaker. "Enough of this flowery oratory! Get to the point!"

Ma Feng took out a brocade handkerchief and wiped the sweat from his forehead. "Yes, yes, there no need for me to continue read-

---

13 The sixth year of Guangyun corresponds to 979 CE. Liu Jiyuan (the young emperor in Jinyang) had been ruler of Northern Han since 968 CE, but did not initially adopt a new era name.

ing from the formal denunciation. General, you know well that after such a long siege by the Song army, Han is at the end of its strength, while the Song ruler Zhao Guangyi has made the conquest of the city a matter of personal honor. His edict declared that 'Han has long disobeyed the will of the rightful ruler, acted heedless to the right way, and governed the people ruinously. For the sake of the land and the people, I personally come to pacify Han in the name of justice.'

"Zhao Guangyi is known for his vicious, vengeful nature. Have you not seen how the King of Wuyue pledged his territories to Song voluntarily and was made a prince, while the ruler of Quan and Tang gave up his lands only after he saw the Song army at his gate, and was thus made a mere regional commander? By now, Jinyang has been under siege for nearly ten months. Zhao Guangyi is beyond furious. Once the city falls, the grandeur of the title he's waiting to bestow our Han emperor will be the least of our concerns. The whole city will suffer the Song ruler's rage! You won't find an unbroken egg in a nest that has tumbled from a tree. General, you mustn't let our people perish in unimaginable suffering!"

Guo Wanchao said, "I'll be honest with you: we military officers haven't been paid in half a month either. The footsoldiers whimper with hunger all day long. If we scrape away all your fancy allusions and circumlocutions, what you mean to say is that our little emperor Liu Jiyuan won't be able to sit on his throne long anyway, so we might as well surrender to Song, am I correct?"

Instantly, the scholars jumped out of their seats in uproar, shouting curses and instructing him of the Confucian duties of ruler and subject, father and son, the respect due to a subject reciprocated by the loyalty due to a ruler, so on and so forth, until Ma Feng was shaking all over with fear. "Everyone! Everyone! The neighbors have ears, the neighbors have ears. . . ."

When the room had finally quieted, the old man hunched his shoulders and rubbed his hands together anxiously. "General, please understand that we're aware of our duty of loyalty to the throne. But if the ruler doesn't do his part, how can the subjects be expected to do theirs? If the emperor is unwise in his governance, we have no choice but to overstep our bounds! The first possibility ahead of us is that the city falls and the Song army slaughters us all. The second is that the Liao army arrives in time to drive away the Song, in which case Han will become nothing more than Liao territory. The third is that we open the gates and surrender to Song, ensuring the survival of Jinyang's eight thousand six hundred households and twelve thousand soldiers, and preserving the bloodline of the imperial family. You too understand the superior choice, General! At least Song follows the same customs and speaks the same language as us, while Liao is Khitan and Tatar. It's better to surrender to Song than let Liao enslave us! Our descendants might curse us for cowards and traitors, but we can't become the dogs of the Khitan!"

Hearing this speech, Guo Wanchao had to revise his opinion of the old man. "Very well." He gave a thumbs up. "You're a righteous man indeed to make even surrender sound so fine and just. Tell me your plan, then. I'm listening."

"Yes, yes." Ma Feng gestured for everyone to resume their seats. "Ten years ago, when the previous Song ruler, Zhao Guangyi's elder brother, was invading Han, Military Governor Liu Jiye and I wrote a memorandum to the emperor begging him to surrender. We were whipped and driven out of court. But today, the emperor spends his days drinking and feasting, careless of the matters of state, a perfect opportunity for us to act. I've already secretly contacted Inspector Guo Jin in the Song army. If you can open the Dasha, Yansha, and Shahe Gates, General, the Song will accept our surrender."

"What about our little emperor, Liu Jiyuan?" asked Guo Wanchao.

"Once he sees that no other options are left to him, he'll wisely surrender too," Ma Feng answered.

"Good enough. But have you considered the most important problem? What are we going to do about the East City Institute?" Guo Wanchao looked around the room. "The prince of East City has people on all the city walls, gates, and fortifications, and they control all the defense mechanisms. If the prince doesn't surrender, the Song army won't be able to get in even if we open the gates."

The room fell silent. "The East City Institute?" The white-robed scholar sighed. "If it weren't for Prince Lu's antics, perhaps Jinyang would have long since fallen. . . ."

Ma Feng said, "We've decided to send a representative to persuade Prince Lu toward the path of reason."

"And if it doesn't work?" asked Guo Wanchao.

"Then we send an assassin and get that fake prince out of the way with one stroke."

"Easier said than done, old man," said Guo Wanchao. "The East City Institute is heavily guarded. With all his strange devices, one might die before getting so much as a glimpse at Prince Lu's face!"

Ma Feng said, "The East City Institute is located right next to the prison. All of the prince's subordinates are criminals recruited from there. All we have to do is plant someone in the prison, and he'll end up next to Prince Lu for certain."

"Do you have candidates? One to persuade, another to kill." Guo Wanchao swept his gaze around the room. The scholars avoided his eyes, focused inward, and began reciting the Thirteen Confucian Classics under their breaths.

Guo Wanchao smacked his forehead. "Wait, *I* have a candidate. He's a scribe from your Hanlin Academy, an old acquaintance of sorts, a Shatuo who goes by a Han surname. He's a middling scholar, but he's strong. He's the sort of muddled self-righteous fool who likes to spend his days complaining on the internet. Let's give him a little money, then hand him a knife and deliver him a speech like the one you gave me. He'll happily do what we want."

Ma Feng clapped his hands. "Excellent! We just need to make sure he has a convincing reason for being thrown in jail so the East City Institute doesn't get suspicious. Too severe a crime and he won't be leaving the dungeon. But it can't be too light, either. At the minimum it needs to justify shackles and chains."

"Haha, that's not a problem. This fellow spends all his time spewing unsought opinions and sowing slander online. His crime is ready-made." Guo Wanchao gripped the armor at his crotch with one hand and turned to leave. "Well, keep today's talk a secret between heaven, earth, you, and me. I'm off to find an internet monitor. I'll bring the fellow over later. We'll talk more next time. Farewell!"

The general's armor clanged as he swaggered out of the room, the contemptuous gazes of the scholars bouncing harmlessly off the backplate. Outside, the fire-oil chariot began its deafening rumble. Ma Feng wiped his sweaty face and sighed. "I do hope that taking care of the East City Institute will really be this simple. Our lives are at stake, everyone. We must act with caution! Caution!"

3.

Zhu Dagun didn't know which magistrate had dispatched his captors, but as Minister Ma Feng had told him, the Department of Justice Penitentiary, the Taiyuan Circuit Prison, the Jinyang County Prison, and the Jianxiong Military Prison were all the same nowadays. Who was to blame but a government of such staggering incompetence that it managed to lose all twelve of its prefectures, with only the lone city of Jinyang left under its rule?

As the soldiers dragged him through Xuanren Ward in chains, many curious gazes followed him through the cracks in the brothels' boarded-up doors. Who among the sisters, clients, and brothel keepers could fail to recognize the penniless scholar? Here was a scribe of the Hanlin Academy, living in the red-light district of all places. Perhaps it would be understandable in a man of passions, but despicably, he had not patronized the sisters even once in all these years. Every time he walked by, he would cover his eyes with his sleeve and quicken his steps, muttering "Sorry! Sorry!" One wondered if he was more embarrassed by the thought of his ancestors seeing his current circumstances, or by the thought of the Xuanren girls seeing whatever he hid in his pants.

Only Zhu Dagun knew that the only thing he was ashamed of was his wallet. With the arrival of the Song army, the Hanlin Academy had cut off his monthly stipend. In the three months of siege, he had received only four pecks of rice and five strings of coins as remuneration for his writing. They called them hundred-strings, but he counted only seventy-seven lead coins on each of them. If he spent a night in the House of Warm Fragrance, he'd be eating chaff for the rest of the month. Besides, he had to pay for internet. He'd chosen his address not only for the cheap rent, but also for the convenience of the network. It had a network management station right on top of the back wall. If anything went haywire, all he had to do was kick the ladder and yell upward. The internet fee was forty coins a month, plus a few more to keep the network manager friendly. Outspending his income was a negligible concern when he couldn't live a day without the internet.

"What are you dragging your feet for? Move it!" Zhao Da yanked on the chain; Zhu Dagun stumbled forward, hurriedly covering his face with his hands as he went down the street. In a moment, they came out of the front gate of Xuanren Ward and turned to travel eastward along the wide thoroughfare of Zhuque Street. They saw few pedestrians, and none who paid any mind to a criminal in chains in this time of war and chaos. Zhu Dagun spent the walk hiding his face and cringing, terrified of bumping into a fellow Hanlin Academician. Fortunately, this was the hour after lunch, when everyone was napping with full bellies. He didn't see a single scholar.

"S-sir." After a while, Zhu Dagun couldn't resist asking in a small voice, "What am I under arrest for?"

"What?" Zhao Da turned to glower at him. "Misinforming the public, starting rumors—did you think the government was ignorant of the trouble you were making online?"

"Is it a crime for concerned citizens to discuss current affairs?" Zhu Dagun asked. "Besides, how does the government know what we say online?"

Zhao Da laughed mirthlessly. "If it's government business, there's government people watching. You untitled little scribe, did you know that spreading slander and rumor about the current situation is a crime on the same level as inciting a disturbance at a governmental office or assaulting a minister? Besides, the internet is another novelty from the East City Institute. Naturally we have to be twice as cautious. You may think that the network manager's there to keep the internet operating smoothly, but he's writing down every word you send out in his dossier. It's all there in black and white. Let's see you try to wriggle out of it!"

Shocked, Zhu Dagun fell silent.

Chug chug chug chug. A fire-oil carriage rumbled past, spewing flame and smoke. It had EAST CITY XII painted on its side, marking it as one of the Institute's repair vehicles.

"The Song army is trying to storm the city again," said one of the soldiers. "Nothing will come of it this time either, most likely."

"Shhh! Is it your place to talk about that?" His companion cut him off immediately.

Ahead, a crowd was gathered around some sort of vendor stand set up under the shade of the willows. A smirking Zhao Da turned to one of his soldiers and said, "Liu Fourteenth, you should save up some money and get your face scrubbed. You'll have more luck finding a wife."

Liu Fourteenth blushed. "Heh-heh . . ."

Zhu Dagun then knew that it was the East City Institute's tattoo removal stand. The emperor was afraid of the Han soldiers deserting, so he had their faces tattooed with the name of their army divisions. The Jianxiong soldiers were tattooed "Jianxiong"; the Shouyang soldiers were tattooed "Shouyang." As for Liu Fourteenth, a homeless wanderer who'd been enlisting in every army he could find since boyhood, his face was inked shiny black from forehead to chin with the characters of every army that had ever patrolled this land. The only blank spot left was his eyeballs; if he wanted to enlist again in the future, he'd have to shave himself bald and start tattooing his scalp.

The East City prince's tattoo removal method had the soldiers rushing to line up. The technique involved taking a thin needle dipped in a lye solution and pricking the skin all over. The scabs were peeled off, and the skin again brushed with lye solution before being wrapped with cloth. The second set of scabs then healed to reveal clean new skin. It was precisely due to the unease of being under siege that everyone wanted a wife to enjoy while they could. Prince Lu's invention showed his deep understanding of the soldiers' thoughts.

The procession walked a bit farther, then harnessed an oxcart at Youren Ward and continued east by cart. Zhu Dagun sat on a stuffed hemp sack, bouncing with every bump in the road, the chains scraping his neck raw. Deep inside, a little part of him couldn't help but regret accepting the mission. He and the General of the Cavalry Guo Wanchao counted as old acquaintances. Their ancestors had been ministers together under old Emperor Gaozu Liu Zhiyuan. The fortunes of their families had gone opposite ways in the time since, but now and then they'd still simmer some wine and talk of things past.

That day, when Guo Wanchao invited him over, he'd been utterly unprepared to see Minister Ma Feng sitting there as well. Ma Feng wasn't just anyone—his daughter was the emperor's beloved concubine, such that the emperor even referred to him as father-in-law. It hadn't been long since he'd stepped down from the position of Chancellor to accept the sinecure of Xuanhui Minister. In all of Jinyang, aside from a few self-important generals and military governors with soldiers under their command, no others could equal his status and power.

After a few rounds of wine, Ma Feng explained to him what they had in mind. Zhu Dagun immediately threw his cup to the floor and jumped up. "Isn't this treason?"

"Sima Wengong once said, 'Loyalty is to give all oneself for the well-being of another.' Yanzi also said that 'Being a loyal minister means advising one's lord well, not dying with one's lord.' One should not take shelter under a wall on the verge of falling. Brother Zhu, consider your gains and losses carefully, for the sake of the people of the city . . ." Old Ma Feng held on to Zhu Dagun's sleeve, his whiskers trembling as he sermonized.

"Sit down! Sit down! Who do you think you're fooling with that performance?" Guo Wanchao hawked out a glob of phlegm. "All you scholars are the same. Powerless to make any difference, you spend all day on the internet pontificating and debating, criticizing the emperor for never doing anything right, and lamenting that Han is going to collapse sooner or later. And now all of a sudden you can't bear to hear a word against the emperor? To put it bluntly, once the Song dogs storm the city, everyone in it is motherfucking dead. Better to surrender while we can and save tens of thousands of lives. Do you really need me to spell this out for you?"

Awkwardly, Zhu Dagun stood there, unwilling to either acquiesce by sitting or defy the general by leaving. "But Prince Lu has those machines on the city walls. Jinyang is well-fortified, and I hear a grain shipment from Liao arrived a few days ago from the Fen River. We can hold out for at least several more months—"

Guo Wanchao spat. "You think Prince Lu is helping us? He's screwing us over! Those Song dogs now control the Central Plains. They have enough grain and money to keep the siege going for years. Back in the third month, a Song army crushed the Khitan at Baima Ridge, killing their Prince of the Southern Domain, Yelu Talie. The Khitan are too scared to come out of Yanmen Pass now. Once the Song army cuts off the Fen and Jing Rivers, Jinyang will be completely isolated. How are we supposed to win? Besides, who knows where that East City prince came from, with all his strange devices. Does he really only care about helping us defend the city? I don't think so!"

For a time, none spoke. A fire-oil lamp crackled on the table, illuminating the small room's walls. The lamp was another one of Prince Lu's inventions, naturally. A few coins' worth of fire-oil could keep it burning until dawn. Its smoke smelled acrid and stained the ceiling a greasy black, but it burnt far brighter than a vegetable seed oil lamp.

"What do you want me to do?" Zhu Dagun slowly sat.

"Try to reason with him first, and if that doesn't work, whip out your knife. Isn't that how things are always done?" Guo Wanchao said, raising his cup.

4.

Prince Lu's origin was a complete mystery. No one had heard of him before the Song army surrounded the city. Then, after the loss of the twelve prefectures, stories of the East City Institute began to circulate through the wards. Seemingly overnight, countless novelties sprang up in Jinyang, three of which grabbed the most attention: the massive waterwheel and foundry in Central City, the defensive weaponry on the city walls, and the city-spanning internet.

Jinyang was divided into three parts, West, Central, and East. Central City straddled the Fen River; the waterwheel was installed right under a veranda, turning night and day with the river's flow. Water wheels had long been used to irrigate fields and mill grain, but who knew that they had so many other uses? Squeaking wooden cogs drove the foundry's bellows, and the water-dragons, fire-dragons, capstans, and gliding carts atop the city walls. The foundry held several furnaces, where the bellows blasted air over iron made molten by fire-oil. The resulting iron was hard and heavy, far more convenient than before.

The changes were even greater on the city walls. Prince Lu had laid down a set of parallel wooden rails atop the wall and ran a strong rope along the track from end to end. Press down a spring-loaded lever, and the power of the waterwheel drove the rope to pull a cart sliding along the track at lightning speed. The trip from Dasha Gate to Shahe Gate normally took an hour even on a fast horse, but with the gliding cart it took only five minutes. On the system's maiden trip, the soldiers tied to the cart as the first passengers had screamed in terror, but a few more trips showed them the fun in it. With exposure came appreciation; they became the gliding cart operators, spending all day aboard the cart and refusing to get off. There were five carts in total, three for passengers and two for catapults. The catapults weren't much different from the preexisting Han ones, except that they used the waterwheel to winch back the throwing arm, not fifty strong men hauling on the oxhide rope; and they no longer threw stones, but pig bladders filled with fire-oil. Each bladder also contained a packet of gunpowder wrapped in oilcloth, with a protruding fuse that was lit right before firing.

Throwing down rocks and wooden beams was a staple of siege defense, but every beam dropped and rock hurled meant one less in the city. If the siege went on long enough, the defenders usually had to take apart houses in the city for things to throw. Therefore, the East City Institute came up with a vicious new invention. Instructed by Prince Lu, the defenders tamped yellow mud into big clay pillars, five feet long and two feet across, and embedded the surfaces with iron caltrops. The construction of the mud pillars followed a specific recipe: yellow mud was covered with straw mats to stew for a week; mixed with glutinous rice paste, chopped-up straw, and pig's blood; and then pounded down repeatedly. The caltrops studding the pillars were doused with wastewater until they rusted an unnatural red-black. Prince Lu said that they'd make the Song soldiers catch a disease called "tetanus." Weighing two thousand six hundred pounds each, glistening a sinister yellowish bronze color, and covered all over with filthy iron caltrops, the pillars turned out to be excellent weapons for slaughter. Hundreds of pillars were secured to the top of the wall with iron chains on each end. When the Song army approached, the pillars smashed down, pulverizing scaling ladders, rams, shields, and soldiers alike. Then, with a turn of the capstan, the waterwheel winched the chains with little squeaks, and the bloodstained pillars ascended sedately toward the parapets once more.

After suffering great casualties from the pillars, the Song army changed tactics and sent Khitan captives and their own old, weak, and sick to serve as the vanguard. Taking advantage of the brief respite after their sacrifices were flattened and while the pillars were still down, the main body of the Song army advanced with ladders, siege towers, and catapults. But now the gliding cart-mounted catapults came into play. In a flash, hundreds of red, stinking, wobbling bladders took to the air, blooming into fireballs as they rained down among the Song troops. Wood crackled and soldiers screamed. The fragrance of meat roasted on fruit tree wood permeated the air. Last came the archers, sniping at anyone with a helmet plume— everyone knew that only Song officers could wear feathers on their helmet. But arrows were limited and had to be used conservatively; once the archers had shot a couple arrows each, they returned to rest, thus ending the battle.

Below the city walls was a field of char, smoke, and wailing. Above, the Han defenders poked and pointed into the distance, counting their kills. For every kill, they drew a black circle on their hand, and used the circles to collect their reward money from the East City Institute. By Prince Lu's calculations, two million Song soldiers had died these months below the city. Everyone else, looking at the Song camps that still covered the horizon end to end, came to an unspoken consensus not to bring up the problem with statistics derived from self-reporting.

With Jinyang securely defended, Prince Lu invented the internet to keep everyone in the city from getting too bored. He first came up with something called movable type (which he claimed was cribbing from an old sage named Bi Sheng, although no one could recall ever having heard of this formidable personage).[14] He'd first carved the text of the *Thousand Character Classic* in bas-relief onto a wooden board, then pressed a layer of yellow mud mixed with glutinous rice, straw, and pig's blood—leftover material from the death-dealing clay pillars—over the printing plate. Finally, he'd peeled the whole thing off and diced it into small rectangles, thus creating a set of individual type blocks that could be freely

---

14 Bi Sheng (毕昇) was an eleventh-century Chinese commoner printer who invented the world's first known movable type using baked clay.

combined and assembled. He'd placed the thousand characters into a rectangular tray, attaching every block in the back to a strand of silk thread with a spring. The thousand strands of thread were then collected into a bundle the thickness of a wrist, termed a "web."

Similar text trays were found all over the city, while the bundles of silk threads passed through the bottoms of the walls to a network manager's station. The end of each bundle of silk was then neatly fitted into a metal mesh by tying a small hook to the end of each thread and hanging the hooks to the mesh. These meshes lined the walls of a station, and if two text trays wanted to communicate, the manager found the two corresponding bundles and brought the metal meshes together with a twist that connected the thousand pairs of metal hooks together. The bundles were thus linked together in what Prince Lu called an "internet."

Once a web connection was established, the users at each end could communicate through the text trays. When one side pressed down on one of the type pieces, the little spring tugged the silk thread, causing the corresponding type to sink down on the other side. Although picking out the desired character out of a thousand densely packed blocks posed quite a strain on the operator's eyes, an experienced user could type with lightning speed. Some pedants worried that the depth and complexity of hanzi writing could not be adequately represented by such an invention. Though the *Thousand Character Classic* was an ingenious primer to introduce the wonders of hanzi, how could a mere one thousand characters be enough to discuss life and the universe? Prince Lu countered that they were one thousand unique characters—never mind discussing the universe, these characters had been enough for the majority of fine essays since antiquity; they were certainly enough for web users to express whatever they needed to say.

In actuality, in the *Thousand Character Classic*, one of the characters—the one for "pure"—did occur twice. The East City Institute removed one of them and substituted a piece of type with a bent arrow symbol. Since it would have been too difficult for two users to simultaneously type and squint at the text tray for a reply, Prince Lu decreed that the current speaker had to press this "carriage return" block when they finished typing to indicate that it was the other person's turn. Why the symbol was called "carriage return" was something Prince Lu never bothered to explain.

At first, only two people could talk on a web connection at once, but Prince Lu later invented a complicated bronze hook rack that linked many internet lines together at once. If one person pressed a character, it would show up on all the other text trays.

This advance in the internet led to a new problem. If eight scholars sat down to chat, the moment one of them pressed the return key, the other seven would fight to speak first, with the result that their text trays would undulate up and down uncontrollably, like the dark waters of Lake Jinyang rippling in the north wind. To solve this problem, the East City Institute sold a new kind of text tray with ten blank type squares. When web users took advantage of the bronze rack to form a chat group, everyone first carved the members' appellations onto the squares. If someone wanted to speak, they pressed the block with their name. Whoever's block moved first had the right to speak until they pressed carriage return. Prince Lu first called this arrangement a "three-way handshake," then "vying for the mic," although he never explained what these terms meant. Zhu Dagun loved to smash his own "Zhu" block nonstop, naturally earning severe rebuke within his circles. Block-mashing not only disrupted the others' ability to speak, but also often caused the internet line to snap.

Though the silk threads were resilient, damage from wind, rain, insects, mice, and bad users like Zhu Dagun was inevitable, and the lines broke from time to time. If you were chatting, only for someone to suddenly call you an "ignorant dog unworthy of the title of scholar sullying the names of past sages," it was a good sign that the threads for some of your type blocks had broken. While you had meant to type "The Master spake, 'even the sage-kings of old were met with failures in this,'" what had shown up in the other text trays was "The Master spake, 'the sage-kings of old were fail-ures,'" thereby not only denouncing the legendary sage-kings, but also smearing great Confucius as well.

At times like this, you had to yell "Manager!" and give the net-work manager a few coins for the trouble of inspecting the web lines while you took the opportunity to go to the market and buy a few pounds of flatbread. Meanwhile, the manager would sever the connection, find the broken silk lines, and knot them back to-gether. If you didn't invest enough into a friendly relationship with the network manager, he'd tie a big fat knot that clogged the net-work so that your lines moved at the rate of a geriatric ox pulling a caravan. But if you did hand over enough coppers, he'd take out a little comb, smooth out the threads until they gleamed, and tie a minuscule square knot. Then you tossed the flatbread through the station window and yelled "All's well!"—that was why Zhu Da-gun had no choice but to reserve money for bribing the network manager, no matter how strained his wallet.

The East City Institute's siege defense weaponry won it the hearts of the soldiers; its peculiar little inventions won the hearts of the commoners; and the internet won the hearts of the scholars. To moralize and debate and weigh in on anything one desired with-out having to step outside one's door—such convenience had never been available to anyone, not even in the time of the ancient sages of legend. With the Song army surrounding the city, the scholars could no longer venture out of the city to climb Xuanwa Moun-tain, sightsee along the Fen River, or drink and admire the flowers. Being shut inside, they had only writing to serve as a pastime, and that dejected them further. If it weren't for West City's internet cov-erage, these destitute, bored intellectuals would have tried to over-throw the government long ago. With an entire state reduced to one city, its three ministries and six departments gone in all but name, no pay for the ministers, and the emperor not even attending court, the scholars had become the most idle and useless group in the city and could only snipe and complain online.

If some loved the internet, of course others kept their distance, as they would for ghosts and gods—and anything else they didn't really understand. If some praised Prince Lu, of course others muttered behind his back. No one had actually seen his person, but he was the hottest topic of gossip among the wards.

Zhu Dagun had never dreamed that the first time he had any contact with the prince would involve being sent by Ma Feng and Guo Wanchao to advise surrender. Whether it was more moral to fight or surrender, he hadn't quite figured out himself. But since both the civil minister and the general charged him with such a weighty task, he could only venture forth, a petition and a sharp knife hidden in his clothes.

5.

The oxcart proceeded creakily past the walled courtyard of an inn. Prince Lu had built it not long after he came to Jinyang. The inn was painted orange, with a blue plaque emblazoned in large characters, BEST WESTERN, presumably to advertise itself as the best inn in West City. It was a somewhat odd name, though rather tame by the standards of the other neologisms that Prince Lu had invented.

After Prince Lu moved to the East City Institute, he had two windows carved in the wall surrounding the courtyard, one for selling wine and another for selling miscellaneous gadgets. The prince's wine was called *weishiji*, presumably a poetic contraction for the phrase "feared and respected by even mighty warriors." It was brewed by soaking and boiling the grain brought from Liao, creating an alcoholic liquid clear as water and crisp as ice that burned a trail of fire through one's guts upon imbibing, far superior in flavor to the rice wine sold in the market. Two pints cost three hundred coins, a high price in a time of abundant moonshine stills, but connoisseurs naturally had their ways of paying.

"Soldiers, give us a volley!"

Zhu Dagun turned and saw a dozen or so hooligans standing at the foot of the city wall, yelling toward the outside. A soldier's head poked out from the parapets above. "Are you short on cash again, Zhao Second? You'd better give us a bigger share of that good wine this time, or else the general's going to crack down and—"

"Of course, of course!" the hooligans laughed. Then they resumed yelling in unison, "Soldiers, give us a volley! Soldiers, give us a volley!"

Soon after came the voices of the Song soldiers, yelling from outside the city. "You'd better keep your word! Five hundred arrows for twenty pints! Don't you dare shortchange us."

"Of course, of course!" With that, the hooligans jumped to action, wheeling out seven or eight haycarts from heaven knew where and arranging them at a distance from the wall. Then they ducked down at the foot of the wall, covering their heads with their arms. "All set. Shoot!"

Bows twanged. A swarm of arrows dense as locusts hissed through the air, arced over the ramparts, and thunked into the piles of hay, instantly transforming the carts into oversized hedgehogs.

Zhu Dagun watched from a distance, fascinated. "I've heard the old story of the Three Kingdoms strategist who propped up straw men to trick arrows from the enemy. I never thought it would still work."

Zhao Da spat. "These hooligans are colluding with the enemy. You could call it treason if you really wanted to prosecute. The city defense is always short on arrows, so the emperor decreed that he'd pay ten coins for every arrow turned in. The five hundred arrows these hooligans collected can be exchanged for five thousand coins, enough to buy thirty-four pints of alcohol. They lower twenty pints in a cask to the Song soldiers, hand out four pints to bribe the watchers on the wall, and drink the remaining ten until they pass out in the streets. Degenerates!" He turned to glare at them, and shouted, "You fellows have some nerve to do this in my sight!" The hooligans only laughed and bowed to him before whisking the carts down an alley.

Zhu Dagun knew that whatever Zhao Da said, he was certainly in the hooligans' pay. But he didn't bother pointing this out; instead, he sighed. "The longer the siege goes on, the worse the thoughts in people's heads. Sometimes it feels as if it's better to let the Song army take the city and get it over with, huh."

"Nonsense!" Zhao Da bellowed. "Any more traitorous talk and I'll whip you!" Zhu Dagun still couldn't figure out if Zhao Da was Ma Feng's agent, dispatched to help him, so he didn't speak further.

The sun beat down ruthlessly. The oxcart plodded forth in the shade of listless willows, down the main road through the internal gate dividing West from Central. Central City was no more than seventy yards across, divided into two levels. The waterwheel, the foundry, and the various other hot and noisy machines were on the lower level. The upper level was for horses, carts, and pedestrians, and on either side of the road were the government buildings for the Departments of Hydrology, Textiles, Metallurgy, and Divination.

The road had been paved with jujube wood wherever possible. Central City had been built in the time of Empress Wu Zetian by the Secretary of Bing Prefecture to connect East and West Cities on either bank of the Fen River. In the three hundred years since, the jujube paving had been regularly polished with wax and tamped down by feet and hooves, until it gleamed a deep brown like dried blood and was hard as stone. When struck, it rang like a bronze bell; swords bounced off it, leaving only white scratch marks. Pried up and used as a shield, it could deflect blades and arrows, even bolts from the Song army's repeating arcuballistas. At this point in the siege, the paving was full of gaps, carelessly filled in with yellow mud. Walking over it, you never knew which foot would start sinking. The soft spots could sprain an ox's ankle.

"Off," Zhao Da said. He instructed a subordinate to return the oxcart, while he personally led his captive through Central City on foot.

The Fen River was shallow and thin from the drought. Zhu Dagun looked at the turbid flow that wound in from the north, babbling through the city's twelve arch bridges before continuing southward without rest. "Liao, Han, Song: north to south, three nations connected by a single river." He sighed unconsciously. "With such a sight before me, I ought to compose a poem to commemorate—"

Before he had the chance, Zhao Da delivered a hard smack to the back of his head, knocking his cap askew and beating the poetic inspiration right out of him. "Enough, you starving scribbler. I sweated buckets getting you here, and I don't need your chattering. The magistrate's office is right ahead. Shut up and walk!"

Zhu Dagun quieted obediently, thinking, *The moment I'm free I'm going to go online and cuss you out to everyone, you corrupt official.* Then he realized that if he succeeded in convincing Prince Lu of the East City Institute, Han would no longer exist. Would the internet still be there when Jinyang belonged to Song? For a time, he walked in a daze.

Wordlessly, they crossed Central City into the modest-scaled East City. They walked past the Taiyuan county building and made two turns on the dusty street to enter a courtyard of gray brick and gray tile. The courtyard walls were tall and smooth; the windows were covered with iron bars. Zhao Da exchanged greetings with the man inside and handed over papers, while the soldiers shoved Zhu Dagun into the west wing. Zhao Da took off Zhu Dagun's chains. "The boss is giving you a cell to yourself. You'll be brought two meals a day. If you want money, more food, or bedding, ask your family to bring them. Try to escape and your crime rises one rank in severity. Trial is in two days. Just tell everything like it is to the boss. Got everything?"

Zhu Dagun felt a sharp burst of pain in his back; he stumbled and fell into a cell. Guards locked and chained the door, then left.

Zhu Dagun pulled himself up and looked around, rubbing his butt. He found that the cell had a bed, a sitting mat, a bronze basin for washing his face, and a wooden bucket serving as a chamberpot. Although the room was poorly lit, it was neater and cleaner than his own home.

He sat on the mat. He groped the pouch inside his sleeve and found that everything was intact: a copy of the *Analects*, so that when he debated Prince Lu he could borrow courage from the writings of sages; an empty wooden box, with a hidden compartment containing Ma Feng's voluminous petition—it may have been an entreaty to surrender, but the impeccable writing and righteous language had Zhu Dagun's abject admiration; a double-edged dagger forged of prime steel, six and three-tenth inches. *Of what import is the anger of a common man?* The First Emperor had asked this of Tang Ju. *A spray of blood five paces long,* answered he. Thinking of this final tactic, the Han words churned Zhu Dagun's Shatuo and Turkic blood.

6.

Only when Zhu Dagun awoke did he realize that he'd fallen asleep in the first place. A ray from the setting sun slanted through the window. It was late in the day now.

Footsteps sounded in the hallway outside. Zhu Dagun slowly climbed to his feet and stretched, looking out through the gaps between the bars.

Earlier, Ma Feng had said that he'd planted agents inside the prison to appear at a suitable time. At this moment, a guard was strolling over, an oil-paper lantern in his left hand and a box of food in his right, humming as he went. He stopped at Zhu Dagun's cell and knocked on the bars with the lantern. "Hey, time to eat." He took two flatcakes from the box, wrapped them around some pickled vegetables, and passed them through the bars.

Zhu Dagun accepted the meal with a friendly smile. "Thank you very much. Does your superior have any words for me?"

The guard glanced around, then set down the food box and took out a scrap of paper. "Here, read this," he whispered. "Don't let anyone see it. The general said to tell you, 'Do what you can, but leave the rest to the will of heaven.' As long as you do your duty, you'll benefit whether it works or not." Then he raised his voice.

"There's water in the basin. Scoop it up with your hands if you want to drink. Relieve yourself in the bucket. Don't get any blood, pus, or phlegm on the bedding. Got it?"

The guard picked up the food box and strolled off. Zhu Dagun devoured the flatcakes in a few bites, poured some water down his gullet, then turned around and read the note by the last fading sunlight. However, once he was done, he felt more confused than before. He'd thought that the guard had been sent by Guo Wanchao, but the note suggested otherwise. It read:

> Dear Sir:
>
> Our state of Han is in big trouble. We're low on soldiers and grain and rely on the siege defense machines to keep going. Lately I heard that the East City Institute people have been uneasy and Prince Lu seems unstable. If he defects to Song, Han is doomed. Woe! If you read this letter I hope you can talk to Prince Lu and make him see the light. He mustn't surrender! He refuses to see any guests at the East City Institute so I can only try to do it roundabout like this. For the sake of our people, please you must persuade him to stay strong! We'll beat Song one day for sure!
>
> —Yang Zhonggui again thanks you

The note was clumsy in language, the handwriting unrefined; clearly, the author was some rough fellow without much education. The name "Yang Zhonggui" seemed unfamiliar. Zhu Dagun thought for a long time before remembering that it was the original name of Military Governor Liu Jiye. He was the son of the Lin Province Inspector Yang Xin. Emperor Shizu had adopted him as a grandson and changed his name to Liu Jiye. In his thirty years as a general, he'd never been defeated in battle, earning him the moniker "Invincible." Currently, he commanded the defense of Jinyang.

Signing the note with his original name showed his desire to distance himself from the current emperor. The reason was no secret. Ten years ago, the previous Song emperor had breached the Fen

River dam in an attempt to flood Jinyang. The streets had disappeared under the waters, and corpses and trash floated everywhere. Liu Jiye had petitioned the emperor Liu Jiyuan to surrender, only to meet with curses and mockery. One of the other signatories to the petition, Guo Wuwei, was publicly executed. Liu Jiye had remained in disfavor ever since, stripped of any meaningful command.

Though he'd once advocated surrender, now he advocated fighting on. Zhu Dagun thought he understood why. The Invincible General might have been a renowned warrior who'd caused the deaths of countless soldiers, but he was also a credulous, shortsighted, gentle soul who wept to see the ordinary people suffer. Ten years ago, the entire city was starving. Commoners swam into the streets every day to eat the bark off the willow trees; if they rolled off their roofs at night while sleeping, they drowned in the stinking water. Liu Jiye's heart had ached so at the sight that he'd only wanted to open the gates and let the Song troops in and end all the suffering.

But this time, the city was comparatively well-stocked. The commoners could eat their fill and still have grain left over to trade for *weishiji*, trade for a few gadgets, or pay a visit to the brothel, satisfying themselves in both body and soul. Naturally this bolstered Liu Jiye's spirit. He wanted nothing more than for the siege to last for a hundred years until the Song ruler died of old age right where he stood, as vengeance for the past. With Prince Lu holed up in his own territory in East City, shut off from all outsiders, only criminals could hope for an audience with him. General Liu had written his clumsy entreaty and left it in the prison in the hopes that some patriotic prisoner could whisper encouragement to Prince Lu.

"Ah . . ." Zhu Dagun blinked. He tore up the note and threw the scraps into the wooden bucket, then pissed over them to destroy the evidence. The guard who brought him food hadn't been the person he was waiting for, but Liu Jiye's agent, in a strange coincidence.

The sky outside the window was soon dark, and there was no lamp in his cell. Zhu Dagun sat with a full stomach and nothing to do. Normally, this would have been a perfect hour for chatting on-line. He flexed his fingers restlessly as he mentally recited the *Thousand Character Classic*. Without sufficient familiarity with this cunning work, one wouldn't be able to quickly find the right character in the text tray. Memorizing it—and thus the layout for the types—had become a requirement for the literati of his generation.

Footsteps once again sounded in the hall; the glow of flames grew as they approached. Zhu Dagun hurried to the bars and waited. A guard stopped in front of him, holding his torch high. "Zhu Dagun?" he said coldly. "In custody for sowing misinformation online?"

Zhu Dagun smiled. "That's me. Though I've never heard of that crime. . . . Does your superior have any words for me?"

"Hmph. Kneel!" the guard suddenly said, in total seriousness. He glanced around, then pulled out something shiny and golden, spreading it to let Zhu Dagun see. Zhu Dagun paled and instantly dropped to his knees. He was only a minor scribe with no governmental rank, but he'd once seen such an object on the incense table of a great scholar of the Imperial Archives. He shivered in fear, obediently touching his forehead to the ground. "The servant . . . the criminal Zhu Dagun a-awaits His Imperial Majesty's instruction!"

The guard stuck out his chin and began to recite, enunciating each character crisply. "In representation of Heaven and the Emperor the edict speaks: We know of you and your abundance of opinions. Often, you debate matters of state on the internet and spin your words very skillfully to corrupt others. However, we understand that you've been falsely reported this time, and we assure you you'll receive proper redress, but you need to help us out first. It's improper for us to lower ourselves by going to the East City Institute, and Prince Lu isn't willing to come to Jinyang Palace. Since we trust no one else in court, we can only put our hopes in you. You and I are both Shatuo, descendants of Yukuk Shad. We trust you, and you must trust us. Ask Prince Lu for us, what are we to do? He once promised that he'd build a flying vessel for us to en-able our one hundred and six household members and four hundred old Shatuo retainers to escape from the city and head straight into Liao territories. But Prince Lu now insists that he is too busy with defending the city to build this 'zeppelin,' a name he glossed as 'stairway to heaven' in an abstruse dialect. It's been two months, and there are no signs of this vessel. The Song troops are fierce and many, and our heart is filled with apprehension. Dear loyal scholar, help us convince Prince Lu to build the zeppelin, and we will reserve a seat for you. When the Liu clan once again rises, we'll grant you the rank of Chancellor. A ruler does not joke."

"Your servant a-accepts this edict." Zhu Dagun lifted his hands above his head and felt a heavy scroll descend into them.

The guard sniffed at him. "See what you can do. The emperor is . . ." He shook his head and left.

Zhu Dagun stood, covered in a cold sweat. He slid the scroll of yellow silk respectfully into his sleeve, his head spinning as he thought of its contents. Guo Wanchao and Ma Feng wanted to surrender; Liu Jiye wanted to fight; the emperor wanted to run away. All of them presented what seemed like reasonable arguments, but upon further thought, none of them seemed so reasonable. Who to listen to, and who to ignore? His heart was a tangle. The more he thought, the more his head hurt.

He didn't know how much time had passed when new footsteps broke him from his torpor. He'd used up all his enthusiasm; he trudged to the bars and waited.

The guard held a fire-oil lamp. He shone the lamp around, then said, "Sorry I'm late. Since you're the only prisoner here today, I couldn't get in until the change of shifts."

"Does your superior have any words for me?" Zhu Dagun said listlessly. He'd already asked this three times today.

The guard lowered his voice. "The General and Elder Ma want me to inform you that the East City Institute will send for you at the hour of the rat tomorrow. Prince Lu is mucking with something new and needs people. Just claim to be knowledgeable in alchemy and you'll be able to approach him."

"Alchemy?" Zhu Dagun said, surprised. "I'm an ordinary scholar. I don't know anything about alchemy."

The guard furrowed his brow. "Who said you have to know anything? You're just trying to get close to Prince Lu. It's not like you're actually going to be smelting pills of immortality. Just mumble something about ceruse, litharge, cinnabar, sulfur, the *Baopuzi*, the *Kinship of Three*, the *Collected Biographies of Immortals*, and so on.[15] No one understands this stuff anyway, so no one can call you out. Go to sleep early, and I'll see you tomorrow. Good luck persuading him!" He turned to leave. Two steps later, he paused to ask, "You did bring the knife, right?"

7.

The sky brightened without fanfare. Sounds of shouting and fighting drifted in; the Song troops were trying to storm the city again. The residents of Jinyang had long since grown accustomed to this, and no one took note.

A guard came to deliver breakfast. Zhu Dagun took the bowl of porridge and looked him over carefully, only to realize he'd only paid attention to the lantern, the torch, and the fire-oil lamp the previous night. He couldn't remember what the guards looked like at all and was unable to tell which faction this guard hailed from.

Zhu Dagun ate the porridge and sat for a while, doing nothing. The clamor of the morning crowd arose outside. A throng of burly men dressed in East City Institute uniforms flooded into the courtyard.

The guards took Zhu Dagun out into the yard. A man with a

---

15 Alchemy in China revolved around minerals and metals, and the primary goal was transcending mortality. The three mentioned texts deal to varying extents with alchemy, Daoism, and the mythical sages who had attained immortality and enlightenment.

yellow beard covering his face walked up and greeted him. "I serve Prince Lu. By his mercy, prisoners here only need to be willing to work for the Institute to obtain pardon for their crime. Your charges aren't too severe. Just sign here and you'll be cleared." The man took out paper and a writing implement. Instead of a brush, the instrument was a goose feather dipped in ink—before Prince Lu, who would have thought that you could pull a feather from a bird, soak it in lye, sharpen the tip, and write with such a thing?

Zhu Dagun automatically reached for the feather, but Yellow-Beard drew it back. "But right now, His Highness needs someone of unusual capabilities and skills. First tell me, are you knowledge-able in alchemy? I'll be blunt, you look like the genteel, bookish sort, so don't try to sell yourself for more than you're worth."

Zhu Dagun quickly dredged up a speech. "I've been studying the *Kinship of Three* since childhood under the guidance of my father. I am thoroughly versed in the ways of Dayi, Huanglao, and the forging flame. Heaven and Earth are my cauldron, water and fire are my ingredients, and yin and yang are my complements. I know when to stoke the flames and when to bank the embers. In my life I've refined one hundred and twenty pills of shining gold and im-bibed them daily. Although I have not ascended to the ranks of en-lightened immortals, my body has become light, nimble and impervious to disease. The pills have the power to cultivate the spirit and extend life." To demonstrate the effectiveness of the golden pills, he sprang up and did two backflips in midair, then grabbed an eighty-pound stone drum lying in the yard. After lifting it above his head and tossing it from hand to hand, he threw it to the ground, where it landed with a thud. He dusted off his hands, his breathing unhurried, his face unchanged in color.

Yellow-Beard stared; his men started to clap. The guard stand-ing behind him sneaked a thumbs up, upon which Zhu Dagun knew that this was Ma Feng's agent.

"Excellent, excellent! We've found a real treasure today." Yellow-Beard laughed and opened the small bamboo case at his waist. He dipped the goose quill in ink and handed it over. "Sign here, and you'll belong to the East City Institute. We're going straight to Prince Lu."

Zhu Dagun signed his name as directed. Yellow-Beard ordered the guards to unfasten the manacles around his ankles, bowed all around to the prison staff, and left the courtyard with his retinue. He and his men escorted Zhu Dagun for half an hour before arriving at a large residence complex, both sprawling in area and dense with buildings. The blue-garbed guards at the gate smiled when they saw Yellow-Beard. "Got the goods? It's been peaceful lately. We haven't had any new people join in a while."

"I know. Prince Lu was frantic about finding an alchemist to help him out," replied Yellow-Beard. "We've finally taken care of that."

A crowd was gathered in front of the gate: imperial messengers, merchants, government officials in search of glory by association, commoners seeking aid in redressing wrongs done to them, craftsmen bringing their own inventions in the hopes of an audience, idlers trying to return the novelties they purchased after they grew bored, laborers looking for work, prostitutes looking for clients. The guard recorded them one by one in his ledger, gently refusing, reporting, and chasing off with a stick as appropriate. If he saw anyone he was uncertain about, he went ahead and took the bribe, then told them to try their luck again in a few days. He was quite orderly and methodical in this work.

Yellow-Beard led his men into the compound. The courtyard was a different scene: behind a privacy wall was an immense pool of water, in the middle of which a geyser rose more than ten feet tall before majestically splashing down.

"Normally the fountain is powered by the water turbine from Central City, but with the Song army regularly trying to storm the city, we need the turbine to power the gliding carts, catapults, and capstans," Yellow-Beard explained. "So instead the fountain mechanisms run on manpower. We have several dozen unskilled laborers in the Institute, whose only trade is doing heavy lifting, nothing like a white collar fellow like you." Zhu Dagun had never heard of the strange words he used, so he simply looked where Yellow-Beard pointed. Indeed, he saw five dull-eyed, muscular fellows to the side, stepping on pedals that went up and down. The pedals drove rotors, the rotors churned a water tank, and the tank valves opened and shut, pumping water high into the air.

They went around the fountain and through an archway to enter the second partition of the courtyard. A dozen or so workshops stood to either side. Yellow-Beard said, "We build the flashlights, sunglasses, clockwork toys, microphones, magnifying glasses, and other things we sell in the city here. Institute staff get a fifty percent discount, and a lot of these gadgets are hard to find in the market. You should come check them out when you get a chance."

As they spoke, they went through a third partition. Heavy, gleaming fire-oil carriage components lay everywhere under a high awning. A piece of heavy machinery puffed away, spewing white smoke and rapidly turning a carriage wheel. Several oil-stained craftsmen were engaged in an animated discussion full of strange words like "cylinder pressure," "ignition timing," and "steam saturation." Two carpenters were hammering together a carriage framework. Several dozen large barrels of fire-oil stood in a corner of the yard, filling the air with their simultaneously aromatic and noxious smell. Fire-oil came from the island of Hainan and was originally used to douse attackers in flames during a siege, before it found myriad uses in Prince Lu's hands. Yellow-Beard said, "All the fire-oil carriages running about in Jinyang were built here. They make up more than half the Institute's income. The newest model will be released soon. It's called Elong Musk—for the long-lasting fragrance of fire-oil after the vehicle darts out of sight. Even the name sounds fast!"

They continued walking, entering a fourth partition. This place was even stranger. There was constantly some shrill squeaking noise, or the crackle of an explosion, or an odd taste to the air, or colorful flashes of light. "This is the Institute's research lab," Yellow-Beard said. "Our prince gets a new idea a minute, and then our craftsmen try to follow up on his ideas and make them a reality. It's best not to linger here; there are lots of accidents."

On the walk here, the other members of their group had gradually dispersed, so that Yellow-Beard and Zhu Dagun were alone by the time they entered the fifth partition. Blue-garbed guards stood at the gateway; Yellow-Beard took out a pass, spoke a code phrase, and wrote down several passwords on a piece of paper; only then were they let inside. Hearing that Zhu Dagun was the newly arrived alchemist, the guards patted him down head to toe. Fortunately, he'd hidden the imperial edict in the rafters of his prison cell and tucked the dagger into his topknot. Zhu Dagun had a big head, covered in a black silk cap with jutting fabric ears in the back. A guard snatched off his cap, but only saw a bulging bun of yellowish hair, and didn't look more carefully. On the other hand, the copy of the *Analects* they found in his sleeve pouch roused suspicion. They looked him up and down, then flipped through the book. "What's an alchemist doing with this?"

This copy of the *Analects* hadn't been printed with Prince Lu's clay movable type. Rather, it had been printed in Emperor Shizong of Zhou's time, using the official carved plates, and had been passed down for generations into Zhu Dagun's hands. Zhu Dagun felt physical, visceral pain as he took back his crumpled and wrinkled treasure and prepared to head in.

Yellow-Beard said, "This row of buildings in the north is where His Highness normally spends all his time. He doesn't like to be disturbed, so I won't go in with you. Don't be afraid; our prince is amiable and kind. He's not hard to talk to . . . Right, I still don't know your name."

"My surname is Zhu," Zhu Dagun quickly said. "I'm the eldest of my siblings and named after Gun, father of the first Xia ruler. My courtesy name is Bojie."

Yellow-Beard said, "Brother Bojie, I've been one of His Highness's helpers since he first arrived in Jinyang. He granted me the name Friday."

Zhu Dagun bowed. "Thank you, Brother Friday."

Yellow-Beard returned the bow. "Not at all, not at all," he said, before turning and leaving.

Zhu Dagun straightened his clothes, cleared his throat, scrubbed at his face, swallowed, and entered the building.

The room was very spacious. Black paper covered the windows, and fire-oil lamps illuminated the inside. Two long tables stood at the center of the room, covered with various jars and bottles. A man stood at one of the tables, head down, working on something.

Zhu Dagun's palms sweated, his heart raced, and his legs wobbled. He hesitated briefly before gathering his courage, clearing his throat stickily, and dropping to a kowtow. "Your Highness! I . . . this criminal is—"

The man turned. Zhu Dagun kept his head down, afraid to look at his face. He heard Prince Lu say, "About time! Hurry and help me. I've been messing with this for days without any progress. Why is it so hard to find someone who understands middle school chemistry? What's your name? What are you doing there on the ground? Get up already and come here."

At Prince Lu's string of words, Zhu Dagun hurriedly stood up and came over, his head down. He thought that this august prince sounded friendly and genial, like someone easy to approach, although he pronounced his words so strangely that Zhu Dagun had to repeat them to himself several times before understanding the prince; he wasn't sure what topolect it was. "Your lowly servant is Zhu Dagun, a criminal." Still keeping his eyes lowered, he made his way to the center of the room. Jars and bottles clanged over as he went, not because of carelessness or poor eyesight, but because the floor was so packed with random objects that he couldn't take a step without kicking something over.

"Hey, Lil' Zhu. You can call me Old Wang." The prince stood on tiptoes to pat his shoulder. "You're really tall. A hundred ninety centimeters, maybe? I heard you're from Hanlin Academy. I really wouldn't have guessed that by looking at you. Have you eaten? If not, I'll get us some takeout to pad our stomachs. Otherwise, let's cut straight to the chase. I still haven't gotten results from today's experiment."

These words threw Zhu Dagun into a daze. He sneaked a glance up and discovered that the prince didn't look like a prince at all. He was of medium height, pale and beardless, and wore a buttoned white cotton coat. His hair was cropped short like a beggar-monk's. He looked to be in his twenties, yet his brow remained creased with worry even when he smiled. "Your servant doesn't quite understand what you're saying, Your Highness. . . ." Zhu Dagun bowed anxiously, unsure of what story lay behind this strange prince.

Prince Lu laughed. "You think my accent is confusing, but all you guys sound like gibberish to me. When I first came, I couldn't understand a single word. Your court speech sounds like Cantonese or Hakka, but nothing like the modern Shanxi and Shaanxi topolects. Since I wasn't a historical linguist, I thought that all the topolects of ancient northern China wouldn't sound very different from what I knew!"

This time, Zhu Dagun understood every individual word coming out of the prince's mouth individually, but their combined meaning fluttered entirely from his grasp. Sweat trickled down his face. "Your servant lacks in erudition. What Your Highness just said . . ."

Prince Lu waved a hand. "That's to be expected. You don't need to understand anyway. Come and hold this flask in place. Oh right, put on a filter mask. You studied alchemy, so you should know that chemical reactions can release toxic gases, I think?"

Zhu Dagun stared.

8.

The crystal bottles on the table held liquids that Zhu Dagun had neither seen nor smelled in his life. Some were red, some were green, some smelled burningly acrid, some stank unbearably. Prince Lu helped him put on a mask, then had him steady a small, wide-mouthed jar. "Take this rod and stir it slowly. Don't stir faster than that under any circumstance, got it?"

Nervously, Zhu Dagun stirred the dark green fluid inside the jar.

It smelled like the sea, and was hot like a bowl of pot herb soup. "This is dried seaweed ash dissolved in alcohol," Prince Lu explained. "You ancients call seaweed *kunbu*. I got this Goryeo *kunbu* from the Imperial Physician. *The Song of Medicine Recipes* said 'kunbu disperses goiter and breaks swelling' . . . oh, wait, *The Song of Medicine Recipes* is from the Qing dynasty. I got mixed up again."

As he spoke, he took out another small jar and carefully removed the sealing clay. The jar was full of an acrid-smelling pale yellow liquid. "This is sulfuric acid. You alchemists call this 'green vitriol,' right? Also *qiangshui*, like in the *Alchemical Classic of the Yellow Emperor's Nine Cauldrons*. 'Bluestone is calcinated to obtain a white mist, which is dissolved in water to obtain strong *qiangshui*. The substance transforms the silver-haired into the ebony-haired. The choking white mist it emits instantly transports one into the realm of spirits, and after eighteen years one departs from senescence and returns to childhood.' You should be familiar with that."

Zhu Dagun nodded as if he was. "That's right, Your Highness."

"Just call me Old Wang. 'Your Highness' sets my teeth on edge. I'll start now; keep stirring, don't stop." He set up a three-paned white paper screen to lean over the mouth of the flask, put on his mask, and slowly poured the green vitriol into the small jar. At first, all Zhu Dagun noticed was a stench that burned its way right through the cotton mask and up his nose, strong enough to make his brain ache and his eyes tear. Then he saw a miraculous purple cloud was floating up out of the jar, unfurling lazily. Zhu Dagun shivered in fright, but Prince Lu only laughed. "Finally! With this crude method for extracting iodine, that's half my big plan taken care of! Don't stop, keep stirring until the reaction finishes. I need to see just how much pure iodine I can extract from one pound of dried seaweed. . . . Are you interested in how I created sulfuric acid and nitric acid? This is the first step in the Long March of establishing basic industry, you know."

"I'd love to hear," Zhu Dagun said automatically.

Prince Lu seemed delighted. "I was pretty good at chemistry back in high school, and I majored in mechanical engineering as an undergrad, so I got a decent foundation. I couldn't have made it this far otherwise. At first I wanted to use the alchemists' method of making sulfuric acid from bluestone, but I couldn't find more than two pounds of it in the city, not nearly enough. Then I happened to see the massive piles of pyrite ore in the iron foundry. Treasure, right for the taking! Heating pyrite gives you sulfur dioxide, and dissolving that gives you sulfurous acid; let that sit for a while and you get sulfuric acid. You can purify that in clay jars; it's how the munitions factories in Communist Shanbei managed, back in the day.

"With sulfuric acid taken care of, nitric acid wasn't hard. The biggest problem was the limited supply of saltpeter, which we also needed to make gunpowder. I had to mobilize everyone in the Institute to scrape crusted urine off the bases of walls to refine into potassium nitrate. Our entire place reeked! Fortunately, people in this city have a habit of pissing anywhere there's a wall. If it weren't for that, we couldn't have built the foundations of industry in Jinyang."

Zhu Dagun flushed. "Sometimes the urges of the bladder are too great. Both men and women commonly take off their trousers and relieve themselves where they stand. Please humor the crude customs of the countryside, Your Highness."

While they were speaking, the contents of the two jars had been combined into one, and the purple cloud had disappeared. Prince Lu spread the white paper screen out on the table and scraped the surface with a flat scrap of bamboo, removing a layer of purplish black powder. "The iodine in seaweed is easily oxidized in air under acidic conditions, creating elemental iodine. Very good, let me send them orders to follow my recipe and manufacture this in batches, and we'll do the next experiment." He crossed the room, sat down in front of the text tray in the corner, and began banging out a missive. Zhu Dagun walked over to look and discovered that this strange prince typed with lightning speed. He didn't even glance at the characters, but typed blind with unfailing accuracy. "Your type tray looks like a different model, Your Highness," Zhu Dagun blurted.

"Old Wang, call me Old Wang," said Prince Lu. "The principle's the same, but each terminal uses two sets of movable type. The bottom set is used for input and the top set's used for output. Watch." He pressed the carriage return to end his message and stood up to grab a crank handle and turn it. The crank turned a roller on which a seventeen-inch-wide length of calligraphy paper had been spooled, passing it smoothly over the text tray. The movable type in the tray, to which ink had been applied, suddenly began to rise and fall, stamping characters onto the paper.

Zhu Dagun bent down to pick up the paper and began to read. "The experiment data is correctly recorded. I've told the chemistry department to oversee it. *Return*." He looked at the prince with admiration. "This is far clearer and more convenient! White paper and black ink simply reads better to the eye. When are you releasing this on the markets? We'll support it with all our might!"

Prince Lu laughed. "This is only a prototype. Version two-point-one will use the same mechanism found in printers to stamp the output on the same line, instead of inking the characters all over the place and making it hard to read. You like the internet too? The thing I was least used to about this era was the lack of internet access, so I racked my brains to come up with this. I finally get to feel like a proper nerdy shut-in again."

"Your August Highness—er . . . Old Wang," Zhu Dagun corrected himself when he saw Prince Lu's expression. "May your servant ask, from which prefecture did you originally hail? Are you a scholar of the Central Plains? You have an extraordinary air about you, after all."

Prince Lu sighed. "The better question is, from what dynasty did I hail? The era I come from is one thousand sixty-one years, three months, and fourteen days distant."

Zhu Dagun didn't know if he was joking or raving. He did the arithmetic on his fingers and laughed obsequiously. "I see that you achieved the Way in Emperor Wu of Han's time, and have lived on to today as an immortal!"

"Not one thousand years in the past," Prince Lu said unhurriedly.

"One thousand years in the future—and nine hundred billion forty-two universes away."

9.

Zhu Dagun didn't understand Prince Lu's ravings, and he didn't have time to dwell on them, because the next experiment had begun. Prince Lu placed a silver-plated copper coin into a small carved wooden chest, set the cup of newly made iodine beside the coin, closed the lid, and lit a small clay brazier next to the chest to heat it a little. Soon, purple vapors came billowing out through the cracks in the chest. *Heavens, we're about to get some pills of immortality,* Zhu Dagun thought, as he carefully waved the fan as Prince Lu instructed, afraid even to breathe too hard.

A while later, Prince Lu pushed the brazier aside, opened the chest, and reached in with a soft cloth. He carefully lifted the copper coin, cushioned on the cloth, revealing that its silver surface was coated with something yellowish. Zhu Dagun peeked inside the chest and didn't see any pills of immortality, but Prince Lu did an excited dance. "It worked! It really worked! Look, this yellow stuff is called silver iodide. All I have to do now is scrape it off into a jar and put it somewhere dark. I can perform another magic trick with this: put this coin somewhere dark, expose it to light for about ten minutes, develop the image with mercury fumes, and fix it with salt water. Once it's rinsed and dry, the coin will be covered with a picture of this room, identical in every last detail! This is the daguerreotype process, which takes advantage of silver iodide's photosensitivity. But we're storing up silver iodide for something else, so I'll have to show you at a later date."

"Without an artist, how can one obtain a picture?" Zhu Dagun asked, confused. "And . . . what miraculous powers does the yellow powder have? Does it impart health and sagehood on one who imbibes it?"

Prince Lu laughed. "It's not that kind of magic. In my day, silver iodide had two main uses. One was photosensitivity, like I mentioned. The other, well, you'll see." He worked as he spoke, scraping the powder off the coin into a small porcelain bottle before pulling off his mask and stretching. "That's all for now. I'm done for the morning. I'll send out the instructions for manufacturing silver iodide, and then I can rest. You haven't eaten, right? We can eat together later. You're tall and strong, and pretty good with your hands—it must be all that alchemy experience. I have some things I want to ask you, so don't wander off. I'll be right back."

Prince Lu sat down at the text tray and began to type at a rattling pace. Now and then he cranked out a length of calligraphy paper and read it, nodding to himself. Zhu Dagun just stood there in the room, afraid to touch anything and accidentally break it, or trigger some mighty magic.

At this point, he finally remembered why he was there. He reached for his sleeve pouch, felt the copy of the *Analects* there, and took a deep breath. "Your Highness, there's something that I don't understand," he said, looking down. "I hope you can advise your servant."

"Go ahead; I'm listening." Prince Lu was still at the text tray, cranking the spool of calligraphy paper, too busy to spare a glance.

Zhu Dagun asked, "Your Highness, are you Han or Hu[16]?"

"Don't be pretentious, call me Old Wang," came the reply. "I'm Han. I grew up in Beijing's Xichen District. My ma's Hui Muslim, but I took after my ba. I may have played in the Niujie and Jiaozi neighborhoods as a kid, but I can't live without pork, so no dice."

Zhu Dagun had already learned to ignore Prince Lu's incomprehensible ramblings. "If Your Highness is Han, why do you live in Jinyang instead of the southern lands?"

"You wouldn't understand even if I explained," said Prince Lu. "I'm Han, but I'm not a Han from your era. I know perfectly well that, of the Five Dynasties and Ten Kingdoms, Liang, Tang, Jin,

---

16   Hu (胡) is an ancient Chinese term for non-Han ethnic groups, used mostly for Central Asians in the era this story takes place in.

Zhou, and even your so-called Great Han were founded by other ethnic groups, and most of your people are Hu too. But once my plan succeeds, I'll be back at my point of departure, and this temporal node of your universe won't have a thing to do with me, got it?"

Zhu Dagun took a step closer. "Your Highness, how are we going to defeat the Song army?"

"We can't," said Prince Lu. "We don't have the soldiers or the food, and we can't mass-produce firearms. Flintlock muskets are easy to manufacture, but we don't have nearly enough sulfur to make gunpowder. We scoured the city and only found a couple dozen pounds. We can't do more than occasionally fire a cannon to give a scare. But that brings me to my next point. Though we can't defeat the Song troops, we can hold out pretty easily. As long as Zhao Guangyi doesn't find out how Liao is sending us grain under the surface of the water, Jinyang survives another day. Tying empty barrels to full barrels and sending them along the bottom of the Fen River is a trick you ancients would never think of."

Zhu Dagun raised his voice. "But the commoners are hungry and weary, and the soldiers wail with pain and exhaustion! The longer Jinyang holds on, the more its tens of thousands of residents suffer, Your Highness!"

"Hey, good point." Prince Lu turned on his stool. "Everyone else is delighted to work here—not only are they pardoned for their crimes, they can even earn some money. But you don't sound like them. Let's talk, then. I haven't had anyone normal to talk to in months. It's been"—he pulled out a piece of paper, took a look, and drew another X on it—"three months, seven and a half days since I was dropped here. I've got twenty-three and a half days before the observational platform automatically returns. The schedule will be tight, but judging from my current progress, I should be able to make it."

Zhu Dagun understood only the faint longing for home that underlay his words. He immediately recited, "The Master said: as long as parents are alive, one should not journey far from them without method. When one's father lives, observe one's aspirations; when he does not, observe one's actions; if in time they do not deviate from the father's way one can be termed filial. Your Highness has long been away from your home and must miss your parents dearly. Foxes die with their heads pointing toward their burrow; crows feed their parents in their old age; lambs kneel before they drink from their mother's teat; stallions will not mate with their dam—"

Prince Lu sighed. "Okay, we're still not on the same frequency here. Can you shut up and listen?"

Zhu Dagun immediately shut up.

Prince Lu spoke slowly. "I'm sure you don't know the alternate universe theory or quantum mechanics, so I'll go over them briefly. My name is Wang Lu. I was an ordinary nerd, amateur writer of *chuanyue*[17] novels, and professional time traveler. In my time, we'd perfected the multiverse theory, so that anyone could go to an agency, rent an observational platform, and go time traveling. At one time, people estimated the number of parallel universes overlaying each other to be around $10^{(10^{118})}$, but more precise calculations later on indicated that, due to overlap between different diverged branches, only about three hundred quadrillion universes exist at any one time. Countless particle-level possibilities cause universes to endlessly emerge, split, merge, and disappear, and yet even the two parallel universes with the most differences are astonishingly similar on a physical level, even as their places on a timeline diverge further and further.

"In a way, this makes things boring, since humanity's exploration of deep space remains stalled, and its understanding of the universe as a whole is very shallow. Even in the most advanced universe I've been to, humanity's reach has gone no further than Alpha Centauri, just next door. But in another way, this makes

17 *Chuanyue* (穿越) is an enormously popular Chinese genre similar to time travel, but with its own distinct tropes. Typically, the protagonist is from the modern day and travels into the historical past (or a secondary-world version of the historical past), often but not always through reincarnating into the body of someone of that era. Their anachronistic knowledge and upbringing sets them apart from others and allows them to break the status quo.

things interesting, since with the invention of the wave function engine it means that we can step across to other parallel universes at our convenience. For topological reasons, the more similar the destination universe, the less energy it takes to travel there. The most advanced observational station we have can send travelers three hundred trillion universes away, though the commercially available equipment only has a maximum range of around forty trillion."

Zhu Dagun kept nodding while he felt his sleeve pouch, inwardly debating whether to take out the dagger and persuade Prince Lu's heart or take out the *Analects* and persuade his mind once he finished his raving. There was no one else in the room, creating a prime opportunity to make his move. It wasn't that Zhu Dagun didn't want to act promptly, but that he himself still felt somewhat undecided as to which esteemed personage he should act on behalf of.

Prince Lu picked up his teacup and took a sip, then continued. "I accepted a job from the Peking University history department, a research task to tally the population of the Sixteen Prefectures during the late Five Dynasties and Ten Kingdoms period.[18] A parallel universe like yours is located toward the front of the timeline, which makes it an excellent place for historical observation.

"Don't think just anyone can get a time travel license. You have to train systematically in quantum theory, computer operation, ground transportation, emergency drills, and more, and pass the test to get a job. If you want to lead tour groups, you have to take the Time Travel Tour Guide Examinations too. Due to the physical similarity between parallel universes, I activated the observational platform at Xuanwu Gate in Beijing to travel nine hundred billion

---

18 The Sixteen Prefectures, comprising a region around Beijing and along the Great Wall, had been under Han Chinese or more Sinicized Hu control for centuries until they were ceded to Liao in 938 CE. The strategically and symbolically valuable territory would remain a major point of contention between Liao and Song for years to come.

forty-two universes and arrive here. By my calculations of revolution and rotation elements, I should have been able to arrive in You Prefecture. Who knew that my observational platform was getting long in the tooth? The wave function engine radiator boiled over, right in the middle of the trip! I had to pour in eight bottles of mineral water and a crate of Red Bull to get it to limp to the destination. The moment I arrived in this universe, the crown bar burst through the tank. That was the end of the engine. I crashed into a gully in Shanxi by the Fen River. My luggage, equipment, and spare fuel tanks were wiped out.

"It took me ten days to patch together the engine, only to discover all the fuel had leaked out. The bit left in the oil lines could hop me two or three universes over at most. What use would a few hours forward be?"

The sounds of shouting and fighting from outside grew louder. The Song army had begun another assault on East City Gate. Prince Lu turned to glance at the report scrolling out above the text tray and typed a few characters himself. "Don't worry." He laughed. "We'll take care of it as usual. I'll move two bladder catapults over . . . Where was I? Ah, right, the wave function engine could just barely start, and raising the angular speed made the engine oil give off blue smoke like a tractor, but the main problem was that I didn't have any fuel. Taking that census was of course out of the question, but even worse, since I hadn't filed this private job with the Ministry of Civil Affairs' Multiverse Administrative Office, I couldn't just call the time police for help when they'd put me in jail for three to five years! If I wanted to get home, I needed some way to gather fuel. I didn't have a choice but to hide my things in the gully and sneak into Jinyang."

"Your Highness, you say you didn't have any fuel, but isn't the city full of fire-oil?" Zhu Dagun couldn't resist interrupting. "Many carriages on the street burn fire-oil."

Prince Lu sighed. "If only it combusted oil. Let me put it this way, the fuel tank didn't hold real, physical fuel, but potential energy, the elastic potential between parallel universes. If I wanted to fill my tank, I needed to create a universe split. When a new universe split off as a result of some decision point, I'd be able to gather this escaped potential energy to power my return. This potential energy isn't something intangible like entropy values. It's more like when you snap a bamboo pole in two, and you hear the *crack* as it splits apart? I don't understand it that well myself, but either way I had to create a big enough event to make the universe split. Now, how could I do this? Let's take an example from history—on the fourteenth of the third month this year, a resident of Jinyang slipped from the parapets and fell to his death in the Fen River. The incident was witnessed by twenty people and recorded in a minor history. If, on the fourteenth of the third month, I grabbed his collar and saved his life, I'd create a change. But it wouldn't be big enough. Out of the one hundred quadrillion universes where this event occurred, he was saved in one quadrillion of them even without me. In that moment, the parameters in one of those universes would change until it perfectly matched the universe we're in, and the two universes would merge. Of course, you and I wouldn't feel anything from where we stand, but the potential would decrease, and even remove fuel from my tank. To cause a new universe to split off, I have to create a big enough change, a change so big that no precedent exists in any one of the one hundred quadrillion universes past this point in the timeline. I managed to use the beat-up wave function computer to find a possibility—one that I could achieve without any modern equipment to help me."

Zhu Dagun didn't speak, only listened intently.

Prince Lu suddenly pulled open a drawer and took out a book. He read from it, "'In the sixth month of 882 CE, the height of summer, Shang Rang led an army from Chang'an to attack Fengxiang. He had reached Yijun Camp when suddenly a great blizzard fell. Within three days, the snow was many feet thick. Thousands died or became frostbitten in the cold, and the Qi army retreated in defeat to Chang'an.' Have you heard of this incident?"

"Huang Chao's rebellion!"[19] Zhu Dagun finally had an opportunity to add to the conversation. "Shang Rang was Grand Commandant of Qi. The story of the blizzard in the second year of Zhonghe is still oft told among the people. It's recorded in the historical annals as well."

"Exactly," said Old Wang. "I'm a modern man, but I don't have death rays or nukes or any kind of sci-fi weaponry, and I don't have the Starship *Enterprise* or *Macross* to back me up. All I can do is use the scraps of knowledge I got from high school and college to alter this era as much as possible. It's a historical fact that Song conquered Northern Han. In the vast majority of universes, the annals record that on the fourth day of the fifth month, the Song army took Jinyang and the Han ruler Liu Jiyuan surrendered. On the eighteenth day of the fifth month, Emperor Taizong of Song drove out all the city's inhabitants and burned Jinyang to the ground. But here, I've already postponed these dates for more than a month. The Song army can't stay here indefinitely; anyone can see that the primitive siege weapons of this era can't break through the fortifications strengthened with my knowledge. Once the Song army retreats, history will be completely rewritten, and the universe will split, without a doubt!" He toyed with the little bottle of silver iodide and laughed delightedly. "And that's without mentioning my new invention. This little thing is going to change history immediately and fill my observational platform's fuel tank! The ancients believed in omens from the heavens more than anything. What could change history more than a snowstorm in the middle of summer?"

"Burn . . . Jinyang? Snowstorm?" Zhu Dagun said numbly.

"It's easier to show than to explain! Follow me!" Prince Lu leapt

19   Huang Chao (835–884 CE) led an agrarian rebellion against the Tang Dynasty, declaring himself the Emperor of Qi after capturing and brutally sacking the capital Chang'an. He was eventually defeated and killed by former subordinates who had defected to Tang, including Shang Rang, but his ten-year rebellion severely weakened the already declining Tang Dynasty.

to his feet and dragged Zhu Dagun by his sleeve to the room's west wall. He pulled some mechanism, a hinge turned, and the entire wall suddenly fell outward to reveal a courtyard hidden among dense overhanging eaves. The blinding sunlight forced Zhu Dagun to squint; it took a few moments before he could clearly see the contents of the courtyard.

He was astonished. Laid out in the courtyard were many extraordinary things that he'd never seen before and didn't know the names of. Several dozen East City Institute workers were laboring under the hot sun. They knelt to pay their respects when they saw the prince. Prince Lu smiled and waved a hand. "Continue. Don't mind me."

"We're testing the hot air balloon," Prince Lu explained, pointing at the workers in the middle of sewing cotton fabric. "I agreed to build an airship for the emperor so he can escape to Liao. An airship takes more time than this, but I'll do what I can and build a balloon for now. When I came to Jinyang, I made a few flashy novelties and bribed some minor officials for an audience with the emperor. I told him I could make Jinyang impregnable for him, and he granted me the convenient title of Prince of Lu right on the spot. I have to repay that kind of generosity."

They turned and came to a group of workers filling a cannon cast of black iron with gunpowder. "This cannon will be used to fire a cloud-seeding canister. Gunpowder isn't a strong enough propellant, so we need the hot air balloon to lift the cannon into the air, and then fire it up at an angle. I've been keeping a close eye on the weather patterns lately. Don't be fooled by how hot it is; the clouds that drift in from the Taihang Mountains every afternoon are full of cold air. By providing enough condensation nuclei at the right time, we can create a snowstorm out of nowhere!" Prince Lu grinned. "I sent the recipe over earlier. The chemical factory off site is currently devoting all its resources to manufacturing silver iodide powder. It won't be long before we can fill a cloud-seeding canister and load it into the cannon. We've already test-flown the hot air balloon. All we have to do is wait for the right weather conditions!"

Zhu Dagun gazed up at the clear and fair sky. The sun shone like fire. The distant sounds of battle were fading; a magpie squawked from the eaves. A fire-oil carriage rumbled along a stone-paved road. The air smelled of blood, oil, and flatcakes. Zhu Dagun stood by the prince, unable to move, his mind in a muddle.

10.

The wall swung shut, returning the room to darkness. They ate a little. Prince Lu sent instructions to the city defense and the workshops through the internet, asking Zhu Dagun questions about alchemy as he worked. Zhu Dagun braced himself and spouted enough smooth-talk and nonsense to pass muster.

"Ah, I need to sleep. I pulled an all-nighter and I'm running out of steam." Prince Lu stretched wearily and headed for the cot in a corner of the room. "Keep an eye out, will you? Wake me if there's any news."

"Yes, Your Highness." Zhu Dagun bowed respectfully. He watched as Prince Lu lay down, pulled the brocade covers around himself, and soon began to snore. He let out a quiet breath and sat down, head spinning, to collect his chaotic thoughts.

Zhu Dagun didn't understand everything Prince Lu had said, but he grasped the tone of his words clearly enough. The master of the East City Institute couldn't care less about the Han Dynasty or the people of Jinyang. He had come from a different land, and he would ultimately return there. He'd created his dazzling novelties and exotic toys to garner public support and earn money. He designed the internet to win over the scholar gentry and relay the East City Institute's orders; he sold the fire-oil carriages, weapons, and fine wine to show goodwill toward the military; and the life-saving grain, deadly fire, and impossible snow were all, in the end, to further Prince Lu's own selfish goals. Han Feizi had written, "Consider one who refuses to enter a dangerous place or fight in the army, who will not for the gain of all the people sacrifice even one hair on their leg . . . you have one who values life above all else." Was Prince Lu not "one who valued life above all else"?

Something was fomenting inside of Zhu Dagun. His chest felt stuffed, his head swollen. His ears rang. He thought of what Ma Feng and Guo Wanchao, Liu Jiye, and the emperor had said. He thought of this state, this prefecture, this city, and the tens of thousands of living beings within. Liang, Tang, Jin, Zhou, and Han had taken the land in turn; Hu and Han were thrown together in this time of chaos. An inhabitant of this turbulent era, Zhu Dagun had once considered abandoning the brush for the sword and carving out some great undertaking. He'd settled in a quiet corner discussing philosophy all day long, not because he was lacking in strength or courage, but because he lacked for direction. The scholars frequently chatted of the grand principles of governing a state and bringing peace to the land. Zhu Dagun always thought that it was empty words, but what aside from their arrogant talk of the halcyon days of the Rule of Wen and Jing, the Restoration of Zhao and Xuan, the Golden Age of Kaiyuan, had they to while away their time? All he wanted was food, a bed, and a roof to sleep under; to spend his leisure time chatting and drinking; to be able to roll into bed after eating, express his aspirations online, visit the brothels when he had the money; to be at ease with the world. But in this era of chaos, to be at ease with the world in itself required swimming against the flow. Even a minor character like him had been dragged into a struggle for the survival of a country. At this moment, he held the fate of Great Han and the lives of everyone in the city in his hands. If he didn't do something, how could he claim to be a scholar, one who spent twenty years filling himself with the words of sages?

Zhu Dagun pulled the fine steel dagger from his sleeve. He knew he couldn't persuade Prince Lu, because Prince Lu wasn't a citizen of Han. Grand principles were a sham to him; only the six and three-tenths inches of steel in Zhu Dagun's hand were real. In this moment, an idea floated into Zhu Dagun's mind, perfect in three ways. He slowly unfolded his large frame and stood, a smile hovering on the corners of his mouth. He stepped soundlessly across the floorboards and reached the cot in a few steps—

"What the fuck are you doing!" Prince Lu snapped up, eyes wide and staring. "I got bitten by a mosquito and got up to burn some bug-repelling incense. What are you doing here with a knife? I'm going to call my me*mmmph*—"

Zhu Dagun had covered Prince Lu's mouth solidly, setting the dagger at his pale, tender neck. "Don't make noise and I'll leave you a way out," he murmured into the prince's ear. "Earlier, I saw you use the internet to move the East City Institute's city defense forces. You had a row of wooden movable type in your text tray. Give me the type blocks and tell me your passphrase, and I won't kill you."

Prince Lu was a prudent man. He nodded frantically, his forehead beaded all over with sweat. Zhu Dagun loosened his fingers, allowing a gap. Prince Lu gasped and panted as he took the movable type of red-colored wood from his pocket and threw them on the cot. "There's no passphrase," he stammered. "My orders pass through a special line straight to the city defense camps and the workshops. No one can fake it. . . . Why are you doing this? I've protected Jinyang and invented countless novelties for every facet of life for soldiers and civilians alike to enjoy. Everyone in the city loves me. Where have I wronged Northern Han, wronged Taiyuan, wronged you?"

Zhu Dagun laughed mirthlessly. "Empty words. You look out only for yourself, while I plan for the benefit of a city's worth of people. First, I'll order the East City Institute to stop the defense. Once the fire-dragons, pillars, and catapults have stilled, General Guo Wanchao will open the gates and welcome the Song army in.

"Second, Minister Ma Feng is waiting inside the palace. Once the city gates are open and the army is thrown into panic, he will persuade the ruler Liu Jiyuan to come out with his family and surrender. But I will take the emperor and help him escape in the chaos, aboard the so-called hot air balloon to the Khitan.

"Third, I will bind you and give you to Zhao Guangyi, trading

you for the lives of the city's inhabitants. The Song army has be-
sieged the city for three months without success; the Song ruler
must be filled with hate for you, the inventor of the city's defensive
machines. If I bring you to him bound hand and foot, he is certain
to be greatly relieved and spare Jinyang from the sword. In this way,
I will not fail Guo Wanchao, Liu Jiye, or the emperor, or the people
in danger of terrible suffering. I can achieve both benevolence and
justice!"

Prince Lu gaped. "What kind of crappy plan is that? Whose
faction are you in? You've cut everyone else a sweet deal, but I
get thrown to the wolves, huh? Do you have to be so extreme? Let's
talk it out; everything is open to discussion. All I wanted was to
gather a bit of energy and go home. Does that make me a bad person? Did I do anything wrong? Did I do anything wrong?"

"You did nothing wrong. I did nothing wrong. No one did anything wrong. So whose fault is it?" Zhu Dagun asked.

Old Wang didn't have a chance to come up with an answer to
this profound philosophical question before the dagger hilt struck
his forehead, knocking him unconscious.

11.

Wang Lu slowly regained consciousness, just in time to see the hot
air balloon slowly rise above the roof of the main building of the
East City Institute. The balloon was sewn from one hundred and
twenty-five panels of thick lacquered cotton, with a basket woven
from bamboo. The basket held a fire-oil burner and the heavy pig
iron cannon. Three or four people were squeezed into the basket
in clear disregard of weight capacity, but as the throttle opened and
the flames roared, hot air swelling the balloon, the massive flying
object continued its swaying ascent. The dark brown lacquer
gleamed in the setting sun, the balloon's long shadow stretching
across Jinyang.

"It worked. . . . It worked!" Wang Lu sat right up, laughing skyward. The north wind was blowing, the summer heat dissipating in its chill. Clumps of water-vapor-rich clouds were gathering in the sky, perfect weather for artificially inducing snow. The time traveler watched the balloon as it rose higher and higher into the heavens, muttering, "Not enough not enough not enough, two hundred meters higher and then it can fire, a little more, a little more. . . ."

He tried to stand and find a better angle to observe from, only to realize that he couldn't move his legs. He looked down and discovered that he was tied onto a fire-oil carriage parked in the middle of the road. The driver lay slumped over in his seat, dead. He looked farther and saw that the road was covered in piles of corpses—Han soldiers, Song soldiers, and Jinyang civilians, all dead in a variety of ways. Blood flowed down the roadside ditch, moistening yellow earth that had lain dry for months. Crying, screams, and the sounds of fighting came from the distance, like the roll of thunder on the horizon. And yet Jinyang seemed abnormally still, except for the crows circling and gathering in the sky.

"Fuck, what happened?" Wang Lu yelled, trying to twist free. His hands and feet had been soundly tied; movement made the coarse fibers slice agonizingly into his flesh. The prince let loose a string of curses, panting roughly, afraid to struggle further. At this time, a cavalry troop shot down the street, their armor and uniform marking them as Song. The riders didn't even glance at Wang Lu as their steeds galloped toward the East City Gate, trampling the corpses. A few snatches of conversation lingered in the air.

"We're too late! What do we do if our arrows can't hit it?"

"It's not a south wind, but a north wind. It'll never reach Liao. It'll only be blown southward—"

"Will we be blamed?"

"Otherwise we'd be too late!"

"Hey! What are you doing! Don't leave me here!" Wang Lu yelled wildly. "Tell your master I know physics and chemistry and mechanical engineering! I can build you a steampunk Song Empire! Hey, wait! Don't go! Don't go. . . ."

The hoofbeats faded. Wang Lu looked up despairingly. The hot air balloon was now a small dot high in the sky, drifting southward with the north wind. *Bang.* He saw the puff of white smoke rise a moment before the sound reached him. The cannon had fired.

Wang Lu's eyes filled with the light of his last hope. He wrenched his head down, bit his clothing, and tore it aside, revealing the skin of his chest. A line of light glowed beneath his left collarbone: the fuel gauge for the observational platform. At the moment, it displayed red to indicate low power. The wave function engine required at least thirty percent to carry him back; snow in July would create a universe split that would fill his tank to at least fifty. "Come on." He was crying, bleeding, talking to himself with gritted teeth. "Come on come on come on and give me a big fat blizzard!"

Each gram of silver iodide powder could generate more than ten trillion particles; five kilograms was enough to create all the ice crystals for a blizzard. It seemed ridiculous, that someone could artificially create snow in an era of such low technology, but perhaps the time traveler's crazed prayer had been fulfilled: the clouds began to gather in the sky, roiling, pitch-black and restless, reducing the setting sun behind them to a thread of golden light.

"Come on come on come on!" Wang Lu roared toward the sky.

A rumble of thunder resonated to the horizons. First, rain fell, cold rain mixed with ice crystals. But as the ground temperature continued to drop, the rain became snow. A single snowflake drifted down, landed on the tip of Wang Lu's nose, and instantly melted from his body heat. But right after it came a second, then a third, heralding their quadrillions of compatriots.

The drenched time traveler laughed heavenward. It was a proper blizzard in July, the snow coming down in clumps; he couldn't wait to see the palaces, buildings, willows, and walls painted powder white. Wang Lu looked down and saw the gauge on his chest glowing green. The engine's energy forecast had crossed the baseline; the moment this universe split into two, the observational platform would collect the energy and automatically activate. In a moment too brief to be assigned a unit, it would send him home to his warm

900-square-foot apartment near the Beiyuan neighborhood round-about, Tongzhou District, Beijing.

"This will be legendary," Wang Lu said to himself, shivering. "I'm going to go home, find a less dangerous job, find a wife, squeeze my way onto the subway every day to go to work, and do nothing but play video games when I get home. I've had enough adventure for a lifetime, truly . . ."

At the rate the snow was accumulating, it would have taken less than an hour to bury Jinyang under a yard of white. But right at that moment, twenty dragons of fire rose from the four directions.

From the dozen gates of West, Central, and East City, the fire-dragon chassis were spraying pillars of flame, accompanied by countless pig bladder catapults hurling fireballs. They were weapons of city defense he'd built with his own hands, weapons the Song army had feared more than any other.

"Wait a . . ." The light went out of Wang Lu's eyes. "No, are they burning Jinyang down anyway? At least they could wait a little, until this snow's done. . . . Wait, *wait*—"

Thick, viscous fire-oil sprayed everywhere; flames roared heavenward. The fires spread with a speed beyond anyone's imagination. Jinyang had been long under drought, and the precipitation called by the time traveler hadn't the chance to soak into tinder-dry timbers.

The fire in West City began in Jinyang Palace, engulfing Xiqing Ward, Guande Ward, Fumin Ward, Faxiang Ward, and Lixin Ward in turn in a sea of flames. The fire in Central City set the great waterwheel alight first, then burned west toward Xuanguang Hall, Renshou Hall, Daming Hall, Feiyun House, Deyang Hall. The East City Institute soon transformed into a brilliant torch. The snowflakes whirling above vaporized without a trace before they had a chance to land. The green light on the time traveler's chest faded. He howled his grief and agony, "Motherfucker, I was so close, so close!"

Bathed in fire, Jinyang lit dusk into daytime. The air boiled in the inferno; a scarlet dragon of flame wheeled upward, dispersing the clouds in an eyeblink. No one saw the fallen snow; they only saw flames that touched the heavens. The ancient city, first built in the Spring and Autumn Era, more than one thousand four hundred years before this moment, wailed distantly in the flames.

Jinyang's fortunate survivors were being driven northeast by the Song army, looking back with every step, their weeping loud enough to shake heaven. The Song ruler Zhao Guangyi sat astride his warhorse, gazing at the flames of distant Jinyang and the figures kneeling before him.

He said, "When you've captured the pretend-emperor Liu Jiyuan, come and see me. Do not harm him. Guo Wanchao, I confer upon you the title of Militia Commander of Ci Prefecture. Ma Feng, I name you Supervisor of Imperial Construction. You two have done me service, and I hope you will turn all your ingenuity and wisdom to my Great Song from today onward. Liu Jiye, why do you refuse to surrender when all the others have? Do you not know the parable of the praying mantis who attempted to block the passage of a chariot?"

Liu Jiye, his hands bound, turned to kneel northward. "The ruler of Han has yet to surrender," he said stubbornly. "How can I surrender first?"

Zhao Guangyi laughed. "I've long heard of Liu Jiye of the East Bank. You live up to your reputation. You can surrender once I capture the little emperor. You should revert to your original name of Yang. Why should a Han try to protect a Hu? If you want to fight, you should turn and fight the Khitan, don't you think?"

Having finished talking to these men, Zhao Guangyi rode forward a few steps. He bent down. "What do you have to say?"

Zhu Dagun knelt on the ground, afraid to raise his head. From the corners of his eyes, he could see the raging flames on the horizon. "I claim no accomplishment," he said, shaking. "I only ask that I be judged to have done no trespass."

"Very well." Zhao Guangyi waved his whip. "Posthumously grant him the title Duke of Tancheng, with a fiefdom of thirty miles square. Chop off his head."

"Your Imperial Majesty! What wrong did I commit?" Zhu Dagun

stood up in shock, flinging aside the two soldiers next to him. Four or five more tackled him. The executioner raised his sword.

"You did nothing wrong. I did nothing wrong. No one did anything wrong. Who knows whose fault it is?" said the Song ruler indifferently.

The head rolled to a stop; the large frame thudded to the ground. The copy of *Analects* fell from Zhu Dagun's sleeve pocket and into the puddle of blood, soaking through, until not a single character could be distinguished.

※

Everything the time traveler had created burned to ashes with Jinyang. After a new city was built nearby, people gradually came to think of those days of wonders as an old dream. Only Guo Wanchao would sometimes take out the "Ray-Ban" sunglasses while drinking with Zhao Da in the Ci Prefecture army camp. "If he'd been born in Song, the world would be a completely different place, huh."

The Song conquest of Northern Han received only a brief description in the *History of the Five Dynasties*. One hundred sixty years later, the historian Li Tao at last wrote the great fire of Jinyang into the official histories, but naturally there were no mentions of a time traveler.

> In [979 CE], the emperor visited Taiyuan from the north through Shahe Gate. He dispatched the residents in groups to the new governing city of Bingzhou, setting fire to their homes. Children and the elderly did not reach the city gates in time, and many burned to death.
> —*Extended Continuation of Zizhi Tongjian, Book 20*[20]

20   The original *Zizhi Tongjian* (资治通鉴, meaning "Comprehensive Mirror to Aid in Government") was compiled from prior sources by the Song Dynasty historian Sima Guang to cover Chinese history in chronological format from 403 BCE to 959 CE, the year before the founding of Song. The *Extended Continuation* was written by the later Song Dynasty historian Li Tao in the style of the original, covering the years between 960 and 1127 CE.

ANNA WU

Anna Wu is an author, screenwriter, and translator. She has a master's degree in Chinese Literature, and her original screenplay, *Mist*, won a Xingyun Award. She has a short story collection, *Double Life*, and has been published in *Science Fiction World*, *Galaxy's Edge*, and other places.

Anna lives in Shanghai and works as a screenwriter for a company specializing in science fiction films. She enjoys going to the movies, attending art shows, swimming, and yoga. An avid cook and foodie, she sometimes contributes to food columns. Her favorite writers are Arthur C. Clarke, Neil Gaiman, Robert Sawyer, and J. K. Rowling.

As a result of her graduate studies, she has a deep knowledge of Classical Chinese literature. Currently, she's working on a science fiction novel set in ancient China. The world-building combines China's legendary engineering marvels with modern science, with hints of fantasy and something darker.

"The Restaurant at the End of the Universe: Laba Porridge" is the first of a series of stories all set in this science fictional eatery. Like the namesake dish, it's a mix of many flavors.

THE RESTAURANT
AT THE END OF
THE UNIVERSE:
LABA PORRIDGE[21]

21 Translated by Carmen Yiling Yan and Ken Liu.

At the end of the universe far away, there was a restaurant, and its name was The Restaurant at the End of the Universe. From a distance, it looked like a conch shell spinning silently in the void of space.

The restaurant was sometimes big, and sometimes small. The furnishings inside its walls changed often, as did the view outside its windows. It had a refrigerator that was always full of fresh ingredients; a cooking box that fried, baked, seared, steamed, and everything else; a clock that could regulate the flow of time within a modest area; and a melancholic android waiter named Marvin. A red lantern shone perpetually at the center of the restaurant.

Two people, father and daughter, ran the place. They came from a place called China on a planet called Earth. Going by the *Traveler's Guide to the Milky Way*, the father was an exemplary specimen of the middle-aged Earthling male—perhaps even a few deciles handsomer than the median. He was black-haired and thin, and there was a scar on his left wrist. He didn't talk much, but was well-versed in Earth cuisine. If a customer could name it, he could make it. The daughter, Mo, looked to be eleven or twelve years old. She had black hair too, and big, round eyes.

The nearest space-time hub was a small cargo station, a singularity primarily used for Earth shipping. Of course, as a singularity, only organisms with a civilization rating above 3A—capable of uploading their physical bodies into the network—could use it.

Few guests came. Most hailed from Earth, but there were the matchbox-sized three-body people of Alpha Centauri, too; Titanians with their vast balloon forms, adapted to the atmosphere of Saturn; even dazzling silver Suoyas from the center of the Milky Way, fifty thousand light-years from Earth. Intelligent beings of every shape and size might be seen in this restaurant's blurred concept of time and space: waving their antennae, dribbling their mucus, crackling and sparking their energy fields.

Virtual reality may hold infinities, but wander long enough in it and your soul feels a little lost. Every once in a while, people still want to put on a real body, eat a real meal, and reminisce.

There was a rule for everyone who ate here. You could choose to tell the owner a story; as long as it was interesting enough, your meal was on the house, and the owner would personally cook you a special dish. And you could eat while you thought of the countless civilizations rising and falling, falling and rising, at every instant and in every corner of the universe outside this restaurant, like the births and deaths of the sextillion stars.

LABA PORRIDGE

He's not a regular, Mo thought. *This is probably his first time here.*

Today, the restaurant was furnished for a Chinese winter's night. There were four or five little tables made of rough-hewn wood and three guests sitting at them. The kitchen station was tucked into a corner. A man and a woman sat at the table under the red lantern. The woman looked to be from Earth, maybe a second-generation clone—her legs were unusually long and slim. The man was probably from Venus, with his bulky cranium and deep purple irises.

And there was an Earth man sitting by himself in a corner, mechanically turning the wine cup in his hand. His pale face was devoid of expression, and his temples were gray. The smell of alcohol poured off of him. Today was the Chinese Laba Festival, and the restaurant had accordingly prepared sweet Laba porridge, whose fragrance filled the room. Yet the man hadn't ordered it.

Mo had never seen eyes like his before: empty and dark as a dry well, they reminded her of the eyes of a dead insect.

While the business was still slow, Mo stuffed the menu into Marvin's hand. She waited.

Marvin took the menu and gazed at the falling snow outside the window, sighing. His eyes glimmered blue to indicate melancholy. "They've been dead for centuries. Why do they bother eating anyway?" he muttered, even as he ambled over to the Venusian's table on his short legs.

"Dad, that Earth man should have a good story." Mo slipped into the kitchen station, grinning. It might count as a gift of sorts— give her a group of people, and she could always pick out the one with the best stories at a glance.

Her father paused in his tasks. He stared at a pile of dishes, silent.

His expression was odd: interest, worry, disgust, perhaps even a little fear?

Time went by. The din of the restaurant floated around them as lightly as the snowflakes outside the window.

"Mo, I think you've heard of the Agency of Mysteries."

"All laws are one; all things are eternal," Mo said without thinking. The organization's motto—one Earth language version of it, at least. It was renowned in many eras and many planets. It ignored all interstellar laws and regulations and could provide any service imaginable—but only if your request was entertaining enough to catch its interest. And you couldn't buy its services with money; you had to . . . trade. What you needed to trade was a secret that no client had ever revealed. No one knew who the boss was, either—he was too clever to be caught by the space-time police.

"His name is Ah Chen. He was a client of the Agency of Mysteries."

Slowly, the father began to tell Ah Chen's story.

Ah Chen wrote novels, and he was twenty when his debut, a romance novel, shot him to overnight fame. At the celebratory banquet, his literary peers greeted him with ingratiating praise and admiration well-laced with envy. He was dazzled and drunk by it all the same.

But achieving fame at a young age is not always a good thing. That night, he met an admirer—his future wife, Ci.

Ci came from a renowned family of scholars. She was pretty and frail, but fiercely stubborn. Against her family's protests, she married the penniless Ah Chen. By day, she worked as a maid, washing and scrubbing until her hands were red from the dishwater. By night, she proofread Ah Chen's drafts and helped him with research.

Three years later, the luster of the awards had long since faded, but the muses had not visited Ah Chen again in the duration. Writing was long, hard work, like a marathon run alone in the night, stumbling by touch and three inches of vision. Moods swooped and plunged, joy clawing into sorrow, as if to torment him with rain and snow.

As editors rejected his manuscripts again and again, Ah Chen came to discover his many weaknesses: he lacked the endurance to carry out plots fully, he wanted sufficient delicacy of touch, he was unable to draw from the strengths of other works and unite them in his own. Some of these weaknesses were real; others were only the specters of Ah Chen's insecurity.

He was young and idealistic. He couldn't endure the publishers' contempt; more than that, he couldn't face his own inadequacy. He began to drink, and every bottle of cheap alcohol was bought with Ci's long days and nights of labor.

One winter night, on Laba Festival, Ah Chen came home with the snow falling outside. He saw Ci smiling warmly at him. There was a pot of mixed grain porridge on the table, steaming.

"They say that Laba porridge originated when a rat stole many kinds of grain and hid them in its hole. Then poor people found the store and made it into porridge. . . ."

Suddenly, Ah Chen's ears were ringing as if a clap of thunder had gone off in his head. Ci went on talking, but he was no longer *listening. He heard nothing of her gentle sympathy, her willingness to live in poverty, her resolute lack of regret.*

He rushed into the night, toward the Agency of Mysteries.

For a long time, Ci sat in the lamplight, alone. Her tears fell into that pot of Laba porridge, slowly cooling.

Ah Chen wanted five abilities from five Earth authors. The agency told him that as the universe conserved energy, abilities couldn't be "copied," only "transferred." Perhaps out of his last vestiges of conscience, or out of fear of disrupting his own universe's timeline, Ah Chen requested that his powers be taken from five other universes parallel to his own.

These five people were all the literary stars of their era.

A, a playwright. His output was great in both quality and quantity, and without equal for the next hundred years. Ah Chen wanted his mastery over plot structure.

B, a poet. The beauty and craftsmanship of his verses had won him acclaim as the greatest of poets. Ah Chen wanted his ear for language.

C, a suspense novelist and psychologist. At his peak, his works had triggered heart attacks in his readers. Ah Chen wanted his grasp of human psychology.

D, a science fiction author. His stories were strange, clever things, well-known throughout the galaxies. Ah Chen wanted his imagination.

E, a scholar of the classics and Buddhism. Weighty and thoughtful, his pen laid out the workings of history and the patterns of the world with the clarity of a black ink brush delineating white cloudscapes. Ah Chen wanted his powerful insight.

"Was Ah Chen a friend of yours?" Mo asked.

Her father smiled cryptically. "One of Ah Chen's targets was an alternate universe version of me. But that version of me found out and stopped him."

Mo wanted to ask further, but in the end, she didn't say anything.

Unlike most people, her memories began from only five years ago. She had opened her eyes to find herself lying in a spaceship with a middle-aged man and a big-headed android, fleeing for the ends of the universe. Before that . . . her memories cut off in an explosion of light.

Afterward, she considered the man her father. But he never told Mo what happened before the start of her memories. He never said anything he didn't want to say.

"Still, four abilities is a lot!"

"The universe obeys the laws of conservation. To get something, you have to give in return."

The Agency of Mysteries delivered A's ability first.

That night, Ah Chen felt as if his brain had been ripped out and forced through a red-hot wire mesh. His head seemed to split open. He howled and howled with pain.

Ci, whom he'd kept in the dark, quaked at his screams hard enough to nearly tumble off the bed. That entire night, wrapped in a thin sleeping robe, she kept Ah Chen's forehead and hands covered with hot towels. Watching him clench his hands into the bedsheets and refuse to go to the hospital, she could only stand helplessly at his bedside. Every time Ah Chen screamed, Ci shivered too. She gripped his hands as hard as she could, terrified that he'd hurt himself as he thrashed and struggled.

By the time the sky began to brighten, Ah Chen's face was as pale as paper, and Ci had wept herself empty of tears. Her mind held only one thought: if this man did not survive, she feared that she would not either.

When Ah Chen awoke in the morning, he found that the world in front of his eyes had taken on a sudden, perfect clarity.

Every piece of furniture, every drawer, every item of clothing, every pair of socks in the bedroom—abruptly, he knew where they were, how big, what color, for what purpose. He looked out the window. A group of neighbors were taking a walk in the commons. Behind every face was an identity, an age, and a list of relationships. Yesterday, Ah Chen couldn't even remember their names.

Her husband had awoken, but Ci saw on his face an eerie expression. Half delighted and half worried, she hurriedly put a hand to his forehead to check his temperature. Ah Chen impatiently brushed her hand away and herded her out of the room without a word.

He snatched up a book at random and started reading at the table of contents. His reading speed had increased five or six times. When he was done, he only needed to glance at the table of contents again, and the events of the book seemed to arrange themselves neatly into twigs and branches growing out of a few main trunks. Every knot, every joint was so clear. When Ah Chen closed his eyes, a few inharmonious branches stood out in sharp relief on the tree, and it seemed to only take him a second to realize how to fix these branches, how to fix this book—this book, which had been so praised and so successful in its sales.

Every edit Ah Chen noticed left him a little more breathless, a little more dizzy. Suspicion, amazement, and overpowering joy drove into him like waves in a tempest. He couldn't even wait long enough to boot up his computer. He grabbed a sheaf of paper and started to write.

With his front door locked tightly, he wrote more than a hundred beautiful plot outlines within the week. The beginnings were stunning, the middles fluid, the climaxes brilliantly fitting, the plot arcs graceful. Every one of them could be called a classic. He shook as he stroked his drafts. Now and then he broke into hysterical laughter.

However, in the course of this week, Ah Chen seemed to have caught some sort of obsessive-compulsive disorder. He rearranged all the furniture in his room, measuring each item's location to the millimeter; he sorted his clothes by color and thickness; he stuck a label onto every drawer. Everything had to be perfectly ordered. A single stain or misplaced scrap of paper was enough to scrape his nerves raw.

That week, Ci was forced to sleep in the living room. She would make three meals a day and bring them to the bedroom. One day, as she tiptoed in, she decided she would clean the room. The moment she opened the wardrobe, Ah Chen flew into a rage and slapped her.

A month later, the Agency of Mysteries brought B's ability. Ah Chen's ears became peculiarly sensitive to sounds; they left indelible marks in his mind. When he heard wind, music, thunder, or even the barking of dogs, every syllable seemed imbued with new significance. Poems, essays, haikus, and colorful slang rose from the pages as if given life, linking their hands and dancing, endlessly dancing, passing before his eyes one after the other like little fairies.

He wrote one beautiful poem after the next, but the sublime melody of his verses gave him no peace, not when A's powers of organization and structure howled at him from the darkness, "Order! Order!" while B's power insisted that the beauty of language came from ineffable spontaneity and inspiration. The two masters' mental states fought like storm and tempest, neither willing to bow to the other. Ah Chen felt as if his body had become a gladiatorial arena for his mind. He couldn't sleep; he shivered despite himself.

C's ability followed. What an abyss that was: a million faces, a million personalities, a million stories, a million different kinds of despair. Ah Chen finally understood the price C had paid to be able to write about those twisted souls and those unimaginable plots, the hell he had made of his own spirit. Ah Chen trembled, navigating through the blood, the tears, the white bones and black graves, as if he walked on thin ice; he very nearly fell. Without C's psychological tenacity, Ah Chen approached the precipice of suicide multiple times. Only through hard liquor, which temporarily numbed his brain, could he seek the smallest scrap of solace.

Day after day, tears washed Ci's face, and she soon fell ill. She couldn't understand how the handsome, scholarly, gentle man she loved could turn into a different person in the space of a night. Truth be told, Ci understood from history that the majority of authors' spouses led unhappy lives, enduring both material poverty and their partners' sensitivity, moodiness, and even unfaithfulness. She had understood it even before she married him.

Unfortunately, for many like her, knowledge and reason had never stood a chance before love.

This was all irrelevant. Ci lay in bed, weakly gasping for air. Remembering the slap, she closed her eyes. A tear slowly wended its way into her hair.

One day at dusk, Ah Chen was awoken by a strange voice.

"You thief."

Ah Chen's eyes snapped open. A man's face appeared in his mind, thin and long, its expression not quite a smile.

The face hadn't materialized in front of his eyes, and it wasn't projected onto anything. It had simply floated to the surface of his mind, clear and blurry at the same time. That's hard to explain. It was as if he had one good eye and one injured eye, and was trying to look at the world with both at the same time.

"Steal my imagination? Who do they think they are?" The man laughed.

Ah Chen grabbed wildly in front of his eyes, but caught only air.

"All laws are one; all things are eternal." The man looked at Ah Chen pityingly, slowly blurring into nothingness.

Ah Chen at last woke from his drunken stupor, and found that his vomit had already been cleared away by Ci, and that his blankets were aired and sweet-smelling. The setting sun shone into the room, and clarity seemed to flow into Ah Chen's heart. That was E's ability.

Humanity always reenacts the same bildungsroman. All the principles you learn through your struggles today had been written down by the ancients thousands of years ago.

There is nothing new under the sun.

"You went to such lengths to steal these things, and all for what?"

What have I done? Ah Chen watched countless motes of dust dance in the setting sun's light.

He seemed to see the history of literature slowly distorting in those four parallel universes as the butterfly effect rippled through space-time. *Countless chains of causality broke apart, then joined again; countless people's fates altered with them.*

He felt as if he was looking into each world: publishers' contempt as A seemed to run out of talent; readers mocking B for his clumsy language; E's wife yelling at him for his uselessness. C flogged himself in the dark of night, sobbing in agony.

He'd stolen each of their most precious possessions, and drowned in alcohol, he'd trampled them into the dirt.

At this point, Ah Chen noticed something strange. E's wise, reasonable voice asked him, "Why do you feel no guilt? Why does your heart hold only regret, and not the pain brought on by your sense of responsibility? Why have you lost the ability to love another?"

Love? Ah Chen thought dazedly. What's love?

Oh. He'd traded love away at the Agency of Mysteries.

"Love was the most important thing of them all," E said tranquilly. "Technique and intelligence will let you see through the world, explain it, look down upon it, but they'll never make you a true master of literature. You have to let go of yourself, join yourself to the world without resistance or hate; use love, admiration, and respect to observe all living things, including humanity. This is the true secret of literature."

Ah Chen stood up and opened the door to the dining room. Ci sat at the table, watching over a pot of steaming Laba porridge.

Ah Chen sat down stiffly across from her, like a puppet.

"You should eat a little." For the first time in many days, her eyes held the light and peace of knowledge.

Ah Chen took a mouthful. It was salty, not sweet. He raised his head, looking at Ci's pale face.

"Ah Chen, I don't know where you went the evening of Laba Festival. I don't know why you changed so much. But you must have a good reason for what you did.

"I waited for you the entire night. The porridge from that day, like today's, was salty." Ci forced a smile.

I should say something, Ah Chen thought. In the end, he didn't say anything.

"Ah Chen, I read your manuscripts yesterday, when you weren't looking. They're wonderful. I'm so happy." Ci finally looked as if she were about to cry. Slowly, she took Ah Chen's hand in hers.

"Promise me, you'll keep writing."

Ah Chen was silent for a long time. "For you, I'll keep writing."

Ci slowly smiled. Her eyes shone with the same sweetness as they'd held just after the wedding, but it couldn't hide the grief at the corners of her eyes. The setting sun shone on her pale face, coloring it with a flush for the last time.

Her hand is so cold, *Ah Chen thought.*

"Ci . . . did she . . ." Mo's heart sank.

Her father continued to operate the cooking box slowly.

"Yes, Ci died the next day. Perhaps she saw that the last spark of light in her life—Ah Chen's love for her—was gone.

"Ah Chen lived alone after that, in the constant clash and torment of the powers in his head. You can't go back on a bargain, no matter how much you regret it. He sporadically wrote many bestsellers, won many awards, but he never remarried, never moved out of the house, and never read his own works. The books piled up in the corner of his study and gathered dust."

So her father was a science fiction author. Mo looked at him, her brow furrowed. *How do you know all this? How do you know a version of yourself from another universe? How many things are you hiding from me?*

The cooking box dinged. It was a bowl of Laba porridge.

Maybe it was just the chill from a snowy night, but when her father carried the porridge past her, it seemed to tinge the air with the cool, faint smell of salt.

At the other end of the restaurant, Ah Chen lifted his head. He saw the owner's long, thin face, and his eyes widened.

They conversed.

Mo hurried over to eavesdrop, but heard only their last words: "All laws are one; all things are eternal." She couldn't help but feel disappointed.

Her father turned and made his way back to the kitchen, leaving

Ah Chen sitting stunned at the table. His gaze followed her father's retreating back for a while, then slowly shifted back.

Gradually, a small smile surfaced on his face. There was a hint of desolation in it, as if he were reliving some memory.

In front of him was the bowl of deep reddish-violet Laba porridge, in which black glutinous rice, kidney beans, adzuki beans, peanuts, longan, jujubes, lotus seeds, and walnuts had been cooked until they'd turned slippery and soft, squeezed together like a family. The cool, faint smell of salt wafted from the bowl.

Ah Chen sat like that until the other guests had left one by one. The porridge had finally cooled.

He got up slowly. Mo hurried to open the door for him.

The smile was like the transient flash of a sparkler in the night sky. His eyes were empty again.

Without a glance for Mo, Ah Chen disappeared into the wind and snow.

The clock struck midnight; a gust of cold wind blew in, carrying powdery snow with it.

"Don't you want to know what we talked about?" her father asked slowly as he wiped a plate dry.

"Yeah!" Mo thought of the look in Ah Chen's eyes and shivered despite herself.

"I told him that, a few days later, a certain book will win an award on Earth. It tells the story of a woman's undying love for a man, and the author's name is Zhang Ci. Ah Chen wrote the book based on Ci's diary. I fear it's the last and only work he can write in this lifetime that will give him satisfaction."

MA BOYONG

Ma Boyong is a prolific and popular fiction writer, essayist, lecturer, Internet commentator, and blogger. His work crosses the boundaries of alternative history, historical fiction, *wuxia* (martial arts fantasy), fabulism, and more "core" elements of science fiction and fantasy.

Incisive, funny, and erudite, Ma's works are deeply allusive, featuring surprising and entertaining juxtapositions of traditional elements from Chinese culture and history against contemporary references. The ease with which Ma marshals his encyclopedic knowledge of Chinese history and traditions also makes it a challenge to translate his most interesting works. For example, he has written a thriller set in Tang Dynasty Chang'an that employs the pacing and tropes of a modern American TV show like *24*, as well as two *wuxia* novellas featuring Joan of Arc, in which the tropes and expectations of *wuxia* are mapped to Medieval Europe. These stories are extremely entertaining for the reader with the right cultural context and shed new light on the genres and sources Ma plays with, but would be nigh-impenetrable for a reader in translation without extensive footnotes.

"The First Emperor's Games" starts off with the absurd premise that Qin Shihuang, China's First Emperor, was an avid computer gamer. Once that premise is swallowed, the mapping of Classical Chinese philosophy onto modern video games is wondrous. However, much of the humor of the story depends on knowledge of Chinese Internet culture and ancient Chinese history, so liberal use of Wikipedia may be necessary for some readers.

More of Ma Boyong's work may be found in *Invisible Planets*.

THE FIRST
EMPEROR'S GAMES

From his magnificent throne in the capital, the First Emperor, Qin Shihuang, issued a new edict: "Now that China has been united, I want to play some games!"

The emperor deserved a break. After conquering the other six states, the Qin Empire had successfully carried out multiple complicated reforms: getting everyone to write in the same script, regrading all roads to be the same width, standardizing units of measurement, and promulgating an all-encompassing encoding for all computer text that subsumed the incompatible encodings used by the former warring states. With this Uni-Code in place, citizens of the Qin Empire could confidently launch any program without worrying about conversion plug-ins or screens filled with random glyphs. Moreover, he had constructed a Great Firewall up north, which shielded the empire from all barbarian attacks as well as pop-up ads.

These tasks had taken up decades of the emperor's youth. With the world at peace, he needed to take a long, relaxing vacation and play some games, just like any ordinary citizen.

The news that the emperor was in search of quality games soon spread throughout the land and became the talk of every teahouse and tavern. Most greeted the news with joy because a good gamer made a good administrator. It was said that Zhang Yi, the great Qin strategist who had furthered the emperor's ambition by sowing discord and suspicion among the other six states, thereby dissolving their anti-Qin "vertical alliance," had adapted his line-breaking strategy from Candy Crush—*swipe, match, gone!* Back when Zhang had been a student, he had devoted all his free time to playing games instead of studying. Yet, look how far he had risen! Obviously, playing games taught important management skills.

However, a few nobles expressed reservations. They thought of games as addictive, cheap entertainment suitable only for plebeians. A great leader like the emperor should stay as far away from them as possible. Their suggestion for curing the emperor of this "electronic opium addiction" was electroshock therapy. The emperor soon declared the nobles guilty of attempted treason and sentenced them to capital punishment.

But the news generated the most excitement among the contending philosophers and scholars of the Hundred Schools of Thought. These wonks, obsessed with putting their ideas for better government into practice, understood the weighty implications right away. As the head of such an extensive empire, the emperor's choice of games would inevitably affect his governing philosophy, and that meant a great opportunity for the scholars to persuade the policymaker under the guise of entertainment. Should the emperor become enamored by a philosopher's game, it was likely that the emperor would push for policies evolving society in the direction of the philosopher's sagacious ideas.

Soon, the capital was filled with representatives from philosophy start-ups and development think tanks. They lined up before the palace with demos of their best games, hoping to impress the emperor.

The first to make a presentation was the Legalist school of thought. To be sure, the Legalists had an unfair advantage because their leader, Li Si, was also Chancellor of the Qin Empire. The day after the emperor issued his edict, Chancellor Li approached the throne, a DVD in hand.

(This is, after all, a story from the ancient days, before solid state drives and fast broadband. Appreciate your good fortune as you marvel at how much trouble the ancients had to go through for a game.)

"My dear minister! What have you brought me?" The emperor was dressed in a loose-fitting, colorful shirt, already looking like a relaxed vacationer.

"It's called *Civilization*."

Li Si handed over the DVD—the demo was made in such a hurry that the title of the game had to be written on the back with a permanent marker (albeit in the chancellor's beautiful seal script). A servant took the disc and slid it into a computer whose case was decorated with golden dragons, and gently pressed the "close" button. As the computer hummed, another servant took the opportunity to place an incense brazier next to the cooling fan, and sweet fragrance soon filled the whole great hall.

A third servant carefully wielded the mouse to begin the installation process. The whole hall waited impatiently as the computer fan sped up and hummed louder.

Five minutes later, the installation was complete. A fourth servant placed a mouse and a keyboard—wireless, nothing but the best in the palace—in a sandalwood tray and brought them to the emperor. A fifth servant knelt before the emperor—his robe was made of the same material as mousepads—and presented his broad, flat back to the throne.

Li Si spoke solemnly: "This game contains the essence of Legalism. The player must assume the role of a great leader and rule with ruthless precision. One must keep the big picture in mind without neglecting micromanagement. The emperor's will is also the fate of all NPCs."

"Sounds great!" The emperor picked up the mouse. Naturally, he picked himself as the leader to play on the opening screen.

At first, he did well. From a single city, he expanded to dominate the region. He even successfully won the race for the Pyramids as well as a few other wonders. The Great Wall, as a wonder, was rather useless, but Qin Shihuang rushed to build it anyway.

After that, he went to war. The "Chinese Civilization," under the leadership of Qin Shihuang, was extremely aggressive. The emperor could not stomach the sight of any city on the map not under his rule. Starting from the Stone Age, he invested most of his resources in military units and was constantly at war. He was having a great time as the game reminded him of his own years of conquest.

But soon, he found the game less than enjoyable. The result of being so aggressive in the early game was that every other civilization viewed him as the enemy. He had no choice but to devote all his resources to military units and buildings. Cities rioted all over the map, protesting high taxes, lack of space, and the constant wars. The fire of rebellion swept the empire.

"Your Imperial Majesty," Li Si broke in. He coughed and tried to make his voice as soothing as possible. "It would be helpful to pay attention to the happiness levels of the citizens in the cities. A few city improvements to promote entertainment may be necessary. Remember, micromanagement. Micro."

Qin Shihuang brushed this advice aside. He was the emperor! How could he possibly be expected to lower himself to worry about the happiness of some plebeians in a game?

"They are supposed to entertain me, not the other way around." The emperor adjusted the entertainment expenditure slider all the way to zero, and then sacrificed a citizen to rush a catapult. "The people in the game are *also* my subjects. They should be glad to be sacrificed for the good of the empire!"

Predictably, this kind of policy did not improve his position. Soon, plagued by invasion and rebellion, his empire collapsed. Angrily, he terminated the game, clicking the mouse so forcefully that the mousepad servant trembled.

Luckily, Li Si had had the foresight to eliminate the feature of the game that evaluated the player's performance against historical world leaders. Otherwise, it was likely that the emperor would have terminated more than the game.

Wiping the cold sweat from his brow, Chancellor Li backed away from the emperor. He had thought the emperor might choose the Emperor difficulty setting; instead, the emperor had picked Deity without hesitation. Well, that was a glimpse into Qin Shihuang's character.

The next presentation came from Kong Fu, the ninth-generation descendant of Confucius himself and the leader of the Confucians. The game he demoed was called *The Sims*.

"This game has its origins in the ancient Zhou Dynasty, and we're the only ones to revive it," said Kong Fu proudly. The fact that the Confucians had inherited the uncorrupted source code of the Zhou Dynasty was something the entire school took enormous pride in, including the great sage Confucius himself.

"How do I play this?" asked the emperor. He had no interest in history, but he was rather curious about the game.

"Your Imperial Majesty, first, you must create a character, and then guide him through a simulated world. There, he must follow the rituals and enact the rites of Confucianism to give his life meaning. For example, you must visit your neighbors often to increase their friendliness toward you. As the Great Sage himself said, 'Broaden the respect you have for your own aged parents to the parents of others; expand the love you have for your own children to the children of others.' The heart of this game is the strengthening of social ties. . . ."

The lecture bored the emperor. If he weren't on vacation, he would have long ago called for soldiers to drag this pedant out. But he was supposed to be having fun, so he forced himself to endure the long tutorial. Finally, Kong Fu relinquished the mouse.

The emperor wanted to dig a swimming pool, but the game informed him that he didn't have the necessary funds.

"What a joke," the emperor muttered. "I possess the whole empire. Are you telling me I can't afford to dig a hole in the ground?"

"As the emperor, you are the role model for all your subjects," said Kong Fu. "Living a simple and frugal life is the right path. Spending so much on luxuries will lead to bankruptcy."

"Why aren't my neighbors coming to my house to honor me?" demanded the emperor.

"You have to visit them often and shower them with gifts to

gradually bring up the level of your relationship. Only then will they come visit you. The game teaches us the importance of kindness and mutual respect, as the Great Sage—"

"Ridiculous!"

The emperor could barely contain his rage. He was the emperor, and everyone else was his subject. Who ever heard of the mighty emperor having to bribe some barbaric tribe with gifts so they'd come to pay their respects? What an insult!

The game was most definitely treasonous.

During the next month, the Qin Empire struck hard at the sale and manufacture of treasonous Confucian games. Thousands of illegal DVDs were confiscated from across the land, and more than four hundred game dealers were arrested. Under the emperor's direction, soldiers dug a giant pit in the ground—not unlike a swimming pool—and the DVDs and game dealers were tossed into the pit and lit on fire.

The third presenter was the leader of the Mohists. Right away, he said to the emperor, "We Mohists are pacifists. We don't advocate war and aggression. Thus, we brought a tower defense game. All you have to do is defend, defend, and defend some more."

The computer screen showed a group of zombies on one side and some plants on the other.

"What are these zombies doing here?" asked the emperor.

"They're the enemies of the empire."

"What about these weeds and flowers?"

"They're the empire's most loyal guardians."

Surprisingly, the emperor had a lot of fun—he loved the sight of the corpses of his enemies strewn across the lawn. He did find it rather annoying that he had to wait passively for waves of zombies to approach, instead of actively dispatching a punitive expeditionary garden into the zombie homeland.

"That is correct, Your Imperial Majesty. We don't need to attack at all. When the enemy realizes that it's impossible to conquer us, they will stop, and war will end."

The Mohist was pleased with his progress. It appeared that the emperor was close to being persuaded.

Qin Shihuang nodded at this explanation, but his gaze was glued to the screen as his finger clicked the mouse feverishly. The Cob Cannons and Gatling Peas demonstrated their fierce firepower as zombie after zombie turned to dust.

Five hours later, the emperor's eyes were bloodshot and his face twitched. Several different servants had to take turns performing mousepad duty.

But the zombies showed no signs of relenting. For just one moment, the emperor's concentration lapsed, and a small zombie rushed over and ate a few Winter Melons. The defenses of the empire collapsed.

"Fraud! You're a fraud!" The emperor tossed away the mouse and rubbed his sore wrist. "You told me that a perfect defense will stop the enemy. But I have already gone through six hundred waves of attacks! Why are they still coming?"

"That . . . that is because you chose infinity mode."

"I think you Mohists are a bunch of naive fools who know nothing about the bloody reality of the world."

The emperor summoned his guards to chase the Mohist away—but he did remember to go to the garden and water all the plants.

As the days passed by, school after school came to present their best games to the emperor. The School of the Military brought *Call of Duty*; the Agriculturalists brought *Harvest Moon*; the School of Names (also known as the Logicians) brought *Ace Attorney*; and the School of Yin-yang came up with something called *The Legend of Sword and Fairy*. But all the games failed after a single test-play by the emperor. Nobody could figure out what the august sovereign would enjoy.

Meanwhile, something else happened that seized everyone's attention. Because he couldn't find a game that truly pleased him, the emperor decided to take his carriage and go on a sightseeing tour. When his procession passed through a place called Bolangsha, a giant iron hammer fell out of the sky and crushed a decoy carriage. The emperor, enraged, vowed to find the assassin and punish him severely.

At first, the investigation went nowhere. It was only after the emperor had executed three chief investigators that the fourth official assigned to the task managed to discover some clues. Based on the trajectory of the hammer, the impact crater, and the scatter pattern of the debris from the decoy carriage, he deduced that the assassin had to be a skilled player of *Angry Birds*.

Not that many people could afford a phone capable of playing this game—remember this was a long time ago—and the narrowed list of suspects soon led the investigation to a young man named Zhang Liang. However, Zhang managed to prove his innocence against the prosecution. As a native of Han State before the unification, he claimed that he was thus by association a person from Hanguk, or Korean. And as all gamers knew, Korean players dominated *StarCraft*, a feat impossible without lots of dedicated practice. Thus, he couldn't possibly have spared any time to waste on *Angry Birds*. The logic was really unassailable, when you thought about it.

Just when the whole empire was stunned by this courtroom turnabout, a Westerner named Xu Fu came to save the day.

Blond-haired and blue-eyed, Xu Fu came to see the emperor in a crisp new suit and well-polished shoes, looking like an iconic member of the global elite.

"What game have you brought me?" asked the emperor. He saw that Xu Fu was carrying a tiny thumb drive.

"Something that you have never, ever, ever, ever seen. It's absolutely amazing."

Xu Fu stuck the thumb drive into the emperor's computer, opened a PowerPoint slide deck, and gave a polished presentation.

"But these are just slides," said the emperor. "Where's the game?"

"Your Imperial Majesty, a state focused solely on immediate, tangible benefits will not flourish for long. We must look far beyond the horizon and invest in the future to ensure lasting prosperity."

"What are you getting at?"

"The game I'm presenting to you is a peerless work of genius. However, it's still under development on the vapor-shrouded island of Penglai. Now, if Your Imperial Majesty would be willing to invest a small amount of venture capital to kickstart the process, I guarantee that within a year we'll have a beta version, and in three years we'll be on the market. As I've shown in the PowerPoint, this is an incredible opportunity: low risk and high reward."

"But . . ." The emperor hesitated. Xu Fu's speech was tempting, but it felt wrong to hand over money without getting a game back. Everyone else had shown up with finished products.

"Indecision is not a trait great leaders should cultivate," intoned Xu Fu. "An opportunity like this may be gone the very next moment."

Qin Shihuang was finally convinced. He prepared a fleet to sail for Penglai Island, laden with treasures that represented his investment in the game. Xu Fu promised that he would return in one to three years with the best game in the universe for the emperor.

"I await your good news!" the emperor called from the wharf.

Xu Fu showed his gleaming teeth and waved vigorously from his ship. "No problem! You can trust me!"

As the ships disappeared below the horizon, the emperor suddenly realized that Xu Fu had never told him the name of the game. He turned to his trusted advisor Zhao Gao. "Did Mr. Xu ever mention to you the name of this vapor-shrouded game?"

Zhao Gao said, "No. But . . . I did steal a look at his laptop."

"So what is the name? Tell me!"

"Let me see . . . Ah, I have it. It's called *The* Real *Duke Nukem Forever*."

"What a great name!" said the emperor, sighing as his mind filled with glorious visions. "I can't wait to play it."

GU SHI

Gu Shi is a speculative fiction writer and an urban planner. A graduate of Shanghai's Tongji University, she obtained her master's degree in urban planning from the China Academy of Urban Planning and Design. Since 2012, she has been working as a researcher at the academy's Urban Design Institute.

Ms. Gu has been publishing fiction since 2011 in markets like *Super Nice*, *Science Fiction World*, *Mystery World*, and *SF King*. Notable works include "Chimera," "Memory of Time," and "Reflection." In 2014, she won the Silver Xingyun Award for Best New Writer. In translation, her work may be found at *Clarkesworld*. Currently, she's working on her first novel, *The Reign of Eternal Delight*, an alternate history set in the court of an empress ruling in the dynasty founded by Wu Zetian, the first Chinese empress.

"Reflection" is an experiment in form as well as narrative technique, but its themes may be found in the oldest tales of our species.

REFLECTION

1.

CLAIRVOYANT

Mark was a very special person—when he told me that he was going to take me to see a clairvoyant, I wasn't too surprised.

"But you are a scientist!" I couldn't help pointing out.

"That doesn't mean I worship science." My expression made him laugh, so he added by way of explanation, "It's like how a butcher doesn't worship pork."

I chuckled. This is what made Mark special. He was an interesting person, and he always took me to see interesting people.

※

"Remember to be polite when you meet her." We were standing in front of an ordinary apartment building. Mark looked reverential, a rare expression for him. "She cares about that."

A bit uneasy, I followed him up the stairs, trying to imagine what a clairvoyant would look like. The light in the stairwell brightened and dimmed as we wound our way up, and the air was redolent of dust. . . . This was not where I envisioned finding a clairvoyant.

He stopped at the top of the staircase—a second later, the door opened. I saw a slender girl whose face was tender and kind.

Yes, a *girl*, maybe fourteen years of age. Her hands and feet were thinner and more elongated compared to an adult's. She was dressed in a black leotard and a pair of black tights, and her pale neck rose like a stalk, topped by a round, childish face. But contrary to her general appearance, her gaze was sharp and tolerant, like an old woman's.

"Ed! You're here!" She wrapped me in a tight hug as though we were old friends who hadn't seen each other in ages. Abruptly, she let me go, took two steps back, and gracefully nodded. "I'm sorry—I forgot that we don't know each other yet."

I wasn't sure what was going on. How did she know my name? Admiringly, Mark said, "I'm so glad you know Ed Lin already. I was worried about disturbing you with a stranger."

"It's good that you brought him. Thank you." She hesitated, as if trying to recall something. ". . . Mark?"

"That's right!" Mark's grin was exaggerated. "You remember me!"

She smiled and gestured for us to come in. "Ed, I prepared your favorite chai."

※

Her home was as unusual as her person. The bed was filled with books, while her desk was covered with snack trays and a tea set. The round dining table's legs had been sawed off, and the top was then covered with a variety of cushions. The eccentric furnishings appeared odd at first, but gave off a sense of comforting familiarity after a while.

"It's too messy," she said apologetically. Then she muttered to herself, "What was I doing?" Turning to me, she smiled and indicated the cushioned dining table. "Please have a seat."

I sat down on the table gingerly while Mark remained standing. I was amused by his hesitancy. Mark was forty-three, with dual doctorates in molecular biology and psychology, and had just been granted tenure. He had always strutted around with a swagger, like an energetic crab—oh, he had been my dissertation advisor, too. But in front of this girl he appeared as awkward and deferential as a kid in elementary school. She poured a cup of chai for me and brought it over.

She stopped and stared at Mark suspiciously. "Who are you? When did you get in here?"

"Just now—"

"No!" Her voice was shrill. Then she turned to me and asked in a much softer voice, "Ed, who is he? Why is he here?"

I was utterly baffled. "Um . . . Mark brought me here. . . ."

"Oh, so it's Mark." She seemed at ease again. "Thank you," she said to him.

Mark scratched his head, embarrassed. "No problem. I came to ask you—"

"I can't answer your question." She handed the chai to me. "I don't know your daughter's test score."

"Right, that's why I came." Mark looked even more anxious than before. "Her grades are dropping. . . . Is there anything I can do?"

"How can I possibly know the answer to that?"

"Because you're a clairvoyant. You can see the future."

She frowned, an expression that mixed youthful arrogance with aged authority. "Fine. What kind of work do you do?"

"I'm a scientist."

"All right, Mr. Scientist, tell me: what is the principle behind warp drives?"

"That . . . ah . . ."

Mark's face turned red.

"Just as you can't tell me what I want to know about science, I can't tell you—"

I started to laugh at her retort when she cried out, "Watch the cup!"

The scalding hot liquid spilled out of the cup onto my hand as I shook from laughing. I winced from the pain.

She took the cup from me in a hurry, muttering, "I'm so sorry. I should have reminded you."

She blew on my hand, her expression focused and tender.

"Have we met before?" I asked, even more confused than before.

She paused for a moment. "We will."

2.
THE INTERVIEW

After graduation, I didn't want to pursue a career in science; instead, I became a reporter. I wanted my life to always be filled with the new and exciting. The clairvoyant didn't strike me as particularly interesting, other than the fact that she made Mark behave like a mouse in front of a cat. The episode soon faded in my memories.

One day, three years later, the editor in chief summoned me into his office.

"Lin, I have an assignment for you." He handed me a slip of paper. "They call her the greatest psychic of this century."

I recognized the address. "The greatest psychic?"

"Look at her record: the World Cup, the US presidential election, the South American earthquake, and so on. She predicted the result perfectly every time. Oh, and look at this, a Weibo post she made the day before yesterday: 'Blood and fire tomorrow at 4:00 p.m.'"

I shuddered. The words were probably a bit too obscure two days earlier, but now it was clear that they were about the plane crash yesterday.

Even the hour was exactly right.

"She never talks to the media. However . . ." The editor paused deliberately. "When I sent her an email query, she agreed to talk to us immediately, provided that we send you."

I was thrilled. "Did she say why?"

He shook his head. "Maybe she's interested in you."

I laughed. "I'm going to demand better treatment around here. Maybe I'm going to be the president someday."

He squinted. "Even if you're the president, I'm still going to hold you to your deadlines."

※

Once again, I stood in front of the building. I was feeling slightly nostalgic for that younger version of myself when a window above me opened.

"Ed!" she called out.

I was pleased by the familiarity in her voice. It calmed me.

She was still living by herself, and a delicious-smelling pot of soup was simmering on the stove. She was taller than I remembered, and more filled out. I was amazed that I remembered her so clearly. Her room had been rearranged, though the furniture remained eccentrically familiar. I sat down and got up again. "I'm here for work."

She grinned. "Grab your list of questions then."

I took out my notepad. It was my habit to draft an outline of questions ahead of time. Apparently, she had foreseen it.

She glanced at the list and turned to rummaging in the pile of books on her bed. Returning, she handed me a sheet of paper. "I remember them well. These should do it."

I read the sheet, growing more astonished with each sentence. She had written out answers to every question I was going to ask.

"How did you know what I was going to ask?"

"Have you forgotten my profession?"

It was a most impressive demonstration.

"You're only allowed to quote from that sheet," she added.

I read the answers with more care. She had been cautious and meticulous, phrasing everything in a way that was ambiguous. The answers seemed to at once say everything and nothing.

"You can't expect me to write a profile with so little—"

"They're more than enough for your article." Her tone brooked no disagreement.

I looked at her helplessly. "Are you telling me to leave?"

"Well . . ." She smiled. "You can stay if you promise that everything we say from this point on is off the record."

"I promise."

"Swear by the name of your father." She raised a hand solemnly.

I almost laughed. But I held up my hand and copied her. "I swear by the name of my father."

She laughed. "I know you'll keep your word, Ed. But I needed you to say it."

"Why?"

"Although the future cannot be changed, I'm still terrified . . . ," she said, handing me a steaming cup.

I could make no sense of her non sequitur. Sitting down, I tried to make myself comfortable and took a sip. The chai was sweet and just the right temperature. "It's delicious."

She smiled with satisfaction. "I know."

"Since you can see the future, you must already know what I want to ask you."

"True. But you should still ask the questions so that we can have a conversation." She sat down and looked into my eyes. "It's better to follow the custom."

"Fine. Can you tell me how you tell the future?"

She took a sip from her cup. Instead of answering me directly, she asked, "Is this the first time we've met?"

"Of course not."

"But I don't remember ever seeing you."

"You don't?" I felt oddly disappointed. "Mark brought me here."

"I don't remember him at all," she said. "I guess that means I'll never see him again."

I couldn't make sense of this. "What?"

"I don't know how to explain this—" She picked up my notepad. "All right, let's suppose that this notebook represents a lifetime."

I waited patiently while she collected her thoughts.

She flipped to the page with my interview questions. "This is today, right now, this moment." Then she turned to the first page of the notepad. "This is the moment of birth, the past."

I could see where she was going. She turned to the last page. "This is death, the future. Most people fill the notepad from front to back. Every page after today is blank. It's possible to recall the past, but impossible to know the future." She flipped the notepad over so that the stiff backing was on top. "I'm different. I fill my notepad from the back to the front. My memories are filled with the future. For me, remembering what will happen tomorrow is like you recalling what happened yesterday."

She paused and took another sip of chai.

I stared at the notepad, stunned. I couldn't accept her explanation.

"Your predictions are . . . your memories?"

"That's right. All the predictions are in my mind. The closer to the present, the clearer they become. Similarly, the past that you recall is the unknown future for me."

"Are you saying"—I licked my lips—"that you've forgotten the past?"

"Yes."

"Then . . ." I struggled to find a logical flaw in her words. "If you've forgotten what has happened, how can you possibly converse with me? How can you even remember what I asked you?"

"The immediate past and future are both deducible from the present," she said. "Look, you can predict that my soup will be ready soon; you can foretell where you'll sleep tonight; you know that I will answer your questions; indeed, sometimes you can even anticipate my answers. That is also how I can guess what you've just asked me."

"But . . . but your answers are beyond my guesses." I held up my hands and gestured wildly to show my confusion and amazement.

She continued in a patient tone. "You have to understand that as the only one living against the stream of time among you, I must dedicate myself to the art of how to converse with you. I have to deduce and guess what you said every moment of every conversation. You don't need to learn a comparable skill."

"So you really don't remember the last time we met?"

"I don't remember that we've seen each other, but I know we will meet again."

※

Oddly, her answer calmed me. She didn't ask me to stay for dinner, and so I missed the sweet, fragrant pumpkin soup. I wrote the profile at home. It was easy with her predrafted answers.

I closed my laptop and gave Mark a call.

He sounded pleased. "You saw her again?"

I told him about our meeting, including the source of her predictions. Mark grew excited. "She predicts the future from her memories? Fascinating!"

I didn't share his enthusiasm. "Don't you understand? If what she told me is true, then the future is unchangeable. Everything we do is wasted effort. How can you not despair at such a world?"

"So what are you going to do?" That was always Mark's style: teaching by asking us to find the answers ourselves.

"I choose to not believe in such a world."

3.
THE FIRST MEETING

After that, I visited her often, and grew more familiar with her home. She always greeted me like an old friend, which made me happy, as I knew that meant we would continue to see each other. I rarely asked her about the future, not even my own—so long as I got to see her, what did it matter?

※

Though she lived alone, she didn't know how to take care of herself well. One weekend, I helped her rearrange things to be more comfortable, and she gladly accepted my help. To thank me, she cooked a meal of my favorite dishes: chicken curry, stir-fried broccoli and beans, and plenty of white rice. I wolfed down everything, sat down on the sofa, and picked up the cup of chai she specifically brewed to my taste. She sat next to me and leaned her head on my shoulder like a cat.

My mistake was taking this gesture as a hint.

Before my hands had even moved, she jerked away. Her gaze was slightly frightened. "Why?"

She never asked questions like "What are you trying to do?" She knew.

"I thought you wanted me," I said.

"No!" My heart clenched at the certainty in her tone. "I meant . . . I want you, but not the way you're thinking."

"Why?" We seemed to be always asking each other this question.

"Because we won't be together. It's impossible. Because—" She stopped, her eyes wide open. Then she went on, emphasizing each syllable. "I. Can't. We. Can't."

A surge of helpless anger. "You have to give me a reason."

"Ed . . ." She looked at me and did not continue.

"Why not?" I wouldn't let it go.

She sighed and sat back on the sofa. "Because . . . because I can't remember the past. Don't you understand? I'm seeing you for the first time in my life right now."

A perpetual first meeting.

The hair on the back of my neck stood up. There was a light in her eyes I had not seen before—unfamiliarity.

She frowned. "Why are you here?"

It was the same expression she had worn years ago when she asked the same question about Mark.

"I came to see you." My voice faded, panic growing in the pit of my stomach.

"Why did you come to see me?" she asked, her voice guarded.

"To talk . . . To have tea."

"You will never come again," she said with absolute certainty.

※

I tried to contact her several times more, but she wouldn't return emails or phone calls. Even her Weibo stopped being updated. I went to her apartment, but there was a FOR RENT sign. I realized that I had so many questions to ask her, though, as she had said, every question had a predictable answer. Sometimes I hallucinated conversing with her, only to realize that I was talking to myself.

My days were a chaotic, unmemorable mess. I asked the editor in chief whether he knew where she was, but he wouldn't answer me, only looking at me with a pitying expression. Finally, I had to go back to the university to find Mark.

After listening to my account, he asked, "Lin, what questions did you ask yourself? What answers did you get?"

"I just want to know where she is!" I was impatient.

"If you can't answer my questions, I can't help you." He looked regretful.

This was, if I recall correctly, the first argument we had. He had always been solicitous of me, despite the fact that I wasn't an outstanding student, and my dissertation was undistinguished. He, on the other hand, was one of the most sought-after advisors in the department.

"Lin, everyone's future is in their heart," he said. "I'm sorry you lost her."

Lost? I didn't know what he meant.

I needed her. That was the only thought in my mind. The thought wouldn't leave me alone, and it was driving me crazy. I needed her; I had to see her; I *must* see her. . . .

I felt dizzy, and Mark steadied me. "I think you need help."

"I have to see her . . . ," I whispered.

He helped me down on a lounge chair. "You need to rest."

His words seemed to cast a spell over me, and I felt exhausted. "You need to sleep," he said.

I closed my eyes. In my dream, I sought her in a mirror maze.

Everywhere I saw my own reflection, but I couldn't see the person I needed.

I want to ask her . . .

"What is it?"

My eyes snapped open. I was sitting in Mark's office. She was sitting across from me. Older. Beautiful.

"What do you want to ask me?" she repeated.

Mark wasn't around. Where had she come from?

"Where's Mark? Did he bring you?" I demanded.

"I don't know who you're talking about." Her gaze was as tender as before. "How are you, Ed? I thought you were doing well."

"I'm fine." My voice cracked. "Before you showed up in my life—before you left me, I was always fine."

"I thought you no longer needed me." She looked away.

"I *do* need you. I've been thinking about you every moment."

"Me too." Her eyes were wet.

"Be with me then," I begged.

"No."

"Why?"

She shook her head. "No. Although I've forgotten the past, I remember one thing."

"What is it?"

"You'll know."

"Damn it! What is this thing that makes you so certain we can't be together? Tell me!"

"You'll find out soon." She pointed at Mark's desk. "The answer is there."

4.

THE OMNISCIENT

I jumped up and rushed over. A lab notebook lay on the desk. *The Omniscient.*

I didn't know this was something Mark was studying.

With a trace of guilt, I opened the notebook.

I'm interested in psychological phenomena that cannot be explained by existing scientific theories. Omniscience in the narrow sense I use the word here is rooted in the proposition that the experience of moving through time from the past to the future is an illusion. Our memories are deceitful because the past and the future coexist in our minds, although the future has been veiled away. The omniscient are those who possess memories of both the past and the future.

I've been looking for someone truly omniscient, or a way to trigger omniscience in a subject. The work has been difficult. Most clairvoyants turned out to be frauds.

Until I met Lin.

I looked up. She was gone.

But her voice seemed to linger in my head. *The answer is there.*

I flipped to the next page.

Lin never knew that he had another personality. But I was lucky enough to meet her, though she never warmed up to me.

To be clear, I never "saw" her. I could only see Lin, and she lived inside his body. I had been under the impression that the clairvoyant was a man until I took Lin to his childhood home (perhaps that was a mistake), where Lin saw her and told me that she was a girl.

I listened to their conversation. Strictly speaking, it was Lin talking to himself. I couldn't record that conversation in any way, since the clairvoyant personality was extremely distrustful of me.

I knew that I shouldn't interfere in their relationship, but Lin had become mired in an emotional trap. It was impossible for him to fall in love with himself, though she was a completely distinct personality.

I couldn't move or speak. Mark was saying that . . . she was me.

She and I were the same person.

I was the clairvoyant.

How was that possible? Had she always been a mere hallucination?

Scenes from the past flashed before my eyes in a montage: the familiar smell of her home; her demand that I interview her; her knowledge of my preferences.... Yes, if Mark's daughter's grades were not within her realm of knowledge, why should everything having to do with me be in her ken? Also, after I ate the food she had made, she had looked so satisfied....

A terrifying chill crawled up my spine. I was a drowning man, and the lab notebook the only piece of driftwood within reach. I flipped through it quickly, though many pages had been torn out. I came to the last page.

As the only known instance of omniscience, Lin proved that the condition was possible—though he exhibited it in an unforeseen manner. True multiple personalities were very rare, and often were associated with extreme trauma. I am thus led to speculate that being omniscient is a condition of great terror and pain, and Lin reacted by splitting himself into two parts: a man who seemed normal, and a woman who predicted the future.

If possible, I would like to interview Lin's family to find out if in his childhood, before the development of the clairvoyant personality, he had exhibited any unusual behaviors. Unfortunately, Lin was an orphan whose parents had died when he was eight in a car accident. He then grew up in a series of foster families who all agreed that there was nothing unusual about him that they could remember.

5.

REFLECTION

My eyes stared at the last page, frozen.

The page turned into a massive stone tied to my feet, dragging me into the murky depths where I couldn't breathe.

I remembered that familiar building. The apartment at the top was always filled with the fragrance of spicy chai and pumpkin soup.

I was eight.

I told Mom and Dad, *Don't go!*

I knew about the accident. I knew they were going to die.

I cried, begged, screamed, threw things on the floor. I tried to cut myself.

They thought I was throwing a tantrum.

They locked me in my room. Their footsteps faded, and never returned.

I knew what had happened. They were dead.

I gazed at myself in the mirror. *This is your fault.*

The reflection gradually changed. It turned into a little baby with wriggling arms and legs.

She was the clairvoyant. She could see the future, but she was unable to alter it. She had once been me, but she would be me no longer.

I told her, *They died because of you. I hate you.*

Although she looked like a baby, she could talk. She reached out, trying to grab my hand.

Ed!

I smashed the mirror. I lay down on the bed and closed my eyes.

I didn't want to see her. I didn't want to hear her.

I knew that tomorrow everything would be better.

Everything would be better.

REGINA KANYU WANG

Regina Kanyu Wang, a science fiction writer from Shanghai, China, has won multiple Chinese Nebula Awards for her writing as well as for her contributions to fandom. She is the cofounder of SF AppleCore and a council member of the World Chinese Science Fiction Association (WCSFA).

Regina has traveled widely in Europe and the US, introducing Chinese SF to international fans and pioneering links between Chinese fan groups and counterparts in other parts of the world. She has been a key member of multiple conventions across the globe (in fact, she has been officially adopted by Finnish SF fandom).

Her short story "Back to Myan" won the SF Comet competition in 2015. *Of Cloud and Mist,* a novella, won the Silver Xingyun Award for Best Novella in 2016.

Besides her fiction, which may be found in venues like *Science Fiction World, Mengya, Bund-pic, Numéro,* and *Elleman,* she is also the author of a book on traditional Shanghainese cuisine. Occasionally, she blogs in English about Chinese SF fandom and other topics at *Amazing Stories Magazine.*

Currently, Regina is the international PR manager for Storycom, a

Chinese company focused on turning speculative fiction stories into movies, games, comics, and other media.

"The Brain Box" is a short, sharp examination of the way we construct the narratives of our lives that end up constricting us.

THE BRAIN BOX

1.

"Mr. Fang, let's just go over the consent form one last time, all right? With the understanding that the technology involved is still experimental; that—"

"Yes."

"I'm sorry, Mr. Fang, but please wait until I've finished reading the whole statement before answering 'Yes, I consent' or 'No, I do not.' The protocol requires it be done this way. Now, where were we . . . oh, right—that we cannot ascertain the full range of potential effects of imprinting into another brain the brain patterns of a person on the verge of death; that possible effects could include, but are not limited to, damage to the target brain, disorientation due to conflicting mental patterns, rejection of imprinted thoughts by the target brain. . . .

"Do you still, after understanding the above risks, voluntarily consent to be imprinted with the data retrieved from Ms. Zhao Lin's brain box, to bear all consequences of the experiment, and to cooperate with the investigative team in preparing a report?"

"Yes, I consent."

"Great. We've authenticated your voice signature. Please lie down here, and place your neck right on the notch at the head of the bed. . . . Perfect, exactly so. We're ready to begin."

Fang Rui closed his eyes. Zhao Lin's face appeared in his mind, and his heart spasmed with pain as he recalled the funeral. *No, not now.* He opened his eyes resolutely, taking in the white walls, white lab coats, and bright white lights of the room. They were taping electrodes to his body, and any abnormal physiological reactions would show up in the waveforms sweeping across the screens. He had to stay calm and let the experiment proceed.

This was his last chance to be close to Zhao Lin, his beloved. She was his everything, the light of his life. He wouldn't be able to forgive himself if he missed the final five minutes of her life.

The technicians inserted his left ring finger into the pulse oximeter, planted the oxygen mask over his face, secured the blood pressure monitor against his left arm, and finally placed the metal helmet over his head.

The implantation process began.

2.

Free fall.

Burning odor.

Smoke and fire sweeping forward from the tail of the plane. Screams punctuated with muttered prayers.

I'm so calm as I grab the dangling oxygen mask and secure it over my nose and mouth that I surprise myself. I'm going to die. Now that I've accepted this undeniable reality, terror and anxiety recede. There's nothing I can do to change my fate.

It's time to let go.

How many minutes do I have left? The capacity of the brain pattern recorder is only five minutes, and it functions as a ring buffer, overwriting old data with new. In the same way that a plane's black box preserves the flight parameters, instrument readings, and cockpit conversation before a crash, the brain box preserves my brain activities before death.

Only another human brain can decode the patterns in the

recorder. Theoretically, it will be possible to reproduce my final thoughts. No brain box has been successfully decoded so far—but that's because everyone with such an implant is still alive. I'll be the first to die.

Most people who've agreed to have brain boxes implanted are young and healthy, still luxuriating in their sense of an unbounded future. Seems illogical, doesn't it? The ideal experimental subject ought to be someone who can already feel the chill of death so that useful data can be quickly retrieved. But for the dying, the pitiful monthly stipend for participating in the trial holds little attraction. And in any event, the desire to disguise our thoughts, to appear better than we really are, hounds most of us. Only the young can be reckless enough to accept the prospect of revealing to the world the nakedness of their thoughts, secure in the belief that the moment of reckoning will not come until decades in the future.

I admit it: I only agreed to be part of the experiment for the money. Fang Rui and I were making too little to satisfy the yawning maw of our mortgage and other expenses, and I thought every little bit helped. But I never could have anticipated that the brain box would lead me to doubt.

Did other subjects experience the same thing? Did the presence of the brain box force them also to start lying to themselves? On the brink of death, does the fear of exposure outweigh the fear of death itself? Such tangled thoughts! If these are truly the last five minutes of my life, whoever ends up having to decode my box will surely have a headache.

"A rationalist to the last," they might say.

Fang Rui said the same thing. After the initial ardor of our romance had cooled, I quickly returned to my analytical approach to life, but he seemed to continue to be driven by sentiment more than sense. After dating for three years, we moved in together, bought a new apartment in the suburbs as an investment, and rented a smaller place to live in the city—he made most of these decisions, and I went along with them. I stayed with him mostly out of habit: I was used to having a warm body to cling to when I woke up from a *nightmare, used to buying just enough groceries to cook for two without worrying about leftovers, used to going out without my keys because he would always be home to open the door for me. But none of these habits was unchangeable, and there was nothing in my life that I wasn't ready to handle alone. There wasn't any reason that we had to be together—though that also meant there wasn't any reason to break up, either.*

We lived like that, unperturbed, unexciting, until I got the implant.

I began to ask myself whether I really loved him. It became impossible to make myself believe that I was living the life I wanted. I had become inured to my uneventful life, but with the brain box in me, I couldn't stop thinking about the scene after my death. What would happen after the data in the brain box was decoded and Fang Rui found out that I didn't love him as much as he thought, or perhaps didn't love him at all? The more I imagined that future, the more it terrified me.

The day he proposed to me, I ran. Turning the proposal into a big, public spectacle was just the sort of sentimental gesture he delighted in. Overwhelmed by the roses spilling from his arms and the joyful cheers of our friends, I ran. I escaped the heart-shaped cage he had constructed from candles and flew away from the city. I told him that he had shocked me and I needed time to think, and he apologized, telling me that he had only wanted to give me a romantic surprise.

"You live such a regular life," he said. "Aren't you tired? I wanted to see you let go."

A week living by myself next to the sea gave me plenty of time to think, but I can't remember any specific thoughts—except the looming presence of the brain box, like a sword suspended above my head. I couldn't eat and didn't sleep well. I didn't know how to explain myself to Fang Rui.

On the last day of my sojourn, the owner of the B&B took me hiking up a hill to see the blooming azaleas. Red, yellow, pink, purple—the flowers were so romantic, so wild. Suddenly, my fear was gone. I was ready to go back to face Fang Rui and tell him the truth.

I'm going to die. Maybe Fang Rui is at the airport right now, waiting with the ring. I'll never get to tell him my true feelings. Everyone's instinct is to shape the presentation of the self so as to maintain a consistent mirage in front of others. His romanticism and my rationalism are both masks that we fear to take off. Maybe he wasn't even aware of it, but his public, melodramatic proposal had been an act designed to cement his reputation as a romantic. My escape wasn't part of his script, but he must have expected it on some level. To maintain his self-image, he has to wait for me, and even come to the airport to put on another show, hoping to change my mind. But fundamentally, he loves himself far more than he loves me—he doesn't actually care what I want.

It's human nature to deceive others through actions and words, but the brain box forces the implanted to be subjected to constant self-reflection: Are my thoughts really my thoughts? Will others discover the unvarnished monologue going through my mind? Is the image others have of me consistent with my real self? Even though the brain box is capable of preserving only the last five minutes, the sensation of being monitored is ever-present, inescapable.

I was naive when I agreed to the experiment. Like the other youthful fools careless of the remote prospect of minds unmasked after death, we didn't realize that we would have to face a life of endless self-reflection and be shackled by such heavy chains of self-doubt.

The plane's dive is accelerating. My ears ache. An intensifying drone fills my head. How many minutes are left? Will these thoughts be recorded over? Will my brain box be recovered? Who will decode it? Will he know Fang Rui and tell him everything?

It's no longer about love. The very existence of the brain box changes everything.

3.

"Mr. Fang! Are you all right? We had to stop the experiment due to irregularities in your pulse and blood pressure."

Fang Rui opened his eyes. His awareness returned to his body from its remote journey. Whiteness everywhere: white walls, white lab coats, and bright white lights. He wasn't on the plane. He had awakened from his nightmare.

"Here, drink some water. You need to take a break and recover. We won't continue the experiment unless you insist."

"No," Fang Rui said, his lips trembling. "Shut it down. . . . I've . . . I've learned everything. Zhao Lin . . . she was ready to accept my proposal as soon as she returned. Her final thoughts were devoted to my well-being, to how to minimize my sorrow. Oh, she's always been so foolishly logical. I miss her so much, so much. . . ."

His voice faded as hot tears overflowed his eyes. But he knew his heart would never ache again.

CHEN QIUFAN

A fiction writer, screenwriter, and columnist—and recently, founder of Thelma Mundi Studio, a multimedia SFF IP incubator—Chen Qiufan (a.k.a. Stanley Chan) has published fiction in venues such as *Science Fiction World*, *Esquire*, *Chutzpah!*, and *ZUI Found*. His futurism writing may be found at places like *Slate* and XPRIZE.

Liu Cixin, China's most prominent science fiction author, praised Chen's debut novel, *Waste Tide* (Chinese edition 2013; English edition scheduled for 2018), as "the pinnacle of near-future SF writing."

He has garnered numerous literary awards, including Taiwan's Dragon Fantasy Award and China's Yinhe and Xingyun Awards. In English translation, he has been featured in markets such as *Clarkesworld*, *Pathlight*, *Lightspeed*, *Interzone*, and *F&SF*. "The Fish of Lijiang" won a Science Fiction and Fantasy Translation Award in 2012, and "The Year of the Rat" was selected by Laird Barron for *The Year's Best Weird Fiction: Volume One*. More of his fiction may be found in *Invisible Planets*.

"Coming of the Light" is one of my favorite stories by Chen, and it captures the anxiety, dynamism, and absurdity of life in contemporary Beijing as a member of the techno-social elite. "A History of Future Illnesses," on the other hand, is far darker and more caustic. Its Hieronymus Bosch–like visions of the future are dominated not so much by an all-powerful, know-nothing brutish state, but an apathetic, amoral, ahis-torical populace for whom the end of history is both a blessing and curse. As always, even in the darkest passages of his tales, Chen injects flashes of humor that I can't be sure should be properly read as hope or despair.

COMING OF THE LIGHT

0.

My mother told me about a Buddhist monk she and I met while shopping on my first birthday.

The monk caressed my head—back then as bald as his—and chanted a few lines that sounded like poetry.

After we returned home, my mom recited a few fragments to my father. Dad, who had had a few more years of schooling than my mom and completed middle school, told her that the lines weren't poetry, but from a Buddhist koan. Only by consulting the village schoolmaster did he finally discover the origin of those fragments, words which would come to determine my life.

As clouds drift across the sky, so Master in the Void is seen.

Dust clings to everything but what is true.

Over and over the monk queries: "What does your visit mean?"

Master points to cypress which in courtyard has taken root.[22]

---

22 The koan behind the verses is attributed to Zhaozhou Congshen (778–897 CE), a Chan (origin of the Japanese "Zen") Buddhist master, sometimes considered the greatest master of the Tang Dynasty. In the koan, a monk repeatedly asks the meaning behind Master Zhaozhou's visit, and each time Master Zhaozhou replies, "The cypress tree in the courtyard." Thanks to Anatoly Belilovsky for the verse rendering used here.

They thought these lines must contain some deep meaning, and so they renamed me Zhou Chongbo, which means "Repeat-Cypress."

1.

I'm sitting in a steamer. I'm a dumpling being steamed.

Everyone keeps on inhaling and exhaling and then staring at the white smoke coming out of everyone else's mouths, like cartoon characters with thought bubbles drifting over their heads containing logical musings, naked women, or frozen obscenicons. Then the smoke dissipates, revealing coarse, swollen faces. The air purifier screams as though it's gone mad, and the young women sitting in chairs along the wall silently put on their face masks, slide their fingers across the screens of their phones, and frown.

I don't need to look at the time to know it's past midnight. My wife won't even respond to my WeChat messages anymore.

I was dragged here at the last minute. My wife and I were on our way home after taking a stroll when we encountered a man dressed in an army coat on the pedestrian overpass. With a booming voice that startled both of us, he said, "The Quadrantid meteor shower will come on January 4. Don't miss it—"

I waited for him to finish with what is known to us marketing professionals as the "call to action"—e.g., "Join the Haidian Astrology Club," "Call this number now!," or even pulling out a portable telescope from his pocket and telling me "Now for only eighty-eight yuan"—which would have made this a reasonably well-executed bit of street peddling.

But like a stuck answering machine, he started again from the beginning: "The Quadrantid meteor shower will come on January 4. . . ."

Mission failed.

Disappointed, we left him. That was when my phone rang.

It was Lao Xu. I glanced apologetically at my wife, who gave me her usual unhappy look when my work intruded on our time together—this was certainly not the first time. I answered the call, and that was how I ended up here, sitting in this room.

The last thing my wife said to me was, "Tell your mother to quit pestering me about a grandchild. Her son is such a pushover he might as well be a baby."

"Chongbo!" Lao Xu's voice drags me back to this room filled with cancer-inducing smoke. "You're in charge of strategy. Contribute!"

Peering through the obscure haze, I struggle to make sense of the confusing notes on the whiteboard: user insights, key selling points, market research. . . . Dry erase marker lines in various colors connect the words like the trails left by the finger on some mobile picture-matching game: triangle, pentagon, hexagram, the seven Dragon Balls. . . .

It's all bullshit. Meaningless bullshit.

The pressure in the steamer is rising. Beads of sweat form on my forehead, slide down my face, drip.

"Is it too hot in here?" Lao Xu hands me a wrinkled paper napkin whose color is rather suspect. "Wipe yourself!"

I obey, too terrified to object.

"Mr. Wan wasn't happy with the marketing plan last time and wanted to switch agencies. I begged and pleaded to get him to stay. If we don't succeed this time, I think you all understand what that means."

The cheap napkin comes apart in my hand, and bits of paper are stuck to my sweaty face.

Mr. Wan is our god, the CEO of an Internet company. Out of any ten random people who accost strangers in the streets of Zhongguancun—"China's Silicon Valley"—one would be engaged in "network marketing," two would be trying to hook you on pyramid schemes, three would be trying to talk to you about Jesus, and the rest would all be founders or C-whatever-Os of some startup.

But if you got these individuals to engage in one-on-one conversion bouts—time limited to three minutes—I'm sure the last group would achieve complete victory. They're not interested in selling you a mere *product*, but an *idea* that would change the world. They're not there to speak for some deity; they're gods already.

Mr. Wan is just such a god.

Due to Lao Xu's persistence and luck, our little agency managed to land Mr. Wan as a client. We are supposed to spend the euros, dollars, yen, and yuan flowing in from angel investors, from private equity funds, from rounds A-B-C-D, and help Mr. Wan's company expand the market for their mobile app, raise product awareness, and improve daily engagement levels so that Mr. Wan could then use the new numbers to attract even more investment.

The flywheel goes round and round.

So where is the sticking point?

"Where is the sticking point?" Lao Xu's dry and thin voice screeches like a subway train shrieking through a tunnel, and an invisible force presses against me until I'm about to black out. Trembling, I stand up, avoiding the gazes of others on purpose. I'm like some two-dimensional inhabitant of a mathematical plane: my body is made up of points, but I can't see any.

"It's . . . a problem with the product." I lower my head shamefully, prepared for an angry tirade from Lao Xu.

"This is your fucking insight?"

I hold my tongue.

Mr. Wan's cofounder—let's call him Y—is a former classmate from USTC who had worked in America for many years. Mr. Wan convinced him to return to China, bringing with him valuable key patent rights to build a business. Y's patent covers a digital watermarking technology, which, because it involves information theory and complex mathematics, is a bit hard to explain.

I'll use a simple example. Let's say you take a picture and use the patented technology to add a watermark invisible to the naked eye; then, no matter how this photograph is subsequently modified or edited—even if eighty percent of the image were cropped—you would still be able to apply a special algorithm to recover the original image. The secret is that the invisible watermark itself carries all the information in the photo at the time it's applied.

This is, of course, only the most basic application for the technology. It could become an authentication/antitampering mechanism with many uses in fields such as media, finance, forensics, military security, and medicine—the possibilities are endless.

However, after Y returned to China, the two cofounders discovered that all the core industries they were interested in had barriers to entry—the difficulty wasn't so much that the fences were high, but that they couldn't even tell where they were. After bumping into walls multiple times, they decided that they had to make an end run around the difficulties by starting with entertainment, hoping to popularize the technology first through grassroots consumer acceptance before gradually infiltrating enterprise business-use cases.

Mr. Wan is always emphasizing the word "sexy," as though this is the only yardstick by which everything should be judged. But their product rather resembles a punctured, crumpled blowup doll left to dry in the shade.

"Why don't you use our client's product?" Lao Xu screams at the young women sitting along the wall. Blood drains from their faces as they pretend to be busy taking notes.

Mr. Wan's mobile app is called "Truthgram," and it automatically applies the special digital watermark to every picture the user takes. No matter how many times the image is transmitted, photoshopped, or otherwise altered beyond recognition, a simple button press would restore the original image. At first, the marketing angle focused on safety: *As long as you stick to Truthgram, Mom will never have to worry about your face showing up in some photoshopped pornographic image.*

Besides priming the sales channels, we also planned a web marketing event called "The Big Reveal." We recruited a hundred women and helped them take selfies with Truthgram, which we then retouched until everyone looked like a supermodel. We posted the photos on the web along with an animated GIF explaining how to use Mr. Wan's app to reveal the truth: "Turn Beauty to Beast in less than one second!"

Male users—maybe *losers* would be more accurate—responded

to the gimmick with extraordinary exuberance, recommending the app to each other and coming up with a veritable flood of variations that fulfilled the promise of user-generated content. Women, on the other hand, detested the marketing trick. They filled the forums with negative commentary about the company, arguing that the app vilified and insulted women by playing up the hoary trope of treating a woman's right to pursue beauty as a twisted form of narcissistic deceit. The marketing event became a PR crisis.

If it were up to me, I would have declared victory. Developing a market is all about pressing the key point, like plunging a sharp needle into the hypothalamus, the emotional center of the brain. If you don't see some blood spill, it probably means your needle is too dull or maybe you haven't stabbed at the right spot.

But Mr. Wan thought our little exercise could only grab some eyeballs temporarily at the cost of damaging the long-term brand value. As it turned out, the data proved him right. After a brief spike, the number of downloads went down and stayed down, and the losers we managed to attract eventually stopped using the app because we couldn't keep them stimulated with a constant stream of new content.

"I'm more interested in whether others see me from the most beautiful angle than in the security of my photos," a perfectly ordinary girl stated in an interview we conducted with our customers. Her phone's photo album was filled with selfies that showed signs of excessive retouching, all of them similar and none resembling her. Still, every half hour or so, she would hold her phone overhead at a 45-degree angle, pout her lips like a duck, and snap a shot.

If a tower's foundations are built on the shifting sands of a beach, how can you expect it to stay standing until the tides come in?

Lao Xu stares at me; I stare at the whiteboard; the whiteboard stares at everyone; everyone stares at their phone. We are like a flock of birds lost in fog, constantly drawn to flashing screens until we've forgotten the direction we were headed in. Yet, cold night has fallen, and hungry predators are approaching in the dark.

My phone beeps, indicating that it's nearly out of battery. My instinctive reaction is not to conserve, but to rush to look through WeChat Moments posted in my network. Every last drop of juice must be used to its fullest extent and not be wasted with invisible background processes. Now you get a glimpse of my values, my philosophy.

I see the latest posts by Mr. Wan. All of a sudden, the dumpling skin has burst, and the fillings spill out.

"I've got it!" I slam my hand down on the table. Everyone jerks awake from their somnambulant state.

I hold my phone under Lao Xu's nose.

Under Mr. Wan's profile, he has posted a new photo, accompanied by the following caption:

On Saturday, the fifteenth of the month under the lunar calendar, I'm going to perform the Buddhist good deed of freeing captive animals on the shore of Wenyu River. I'll purchase and free river snails laden with eggs; birds; reptiles; fish; and other animals. By this compassionate deed, I hope the Buddha brings blessings to everyone so that the aged may live longer, the middle-aged may have harmonious families, and children may gain wisdom and health! Happy Saturday! (Donations to help purchase more animals to free gratefully accepted: more animals = more good karma for all! Funds may be sent to this account: XXXXXXX. Sharing and reposting this message will also gain you blessings.)

"Err—I hadn't realized that they were running so low on funds." Lao Xu's eyes are wide as teacups. "They haven't paid us our last invoice yet!"

"Keep on reading," I say. I continue to slide my finger up the screen. Mr. Wan's dynamic timeline is woven from high-tech news and pop-Buddhism, a mixture of concentrated caffeine pills and chicken soup for the soul. "I think we've discovered his other passion."

"So what?"

"Let's think about why, every day, so many people share and

forward these posts about how to do good deeds to build up merit and gain the Buddha's protection. Are they really that faithful? I doubt it. Maybe preventing their photographs from being tempered with isn't a core need for people, but the anxious contemporary Chinese are obsessed with personal security, especially the psychological sense of being safe. We have to connect Mr. Wan's product with this psychological need."

"Be specific!"

"Everyone, what kind of posts would you share to feel more secure?" I ask.

"Powerful mantras!" "Pictures of Buddhas!" "The Birthday of the Buddha, and other festival birthdays!" "Wise sayings by famous master monks!"

"What sort of posts would make you believe and willingly hand over money?"

There's a pause as everyone in the room ponders my question. Then, one of the girls timidly speaks up. "Something that's been con-consecrated . . . um, you know, when the light has been—"

"Bingo!"

The room falls silent. Lao Xu gets up and, poker-faced, walks behind me. I hear a loud slam, and a chill wind pours into the back of my shirt as though a bucket of ice has been emptied into it. The haze in the room instantly dissipates.

"Awake now?" Lao Xu closes the window. "Explain what you mean again, but stop being so damned mystical."

I hold his gaze and speak slowly. "Let's find a famous and respected monk to consecrate this app—'bring light into it'—so that every picture it takes becomes a charm to ward off evil. We'll create a sharing economy of blessings."

Everyone shifts their gaze from the phone screen to me; I gaze at Lao Xu; Lao Xu says nothing but gazes at the phone.

After a while, he lets out a held breath. "You know, all those Rinpoches in Chaoyang District are going to get you for this."

I have no idea what's in store for me.

10.

My wife is a Neo-Luddite.

Once, she had been a heavy gamer. She spent so much time on the computer that her parents sent her to a summer camp that specialized in curing Internet addiction. The experience caused her attitude toward technology to turn a hundred and eighty degrees.

Many times I asked her, what really happened in that campground located on Phoenix Mountain called "The Nirvana Plan"?

She never answered me directly.

This was the biggest philosophical difference between us. She believed that despite the appearance of unprecedented novelty, the high-tech industry was ultimately no different from another ancient trade: they both took advantage of the weaknesses of ordinary men and women, and, under the guise of words like "progress," "uplift," and "salvation," manipulated their emotions. Whether you put your hand on a Bible or an iPad, in the end you were praying to the same god.

We only give the people what they want. They desire comfort, joy, a sense of security. They want to improve themselves, to see themselves stand out in the crowd. We can't take such desires away from them. That was how I always argued back at her.

Oh, please! Don't give me that. You're just playing a game to satisfy your own yearning for control, she said.

Come on; give people a little credit! I said. *Everyone's got a brain. How can anyone "control" anyone else?*

There are always NPCs.

What are you talking about?

Non-Player Characters. What if everything is controlled from behind the scenes by some invisible background process? Then every action you take will affect the game logic. The system will react with NPCs and they will carry out their predetermined programming.

I stared at her face as though I'd never really known her. I even wondered whether she had just joined some new cult.

You don't really believe that, do you?

I'm going to walk the dog. There shouldn't be much dog poop in the streets this early in the morning.

11.

Every day, as the temple bell tolls five, I have to get up to sweep the grounds. I sweep the wooden floor of the gallery from the new library to the stone steps, and thence to the temple gates, where the ancient pagoda tree grows, its gnarled branches spread like the talons of a rampant beast.

As for whether I will be quietly reciting the *Surangama Sutra*, the *Lotus Sutra*, or the *Diamond Sutra* as I sweep, that depends on the day's PM2.5 air quality index. My throat hurts when I breathe the polluted air; I don't need the distraction.

Any of the faithful coming to the temple to make offerings can see that I haven't been truly called by the Buddha. Just like all the other "disciples" flocking here on weekends to study Buddhist doctrine, I'm here to hide from the real world.

In a way, I'm not too different from the throngs of shoppers at the Buddhist shop outside Yonghe Lamasery vying to buy electronic "Buddha boxes." They bring the box home, push a button, and the box starts chanting sutras. On the hour (or at designated times), the box will even emit a tranquil, meditative *duannnnng*, like the ringing of the bell in a temple. The purchasers apparently think this will bring them blessings and cleanse bad karma. I often imagine all the passengers squeezed like canned sardines into the number 2 subway train leaving from the lamasery station, all of their Buddha boxes ringing harmoniously together on the hour. Perhaps the so-called *Chan* state of mind refers to the detachment of such a moment from real life.

And now that I have to commit to a Buddhist vegetarian diet, I miss the restaurant at Beixinqiao where they serve chitterlings soup made from ancient stock that has supposedly been accumulating flavor for years.

I've canceled my mobile number and deleted all my accounts on social media; my wife has left me and returned to her hometown; I've even been given a Dharma name: "Chenwu"—"Free of Worldly Dust." All I want is for those crazy people to never find me again.

I've had enough.

Everything began that night with the crazy marketing scheme that seemed to make no sense.

Mr. Wan bought my idea. Overnight he summoned the engineers to develop the new product. Lao Xu laid out the marketing plan and strategy. The most important piece of the project, of course, was assigned to me, the originator.

I had to go find a respected master monk willing to consecrate our app, to bring it light.

Lao Xu demanded that the entire process be filmed and turned loose online to go viral. I ran through every excuse I could think of: *My family have been Christians for three generations; my wife is pregnant and can't come in contact with raw foods, animal fur, or anything having to do with spirits. . . .*

Lao Xu responded with only one line: *This is your baby. If you don't want to see it through, get out and don't come back, you get me?*

I visited every temple in Beijing, begging and pleading with the master monks, and I sought out every lama secluded in spiritual solitude in the city's various nooks and crannies. Each time, however, even after having come to an agreement on the price, as soon as I brought out my camera, the monks' faces turned stony, and after a few "Amitabha," they would cover their faces and escape my presence.

We tried using hidden cameras a few times, but the combination of incense haze and camera shake made the results unwatchable.

As the deadline approached, I could no longer sleep, but tossed and turned all night. My wife asked me what I was doing.

"Rolling dough for pancakes," I said.

She kicked me. "If you want to do that, get on the floor. Don't pretend you're a rolling pin in bed. I'm trying to sleep."

The kick managed to free my clogged neural pathways. Instantly, I was inspired.

Mr. Wan's new app went on sale on time. Lao Xu, energized like his Land Rover, shifted into high gear and whipped us into a frenzy. Videos, new concepts, and new campaigns were released one after another. Soon, a video depicting a master monk consecrating a mobile phone went viral, and Buddhagrams began to conquer Weibo and WeChat. The number of downloads and daily engagement level rose exponentially like rockets heading for the clouds at escape velocity.

Don't ask me the impact of such growth on the long-term brand value; don't ask me what this meant for the subsequent development and application of the digital watermark technology. Those are problems Mr. Wan had to solve. I was only a strategist for a third-rate marketing company who had some crazy ideas. I could only work on problems that I was capable of solving with my own methods.

In the end, we underestimated the creativity of users. It turned out that Buddhagram pictures, due to the presence of the watermark, could be recovered from even low-resolution copies or cropped fragments. This meant they could be shared and forwarded without taking up much bandwidth or time. Trying to take advantage of the situation, we released a series of new ads touting this newly discovered advantage.

Downloads spiked again, but no one anticipated what happened next.

It started with a picture of an apple taken with Buddhagram. A week later, the poster shared a second picture of the same apple: it was apparently rotting at a much slower rate than other apples.

Next came the various pictures of pets that miraculously recovered their health after having had their pictures taken with Buddhagram.

Then, an old lady claimed that after she had taken a Buddha-selfie, she managed to survive a deadly car accident.

Rumors multiplied. Taken individually, each seemed some preposterous April Fool's joke, but behind every story stood a witness who swore it was true, and the number of believers snowballed.

The posts grew stranger. Patients with terminal cancer posted selfies showing their tumors diminishing daily; couples who had trouble conceiving took nude selfies and became pregnant; migrant laborers took group selfies and won the lottery. The kind of news that one would normally expect to find only on tabloids on the subway filled every social media platform. All the pictures had the Buddhagram watermark, and all of us thought they were from astroturfers hired by the company.

We thought wrong.

Supposedly, Mr. Wan's phone was ringing nonstop with calls from interested investors. Other than asking about a chance to invest, the next most popular question was: *Who is the master monk who brought light to the app?*

The logic was simple: if a consecrated mobile app could have such magical effects, then asking the monk himself to perform some rite would surely result in earthshaking miracles. The investors thought of this, and so did millions and millions of users.

In this age, truth was as rare as virtue. Even more tragic, when faced with the truth, most people preferred to doubt its veracity because they would rather believe the truthy mirage created by their own minds.

Soon, my contact details were leaked. Email, phone, text. . . . Everyone screamed the same question at me: *Who is the master monk???*

I refused to answer. I knew they would figure it out sooner or later.

Crowdsourcing the search, they finally managed to locate the master monk and the disciples in the viral video—a bunch of actors my friend had found for me among the crowd of extras congregated at Hengdian World Studios, hoping to get a role. They were supposed to portray commoners during the Qing Dynasty, which meant they were already shaved bald—just like Buddhist monks. This made negotiations rather easy. The extras who harbored dreams of making it big in the movies were especially diligent, and the lead even argued with the makeup artist over the correct placement of the burn marks over his head to indicate his ordained status. Watching the scene, I grew concerned.

They were all good people. The fault was entirely mine.

The poor actors who had been located by the "human flesh search engine" could no longer live in peace. The enraged netizens hounded them and their families using the vilest language, forcing them to acknowledge what was obviously true: they were mere extras hired by the company to portray the master monk and his disciples.

Except that the crowd still wasn't quite on the same page as me: they continued to believe that my company—or more precisely, I—was hiding the real master monk. Out of greed or selfishness, I was refusing to disclose his identity to the public so that everyone could benefit from the master's powers.

I really wasn't.

Lao Xu closed the company temporarily. Every day, groups of middle-aged women congregated at the foot of the building, holding up protest banners. Even if we could endure the pressure, the building's property manager couldn't. Lao Xu put us all on paid leave, hoping that the storm would quickly blow over. Kindly, he told me that it was best for me to leave the city and return to my parents' home for a few days. It was just a matter of time before one of the netizens who was terminally ill might arrive at my door with his family, pleading with me to give up the master monk's WeChat ID.

I realized that Lao Xu was right. I couldn't put my family at risk.

And so, after I settled my affairs, I came to this ancient temple to become a grounds sweeper.

The bell tolls nine times, indicating the end of morning lessons.

The staff of the temple, including me, assume our positions. The temple is open to the public today, and the abbot, Master Deta, will be greeting a group of VIP faithful from the Internet industry and conducting a salon to discuss the connections between Buddhist doctrine and the web.

My assigned job is to hand out the visitor's badges. On the list of VIPs, I see more than a few familiar names, including Mr. Wan.

Though it's thirty-eight degrees Celsius, I put on my cotton medical face mask. Sweat pours off me as though I'm drenched by rain.

100.

The faithful, now dressed in the yellow robes and yellow shoes normally reserved for monks, stream in one after another, their colorful badges swaying on lanyards before their chests. For a moment I suffer the illusion of having returned to my old life from a few months ago: the China National Convention Center, JW Marriott Beijing, 798 D Park. . . . I was either at meetings or on my way to meetings, handing out my business card, adding people's WeChat IDs, puffing up our clients, sketching incredible visions, peppering my speech with "Internet thinking" buzzwords—like some updated version of a Red Guard clutching his Little Red Book.

The faces before me are still the same, but now their badges have been stripped of the eye-catching titles. "CXO," "Cofounder," and "VP of Investment" have been replaced by "Householder," "Believer," and "Benefactor." At least for the moment, they've retracted their typical arrogance and protruding bellies. Mumbling mantras, they take their seats and piously hand their phones, iPads, Google Glasses, smart wristbands, and so on to the waiting novice monks in exchange for a numbered ticket.

I see Mr. Wan. His face looks pallid and thin, but his gaze is steady and his steps airy. Placidly, he places the palms of his hands together and bows to the guests on either side of him, showing no trace of his former domineering air. As he passes me, I lower my head, and he lowers his in turn to acknowledge my greeting.

Many things must have happened in the intervening months.

Supposedly, Master Deta had once been a promising student at the Computer Science Department of Tsinghua University. However, as a result of his enlightenment, he gave up offers for graduate study at Stanford, Yale, UC Berkley, and other ivy-clad campuses, took up vows, and became ordained as a monk. With him as an example, a group of other graduates of elite colleges also joined our temple and began to spread the teachings of Buddhism online, bringing relief to all mortal beings with methods adapted to the Internet age.

The master's lecture today roams over many subjects—so many that I barely remember any of them. I do see Mr. Wan holding a pious pose and nodding frequently. When the master discusses how big data techniques could be used to help locate the young reincarnations of tulkus, his eyes even grow tearful.

I'm trying to hide from him, but I also can't suppress the urge to go up to him and ask if the storm has finally blown over. I don't miss my old life, but I miss my family.

Here, only monks who have achieved a certain status have the right to use the Internet. The layered green branches of the ancient cypress grove, like a firewall, separate us from the noise and dust of the secular world. My daily life, however, is not boring at all: sweeping, working, chanting, debating, and copying. Uncluttered by material possessions, I've been sleeping without trouble for the first time in years, and no longer live in constant dread of sudden vibrations from my phone—though occasionally my right quadriceps still suffers phantom pulses. But my teacher tells me that if I count my prayer beads—all one thousand and eight hundred of them—every day for a hundred eighty days, I shall be fully cured.

I think it's because we want too much, more than what our bodies and minds are designed to withstand.

My old job was all about creating need, encouraging people to pursue things that didn't matter for their lives, and then I used the money they gave in exchange to purchase illusions others had created for me. Round after round, we never seemed to tire of the game.

I think about my wife's words: *Her son is such a pushover he might as well be a baby.* Fuck, I'm even more useless than a baby.

This is my sin, my bad karma, the blockage I need to clear for my progress.

I'm starting to understand Mr. Wan.

After the lecture, Mr. Wan and a few others surround Master Deta, apparently because they have many questions that need his insight. Master Deta beckons to me. I gird myself and walk over.

"Would you bring these honored guests to meditation room three? I'll be over in a moment."

I nod, and lead the group to the room in the back reserved for VIPs.

I ask them to sit, and I pour tea for everyone. They nod and smile at each other, but their conversation is restricted to small talk. I'm guessing that they are competitors outside the temple.

Mr. Wan doesn't look at me directly. He sips his tea and closes his eyes, meditating. His lips move as he silently recites some mantra, and his hands are busy with a string of rosewood prayer beads. After the forty-ninth time through the beads, I can't hold myself back any longer. I walk up to him, bend down, and whisper next to his ear, "Do you remember me?"

Mr. Wan opens his eyes and scrutinizes me for half a minute. "You are Zhou. . . ."

"Zhou Chongbo. You have an excellent memory, sir."

Mr. Wan grimaces and lunges at me, wrapping the string of prayer beads about my neck and pushing me to the floor.

"You fucking idiot!" He curses and strikes me. The two guests next to him stand up, startled, but they don't dare to intervene. "Amitabha. Amitabha," they murmur.

I protect my face with my hands, but I don't know what to say. "Mercy!" I cry. "Mercy!"

"Stop!" Master Deta's voice booms. "This is a sanctified place! Such violence has no place here."

Mr. Wan's fist, suspended in midair, stops. He stares at me, and tears suddenly spill from his eyes and fall onto my face, as though he's the one wronged.

"All gone. . . . I've lost everything . . . ," he murmurs. Then he falls back into his seat.

I get up. I guess someone who's lost everything can't even strike very hard. My body isn't hurting at all.

"Amitabha." I put my palms together and bow to him. I know he's not feeling much better compared to me. Just as I'm about to leave the meditation room, the abbot stops me, and strikes me with his ferule: twice on the left shoulder, once on the right.

"Don't discuss what happened today with others. You still have too much worldly arrogance about you and cannot handle important tasks. You must study harder and reflect on your actions."

I'm about to argue the point, but then remember that I once tolerated much worse from Lao Xu and Mr. Wan. Master Deta is basically the temple's CEO. I have to swallow my pride.

I bow to him and back out.

I lean against the wall of the gallery and watch the woods in the setting sun. Smog glistens above the city like the piled layers of a sari. The bell tolls on the hour, and startled birds take to the air.

A thought flashes through my mind. I am reminded of how Master Subhuti once struck Monkey three times on the head with a ferule and then walked away with his hands held behind him, which was a message for Monkey to come to the back door of the master's bedroom at the hour of the third watch for special lessons.

But how am I supposed to interpret two strikes on the left shoulder and one on the right?

101.

At around nine o'clock at night—that's when first watch turns to second watch under the ancient time system—I head for the abbot's chambers via backwoods trails. My journey through the dark woods is accompanied only by the gentle susurration of pines, with not even a chirp from a bird.

I knock twice on the door, and then once. Someone seems to be stirring inside. I knock again. The door opens automatically.

Abbot Deta is sitting with his back to the door. Before him is a giant screen, completely dark. I seem to hear the low-frequency buzzing of electronics. He sighs loudly.

"Teacher! Your student is here!" I fall to my knees and prepare to kowtow.

"I think you've read *Journey to the West* too many times." The abbot gets up, and I can see that his expression isn't one of joy. "I told you to come at one minute past ten o'clock."

I'm stumped for words. Apparently the master was using binary notation.

I hurry to hide my embarrassment. "Um . . . this afternoon—"

"It wasn't your fault; I know what happened. As soon as you stepped into this temple, I learned everything about you."

". . . Then why did you accept me?"

"Though your heart wasn't directed toward the Buddha, you have within you the root of wisdom. If I didn't take you in, I'm afraid you might have sought refuge in suicide."

"Master is indeed merciful." I'm still completely as a loss.

"I know you don't understand." Master Deta isn't actually that old. He's barely in his forties. As he laughs with his glasses perched on his nose, he resembles a college professor.

"Forgive your foolish student, master. Please enlighten me."

Master Deta waves his hand. The giant screen, apparently controlled by body motion, lights up. The image on the screen is difficult to describe: a gigantic, compressed oval whose background is various shades of blue, studded with irregular patches of orange-red dots. Or maybe it's the other way around. I think the image resembles the false-color version of some planet's topographic map, or maybe a slide full of multiplying mold seen through a microscope.

"What is this?"

"The universe. Or more precisely, the cosmic microwave background. This is the image of the universe about 380,000 years after the Big Bang. You're looking at the most precise photograph of it so far." His enthusiastic admiration contrasts sharply with his humble monk's garb.

"Um . . ."

"This was made by computation based on the data gathered by the European Space Agency's Planck space observatory. Look here, and here—do you see how the pattern is a bit odd?"

Other than patches of orange-red or cobalt mold, I can't see what's so special.

"Are you saying that . . . um . . . the Buddha doesn't exist?" I ask tentatively.

"The Buddha teaches that the great trichiliocosm consists of a billion worlds." He glares at me, as though forcing me to retract my words. "This picture proves that multiple universes once existed. After so many years of effort, humanity finally proved, through technology, the Buddhist cosmology."

I should have realized this would happen. The abbot is just like the pyramid schemers in Zhongguancun—anything, no matter how unrelated, could be seen by them as powerful proof for their point of view. I try to imagine how a Christian might interpret this picture.

"Amitabha." I put my palms together to show piety.

"The question is: why has the Buddha chosen now to reveal the truth to all of humanity?" He speaks slowly and forcefully. "I pondered this question for a long time, but then I saw your scheme."

"Buddhagram?"

Master Deta nods. "I can't say I approve of your methods. However, since you ended up coming here, that proves that my guesses were correct."

Cold sweat seeps onto the skin at my back, not unlike that night so long ago that it seems unreal.

"This world is no longer the same as its original form. Put it another way: its creator, the Buddha, God, Deity—no matter what name you give it—has changed the rules by which the world operates. Do you really believe that the consecration was what allowed Buddhagram to perform miracles?"

I hold my breath.

"Suppose the universe is a program. Everything that we can observe is the result of the machine-executable code. But the cosmic microwave background can be understood as the record of some earlier version of the source code. We can invoke this code via computation, which means that we can also use algorithmic processing to change the version of the code that's currently running."

"You're saying that Mr. Wan's algorithm really caused all of this?"

"I dare not jump to conclusions. But if you forced me to guess, that would be it."

"I'm pretty science-illiterate, master. Please don't joke with me."

"Amitabha. I am a Technologist-Buddhist. I believe in the words of Arthur C. Clarke: 'Any sufficiently advanced technology is indistinguishable at first glance from Buddhist magic.'"

I know there's something not quite right here, but I don't know how to debate him. "But . . . but that project failed. Look at what a sad state Mr. Wan is in. I don't think I have anything more to do with this."

"*What is not real? That which form possesses.*
The Tathagata will be seen
When mind past form progresses."[23]

"Master, please allow me to leave the temple and return to the secular world. I miss my wife." A nameless fear suddenly seizes me like a bottomless pit rising out of the screen on the wall, trying to pull me in.

Master Deta sighs and smiles wryly, as though he has long since predicted all this.

"I was hoping that by studying Buddhist doctrine with me, you would be sufficiently calmed to stay here and wait out the

23 This is a quote from the *Diamond Sutra*.

catastrophe. But . . . you and I are both caught in the wheel of samsara, so how can we escape our destinies? All right. Take this as a memento of our time together."

He hands over a gold-colored Buddha card. On the back is a toll-free number as well as a VIP account number and security code.

"Teacher, what is this?"

"Don't lose it! The resale value of this card is 8,888 yuan. If anything happens, you can give me a call."

Master Deta turns and waves his hand, and the moldy image on the screen is replaced by regular TV programming. An American quantum physicist has been killed by gunshot. Bizarrely, the shooter claims that it was an accident because he thought the victim was someone else.

110.

Half a year passes. I meet Lao Xu at Guanji Chiba, a popular barbecue restaurant in Zhongguancun.

Lao Xu hasn't changed much. He's still pathologically in love with barbecued lamb kidneys. Like a stereotypical Northeasterner, after a few bottles of beer, his face glowing with grease and jittering with emotion, Lao Xu begins to say what's really on his mind.

"Chongbo, why don't you come and join me again? You know I'll take care of you."

Animatedly, Lao Xu tells me what's been going on with him, spewing flecks of spittle through the smoky haze. After he hid and rested for a while at home, another phone call drew him back into the IT world. This time, he didn't start a marketing company with no future, but became an "angel investor." With all the contacts he made among entrepreneurs, now he gets to spend other people's money—the faster the better.

He thinks I have potential.

"What's going on with Mr. Wan?" I change the subject. My wife has just found out that she's pregnant. Although my current job is boring, it's stable. Lao Xu, on the other hand, isn't.

"I haven't heard from him for a while . . ." Lao Xu's eyes dim, and he takes a long drag on his cigarette. "Fortune is so fickle. Back when Buddhagram was on fire, a whole bunch of companies wanted to invest. An American company even wanted to talk about purchasing the whole company. But at the last minute, an American man showed up claiming that Y's core algorithm was stolen from one of his graduate school research labmates. The American sued, and he just wouldn't let it go. So the patent rights had to be temporarily frozen. All the investors scattered to the wind, and Lao Wan had to sell everything he owned . . . but in the end, it still wasn't enough."

I drain my cup.

"It wasn't your fault," Lao Xu says. "Honestly, if you hadn't come up with that idea, I bet Lao Wan would have failed even earlier."

"But if they hadn't made Buddhagram, maybe the Americans wouldn't have found out about the stolen algorithm."

"I've finally got it figured out. If what happened hadn't happened, something else would have. That's what fate means. Later, I heard that the labmate Y stole from was shot and killed in America. So now the patent case is in limbo."

Lao Xu's voice seems to drone on while time stands frozen. My gaze penetrates the slight crack between his cigarette-holding fingers, and the background of noisy, smoky, shouting, drinking patrons of the restaurant fades into the distance. I remember something, something so important that I've managed to forget it completely until now.

I thought everything was over, but it's only starting.

After saying goodbye to Lao Xu, I return home and begin to search, turning everything in the house upside down. My wife, her belly protruding, asks me if I've had too much to drink.

"Have you seen a golden card with a picture of the Buddha on there?" I ask her. "There's a toll-free number on the back."

She looks at me pitifully, as though gazing at an abandoned Siberian husky, a breed known for its stupidity and difficulty in being trained. She turns away to continue her pregnancy yoga exercises.

In the end, I find it tucked away inside a fashion magazine in the bathroom. The page I open to happens to be the picture of a Vaseline-covered, nude starlet lounging among a pile of electronics. Each screen in the image reflects a part of her glistening body.

I dial the number and enter the VIP account number and security code. A familiar voice, sounding slightly tired, answers.

"Master Deta, it's me! Chenwu!"

"Who?"

"Chenwu! Secular name Zhou Chongbo! Remember how you struck my shoulders three times and told me to go to your room at ten-oh-one to view the picture of the cosmic microwave background?"

"Er . . . you make it sound so odd. Yes, I do remember you. How've you been?"

"You were right! The problem is with the algorithm!" I take a deep breath and quickly recount the story as well as give him my guess. Someone is working really hard to prevent this algorithm from being put into wide application, even to the point of killing people.

The earpiece of the phone is silent for a long while, and then I hear another long sigh.

"You still don't get it. Do you play games?"

"A long time ago. Do you mean arcade, handheld, or consoles?"

"Whatever. If your character attacks a big boss, the game's algorithms usually summon all available forces to its defense, right?"

"You mean the NPCs?"

"That's right."

"But I didn't do anything! All I did was to suggest a stupid fucking marketing plan!"

"You misunderstand." Master Deta's voice becomes low and

somber, as though he's about to lose his patience. "You're not the player who's attacking the boss. You're just an NPC."

"Wait a second! You are saying . . ." Suddenly my thoughts turn jumbled and slow, like a bowl of sticky rice porridge.

"I know it's hard to accept, but it's the truth. Someone, or maybe some group, has done things that threaten the entire program—the stability of our universe. And so the system, following designated routines, has invoked the NPCs to carry out its order to eliminate the threat and maintain the consistency of the universe."

"But I did everything on my own! I just wanted to do my job and earn a living. I thought I was helping him."

"All NPCs think like that."

"So what should I do? Lao Xu wants me to go work for him. How do I know if this is . . . Are you there?"

Strange noises are coming out of the earpiece, as though a thousand insect legs are scrabbling against the microphone.

"When you are confused . . . *hiss* . . . the teacher helps . . . Enlightened . . . *hiss* . . . help yourself. All you have to do . . . *hiss* . . . and that's it . . . *hiss* . . . Sorry, your VIP account balance is insufficient. Please refill your account and dial again. Sorry . . ."

"Fuck!" I hang up angrily.

"What's wrong with you, screaming like that? If you frighten me and cause me to miscarry, are you going to assume the responsibility?" My wife's voice drifts to me slowly from the bedroom.

In three seconds, I sort through my thoughts and decide to tell her everything. Of course, I do have to limit it to the parts she can understand.

"Tell Lao Xu that your wife is worried about earning good karma for the baby. She doesn't want you to follow him and continue to do unethical work."

I'm just about to argue with her when the phone rings again. Lao Xu.

"Have you made up your mind? USTC's quantum lab is making rapid progress! Their machine is tackling the NP-completeness problem now. Once they've proved that P equals NP, do you realize what that means?"

I look at my wife. She places the edge of her palm against her throat and makes a slicing motion, and then she sticks her tongue out.

"Hello? You there? Do you know what that means—?" I hang up, and Lao Xu's voice lingers in my ear.

Every program has bugs. In this universe, I'm pretty sure that my wife is one of them. Possibly the most fatal one.

111.

I still remember the day when Lailai was born: rose-colored skin, his whole body smelling of milk. He's the most beautiful baby I've ever seen.

My wife, still weak from labor, asked me to come up with a good name. I agreed. But really, I was thinking: *It makes no difference what he's named.*

I'm no hero. I'm just an NPC. To tell the truth, I've never believed that all this was my fault. I didn't join Lao Xu; I didn't come up with some outrageous idea that would have caused the whole project to fail; I didn't prevent that stupid quantum computer from proving that P equals NP—even now I still don't know what that fucking means.

If this is the reason that the universe is collapsing, then all I can say is that the Programmer is incompetent. Why regret destroying such a shitty world?

But I'm holding my baby son, his tiny fist enclosed in my hand, and all I want is for time to stop forever, right now.

I regret everything I've done, or maybe everything I haven't done.

In these last few minutes, a scene from long ago appears in my mind: that guy wearing the army coat on the pedestrian overpass.

He's staring at me and my wife, and like some stuck answering machine, he says, "The Quadrantid meteor shower will come on January 4. Don't miss it. . . ."

No one is going to miss this grand ceremony for going offline.

I play with my son, trying to make him laugh, or make any sort of expression. Suddenly, I see a reflection in his eyes, rapidly growing in size.

It's the light coming from behind me.

A HISTORY OF
FUTURE ILLNESSES

Call me Stanley. I come from your future.

Let me begin with what's already familiar to you, and by following the flow of the river of time, explore the diseases, both physical and mental, that have plagued the humanity of tomorrow, until the end of history.

IPAD SYNDROME

It began with the iPad 3, with its Retina Display whose subpixel rendering technology achieved a resolution in excess of 300 PPI, higher than conventional print. The display quality of electronic books could finally compete with paper. Pundits hailed it as another Gutenberg revolution and predicted the death of the traditional print industry. Humanity was about to enter a new era of reading.

As usual, the pundits were as myopic as bats hanging in a dark cave.

Apple first pushed for a revolution in education. They gave every child an iPad, and invested vast resources in making textbooks that were electronic, multimedia-enhanced, and integrated with social media. Schoolchildren, especially those in East Asia, said goodbye to their heavy backpacks. Their spines straightened; their shoulder and neck muscles relaxed; the deformation fatigue of the lenses in their eyes slowed due to broader viewing angles, sharper, more detailed images, and light sensors that automatically adjusted screen brightness.

The future seemed bright, until parents began handing the magic tablets to even younger children.

The youngest recorded iPad user was aged four months and thirteen days. The iPad's direct manipulation interaction model allowed even babies to slip into fingertip adventures and become seamlessly immersed in them. Many uploaded YouTube clips of babies playing with iPads, and their pure, undisguised delight garnered millions of hits and likes. The amused audience did not quite realize the danger hidden behind the joyous scenes.

The first confirmed case came out of South Korea. Six-year-old Park Sung-hwan was diagnosed with autism, though fMRI and PET scans revealed no unusual neural variations. His symptoms included flat affect, language impairment, and lack of muscular coordination. He did not respond to the emotional states of his parents in an age-appropriate manner and showed a lack of interest in the world. In fact, the only thing he was interested in was the iPad. But all he did was repeatedly open and close apps, unable to actually browse the web, play a game, or otherwise engage with the functionality of those apps.

It seemed that the world, for him, consisted solely of the force feedback vibrations generated by fingers sliding across the screen.

An astute clinical child psychologist observed Park and compared him against other similar cases before announcing the shocking concept of "iPad syndrome." The discovery struck a chord around the world, and soon tens of thousands were diagnosed with it.

The academic consensus was that this special type of perceptual dysfunction occurred because babies were exposed to the intense visual and tactile feedback of the iPad before their sensory neural connections were fully developed. Aimless hand movements led to an overabundance of concentrated visual and tactile sensory information, which had to be adequately integrated and coordinated with the rest of the body to form a solid foundation for the development of bodily self-image. This was precisely the key step missing in the development of those afflicted with iPad syndrome.

To them, the regular world was dim, blurry, low-resolution, unresponsive to the sliding finger and utterly devoid of wonder. Trained by early and long exposure to the iPad, their vestibular systems developed a special sensory signal filter that only permitted the intense signals of the iPad to enter the cortex and stimulate the neurons. Other signal sources, on the other hand, were simply shut out.

Parents of children with iPad syndrome filed a class-action lawsuit demanding tens of billions in compensation since Apple had not disclosed the serious side effects of iPad use on young children with prominent labeling. The case slowly wound through the courts until the two sides finally settled. Besides an undisclosed amount paid to the plaintiffs, Apple also agreed to invest significant resources into researching rehabilitation for the disorder.

As the impacted children grew up, they learned, through therapy, a unique way of life. iPads became extensions of their bodies. Through the tablets, they spoke, expressed emotions, and exchanged thoughts. Besides text and voice, they also transmitted information via vibrations as though they were sharks in the abyss or worms deep underground, by holding fingers or palms against one another's iPads, experiencing sensations that outsiders could never know.

They were like extraterrestrials concealed in human society and, other than the minimal exchanges required to survive in a human economy, refused to interact with regular humans at all.

They formed family-like structures. Following rules and rituals unknown to others, they found each other, copulated, had children. After offers of large sums of money failed to produce results, some journalists tried to surreptitiously film the family lives of those with iPad syndrome. The result? The offending journalists disappeared.

Don't worry; the worst was still to come.

There was a one-in-eight chance that their children would also inherit this more-than-pathological love for the iPad.

DISEASE-IMITATION AESTHETICS

As changing beauty standards gradually decentered the straight male gaze, plastic surgery reached a peak of inventiveness in the mid-twenty-first century. But modification of the body's external characteristics was no longer sufficient to satisfy the shifting tastes of a diverse population. A new—or more accurately, ancient—aesthetic trend came back into fashion spectacularly.

It was possible to trace this trend all the way back to the Three Kingdoms and Jin Dynasty period (220 to 420 CE). He Yan, the founder of the Xuanxue school of Daoism, developed a new medicinal formula called "Five Minerals Powder," which was based on the famed Eastern Han Dynasty doctor Zhang Zhongjing's cure for typhoid fever and made from a mixture of stalactite, sulfur, quartz, fluorite, and red bole clay.

He Yan himself had this to say of his invention: "Not only does it cure disease, but it also opens up and enlivens the mind." Consuming Five Minerals Powder for its psychoactive properties became the fashion among scholar-officials. After ingesting the powder, the typical user became restless, anxious, flushed, and had to walk about in loose clothing to cool down as their mind wandered a different plane. Habitual use led to irritability, explosive temper, and a proclivity for trances—not unlike the man of legend who reacted to a nettlesome fly by chasing after the insect with an unsheathed sword.

The fashion for taking Five Minerals Powder in China lasted for almost six centuries, until the Tang Dynasty. "Rambling Powder" became a poetic marker for those of an elevated social class—a metonymic process similar to the social signals attached to marijuana or LSD use later.

Similarly, in order to satisfy the pursuit of morbid beauty standards, Medieval European nobles contracted tuberculosis or even consumed arsenic to give their skins that unique, white glow. The elevation of the symptoms of illness to signs of beauty was certainly not limited to any one time or place.

And now, technology could help.

Ligament tightening agents temporarily reduced the joints' range of motion; combined with trace amounts of tetrodotoxin injected into facial muscles, the result was a simulation of the stiff poses and expressions associated with classical East Asian beauty standards. In the Roppongi district of Tokyo, one might often encounter tall Caucasian women whose hair had been dyed pure black, shuffling along with rigid smiles that carefully concealed their teeth. In fact, they were the executive assistants of multinationals who had decided to undergo periodic cosmetic treatments to induce partial paralysis in the face and a constrained gait in order to satisfy the demands of "cultural integration," the morbid fashion of the social elite, as well as the fetishistic needs of their Asian bosses.

And then there were the Blinkers, whose name came from a neurological tic that caused them to blink irregularly as their orbicularis oculi and levator palpebrae superioris muscles twitched. People suffering from social anxiety disorder implanted under their eyes chips that could control muscle movement by stimulating the nerves. They formed a complicated, intricate read-decipher-feedback system, capable of communicating by blinking their eyes alone, without any need for spoken language or facial expressions. At Blinker gatherings, one could see a group of silent, blank-faced individuals gazing into one another's eyes like lighthouses broadcasting Morse code at high frequency. Indeed, some could communicate with two interlocutors at the same time, blinking with each eye separately.

Aesthetics has always been inseparable from politics. Against the fractured background of a multipolar world, humanity could not come to a consensus regarding the definition of "beauty." In the seams and amid struggles, those who imitated sickness flourished.

At the mass parade in Saigon to celebrate the one-hundredth anniversary of the end of the Vietnam War, the "Agent Orange Phalanx" gathered in Ho Chi Minh Square put on a show based on the aesthetics of illnesses, an event that attracted the attention of media from around the globe.

During the Vietnam War, the Americans dispatched low-flying aircraft to spray seventy-six million liters of dioxin-containing defoliant over ten percent of the forests, rivers, and soil of South Vietnam in order to eliminate the hideouts of the Viet Cong. Agent Orange—named after the orange-striped barrels in which the poisonous brew was shipped—contained extremely toxic 2,4-dichlorophenoxyacetic acid and 2,4,5-trichlorophenoxyacetic acid and was very stable chemically. Once released into the environment, it took more than nine years for fifty percent of the compounds to break down, and they persisted for more than fourteen years in the human body. The chemicals also could cycle through the food chain without being destroyed.

The marchers who made up the phalanx came from all over the world and were well prepared. In the front were what appeared to be a group of deformed children. Some were curled up in electric wheelchairs, their limbs flopping uselessly as though made of rubber—indeed, a few had no limbs at all; some showed smooth skin where eyes should be; some had swollen heads with bulges that resembled the lobes of a heart; some had legs fused together like the lower body of a mermaid.

In fact, they were not really people at all, but genetically modified pets who wore synthetic human skin. Speakers on their bodies played loops of prerecorded political slogans chanted in eerie voices.

Behind them stood the "festering detachment": Hodgkin's lymphoma, chloracne, scarlet warriors who looked as if their skin had been stripped off. As the marchers moved, the sarcomas and swellings covering their bodies quivered, and fluids of various colors seeped from bursting boils and sacs to paint symbols of peace on the ground. They embraced each other, kissed each other, spat and smeared and sprayed bodily fluids at the camera, and shouted in indistinct voices. The time and resources they must have invested to pull off such a stunt were unimaginable.

Then came the "crawlers," who had to march very slowly because they had lost the use of arms or legs. Most of them were truly physically disabled, but enhanced their deformity through prosthetics connected to their bodies with loose flaps of synthetic skin, or by exaggerating the unnatural angles at which their limbs were twisted. They resembled creeping creatures with segmented bodies and limbs from horror movies, and the more they exposed their bodies, the more they attracted the gaze of the cameras.

The climax of their performance was a re-creation of *V-J Day in Times Square*, except that Ho Chi Minh Square replaced Times Square, and a deformed child and a patient covered in tumors kissed instead of the nurse and the sailor. Magnesium bulbs flashed, satellites beamed the scene live, and billions witnessed the juicy *Kiss of Agent Orange*.

Who was to say it wasn't beautiful?

CONTROLLED PERSONALITY SHATTERING

If you could choose to become a different self, would you?

Don't mistake this for some self-help platitude, a sip of chicken soup for the soul. I mean literally a different self.

Jung, the disciple who rebelled against his master Freud, once said, "I simply believe that some part of the human Self or Soul is not subject to the laws of space and time." The quote might appear as an attempt at footnoting his concept of archetypes, but in reality it came about after Jung was struck by the ideas of the *I Ching*, as introduced by Richard Wilhelm, a German sinologist.

Together, Wilhelm and Jung were responsible for *The Secret of the Golden Flower: A Chinese Book of Life*, which had been described as a practical guide for using ancient Daoist philosophy to integrate personality. The 1962 publication turned out to be a visionary prediction of humanity's increasingly fractured lifestyle.

Sociologists speak of the "role set" as a competitive strategy humans developed over the course of their evolution. A role set refers to the collection of roles and behaviors associated with one's social status, an adaptation for social interactions under specific environmental conditions. Still, the role set is about controlled role shifts because it is limited to the Freudian ego and does not influence the unconscious id.

Technology accelerated evolution.

Many early Internet users seemed to experience a mild form of dissociative identity disorder which allowed them to easily switch personalities between different windows. One second and an Alt-Tab were all it took to change from a hardworking single career woman to a seductive sex-starved minx. As time spent on the net became fragmented, pervasive, and nonlinear, many surplus personalities were created without being handled appropriately. Like fragments of an operating system, these personalities accumulated in the subconscious, where they silently eroded the foundation of all personalities and erupted from time to time in the form of harrowing news stories about murderous rampages committed by the mentally ill.

At the beginning of the twenty-second century, the brain-computer interface became a viable commercial product. Developers created many brain-network apps that allowed users to consciously operate datalinks. As parallel programming proliferated, an operating system called "Sliding Windows" was developed, which gave users the ability to smoothly switch between cognitive processes. Predictably, the Far East fundamentalist terrorist organization SHAJI released a trojan called the Window-Breaker, engineered specifically to attack Sliding Windows. The malware spread through social networks and embedded itself in the innermost part of the user's installation of Sliding Windows, where it proceeded to sow complete chaos in the operating system's process-switching mechanism.

When an infected user flirted with her lover, the personality for dealing with the boss came to the front; when she endured a tongue-lashing by the boss, the personality for caressing a pet became active; and when the puppy rubbed itself against her legs, begging to play, the user instead panted with sexual desire.

Over three billion were infected with multiple-personalities switching disorder (MPSD), the great plague of the cyberpunk age.

To halt the spread of the malware, social networks were partitioned into quarantine zones. A twenty-second-century version of medieval witch hunts played out on the net as AI network officers, disguised as random programs, interacted with users on social networks to evaluate whether they had been infected by the trojan. And if the answer was yes, the user was forcibly cut off from the network and placed into off-grid rehabilitation. After completing the treatment process, patients were evaluated on their ability to control multiple personalities, which determined whether they would be allowed to return to the beautiful new digital world.

Overnight, the valuation of the brain-computer industry fell to a low not seen in twenty years.

Amazingly, mainland China was scarcely affected by this network storm. On the map tracking the malware's progress across the globe, China remained the only patch of healthy dark green, a fact that attracted worldwide interest. After extensive analysis, experts came to the conclusion that China was spared because of three reasons: one, the highly regulated nature of China's Internet industry; two, the latest version of China's Great Firewall; and three, a surprising discovery made after a detailed comparison of the fMRI and ECoG data from Chinese users and a control group, which showed that Chinese users' subconscious was already fundamentally fragmented and could seamlessly switch between different egos. Most important, each fragmentary personality was absolutely and sincerely convinced that it was the true self.

The discovery shocked the world. People dug up Wilhelm's forgotten dusty tome, hoping to find inspiration within. They discovered the secret of personality management from the mysterious ancient East, and by integrating the newest neural language programming (NLP) techniques, they hoped to rescue a world on the verge of total breakdown.

Several schools of Eastern mystical philosophy became trendy, including traditional Tantric Buddhist techniques for integrating mudras and poses to indicate the anchoring of personalities, I Ching–derived methods for using military-grade software to stimulate the cortex in order to integrate yin-yang neural patterns, and so on and so forth. But the most influential school of philosophy was without a doubt spread by the Chinese government's army of retired government cadres, who went overseas to set up "Lao Tzu Institutes."

The Lao Tzu Institutes taught a whole systematic curriculum that helped MPSD-sufferers find the way back by the Daoist Path, utilizing techniques such as traditional mystical exercises and Chan Buddhist–style meditation to help the practitioner achieve enlightenment on the nature of life, until the spiritual universe had been rearranged to the harmonious, yin-yang-balanced state of the primeval Innocent Babe.

I'm not going to tell you the result of this effort—the known Path is not the True Path, as Lao Tzu would say.

But suffice it to say that the Chinese nation, for the first time since the thirteenth-century *Il Milione* composed by Marco Polo, had once again managed to export its wondrous values to the world.

TWIN ELEGIES

It all began with the discovery of a woody perennial in the Amazon called *Duoliquotica*. Native legends claimed that the plant was made of the blood and essence of an ancient god, who appeared as a single head atop two bodies. This was reflected in the biology of the plant, which was dioecious. The male and female plants grew side by side, and entwined around each other as they reached maturity. After fertilization, large fruits grew atop pairs of plants, not unlike an outsized head on top of two slender bodies.

Scientists extracted from the plant a previously unknown compound with mysterious properties, also named "duoliquotica." After accidental exposure to the compound during a trial, a pregnant subject, Julia Kristeva, found herself the mother of a pair of identical twins. Thus did the mystery of the compound begin to be unveiled. In subsequent trials, twenty-three more pairs of identical twins were born. Later, researchers would refer to them as the "Duo 24," though the media preferred the more sensational B-movie moniker "Twinning God's 24."

The first pair of twins, Adam and Eva, were famous around the world even before they had learned to talk. The babies' laughter and cries were completely in sync. No matter how far apart they were placed from each other, their expressions mirrored each other's within 0.3 seconds. As their vocabulary grew, their strange talent developed into an intolerably eerie performance.

They seemed to always speak simultaneously, and stopped and started again in perfect sync. At first, an observer might think they were just speaking their own thoughts, but recording the twins' speech and playing it back showed that it was a highly efficient dialog. There was no delay introduced by the need to comprehend the other; the two sentences, overlaying the same segment of time, were statement and response.

Indeed, electroencephalograms showed that they could understand each other without any speech. The simultaneous speech was nothing more than a parlor trick for showing off.

Scientists were excited by this first verifiable example of telepathy in history. Shortly, the other twins also displayed various degrees of psychic connection. Bafflingly, the connections did not seem to depend on any kind of detectable signal exchange: electromagnetic waves, biochemical signals, vibrations through the air. . . . Even when each member of a pair was enclosed in a separate full-isolation chamber, they still could sense the other's emotions and thoughts.

Everything indicated the power of the ancient god, similar to quantum entanglement. No matter how far the particles were separated, as soon as one member of an entangled pair changed state, the other changed the same way.

Back then, humanity's understanding of basic theory had not yet advanced to the point where this phenomenon was seen as innate to nature. Thus, after the initial explosive media coverage died down, the research project, unable to make any real progress, became classified. All the research subjects were drafted into military service to act as long-distance communication devices, far more sensitive and secure than any cryptographic equipment.

The American military relied on the twins to gather a great deal of intelligence. Russia, the Middle East, East Asia, the EU—in each area the Americans first relied on bribes to open key doors, and then deployed the twins to transmit intelligence without fear of detection. This method worked well until a rather unexpected romance exposed the whole plot.

The ninth pair of twins, David and Peter, fell in love with the same Japanese woman—more precisely, it was Peter who, through long-distance entanglement with David, fell in love with Minako Noda, a Self-Defense Forces officer. Unfortunately, Peter could only experience this love secondhand through his brother. Peter requested David swap places with him multiple times, but David refused. Driven by jealousy, Peter sought revenge in a manner befitting a member of Duo 24.

Night and day, Peter transmitted paranoid delusions to David without cease, even when they were asleep. David was powerless to resist the torrent and sank into delirium, at which point Peter directed him to kill his lover, turn himself in, and confess his role in the American plot.

After recovering his senses, David committed suicide. At the moment that he stopped breathing, the smiling Peter, three thousand kilometers away, tumbled from a park bench and lay motionless in the fallen leaves, as though he had expected this fate for himself.

The tragedy sent shock waves through the remaining members of Duo 24. All their lives, they had lived as the mirror of each other's souls, but never faced the fact that each of them was also an individual, with his or her own desires, fears, and death. Some, in despair, saw their gift as a divine curse, a genetic defect in the guise of a benefit. The twins were tragic puppets entangled in one life, powerless to dissolve the invisible bonds of fate and doomed to die at any moment to accompany the other.

Five pairs of twins chose to commit suicide. Their bodies were buried in double coffins, sunken deep in cement graves.

The military offered the rest of the twins a way out: they could choose to enter long-term cryogenic storage and await a solution for their curse in the far future.

Six pairs chose to continue to live in the world and support each other; another six pairs chose to enter the cryogenic chamber, placing their faith in the future; and the remaining six pairs were mired in conflict: one member of each pair wanted to be frozen to escape their unknown fate, while the other member would not let go of the life they already had. If only one twin were frozen, he or she was very likely to die in hibernation when the other one expired.

In the end, the conflict-riven pairs reached a compromise: they would swap places once every ten years. As each entered cryogenic sleep, they placed their life in the hands of their identical twin, trusting they would treat their twin with benevolence. It was like the words of the Gospel of John: "A new commandment I give unto you, That ye love one another."

THE NEW MOON

Scientists told us that 4.4 billion years ago, a body about the size of Mars slammed into the Earth, and the resulting fragments coalesced into the moon. Sixty-five million years ago, a large asteroid impacted the Earth, causing the extinction of the dinosaurs. Twelve thousand and nine hundred years ago, fragments from a comet breaking apart fell on the frozen tundra of North America, leading to the deaths of the mammoths and other mammalian megafauna as well as the collapse of the ancient Clovis civilization. Thereafter, an extremely frigid climate reigned for a thousand years.

Archaeologists told us that the cataclysmic end of the world prophesied by the ancient Maya to occur in 2012 would be brought about by Planet X, the legendary Nibiru—meaning "ferry boat" in

Sumerian—which would cross the orbit of the Earth once every 3,630 years as it careened along its long elliptical journey around the sun. Its intense gravity would lead to shifting tectonic plates, deviation in the Earth's magnetic poles, earthquakes and tsunamis, climate change, and volcanic eruptions. Humanity would thus be ferried into a new era.

The Little Astrology Prince of Hong Kong told us, in his dulcet voice, that Venus retrograde was over. The key thing to understand about Venus retrograde was that *it was always going to be over*. It gave you a chance to think about relationships that no longer had meaning, and to stop maintaining them out of habit.

Of course, humanity did not enter a new era in 2012—at least not on my timeline. Instead, the human race experienced a transformative event in the twenty-third century. A large asteroid nicknamed "the Wanderer" (about the size of Shanghai), after a long journey through the vastness of space, was captured by the gravity well of the Earth-Moon system and eventually stabilized itself at one of the Lagrange points. The Earth, from then on, had a second moon, which was called the New Moon.

Humans, a species prone to romanticism, began to contemplate subtle changes in themselves once they had become habituated to new tidal patterns and new heavenly sights. Women's monthly cycles grew chaotic, and moods swung to extremes. Tens of thousands of fetuses stopped developing due to hormonal imbalances induced by the New Moon—a phenomenon described as "the dark side effects of the New Moon." An invisible force began to influence the development of the human race.

Some people exhibited strange allergic reactions on nights when the New Moon was full. Eerie patterns appeared on their skin, muscle fibers tensed, pupils dilated, and their minds became confused and extremely aggressive. They would tear off their clothes, and run naked on all fours through city streets or the wilderness, as though returning to primitive worship of totemic animals. Subsequent examination of these individuals revealed that branches of their Y chromosomes still retained vestiges from the earliest stages of human evolution. After filtering for such signs in the DNA profiles of the population, a classified marker was added to the files of individuals with such genes.

Due to antidiscrimination legislation, their identities were kept secret; however, they were required to take suppressant medication and to wear special light-filtering contact lenses to counter the awakening effects of the New Moon. Some urban youths saw this as a new trend, and held transformation parties on full New Moon nights, where they turned into beasts with the aid of drugs and machinery and engaged in mass orgies.

The growth cycles of crops and livestock also changed, and astronomers had to work hard to devise new months, solar terms, and calendars. They became so complicated that it was impossible for anyone to understand or to derive based on simple astronomical observations; instead, farmers and farming machines had to rely on constant official updates.

The truly shocking new phenomenon involved those who were conceived during the full New Moon, known as the "New Mooners."

Scientists never could explain the specific role played by the light of the New Moon at the moment when the sperm fertilized the egg or during cell division. No satisfying explanation emerged through analysis of the light spectrum, gravity, magnetic field, or any other possible factor. The only thing scientists knew was that the fetuses in the womb were developing into a new population distinct from all known human populations. A terrified humanity came to the conclusion that the normal fetuses whose development had been halted by the New Moon previously had perhaps been the victims of evolutionary competition against this new race.

Still, over 97.52 percent of the parents of such fetuses chose to carry them to full term, regardless of whether they would turn out to be angels or demons.

The New Mooners were not too different from normal humans in physical appearance, other than a change in the refractive index of the epidermis that gave their skin the sheen of plastic or thin membranes. Their metabolism, however, was three to five times slower than normal humans, which meant that they were also exceptionally long-lived. Most suffered mild depression, which caused many parents to worry that they would commit suicide. But after long observation and understanding, people came to realize that the depression-like symptoms were really the effects of a mental barrier that allowed them to filter out the information overload of the external world and to reduce cognitive load and mental stress. The New Mooners needed to focus their attention on a far more important problem, a problem that would require the efforts of thousands of generations.

The problem was this: the New Moon, which they viewed as a creation god, was going to be inexorably worn down by the passage of time. As the stability of the gravitational system decayed, the New Moon would depart from the Lagrange point and, pulled by gravity, fall onto the surface of the Earth, slowly and poetically destroying everything.

They wanted to save the New Moon.

NEOTENY

At the beginning of the twenty-first century, people thought of it as a mental illness, and specialists called it "Peter Pan syndrome." Though these individuals were in their thirties and forties, they refused to grow up, instead speaking and behaving immaturely as though they were living the fantasy of Neverland. They were terrified of reality, shied away from competition, avoided responsibility and duty, fled from commitment by constantly changing partners, and sought refuge in the illusory joys of drugs and alcohol.

They attributed all these symptoms to overly protective families, and some even resented their parents for how much they'd indulged them in childhood.

Like our age-old pursuit of beauty and eternal youth, this development was but another tiny step on the ladder to the next stage.

In the middle of the twenty-second century, a developmental disorder that slowed down growth began to spread. Patients' biological clocks seemed to tick at a pace many times slower than normal, and secondary sexual characteristics did not develop until they were in their thirties. Menopause and andropause were correspondingly delayed. Scientists came up with the explanation that since human lifespans had been extended by various technical measures to exceed 150 years, it was not surprising that youth would also last longer. Numerous literary and multimedia works celebrated the long youth, and patients with the developmental disorder became models for the future direction of human evolution. Many sociologists and anthropologists offered arguments as to why the disorder had the potential to reshape culture and redefine what was "normal," and the "normals" of the past would be abandoned by Darwinian progress.

But they saw only a part of the problem.

Compared to other animals, humans remain in their juvenile state for a proportionally much longer time period. Among primates, the juvenile stages of lemurs, rhesus monkeys, gorillas, and humans last 2.5 years, 7.5 years, 10 years, and 20 years, respectively. The sexual maturation of humans comes five years later than chimpanzees, and similarly with the replacement of baby teeth. Why do we need such a disproportionately long childhood?

As early as the mid-twentieth century, scientists had discovered physiological correspondences between human children and young chimpanzees, such as small jaws, flat faces, and sparse body hair. Humans and chimpanzees share 99.4 percent of their genes, but almost 40 percent of the genes whose expression changed over time activated far later in humans than in chimpanzees, especially those responsible for growth of the gray matter in the brain responsible for higher thinking.

Most child development authorities informed parents that brains in the process of maturation, while synapses were still in their formative stages, were most receptive to new information and held enormous potential for future capacity.

Homo sapiens, with its long juvenile stage, pulled ahead in the primate evolutionary race and achieved first place. We retain our juvenile features, such as the lack of body hair and a disproportionately large head, into adulthood. Similarly, we hold on to childish cognitive characteristics such as curiosity and a desire to learn throughout our lives. Some people even have a genetic mutation that allows them to keep generating all through adulthood the lactase necessary to digest milk, an ability generally lost once children are weaned—indeed, they call other humans without the mutation the "lactose-intolerant," as though they have a disorder.

Neoteny was critical to our species; was it time for a second wave?

The scientific world wished to take advantage of this opportunity to push human evolution forward, but they were faced with a legal problem. Patients affected by the developmental disorder were legally adults, but their physiology and psychology remained childish. Controversy erupted over whether the patients had the capacity to agree to be experimental subjects on their own, or whether it was necessary to secure the permission of guardians. As the issue dragged out in the courts, online mobs exposed the personal information of the patients' relatives and derisively criticized them as "selfish monkeys." The online mobs argued that those who, out of concern for their own security, ignored the far greater mission of advancing the human race did not deserve to be called *sapiens*. Historically, of course, such arguments had been raised again and again, like recurring waves in the river of time.

In the end, logic won over emotion. States assumed responsibility as guardians of the patients. After signing human experimentation agreements on behalf of their wards, the governments purchased expensive insurance and named the patients' relatives as beneficiaries, by way of compensation. Everyone shut up, and the experiments could finally proceed.

Like an upgraded version of the therapists in *A Clockwork Orange*, scientists prodded and poked and stimulated the patients in various ways, injecting them with torrents of information. They couldn't wait to expose the experimental subjects to the entirety of human knowledge and history during their long-but-still-all-too-brief periods of plasticity, hoping to stimulate the formation of more complex synaptic connections in the human brain, which had not evolved in ages, and thereby push back the frontiers of knowledge and derive solutions for the many complicated problems plaguing humanity. Subconsciously, the researchers thought of themselves as God, hoping to create a new race of Man on the sixth day.

They ended up with bedlamites, imbeciles, depressives, sex addicts, and vegetables.

The arrogant researchers didn't even know where they had gone wrong. They did not understand the secret of the genetic switches; they were not the ones who had set the trap.

Humans had once tamed wolves into dogs. They tried to breed canid adults to retain juvenile features such as floppy ears, short snouts, large eyes, playfulness, the desire to please people, and to eliminate the bloodthirst and ferocity of the mature wolf. Humans did this not because they wanted to help wolves evolve into *Canis sapiens*; they simply wanted to bend the wolves to human aesthetics.

It was a misunderstanding over a subtle—if rather sick—preference for cuteness.

RITUAL DEPENDENCY/WITHDRAWAL

You walk a long way to the newsstand and ask for the magazine; you pay for it, put it in your bag, and after a long journey involving various forms of transportation, return to a secluded space; you turn on the light, orange or pale white, and rip open the nonbiodegradable plastic wrap; you pour yourself a cup of tea, or open a can of diet soda; you caress the pattern in the paper and, deliberately or randomly, open the magazine to this page.

You start to read. When you're done, you're thoughtful or weary; you tell others to read or not read this story.

You have completed one insignificant ritual out of the millions in your life.

Humans are ritualistic animals. From the ancient past to the present, from cradle to grave. Rituals solidify in our minds, glue together groups and cultures, chase away the terror of death, help us find our places, define the meaning of existence. The powerful in every culture have used rituals to assemble multitudes, to extract wealth, to form parties and factions, to consolidate rule. Rituals give endless labels to people, in addition to their names, telling them where they belong, but in the end there was no label for the self.

In my era, technology allows ritual to become an indivisible part of everyday life. It's implanted into you and becomes part of your genetic heritage to be passed on to your children and their children, multiplying and mutating, more vigorous than its host.

Maybe it's true in your age as well?

You cannot control the impulse to refresh the page. Information explosion brings anxiety, but can fill your husk of a soul. Every fifteen seconds, you move the mouse, open up your social networking profile, browse the comments, retweet and reblog, close the page, and do it all over again fifteen seconds later. You can't stop.

You can no longer talk to people in real life. Air has lost its role as the medium for transmitting voice. You sit in a ring, your eyes glued to the latest mobile device in your hand as though worshiping the talisman of some ancient god. Your thoughts flow into virtual platforms through the tips of your fingers. You're arguing, laughing, flirting, joking. But reality around you is a silent desert.

You cannot free yourself from the control of artificial environments. Ritual is omnipresent. It is no longer restricted to sacrifice, sermon, mass, concert, or game—performed on a central stage where the classical unities hold. Ritual itself is evolving, turning into distributed cloud computing, evenly spread out into every nook and cranny of your daily life. Sensors know everything and regulate the temperature, humidity, air currents, and light around you; adjust your heart rate, hormonal balance, sexual arousal, mood. Artificial intelligence is a god: you think it's there for your welfare, bringing you new opportunities, but you've become the egg in the incubator, the marionette attached to wires. Every second of every minute of every day, you are the sacrifice that completes this unending, grand ritual.

You *are* the ritual.

Radical thinkers obsess over how to withdraw from all this. The power of ritual comes from repetition, not its content. Day after day, the repetition of poses and movements gradually seeps into the depth of consciousness, like a hard drive's read-write head repeatedly tracing the pattern of an idea, until the idea becomes indistinguishable from free will itself. It's like that sci-fi flick from the beginning of the twenty-first century. Romantic love is ritual's most loyal consumer, along with patriotism.

The radicals try to imitate the Luddites of old: destroy the machines, hack into systems, awaken the people, exhort everyone to abandon technology and return to the wilderness, where everyone can sharpen their character against the grindstone of severe nature and hope to recover a primitive, pure simplicity. The media, rather mercilessly, point out that what they are advocating is a good fit for the ritualistic habits practiced by Zen Buddhists of seventh-century Japan.

The only thing that can be done is to do nothing.

Like marionettes with their strings cut, the radicals fall wherever they are: bedrooms, subways, airports, public squares, offices, beaches, assembly lines, cafeterias, streets, restrooms. . . . They do nothing, say nothing, only lying still and quietly, waiting for their bodies to waste away, waiting for their lives to be exhausted. They wield nothingness in their war against meaning, use the lack of will to dissolve freedom, employ the loss of the self to construct the self.

Sensors detect the fading of their vital signs, and artificial intelligences activate robotic helpers to take the withdrawing bodies to medical facilities via the transportation network. Like skiffs floating over the river of normal people, the bodies are gathered into clean, white, therapeutic rooms where various life-support systems and cables are plugged into them. They are now caught in a dilemma: a new paradox rises from nothingness. They will use their bodies to complete this unmoving struggle in human history's first instance of mass suicide committed in imitation of natural death.

They have completed one of the greatest rituals.

CHAOTIC CHRONOSENSE

Time is a human illusion, said a Jewish scientist in Europe in 1915. From then on, the smooth and unchanging steel plate that was time melted, like the soft clocks draping from tree branches under Dalí's paintbrush.

Scientists attempted to control time via multiple paths: speed, gravity, entropy, quantum entanglement . . . but had to concede defeat in the end. Humanity tried everything to conquer this shapeless and colorless but omnipresent specter. It was there at the start of life, but even at the doorstep of death, the cleverest mind could not understand its secrets. Time's arrow is bound up with all human civilization's fears: it has a single direction, and once loosed it never stops, never turns back, all the way to the heat death of the universe.

Since it was impossible to change the world, the only choice was to change the self.

Researchers then focused on the sense of time in the human brain. Every day, fragments of memory surfaced in the neurochemical webs of billions of heads—wasn't this phenomenon a form of time travel? Experiments showed that by stimulating specific areas of the hippocampus, it was possible to induce the feeling of déjà vu in test subjects and cause them to treat the scenes they were experiencing in their lives as though they had already been previewed in childhood. It was as if a marvelous editor had cut a life into segments and then pasted them back together in a new order to create the sensation of traveling through time.

With mastery of this secret, time turned into putty in the magician's hand, capable of being stretched and sculpted into any shape. It was a fascinating paradox wherein speeding up brain activity slowed the passage of external time, and vice versa—it was the theory of relativity applied to the world of consciousness. Those truly skilled in the art could even implant a closed loop in the subject's brain so that the poor fool lived out a real-life version of *Groundhog Day*, repeating the same day over and over again, even though it was just an illusion created by manipulating memory.

Chronosense, Ltd., was formed in response to this opportunity. Based on the needs of the individual customer, they offered different levels of adjustment to their time sense and charged a fortune for such services. Of course, the fee was calculated precisely based on the passage of time in the physical world.

In East Asia, students trapped in a culture based on tests needed to make the most of the little time they had. The night before big exams, with Chronosense's help, they could stay up and swallow a semester's worth of knowledge and examination-fu, like the memory bread from *Doraemon*. There was a 0.5 percent probability that this technique would lead to a stroke, and so a drug that counteracted the effects became a popular purchase for the students as well.

Those seeking the thrill of psychoactive substances, on the other hand, wanted the exact opposite effect, which was for the subjective experience of time to slow down until it seemed to stop. They wanted to make the drug-induced high gradually expand like an explosion frozen in a glacier, each blooming firework as Zen-like as an unmoving mountain. They sat in the dark, waiting to submerge in the chemical ecstasy, until the mushroom cloud devoured the last trace of their consciousness, leaving the flesh on life-maintenance. For them, time ceased to exist, and only hallucination was reality.

The aged were the most fervent fans of memory, and they made the most meticulous demands of Chronosense, careless of what the offerings cost. After locating the most joyful days of their lives, they edited them together into a highlight reel that they looped over and over in what little time they had left. It was the best way to squeeze the most out of the end of life, so they could die with smiles on their faces.

Human ingenuity would never go to waste. Always, evil genius knew exactly what to do with it.

Authoritarian regimes soon discovered the vast potential of this technology. By employing a special edition of the tech, they enslaved their people and managed to squeeze twelve hours' worth of physical and mental labor from the population in every legally mandated eight-hour shift. While the ordinary people teetered on the edge of exhaustion and collapse, GDP rose and rose. In order to release some of the dangerous pressure of overwork, governments opened resorts specifically for vacationing workers where their overwound sense of time could be adjusted via technical measures to achieve some semblance of balance.

The laboring masses, kept in the dark about the truth, worked even harder to earn the right to vacation, where all they recovered was the time that had been stolen from them.

Their children, on the other hand, seemed to be born with their sense of time out of balance. As they also entered the labor force, and their sense of time was further twisted, things began to spin out of control. The next generation learned to forget, an instinctual strategy for bringing relief to the overburdened brain. Periodically—the exact length of time differed from individual to individual—the memories of these people reset themselves, and they woke up as newborns with blank slates. As those with reformatted brains imitated each other, a primitive savagery began to spread like a plague, and violence and lust broke through the barriers set up by civilization and technology.

The wild people took over the streets and cities and destroyed every machine and institution that tried to change their raw nature.

They truly possessed time. They no longer needed time.

EPILOGUE: SPEAKING IN TONGUES

In the beginning was the Word, and the Word was with God, and the Word was God.

Or, as a structural linguist would put it: language constructed thought; thought understood and transformed the world; and so language was the world's prime mover, was God.

Wherever God was, so was the Devil, just as light could not be separated from darkness.

It was language, not tools, that separated humans from apes. The bridge between the signifier and the signified connected the world of subjectivity with the physical world. Meaning was like the water of the Ganges, a wide-flowing torrent. Humans extracted drops of sensory experience, saved them, classified them, generalized them, and sublimated them until the border between the self and objective reality was defined. Then they learned to exchange thoughts between different individuals, to communicate intent, and society began to form: division of labor, work, family, power, state, war— everything was built on this foundation. Language was the measure of understanding, and every debate among humanity was based on our shared linguistic system.

The gaps and seams persisted in the places that could not be encompassed by words.

Religion, music, painting, love, pain, joy, loneliness—these words are like the tips of icebergs, concealing the unfathomable, vast, complicated feelings beneath the surface. They accompanied humanity's cultural genes from ancient times, and like the sedimentary strata of geology, folded and overlapped one another, interpenetrating and merging, evolving until today.

When you discuss these topics, you know not what you're discussing.

All societies wish to promulgate an effective set of linguistic regulations in order to rectify the thoughts of the masses. From Qin Shihuang's edict for all China to write the same way, to the Newspeak of *1984*, words have vanished and new idioms have been invented. Some expressions were usable only by certain classes in certain places, while the masses were required to avoid these formulations reserved to the noble and highborn, and so they invented slang that required the overactive associative brain to smoothly wield its store of homonyms, puns, metonyms and rhymes, a celebration of the tongue and the vocal cords.

In a certain age, even revelry was a disciplined ideological tool, realized through technology.

The government installed firewalls in the language center of the brain of every newborn, thus achieving for the first time in history a real-time language surveillance network. When what an individual wished to say triggered the filters in their firewall—which were constantly kept up to date—the firewall cut off the person's speech and punished them with an appropriate level of pain. On the other hand, when the person spoke the words that satisfied the desires of those in power, the firewall rewarded them with a pleasure similar to drugs.

A brave new world of reward and punishment.

The system worked so well that people, of their own initiative, devised a way to integrate the filters into their genes so that they could be passed on to their children, allowing them to meld with the firewall even more seamlessly. Eventually, even the merest hint of an undesirable thought would be eliminated before it could take root, maximally reducing the potential for being punished. The mechanism gradually became a part of the unconscious, assimilated into the part of the cortex that we inherited from our amphibious, piscine, reptilian ancestors, meshed with the most primitive part of human language.

Then things took a different turn.

Humanity never fully understood what happened next, not even now in the time I'm from. One theory is that humanity was indeed the creation of some higher intelligence, who implanted into the human mind a highly designed language system. The system evolved as civilization developed, but when a foreign invader threatened its fundamental principles, it would reset the system to factory defaults and return everything to the origin. The system was also highly infectious.

Can you imagine it? A world without language. Everything collapsed.

The problem wasn't that it was impossible to talk; rather, humanity lost the very tool necessary to understand the world and the self. The universe returned to primeval chaos.

I am the product of a second system. Very few individuals showed symptoms of it—maybe in your time, it would be called "divine inspiration."

It was no longer I who spoke words, but words that spoke me.

It was as if the divine intelligence had lost patience with foolish humans. The chosen ones who brought with them a brand-new linguistic logic had to direct the unenlightened primitives to reunderstand the world and rebuild civilization. The new world did seem to be more peaceful, more enlightened, more perfect. Scientists invented time machines and discovered the theory of timelines. They dispatched envoys to parallel universes along different timelines to spread the gospel so that the humans in these other worlds could avoid their mistakes. Many of these envoys did not meet happy fates.

This is why I, Stanley, have come from the future to speak to you. For reasons that I cannot reveal, I will terminate my sojourn here shortly and leave your timeline to leap into another unknown world.

In your universe, the number nine is special, symbolizing permanence, rebirth, the supreme. I hope the nine chapters of my gospel can accompany the lost souls of this world through the door at the end of time, to achieve eternal recurrence.

ESSAYS

A BRIEF INTRODUCTION TO CHINESE SCIENCE FICTION AND FANDOM[24]

by *Regina Kanyu Wang*

Chinese science fiction has remained largely mysterious to the outside world until recently. In 2015, Liu Cixin (刘慈欣) won the first Hugo Award for Asia with his novel *The Three-Body Problem* (《三体》), and in August 2016, Hao Jingfang (郝景芳) won the second with her novelette "Folding Beijing" (《北京折叠》)—both translated by Ken Liu, who is himself a Hugo-winning American author. Now, as more and more Chinese science fiction is translated into English and other languages, it is the perfect time to explore its history.

This essay mainly focuses on science fiction, not fantasy, but a few words on fantasy may be helpful. In China, the boundary between science fiction, or *kehuan* (科幻), and fantasy, or *qihuan* (奇幻), is seen as quite rigid. However, due to our historical tradition in

---

24 Originally written in English.

myths and kung fu stories, it is hard to define Chinese fantasy as a whole. You will find it hard to tell *qihuan* (奇幻: fantasy) from *xuanhuan* (玄幻: mostly referring to online fiction with Chinese-style supernatural elements) and *mohuan* (魔幻: mostly referring to fiction with Western-style magic elements). Narrowly speaking, though, current Chinese fantasy literature excludes themes such as grave robbery (盗墓, *daomu*: stories involving a group of treasure-seekers breaking into ancient graves, where they come across ghosts and all sorts of other evil creatures), time travel (穿越, *chuanyue*: stories featuring a contemporary person traveling back in time to ancient dynasties for some unexplained [and unimportant] reason, where they become involved in complicated courtly intrigue or some other soap-opera-like plot), and Daoism immortality-chasing (修真, *xiuzhen*: stories featuring a protagonist overcoming various challenges to pursue immortality by Daoism method), which stand as popular genres by themselves.

There have been fantasy magazines and fan groups throughout contemporary China, but compared to science fiction, Chinese fantasy literature is not at its peak. Having said that, TV series and movies adapted from successful early works are starting to come out in recent times. For example, in 2016 we have *Novoland: The Castle in the Sky* (2016), a TV series based on the Novoland fantasy universe, which is meant to be China's Dungeons & Dragons and is the collaborative effort of many fans and writers; and *Ice Fantasy* (2016), a TV series adapted from the bestselling *City of Fantasy* (2003), written by Guo Jingming, a famous Chinese YA author. However, for this essay, I will only talk about science fiction in mainland China.

1.

PREHISTORY AND EARLY HISTORY OF CHINESE SF

Like all cultures, Chinese legends and myths have fantasy elements in abundance. In China, however, the first text in the science fiction genre can be found as early as 450 BC to 375 BC. In one of the classics of Daoism, *Liezi* (《列子》), we can find a story called "Yanshi" (《偃师》) in the chapter "The Questions of Tang" (《汤问》). Yanshi, a skilled mechanic, builds a delicate automaton resembling a real human being, which can move, sing, and dance. He shows the dummy to the king to prove his skill. The dummy is so delicate and convincing that the king suspects Yanshi is cheating him by using a real human. At the end, Yanshi has to break the automaton to prove that it is only made of wood and leather. Yanshi's automaton can be seen as a prototype for an early robot.

Science fiction as we know it today first came to China in the late Qing Dynasty. Chinese intellectuals like Lu Xun (鲁迅) and Liang Qichao (梁启超) emphasized the importance of science fiction as a tool to help the country prosper. In 1900, the Chinese translation of French author Jules Verne's *Around the World in Eighty Days* was published—it was the first piece of translated foreign science fiction published in China, translated by Chen Shoupeng (陈寿彭) and Xue Shaohui (薛绍徽) from an English translation (Geo M. Towle and N d'Anvers; Sampson Low, Marston & Co., London, 1873, *The Tour of the World in Eighty Days*, then changed to *Around the World in Eighty Days*). Lu Xun, arguably the most famous writer in modern Chinese literature, also translated several science fiction novels into Chinese, such as Verne's *From the Earth to the Moon* and *A Journey to the Centre of the Earth*, published in Chinese in 1903 and 1906 respectively. Lu Xun translated the novels from the Japanese translation by Inoue Tsutomu since he didn't know French. The earliest original Chinese science fiction novel we know of is *Colony of the Moon* (《月球殖民地》), written by Huangjiang Diaosou (荒江钓叟, pen name of an anonymous author, which means "Old Fisherman by a Deserted River"), serialized in a journal called *Illustrated Fiction* (《绣像小说》) in 1904 and 1905.

For a long time in China, literature has been regarded as something which should carry social responsibilities. During the early years of the twentieth century, science fiction in China was supposed to play the basic role of teaching advanced science as well as democracy from the West. Most of the Western SF that was translated into Chinese was adapted to serve this role. For example, Verne's original text for *From the Earth to the Moon* contains twenty-eight chapters, but Lu Xun's translation only has fourteen; *A Journey to the Centre of the Earth* has forty-five chapters in its original French text, but Lu Xun rewrote it into twelve chapters. Much of this effort was, ironically, devoted to cutting out some of the highly technical messages to make the story more exciting to readers.

Wars and political turmoil lasted from the late Qing Dynasty (1833 to 1911) to the Republic Era (1911 to 1949). Lao She (老舍)'s *Cat Country* (《猫城记》) came out in 1932. It may be the best-known Chinese SF around the world before the founding of the People's Republic. In this novel, the first-person narrator flies to Mars, but the aircraft is crushed as soon as it arrives. As the only survivor, the narrator is taken to the City of Cats by feline-faced aliens, where he then lives. With his ironic description of the alien community, the author criticizes his own society.

After the establishment of the People's Republic of China in 1949, the first wave of new Chinese SF came in the 1950s. *A Dream Tour of the Solar System* (《梦游太阳系》), by Zhang Ran (张然), was regarded to be the first story with SF elements in the PRC.[25] Published in 1950, it introduces astronomical bodies in the solar system in the format of a dream narrative, more like science fairy tale than hard sci-fi. Some of the big names at that time were Zheng Wenguang (郑文光) and Tong Enzheng (童恩正). Zheng Wenguang's *From Earth to Mars* (《从地球到火星》, 1954) was regarded as the first SF short story in the PRC. It's about three Chinese teenagers stealing a spaceship and flying to Mars for adventure. SF writers of the period were largely influenced by SF from the former Soviet Union. The complete collection of Jules Verne was translated from Russian into Chinese from 1957 to

25 Author's Note: Zhang Ran (张然) is not the same person as, and not related to, the science fiction author Zhang Ran (张冉), who began publishing in the 2000s and whose "The Snow of Jinyang" is in this anthology.

1962 because it was highly praised in the former Soviet Union. Works by former Soviet Union writers like Alexander Belyayev were also translated. Most science fiction of the period was written for kids or as popular science texts, optimistic and limited in scope.

Then came the Cultural Revolution, leaving little space for literature, and even less for science fiction. Anything that bore any relation to "Western capitalism" was regarded as harmful. Many writers were forced to stop writing. After the reform and opening-up policy, the golden age of Chinese SF finally arrived in the late 1970s. A large body of work emerged, along with a growing number of fan groups and magazines specializing in SF. During this time, Ye Yonglie (叶永烈) was one of the most prestigious writers. His *Little Know-It-All Travels around the Future World* (《小灵通漫游未来》, 1978), has sold more than 1.5 million copies, and its comic book adaptation sold another 1.5 million copies. Zheng Wenguang and Tong Enzheng started to write SF again. Zheng's *Flying to Sagittarius* (《飞向人马座》, 1979) became a milestone of Chinese SF. It tells the story of three teenagers trying their best to return to the Earth after roaming outside the solar system for years. And Tong's most famous work, *Death-Ray on Coral Island* (《珊瑚岛上的死光》, 1978), is about scientists fighting against evil corporations to protect the peace of humanity. *Coral Island* was adapted into the first SF movie in China in 1980 with the same title.

In 1983, the anti-spiritual-pollution campaigns wiped SF from the map again. Since 1979, there had been arguments on whether science fiction should be literature or popular science. The charge of pseudoscience was leveled against science fiction. In 1983, Deng Xiaoping, the Chinese paramount leader at the time, spoke against capitalism and exploitation in literary works. Science fiction was regarded as spiritual pollution because of the elements of capitalism and commercialism in it. Stories that talked about more than science were regarded as being harmful politically. Very few—or more accurately, none—dared to write or publish SF during the period. It wasn't until late 1980s and early 1990s that Chinese SF recovered from the attack and flourished again.

2.
PUBLICATION OF PROZINES

The definition of prozines in China is a bit different from the definition used in America. In China, you have to get a special number
called a "CN," similar to an "ISBN," certificated by the government,
to be allowed to publish prozines.

In the late 1970s and early 1980s, lots of SF magazines popped up
in China. In 1979, *Scientific and Literary* (《科学文艺》) began to publish in Sichuan Province. *Age of Science* (《科学时代》), *Science Literature Translation Series* (《科学文艺译丛》), *SF Ocean* (《科幻海洋》),
Wisdom Tree (《智慧树》), and *SF World–Selected SF Works* (《科幻
世界——科学幻想作品选刊》) appeared within the following three
years. However, all these magazines except *Scientific and Literary* stopped publishing during the anti-spiritual-pollution campaigns.

In 1980, *Scientific and Literary* sold about 200,000 copies of
each issue, but after the anti-spiritual-pollution campaigns, the
number dropped as low as 700 copies. After 1984, Yang Xiao (杨潇),
editor of the magazine, was selected as the president of *Scientific
and Literary*. Together with her team, she made great efforts to
hold the fort for Chinese SF. In 1991, the name of the magazine
was changed to *Science Fiction World* (《科幻世界》), and that year
in Chengdu, they held the annual conference of World SF. We can
look back to 1991 as the year Chinese SF started to flourish again.
By 1999, an essay question in China's National Higher Education
Entrance Exam, "What if memory could be transplanted?," was the
same as the title of an article published in *Science Fiction World*
that year. This partly pushed sales of *Science Fiction World* to its
peak: 361,000 copies of each issue in 2000.

As the twenty-first century drew closer, another important Chinese SF magazine came to life in the Shanxi Province. *Science Fiction King* (《科幻大王》) started to publish in 1994, changing its
name to *New Science Fiction* (《新科幻》) in 2011. The peak sales
were around 12,000 copies per issue in 2008. Unfortunately, at the

end of 2014, *New Science Fiction* stopped publishing due to its relatively low sales. *Science Fiction Cube* (《科幻Cube》) is the youngest member of the current existing SF prozine market in China. Its first three issues only came out in 2016, and each issue sold about 50,000 copies. Some other SF magazines appeared and disappeared in this period, including *World Science Fiction* (《世界科幻博览》) and *Science Fiction Story* (《科幻-文学秀》). Other publications, like *Mengya* (《萌芽》), *ZUI Found* (《文艺风赏》), and *Super Nice* (《超好看》), publish science fiction as well as other genres.

3.

BIRTH OF EARLY CHINESE FANDOM

The first Chinese SF fan group appeared in Shanghai in 1980. Philip Smith from the University of Pittsburgh visited Shanghai International Studies University (SISU) and delivered a course on science fiction literature. A scholar who worked at SISU at the time, Wu Dingbo (吴定柏) regards the science fiction club formed there as the first Chinese SF fan group. In 1981, Science Fiction Research Associations were founded in several cities like Shanghai, Guangdong, Heilongjiang, Ha'erbin, Liaoning, and Chengdu, and then all were swept away by the anti-spiritual-pollution campaigns. And it wasn't until 1988 that the Science Fiction Literature Committee was founded in Sichuan Writer's Association, chaired by Tong Enzheng. The committee aimed to unite science fiction writers in Sichuan and make Chinese SF writing prosper from its nadir.

In 1990, Yao Haijun (姚海军) established the Chinese Science Fiction Readers' Association with the help of his fanzine *Nebula*.

In the 1990s, regional fan groups and university clubs boomed all around China. The *Science Fiction World* magazine also founded its own fan club.

In 1998, the first online SF fan groups appeared in China. Chinese Science Fiction Online Association (中华网上科幻协会) and Feiteng Science Fiction Writing Group (飞腾科幻创作小组) were established.

The latter one was renamed Feiteng SF Corps (飞腾科幻军团) after it expanded. Some of the other important online fan groups were SF Utopia (科幻桃花源), River of No Return (大江东去科幻社区), and Space Lunatic Asylum (太空疯人院). Unfortunately none of them exist today. Some of the active members continued their discussion in the Science Fiction World group (with no relation to the magazine) on douban.com (a social networking website popular in China based on hobbies).

Quite a number of Chinese SF authors were active members of these fan groups.

4.

FANZINES

China's first fanzine was *Nebula* (《星云》), edited by Yao Haijun from 1989 to 2007. During these years, forty issues were published. Yao Haijun was a worker in a logging factory in Heilongjiang when he started the fanzine. Now he is the editor in chief of *Science Fiction World* magazine. *Nebula* played an extremely important role in the development of modern Chinese fandom, and even in the history of Chinese science fiction at large. It was the bridge between editors, writers, researchers, and readers. The peak circulation was more than 1,200 copies per issue.

Some of the other fanzines prevalent in the 1990s were *Galaxy* (《银河》), edited by Fan Lin (范霖) in Zhengzhou; *Up to the Ladder toward the Sky* (《上天梯》), edited by Xu Jiulong (徐久隆) in Chengdu; *Planet 10* (《第十号行星》) and *TNT*, edited by Wang Lunan (王鲁南) in Shandong; and *Universe Wind* (《宇宙风》), edited by Zeng Deqiang and Zhou Yukun (曾德强、周宇坤). There were also letterzines, such as *Nebula*, sent to subscribers all around the country. However, most of these only survived a couple of years due to lack of money and time.

Regional SF fan groups also published their fanzines. *Cubic Light Year* (《立方光年》) in Beijing and *Supernova* (《超新星》) in Tianjin were two of the key representatives. Receiving the support of many SF writers, *Cubic Light Year* was of quite high quality. However, both zines only published a few issues because it was hard for the editors and writers to keep running the projects on a voluntary basis.

University SF clubs also publish their fanzines, but these too have a short lifespan. One exception to the rule is *Critical Point* (《临界点》) published by Sichuan University Science Fiction Association, which published its special twentieth-anniversary issue in 2013.

With the dawn of the Internet era, numerous netzines appeared. Chinese Science Fiction Online Association published *Sky and Fire* (《苍穹火焰》) in 1998 and 1999, with a total of seven issues, and River of No Return published *Edge Review* (《边缘》) in 2005 and 2006, with a total of four issues. *New Realms of Fantasy and Science Fiction* (《新幻界》) published thirty-two issues from 2009 to 2013, which seems like a miracle, since all the issues are of very high quality and could be downloaded online for free. They even published two printed anthologies. Some of the stories published on *New Realms of Fantasy and Science Fiction* have since been translated into English, such as "Invisible Planets" (《看不见的星球》, 2010), by Hao Jingfang.

Some of the other netzines that are still active today in China are *Chinese New Science Fiction* (《中国新科幻》) and *Science Fiction Collects* (《科幻文汇》). Hopefully, they can live long and prosper.

5.
AWARDS AND MAJOR EVENTS

The Galaxy Award (银河奖) is the highest honor an author can achieve in the Chinese science fiction field, and for a long time, it was the only one. The Galaxy Award was first established in 1986 by two magazines, *Science Fiction World* (previously *Scientific and Literary*) and *Wisdom Tree* (《智慧树》). After *Wisdom Tree* ceased publication, *Science Fiction World* became the only organizer of the

Galaxy. The Galaxy is only awarded to works published in or by *Science Fiction World*, with readers voting for their favorites. However, the Best Short Story of 2016 Galaxy Award was awarded to "Balin" by Chen Qiufan, which was published in *People's Literature*, making the first exception.

An award open to all SF works published in the Chinese language thus became necessary. The Chinese Nebula Award (全球华语科幻星云奖) was established in 2010, organized by the World Chinese Science Fiction Association. All members of the association can nominate their favorites and vote for them; the vote is also extended to the public. The final winner is selected by a panel of judges from five shortlisted works or candidates.

The major annual SF events in China take place around these two awards. Usually, there are con-like carnivals for fans. They do not follow specific rules, but usually involve award ceremonies, red-carpet walks, late night roadside barbecues, and drinking. *Science Fiction World* also hosts a seminar on writing after the Galaxy Award Ceremony every year, while World Chinese Science Fiction Association events have started to look like international cons. Cat Rambo, president of Science Fiction and Fantasy Writers of America; Taiyo Fuji, president of Science Fiction and Fantasy Writers of Japan; and Crystal Huff, cochair of Worldcon 75, were invited as guests for the 2016 Chinese Nebula Award Weekend.

Thanks to the prosperity of Chinese science fiction in recent years, new awards keep appearing. For example, The Morning Star & Jinkang Award was established in 2015 by Science & Fantasy Growth Foundation; The Coordinates Award was established in 2015 by several hard-core fans; and Union Writing Competition was established in 2012 by a group of fans in Sichuan University and renamed as Masters of the Future Award in 2016 by the same crew, who started their own company to build both an online hub and an offline space for science fiction fans.

In the history of Chinese science fiction, three international conventions were held in China: the annual conference of World SF in 1991, the 1997 Beijing International Conference on Science Fiction, and the 2007 International SF&F Convention. Yang Xiao, the president of *Science Fiction World* at the time, attended the annual conference of World SF in 1989 in San Marino and won the hosting right for Chengdu, China, in 1991. Yang was not fluent in English, and neither had she attended international professional conferences before. There were both domestic and foreign obstacles, but Yang and her team fought hard to conquer both. The conference was largely supported by the government and turned out to be a great success.

The '97 Beijing International Conference on Science Fiction was also organized by *Science Fiction World* and supported by the China Association for Science and Technology. It played an important role in promoting science fiction culture in China. One of the results of the conference was the rocketing of sales of *Science Fiction World*.

The 2007 International SF&F Convention was organized by *Science Fiction World* in Chengdu just before Nippon 2007, designed to promote science fiction culture. That year, European and American writers visited China before heading over to Worldcon in Japan.

6.

CONTEMPORARY CHINESE SF FANDOM

There is a bus theory describing Chinese SF fans. The fans' love toward science fiction is just like taking a bus. When they are young, they get on the bus and start to read science fiction. When they grow older (and reach their destination), they stop to read it and get off the bus. It is true that the majority of the readers of *Science Fiction World* are middle school, high school, and university students. In comparison, adult fans read more foreign SF works, either in English or in Chinese translation.

Active SF fans do exist, but despite this, no regular national "cons" have been established. University SF clubs prosper and decline. Regional fan groups appear and disappear. Chinese fandom is quite dispersed, and it is hard to find a particular fan group in China with a "long" history.

However, two fan groups in China with a relatively long history function well to this day.

The first one is SF AppleCore. In 2009, SF clubs in four universities in Shanghai decided to collaborate and organize a big event. During the preparation of Shanghai Science Fiction and Fantasy Festival (SSFFF), AppleCore was founded as the association of university SF clubs in Shanghai. SSFFF was held in 2009 and annually from 2011 till now. It is based in universities, and most of the organizers and attendants are university students. During the weekends of a certain month, usually May, various events like debates, panels, lectures, and LARPs (live action role-playing games) are held in member universities, organized by university SF clubs. A single event can attract 30 to 200 attendants, depending on the guests and contents.

AppleCore has grown to be more than an association of university SF clubs. In October 2013, AppleCore started monthly meetings targeting alum fans. Usually, during these gatherings, there are movie screenings and themed lectures, panels or short talks in the afternoon and dinner in the evening. The topics explored range from science to fantasy, and from art to astronomy. Some examples include: a screening of the movie *A Scanner Darkly* would be followed by a lecture on Philip K. Dick; talks on depression and autism; a visit to the contemporary art exhibition "Heman Chong: Ifs, Ands, or Buts"; and a steampunk accessories DIY workshop. On average, 30 to 120 members show up for the afternoon activities, and 5 to 20 stay for dinner.

In November 2014, the AppleCore Reading Group was formed. Fans are encouraged to read a specific book every month and meet to discuss it. The very first discussion was on *The End of Eternity* by Isaac Asimov. *Annihilation* by Jeff VanderMeer was discussed in December 2015. A special discussion on Chinese Nebula nominees was organized in September 2015, with a focus on Chi Hui's *Artificial Human 2075: Awareness Restructuring*

(《伪人2075: 意识重组》, 2014). The aim is for the reading group to start with a limited circle of members and gradually expand to a larger scale.

The AppleCore Writing Workshop was also established in 2015 as a trial and put into official operation in 2016. Small groups of writers meet monthly and discuss each other's works.

AppleCore is not only the largest SF fan group in eastern China, but is perhaps also the one with the most international contacts. In its seventh year, it won the Gold Xingyun Award for Best Fandom in 2016.

The other organization is the World Chinese Science Fiction Association (WCSFA), our largest fan group, established in 2010 in Chengdu and registered in Hong Kong. AppleCore is more fan-driven and works as the regional fan hub in Shanghai, while WCSFA is an official organization and works as the national fan hub in China.

The World Chinese Science Fiction Association has around 300 members, and most of them are "professionals": writers, translators, editors, researchers, etc. WCSFA has been organizing the Chinese Nebula Award every year since 2010. With the aim of nurturing Chinese SF, the organizing committee works hard to improve it year by year. The award ceremonies have been held in Chengdu, Taiyuan, and Beijing, and it is expected future ceremonies will travel to more cities.

What should also be mentioned here is that Beijing tried out the first Worldcon bid in China in 2014. Though we lost to Kansas City in the end, it was a good beginning, and we can now expect a large group of Chinese representatives at future Worldcons.

7.
CURRENT CHINESE SF IN LITERATURE AND ACADEMIA

Liu Cixin (刘慈欣) is the biggest name in contemporary Chinese SF thanks to his grand universe-spanning imagination. His "Three-

Body" trilogy (《三体》三部曲) is extremely popular and is due to be adapted into a six-part movie series. The English translation of the first book was published in November 2014—the first contemporary Chinese SF novel translated into English—and won a Hugo. The next two books were published in English in 2015 and 2016 respectively.[26]

Wang Jinkang (王晋康), who spent his twentieth year of writing SF in 2014, is another heavyweight in Chinese SF. His stories are deeply rooted in the tradition of realism and usually with a focus on biology. Some of his representative works include the short story "Adam's Regression" (《亚当回归》, 1993) and the novel *A Song for Life* (《生命之歌》, 1998).

Han Song (韩松), who works for Xinhua News Agency, is known to have said that the news pieces he writes during the daytime are more science fictional than the science fiction stories he writes at night. His stories, influenced by Kafka, are unusual and surreal, and his pioneering writing style garners him special attention. Some of his representative works are the short story "Gravestone of the Universe" (《宇宙墓碑》, 1991) and the novel *Red Ocean* (《红色海洋》, 2004).

He Xi (何夕)'s stories are effective at exploring emotions and feelings, which really touch the reader. "The Sad One" (《伤心者》, 2003) is his most famous short story, about a lonely mathematician figuring out a theory that cannot be understood by his era, and a mother always having faith in her son. He Xi published his first novel, *The Doomsyear* (《天年》), in 2015.

Arguably, these are the "Big Four" of Chinese SF today.

Younger writers like Chen Qiufan (陈楸帆), who leads science fiction realism; Fei Dao (飞氘), who applies skills and concepts from literary fiction to his SF writing; Baoshu (宝树), who is good at telling interesting stories with a focus on philosophy; Zhang Ran (张冉),

---

26 The first and third books in the series were translated by Ken Liu, and the second book was translated by Joel Martinsen.

who benefits a lot from his earlier experience as a journalist; Jiang Bo (江波), who has deft control of large scenes; and A Que (阿缺), who is a master of storytelling born in the 1990s—they are all from the most well-educated group in China.

The writers described in this section so far are male, but there are also quite a few prestigious female writers in China: Zhao Haihong (赵海虹), Ling Chen (凌晨), Chi Hui (迟卉), Xia Jia (夏笳), Hao Jingfang (郝景芳), Chen Qian (陈茜), and Tang Fei (糖匪). They approach the genre with their unique perspectives. Zhao Haihong's stories feature an emphasis on emotion and romantic atmosphere; Ling Chen takes good control of hard SF elements; Chi Hui is very prolific, making it hard to conclude her style; Xia Jia is good at creating fantastic scenes and dreamy atmospheres, and recently has started to focus on near-future scenes in China; Hao Jingfang regards her own writing as "nongenre," as she cares about what happens in real space but sets her stories in imaginary space; Chen Qian's stories have simple language but hard SF cores; and Tang Fei's writing, which carries characteristics of the New Wave, is regarded as "nontypical SF" by herself. Among them, Xia Jia is probably the most well-known writer, and after her Hugo win, Hao Jingfang is also receiving a lot of attention.

In terms of academia, there are a group of Chinese SF researchers led by Professor Wu Yan (吴岩) from Beijing Normal University. There has been a master's program focusing on science fiction in Beijing Normal University for years, and the first Ph.D. student in the same major was recruited in September 2015. Before the specialized Ph.D. program in science fiction was established, young researchers and writers like Xia Jia and Fei Dao tended to combine their interest in science fiction within the field of comparative literature. Many of them share research interests in late Qing Dynasty SF in China, while others are more interested in modern and contemporary Chinese SF. And it's fascinating to see these researchers explore the works of their contemporaries and friends.

8.
CHINESE SCIENCE FICTION MOVIES

Science fiction IPs (intellectual properties) are extremely hot in China these days. Liu Cixin sold the film rights of the "Three-Body" trilogy long before the upsurge, making it one of the earliest Chinese science fiction "big" movies to be adapted from literature. The movie has not been released as of this writing (early 2018), but a stage adaptation has been received enthusiastically in Shanghai and Beijing. The first Nebula Award for Global Chinese Science Fiction Films, also organized and awarded by WCSFA, was just awarded in August 2016. The Best SF Movie award went to *CJ 7* («长江七号», 2008), directed by Stephen Chow; and Lu Chuan won Best Director for his *Chronicles of the Ghostly Tribe* («九层妖塔», 2015).

There are dozens of projects in development, and we can certainly expect to see more Chinese science fiction movies in the coming years.

CONCLUSION

Chinese SF is winning more attention on the international stage than ever before. The Hugo-winning magazine *Clarkesworld* started a Chinese SF translation project in 2015 in partnership with Storycom, a Chinese company dedicated to turning science fiction stories into movies/comic/games. *Clarkesworld* has been publishing one Chinese SF short story in translation each month since.

Led by Li Zhaoxin, a senior SF fan and critic, SF Comet, an international SF short story writing competition, runs monthly. Chinese and foreign writers compete by writing a short story to a certain theme within a limited time frame. The stories are published in both Chinese and English. Both Chinese and foreign fans can vote for the anonymized stories and choose their favorite. Currently, the competition is on hiatus and we hope it will continue soon.

The first anthology of contemporary Chinese SF stories, *Invisi-*

ble Planets, edited and translated by Ken Liu, was published in November 2016.

It is becoming easier and easier to find translated Chinese SF these days. Check them out and you won't be disappointed!

AUTHOR'S NOTE

Special thanks to Zhang Feng, Jiang Qian, Zhao Ruhan, Zheng Jun, Xia Jia, and Dong Renwei for their writings on Chinese science fiction.

A NEW CONTINENT FOR CHINA SCHOLARS: CHINESE SCIENCE FICTION STUDIES[27]

by Mingwei Song

Seven years ago, I attended a conference in Shanghai, a major event celebrating contemporary Chinese literature coorganized by Harvard and Fudan (one of the top universities in China), which featured China's A-list novelists, poets, essayists, and literary critics. The dignitaries attending it included the Nobel Laureate-to-be Mo Yan, dozens of his peers, chief editors of major literary magazines, famous professors, as well as some younger popular authors. Almost nobody had heard of Chinese science fiction before this conference concluded with a late-afternoon roundtable discussion that gave two SF authors, Han Song and Fei Dao, ten minutes to talk about their genre. Han Song, a major author of Chinese SF's New Wave, and Fei Dao, a promising young author, I later learned, spent a huge amount of time preparing for the ten minutes' talk. I

27 Originally written in English.

remember I was sitting in front of Yu Hua and Su Tong, two literary giants who kept chatting in low voices. But they suddenly became silent, and they listened attentively when Han Song began to talk about the amazing new development of SF over the past decade, and when Fei Dao strategically linked the contemporary authors' artistic pursuits and social concerns to Lu Xun, the founding father of modern Chinese literature, who was also an early advocate for "science fiction" (*kexue xiaoshuo*) at the turn of the twentieth century, I could say that the entire audience, during the ten minutes, kept silent and listened with great interest to Han Song and Fei Dao.

It was a moment that changed the field.

July 13, 2010, 3:30 p.m.

Two days earlier, I introduced myself to Han Song and Fei Dao. We had a pleasant conversation. Before meeting with them, I had read all their publications I could find. Three years earlier, my friend Yan Feng (a Fudan professor) sent me a manuscript called *Santi* (later rendered into English as *The Three-Body Problem*). He highly recommended that I read it. But I was busy with something else at that time; I didn't even read through the second chapter (the chapters were in the same order as they appeared in the English translation by Ken Liu). It was not until 2008 that I picked it up again, felt awed, and was soon obsessed with this new wave of Chinese science fiction: Liu Cixin, Han Song, Wang Jinkang, He Xi, La La, Zhao Haihong, Chen Qiufan, Xia Jia, Fei Dao, Hao Jingfang, Chi Hui, etc. I read every piece I could find written by them, and I strongly suggested to the Shanghai conference organizers that we invite Liu Cixin to the conference. However, Liu Cixin couldn't come due to a schedule conflict. But Han Song and Fei Dao did not fail their mission; in a very humble and yet powerful way, they succeeded in making science fiction *the* hot topic for the conference. By the time Han Song and Fei Dao finished speaking, I felt that I had come to an epiphany: Chinese science fiction had already experienced a decade of its own golden age, 1999 to 2010.

Unfortunately, it was almost unknown to people outside the circle of SF fans. The mainstream literary scholars knew nothing.

During his presentation, Fei Dao compared this new wave of Chinese science fiction to a lonely hidden army. Perhaps it would have perished without anyone paying attention to it. Indeed, if no one from the literary establishment bothered to pick up a copy of *Santi*, or had the patience to read the labyrinthine narrative of Han Song's bizarre story about China's invisible reality, the new wave of Chinese SF could perhaps only serve as self-entertainment for SF authors and fans. But in July 2010, thanks to Han Song and Fei Dao, this lonely hidden army was brought to the center stage of a convention of literary elites.

Right after the roundtable, Theodore Huters (UCLA), a professor I respect tremendously, began to think about doing an anthology to introduce these new Chinese SF authors. He commissioned me to edit a special double issue for *Renditions*, a literary magazine that introduced some of China's most famous authors to the world. It took me two years, with the support of dozens of writers and translators, to complete this job. In 2012, the *Renditions* special issue was published, featuring ten stories by contemporary Chinese SF authors. It's about the same time that Ken Liu, the most devoted translator of Chinese science fiction, began to enter the field. Other publications, such as *Pathlight*, also ran special issues featuring translations of Chinese science fiction. In other countries, such as Italy and Japan, Chinese science fiction has also gained new life in new languages.

When Ken Liu's translation of *The Three-Body Problem* appeared in 2014 and won the Hugo Award in 2015, this new wave of Chinese science fiction became an international sensation. What happened later is perhaps familiar to most of the readers: Obama and Mark Zuckerberg both praised the novel; its sequel, *Death's End*, was on the bestseller list of the *New York Times*.

※

Scholars are usually a little late to trends. But this time, the tremendous popularity of Chinese science fiction is impossible to ignore. Within only three to four years, Chinese science fiction has quickly become one of the most prosperous subfields for China scholars. Major academic conferences such as MLA, AAS, ACLA, ACCL, and the like all feature panels, roundtables, workshops devoted to Chinese science fiction. As one of the first Chinese American scholars paying attention to this new development of the genre, I was frequently commissioned to contribute to academic journals/volumes in both the US and China (and France and Germany as well), edit special issues, and even organize conferences and workshops. I am not alone in this campaign. I have such comrades-in-arms as Hua Li, who wrote several articles on contemporary SF, and Nathaniel Isaacson, who recently published *Celestial Empire: Emergence of Chinese Science Fiction*, the first monograph completely devoted to the study of early Chinese science fiction. More importantly, an entire new generation of younger scholars engaged the topic seriously, producing more systematic research and presenting more provocative arguments. It was almost like a miracle: a new continent for scholarly adventure emerged in front of our eyes.

Still, I need to emphasize that the field has its own history. Its current momentum is new, but it still has a heritage that set up some framework for the contemporary research, just like this new wave that also has its precedents—at least a few short-lived booms that took place in the first decade of the twentieth century: the 1950s to 1960s as children's literature in China, 1970s to 1980s in Taiwan, and a major revival on the mainland during the early Reform Era. However, the history of Chinese science fiction has never been a continuous one. It is full of gaps and interruptions caused by politics or the change of cultural paradigms. Each generation of new authors had to reestablish the paradigm. Only on a few occasions could they get access to earlier authors' work, but they rarely received obvious, substantial influences from them.

But for literary scholars, the task is not just to test how earlier generations influenced later ones, or to try to create a literary history that pretends to be coherent and consistent. Literary scholars put more emphasis on texts and contexts. I need to pay homage to three scholars who made major research on the genre before its recent revival. In the early 1980s, German sinologist Rudolf Wagner published a lengthy article "Lobby Literature: Archeology and Present Functions of Science Fiction in China." It mainly discusses science fiction of the early Reform Era. Wagner defined it as lobby literature without labeling it as propaganda, but gave a subtle and sympathetic analysis of the genre's rich meanings at the turning point of China's political situation. His article is an inspiring piece that connects the future-oriented SF to past history and present challenges.

By the end of the 1980s, Wu Dingbo collaborated with Patrick Murphy to publish the first translated anthology of Chinese science fiction from the 1980s, titled *Science Fiction from China* (New York: Praeger, 1989). Wu wrote an introduction that serves as a concise history of Chinese science fiction, presenting most of the important authors and advocates for the genre from the early twentieth century to the early 1980s. He spent more time introducing the rise and decline of Chinese SF during the early Reform Era. Wu's introduction was the most complete discussion on the genre published in English by that time.

In 1997, David Der-wei Wang's paradigm-making book *Fin-de-siecle Splendor: Repressed Modernities of Late Qing Fiction, 1848–1911* (Stanford, 1997) was published. One of his chapters, "Confused Horizons: Science Fantasy," is the defining study of late Qing science fiction, which was first promoted by Liang Qichao and later prospered for nearly a decade (1902 to 1911). Wang's approach is to combine textual analysis and cultural history, looking into the imaginative and epistemological levels of the narrative. Wang's study has had a deep impact on later scholars' work on late Qing science fiction. It is no exaggeration to say that after Wang's book was published there was a revival of scholarly interest in late Qing literature, including science fiction.

In China, the pioneer in Chinese science fiction studies is no doubt Wu Yan. He was almost the sole serious scholar working on the genre for decades before it received recognition from more scholars. In addition to a series of academic articles, Wu published in 2011 a monograph titled "Kehuan wenxue lungang" (Outline of Science Fiction Studies). Unlike Rudolf Wagner, Wu Dingbo, or David Der-wei Wang, Wu Yan focuses his study on contemporary Chinese science fiction writers, comparing them to Western authors and applying a number of theories (including cyborg, feminism, and globalization) to analyzing these writers. In China today, Wu Yan, as the only advisor qualified to advise Ph.D. students to do projects on SF, is definitely the leader of the community of Chinese science fiction researchers.

By the time Chinese science fiction began to gain international recognition, Wu Yan edited a special issue for *Science Fiction Studies*, a collection of about ten research articles covering the entire history of the genre in China, from late Qing science fantasy to Lao She's *Cat Country*, from the 1980s to the very recent boom of the genre after 2000. Both Liu Cixin and Han Song also contributed to this special issue, which is a landmark in the development of the field.

My own research on Chinese science fiction is rather limited to contemporary works, particularly the New Wave, a term I borrowed from British SF history to baptize this new trend of the genre that shows both social concern and artistic innovations. It is a controversial definition, I know. I have published four articles in English (two translated into French and German), and numerous articles and essays in Chinese. In one recent article, "Representations of the Invisible: Poetics and Politics of Contemporary Chinese Science Fiction," I argued that the trend called the New Wave grew out of the post-1989 political culture, and it has not only resurrected the genre but has also subverted its own conventions, which used to be dominated by political utopianism and technological optimism throughout nearly the entire twentieth century in mainland China. Contemporary science fiction reenergizes the genre by consolidating and reinventing a variety of generic conventions, cultural elements, and political visions—ranging from space opera to cyberpunk fiction, from utopianism to posthumanism, and from parodied visions of China's rise to deconstructions of the myth of national development. In a peculiar way, Chinese science fiction has entered its Golden Age at the same time that it generates a new wave subversion of the genre. The new wave has a dark and subversive side that speaks either to the "invisible" dimensions of the reality, or simply the impossibility of representing a certain "reality" dictated by the discourse of mainstream realism. On its most radical side, the new wave of Chinese SF has been thriving on an avant-garde cultural spirit that encourages one to think beyond the conventional ways of perceiving reality and to challenge the commonly accepted ideas about progress, development, economic miracle, and nation and people.

I should also mention that in addition to mainland writers, a number of authors in Taiwan and Hong Kong have also made important contributions to the field, particularly those authors of experimental fiction, like Lo Yi-chin, Dung Kai-cheung, and Ng Kim-chew, who all appropriate elements of science fiction to achieve a more sophisticated level of literary experimentation with motifs of heterotopia, the posthuman, and metaphors of identity. Sinophone science fiction could be the next goldmine to be discovered, explored, and brought to attention for a world audience.

※

Through editing a few special journal issues and organizing conferences, I got to know a number of scholars working on interesting topics. For example, Adrian Thieret writes about Liu Cixin's version of cosmopolitanism; Cara Healey studies genre transgression and transnationalism in science fiction; Hua Li explores a variety of topics in the political, environmental, and metaphorical in Chinese SF; Jiang Jing studies both late Qing science fiction as the origin of modern Chinese literature and the socialist science fiction from the 1950s to 1980s; Nathaniel Isaacson, after his book on late Qing SF was published, is working on variations of science fiction in other genres during the Republic Era and early PRC; I myself prepare to write about heterotopia in the variations of science fiction by Taiwanese and Hong Kong authors. Scholars like Li Guangyi, Ren Dongmei, Liang Qingsan, and Zhang Feng (Sanfeng) have unearthed important materials for further research in the genre. Some more comprehensive bibliography and collection of materials will hopefully be made accessible to researchers soon.

The field keeps growing, and the new continent is full of wonders. I hold a firm belief that Chinese science fiction is going to be, or has already become, the most rapidly growing subfield of modern Chinese literary studies. It is changing the field. It reshapes our understanding of Chinese literary modernity as well as its potentials for future development.

SCIENCE FICTION:
EMBARRASSING NO MORE

by Fei Dao

Some years ago, I attended a speech by an arthouse director I admired. He was known for unflinching realism in his work, and the small Chinese towns buffeted by the tsunami of modernization portrayed in his films always reminded me of my hometown.

In his speech, he opined that contemporary Chinese society was obsessed by the present, and was without a clear vision of either the past or the future. Therefore, for his next film, he wanted to return to the past, to reexamine and reevaluate Chinese history. So, during the audience Q&A, I asked him whether he would eventually make a film about the future, or, in other words, a sci-fi film.

The audience roared with laughter.

For most in attendance, the appearance of the word "sci-fi" in the cultured and sophisticated setting of this speech was utterly incongruous. My question shocked them in the same way the audience at an opera would be stunned if someone had asked whether Pava-rotti was considering taking up beatboxing.

To be honest, I was terribly embarrassed. No one wanted to be *that guy* who asked odd questions that made everyone feel awk-ward. Of China's 1.4 billion people, the number of science fiction fans was a vanishingly small minority. For most Chinese, "sci-fi" conjured up images of young, gawky teenagers obsessed with an-ime, *wuxia* novels, outrageous clothing, and ridiculous hairstyles. Like those other juvenile pursuits, sci-fi was to be abandoned when one reached maturity. Science fiction was neither practical nor useful and had nothing to do with real life. In most people's minds, it was no more real than distant countries whose capitals they couldn't even recall. Once in a while, they might hear the genre mentioned, but they knew nothing about it and had no desire to find out more. Indeed, if "sci-fi" happened to pop up in conversation, their faces would twist into expressions of bewilderment, and they would ask, "Are you talking about Harry Potter? That's sci-fi, isn't it?"

In any event, I was younger back then, and my courage had not yet been dulled by experience. Thus, when I attended an interna-tional academic conference meant to discuss Important And Intel-lectual Subjects, the inexplicable urge to bring up science fiction once again gripped me. Taking advantage of a coffee break, I walked up to a renowned German sinologist and asked him if he had ever read any Chinese science fiction.

This aged and respected scholar had once declared that after the founding of the People's Republic of China, Chinese authors had produced no work that would be considered great by the rest of the world. I did not agree with him.

At that time, Mo Yan hadn't yet won the Nobel, but I wasn't thinking of him anyway. The second book in Liu Cixin's "Three-Body" series, *The Dark Forest*, had just been published, and every Chinese sci-fi fan was thrumming with excitement. I was certain that at least in the realm of science fiction, a contemporary Chi-nese author had indeed written something the equal of any of the great Western classics.

But the renowned sinologist interrupted my disquisition politely, "I don't even read German sci-fi!"

There was nothing I could say in response to that. Heck, even Chinese readers for Chinese sci-fi were few and far between.

I wasn't some rabid superfan who believed that my beloved genre was the best thing ever to happen to literature and anyone who couldn't appreciate sci-fi was a philistine. In fact, I didn't even like to argue with people. My questions were a kind of performance art: out of a desire for security or mental peace, everyone built around themselves a mental firewall that filtered the torrents of information in which modern life inundated all of us. "Sci-fi" was one of the keywords tagged by most people's firewalls as useless information, and I simply wanted to toss it over the firewall so that they had to evaluate it anew instead of automatically ignoring it. I suppose many would think what I did was foolish and pointless, but at least I didn't harm anyone with my questions.

Here, I have to explain to my readers in the West that for a long time, science fiction in China was like subatomic particles or radiation, undetectable to most. A student majoring in literature would find virtually no information concerning sci-fi in textbooks or academic histories of Chinese literature. (To be sure, in histories of Western literature one would occasionally find the names of writers like Margaret Atwood, Kurt Vonnegut, and Thomas Pynchon—but the text would go on to emphasize that these writers only used the techniques of science fiction as a form of "literary experimentation," as though it would be a terrible thing to sully the august tomes of literary history with the presence of any pure genre writer.)

Within the elegant, highly intellectual, awe-inspiring atmosphere of "serious" academic conferences, it was almost impossible to find a science fiction author or a scholar of sci-fi. It was rare to see sci-fi covered in the mainstream media. If some newspaper or magazine happened to publish a 200-word snippet about sci-fi or if a popular magazine founded by a bestselling YA author published a story by a sci-fi writer, fans celebrated the occasion and rushed to share the news with each other. Even the publisher of Doris Lessing's

Mara and Dann: An Adventure and the writer invited to provide an introduction for the book avoided mentioning the book's obvious genre classification, fearful of harming sales.

In the face of so much apathy and ignorance from society at large, sci-fi fans in China rallied to *Science Fiction World*, a magazine dedicated to serving them. Through college fan clubs, Internet forums, and other grassroots activities, fans found each other and banded together, forming a distinctive subculture. Hidden in their refuge, protected by their isolation, they entertained themselves, feeling sorry for those who didn't understand or experience the sense of wonder in gazing up at the stars.

Once, when speaking to a group of prominent Western authors and scholars who had never heard of Chinese sci-fi, I used the metaphor of a "hidden army." Forgotten by everyone in the cultural landscape, they lay concealed in silence, alone on the desolate heath. Perhaps someday an opportunity would arise when they would burst into action and change the world, but it was also possible that such an opportunity would never come, and they would fade into oblivion. Future explorers might find the remains of their mysterious, unfinished war engines, but those who had constructed the weapons and practiced with them would be forever forgotten.

However, soon after, the third volume of Liu Cixin's magnum opus, *Death's End*, was published. An unanticipated sea change came over China's literary scene. The isolation that had kept sci-fi out of view had also acted as a dam storing up the potential for an explosive release. As young Chinese fans grew up and entered society, they persisted in their love of genre literature. Like faithful fans at a concert, they waved their faint glow sticks to support their beloved art. As night fell, thousands of tiny lights danced with more urgency and force, and thousands of lonely voices coalesced into a powerful rhythmic chant. Finally, Liu Cixin, the star of the show, came onto the stage to perform his masterpiece, and the crescendo of wild cheers that greeted him seemed to shake the stars suspended in the sky above.

Society at large was consumed with curiosity. Literary critics, numbed by the clichéd portraits of urban life and listless middle-class affairs that filled "literary fiction," were surprised to find that fiction written in Chinese was capable of narrating grand space epics and painting magnificent portraits of an imagined future. A fresh literary terrain materialized out of nowhere, waiting to be cultivated by page-plowing scholars and critics.

All of a sudden, literary theory became a hot topic again, and the number of dissertations and papers focused on sci-fi exploded. Established scholars gave lectures on the "meaning of sci-fi," and even avant-garde artists enthusiastically invited sci-fi writers to collaborate with them to explore the revolutionary ideas made possible by science and the infinite potential of humanity. Agents and producers always on the lookout for the next piece of valuable IP buttonholed every sci-fi writer, demanding to know, "Do you have any stories suitable for screen adaptation?"

Within but a few years, sci-fi authors had turned from invisible and forgotten bookworms to superstars in hot demand. They took off their simple, outdated plaid shirts and became sharp dressers—no, really, some of them could even be glimpsed in the pages of fashion magazines. Everyone acted as if each sci-fi author was a walking mine of brilliant ideas.

The symbols and memes of sci-fi also injected themselves into the popular imagination. Internet CEOs interpreted the "dark forest" of the "Three-Body" series as a metaphor for the ruthless competition in their domain, while a government spokesperson employed the "dark forest" to describe the worst-case scenario for the crisis on the Korean Peninsula. Sci-fi had never touched so many in China. The vice president of China affirmed that sci-fi was a "positive force" for the development and progress of the country, and even declared himself a fan. Everyone agreed that this was the most encouraging, most supportive environment sci-fi had ever experienced in China.

Still, mere novelty wears out quickly, and it's impossible to predict whether the hidden army, once revealed, can really become a force to be reckoned with and sustain the wave of cultural enthusiasm for sci-fi. Readers expecting more of *The Three-Body Problem*, or even *The Four-Body Problem* and *The Five-Body Problem*, would no doubt be disappointed. No one could (or should) replicate Liu Cixin. Today, although he hasn't published a new novel since *Death's End*, "Da Liu" remains peerless in China (some have estimated that yearly sales of his books exceed the sum of the yearly sales of all other science fiction books combined). After Chinese authors managed to bring home Hugo rockets two years in a row, what else can they do to keep the attention of mainstream society? If the ambitious sci-fi films currently in production don't achieve commercial success—remember, Chinese audiences have been trained to have very picky tastes by a steady diet of big-budget Hollywood sci-fi blockbusters—how much longer will the financiers remain excited?

I imagine the answers to many of these questions will reveal themselves shortly. Most of the sci-fi authors I know are not concerned about them because they have day jobs—engineer, reporter, university instructor, science researcher, judge, entrepreneur, and so on. Even if the current wave of enthusiasm burns out and sci-fi once again retreats from the view of most people—I'm reminded of little Pluto, which was unknown until 1930, and which then enjoyed a brief few decades of attention before scientists mercilessly ejected it from the ranks of the planets—sci-fi authors will simply shrug and return to their hidden base, away from the bright and fickle beam of public attention, and continue to let their imaginations roam.

As for myself, I'm glad that I got to witness this wave of interest and so many fantastic happenings. Let me tell you a bit more about that arthouse director I mentioned at the beginning. At the time of his speech, I asked him why it was that Chinese films rarely showed the future. He answered perfunctorily that "exploration of history and the present already encompasses within it anticipation for the future." At that moment, he probably wouldn't have believed that in a few years he would make a film about the year 2025. When that film was released, some in the media praised the director for "opening a new path for expressing realism through the experimental techniques of science fiction." I knew then that my long-held dream had been fulfilled: when I talk about sci-fi with others, none of us need feel embarrassed anymore.